NIGHT-THREADS
The spellbinding fantasy series by
Ru Emerson

Book One: *The Calling of the Three*
Book Two: *The Two in Hiding*
Book Three: *One Land, One Duke*

And the adventures continue in . . .

The Craft of Light
and
The Art of the Sword

D0483297

NIGHT-THREADS

THE ART OF THE SWORD

RU EMERSON

ACE BOOKS, NEW YORK

This book is an Ace original edition,
and has never been previously published.

THE ART OF THE SWORD

An Ace Book / published by arrangement with
the author

PRINTING HISTORY
Ace edition / December 1994

All rights reserved.
Copyright © 1994 by Ru Emerson.
Cover art by Donald Clavette.
This book may not be reproduced in whole or in part,
by mimeograph or any other means, without permission.
For information address: The Berkley Publishing Group,
200 Madison Avenue, New York, NY 10016.

ISBN: 0-441-00032-0

ACE®
Ace Books are published by The Berkley Publishing Group,
200 Madison Avenue, New York, NY 10016.
ACE and the "A" design are trademarks
belonging to Charter Communications, Inc.

PRINTED IN THE UNITED STATES OF AMERICA

10 9 8 7 6 5 4 3 2 1

To Doug

*And with fond memories of the best possible
Scaramouche—Stewart Granger*

*And also my thanks to Ramblin' Jack Elliot,
for the song about
the son of the Spanish Grandee.*

Cast of Characters

Jennifer Cray: Once a hard-working associate lawyer in a Los Angeles firm, she is now married to the Thukar of Sikkre, Thukara in her own right, a powerful Wielder of Night-Thread Magic, and legal advisor to the Emperor's Heir.

Dahven: Thukar of Sikkre

Aletto: Son of the murdered Duke Amarni, nephew to the usurper Jadek—and the reason why three Angelenos were drawn into Rhadaz four years ago. He is now Duke of Zelharri.

Robyn Cray: Jennifer's older sister, Aletto's duchess, shape-shifter.

Chris Cray: Robyn's twenty-year-old son, previously a high-school senior and computer gamer, now a trader and importer of current foreign technology into Rhadaz.

Edrith: Former Sikkreni market thief and close friend of Dahven's; now Chris's business partner and fellow traveler.

Enardi: Bezanti son of a wealthy merchant and also Chris's partner, Enardi handles finances and diplomacy.

Lialla: Aletto's sister, the sin-Duchess of Zelharri; both Wielder of Night-Threads and Shaper of Light.

Shesseran XIV: Current Emperor of Rhadaz—an aging and ill man who has put most of his duties into the hands of his brother and Heir, Afronsan.

Afronsan: The man who will become Shesseran XV spends most of his days in the civil service building and thus is regarded by his enemies as a "paper pusher."

Vuhlem: The harsh, patriarchal Duke of northern Holmaddan, who nurses his own ambitions.

Ryselle: Young Holmaddi village woman who has become friends with Lialla.

Kepron: Son of a Holmaddi village woman and one of Vuhlem's guards, and Lialla's most recent novice.

Henri Dupret: Second son of the French Duc D'Orlean, in charge of his father's sugar fields and estates in French Jamaica and, like Vuhlem, a man with secret ambitions.

Ariadne Dupret: Henri's daughter by an indentured servant; Ariadne knows more of her father's secrets than is safe.

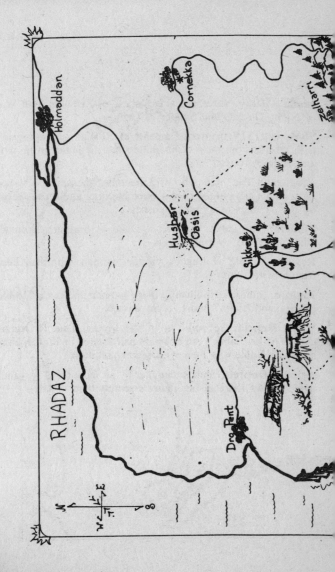

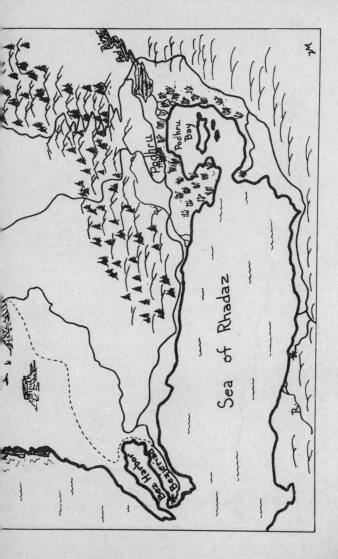

i

⊠

IT was warm and close along the northern Holmaddan shore;
unusually and unpleasantly warm, particularly for so late in
summer—nearly autumn. The sun hung midway in a clear, deep
blue sky, turning the water a rich, white-capped aqua, reflecting
blindingly off knee-deep tide pools.

A ragged line of women came slowly along the sand. Behind
them, above the southern bluffs that separated the shore from the
village of North Bay, a line of thick black cloud was just visible.
And against the cloud, upon the leading edge of one high ledge,
the motionless outline of a boy. He stood very still for a long
moment, watching as the women straggled across hot sand, their
scarves and carry-bags flapping in a sudden gust of wind. Their
heads were down; if they talked to each other, he couldn't tell
from here. He raised his own head to gaze beyond them, at the
Lasanachi wreck the storm had tossed ashore, then brought his
eyes back to the women, studied them for such signs of trouble
as the headman had spoken of—but no, they weren't gabbling,
out there, gossiping, wasting time. Spreading—sedition, that city
guard had called it. Getting above themselves, the headman said,
using words a man could understand. Making trouble for those
they were created to serve, he'd said. But the women had been
very subdued since the Duke's men came and took that outsider
woman away. *Afraid their own heads are for the block, like hers
nearly was*, he thought and nodded sharply, pleased with his
analysis of things. He ran a hand through sparse, silky beard,
turned and began working his way back to level ground, glanc-
ing over his shoulder one last time before the beach was out of
sight.

The headman was right; after that early morning raid on the

village witch's house and its aftermath, even stupid women such
as theirs would know better than to try the city women's tricks
here. But that foreign female who called herself a Duke's sister
hadn't been here long enough to subvert anyone, fortunately, and
with her gone, there wouldn't be any further trouble. The women
were following the headman's orders: Go out to gather shells for
trade, shellfish for eating. Pick thereafter through the remnants of
the Lasanachi longship, and bring back any treasures the men
might have missed. Waste no time. They were moving across
that hot sand as quickly as he'd ever seen them move.

The boy shook dirt and stones from his trous and sandals at
the base of the hill, grinned and groomed his moustache with
careful hands as he caught his breath so he could run the rest of
the way to the men's house. Make a good show of it, he thought,
of obeying the headman's orders himself. Because among the
things the men had removed were several wooden crates contain-
ing pale glass bottles of truly wondrous liquors—sweet and
fruited, and strong enough to turn even the old men's heads.
Make a good enough show of his willingness to serve his elders,
and he might be given another small skin of the stuff.

OUT on the sand, one of the women stopped suddenly and caught
hold of her foot, as if she had stepped on something sharp; another stopped and knelt to check the sole of it, then shook her
head. Her eyes were searching all along the high ground behind
them. "It's all right," she said quietly. "He's gone." She stood,
stared back at the bluff where the boy had been, shaded her eyes
and looked carefully along the bluff as far in each direction as he
might have gotten, then shook her head again. "Truly gone. I
told you they were growing bored with this constant watching,
and Harana's son was always impatient. He'll be halfway to the
men's house already." She shoved the scarf back from short-cut
red hair.

The Wielder Sretha put her foot down, pressed her own scarf
aside, and stood very still, eyes closed for a long moment. The
other women waited. "You're right, Ryselle. He's gone."

"I *wish* you would not do that, Sretha," one of the older
women said fretfully. "It's not—"

"Not what?" Sretha demanded in a crisp voice as the other
hesitated. "Not proper? Not right? And what do you know about
Wielding, Aleria, that I do not?"

"It isn't safe!" Aleria replied sharply. "The sin-Duchess Wielded during daylight hours, and look what became of her!"

Sretha shrugged. "One doesn't follow the other; if that woman had not been able to Wield the ways she did, things might have gone much worse—for all of us. And I was wrong. Thread simply is, just as she said; there's no right and wrong time for it, or way to handle it. It's more difficult to use during the day, of course—for me, at least, but I'm older and more set in my ways than the sin-Duchess, of course. It's harder to see by far. But anyone can use the red sensing Thread. I could even have taught my sister's son——" Sretha shrugged again as the other woman made a wordless, unhappy little sound. "Let it pass. Kepron is gone to the city with his father's company, the sin-Duchess is gone. More importantly, Harana's stupid son has become bored with watching to see if we intend rebellion. But it has been ten days; I think Ryselle is right: Even the headman is bored with it, and content that we have learned not to thwart him or the Duke, in any fashion."

Ryselle shook her head impatiently. "We'd better get on, though. You yourself said not to do anything to make them curious. And there is no second-guessing Father these days, if there ever was." She turned and strode out across the sand. Her mother made a vexed noise, sighed faintly, and followed.

It was also close and warm in French Jamaica, particularly along the southern coast, but that was natural for the season. There had been one hurricane already, which had missed the island as the old women with their smokes had said it would. It had tossed enough debris high on the northeastern shores that the boys would be busy for many days to come, clearing the wharves where the small fishing boats put out, and word had it another of the storms was on its way. The smoke-women weren't needed to tell that; there was a feel to the air, as though it were liquid—a brassy look to the sea and the sky.

On such an afternoon, the streets of Philippe-sur-Mer, protected from storms and from all cooling breezes but the rare southerly sea winds by its deep bay, were nearly deserted. Only a few men moved along the docks, which reeked of tar, fish, and other less pleasant things. On the heights above the city itself, where many of the nobles and wealthy lived, only a faint, occasional breath of air moved the trees; at the cemetery reserved for

the upper classes, set against a ridge as it was, there seemed to
be no more moving air than on the docks.

Women swathed in full-skirted black and dull gray gathered
beneath a small, square canvas awning, installed to protect fair
skin from the sun; a few men clustered a distance away and
spoke in low voices. Between the two groups, just under the
edge of the canopy, a coffin, its dark wood smelling faintly of
wax and lemon; brass handles gleamed in the rays of a late afternoon sun.

The widow sat where she could have touched the box, her face
and shoulders draped in black gauzy stuff. An older woman
whose gown bore damp patches beneath the bosom and at the elbows patted her shoulder; two others bent to speak with her.
From behind the veils, a steady, low voice asked: "Are any of
the men near?"

"No." A girl whose blue-black hair was scarcely restrained
under a broad hat glanced toward the men, away at once.

"Well done," the older woman murmured. "All of you. *They*
saw nothing but what we wished: an old and overweight man
with a weak hea.t, too much wine on a hot summer's day—even
his doctor said as much, did he not, Helene?"

"There is still the chance—" the widow began doubtfully. The
older woman knelt to grasp her hands.

"No, Helene. He is dead, your husband—and not greatly
missed by any of them, I should think. But why should they
doubt his end to be caused by other than his heart? We bring no
attention upon ourselves by wholesale slaughter among them, we
only cull those like Lord D'Etarian who—" She hesitated.

"Who deserve to die, for treating their women like cattle," the
girl said flatly.

"Hush, Ariadne," the widow whispered urgently. "If anyone of
those men heard you—!" Ariadne shook her head; the widow
sighed very faintly. "But you are wrong, Ariadne Dupret. What
man of my husband's—my *late* husband's—friends and relatives
would beat his cattle? Or even treat indentured servants as he
treats his women?" She pressed veils from her face; one side of
her mouth sagged oddly, as though the nerves there did not function properly; the greenish yellow of an old bruise showed
faintly against her temple. "Two good things at least have come
of this; that Marcel will no longer beat upon me—any more than
he will petition your father—"

"I would not marry your son," Ariadne said flatly. "I would

die first—or *he* would, another victim of too many rums and the wrong alley." She smiled grimly.

"Caution, Ariadne—" the older woman began.

"Yes, of course. But what man of them would believe it—that any of their daughters could do such a thing? To stalk a man down a black dockside alley and stab him dead—" Her fingers curled; she flattened them against her skirts. "You know what *my* father is, Aleyza. If he does not suspect the least thing, why, then, which of them ever would?"

"All the same—have care, girl," the older woman whispered sharply. "The priest comes, the men will follow." She drew a length of pale gray across her own face and helped Helene D'Etarian lower her veils.

"If we *could* remove Henri," Helene murmured. "He is the worst of them all, I think." But Ariadne Dupret shook her head.

"No, not the worst. There are two others, much more vile than my father, and I can manage him—for now. But be careful, Helene, here he is."

IT was cool in Zelharri, damp and foggy in Duke's Fort even at midday, but all along the eastern mountains there had been little true summer this year. The young Duke was seldom seen in the city these days; the few times he had come into the market with his outlander wife, he had been limping and his face was tight with pain. The par-Duchess Lizelle never came out of the Fort anymore, and only rarely did the Cornekkan twins who served her come in search of the special delicacies she liked to eat. Duchess Robyn seemed distracted and frequently worried. The market buzzed with low-voiced, worried gossip—but for all the talk, no one really knew what was wrong in Duke's Fort just now.

1

2

IT was hot and still in Sikkre, hotter than normal in the Thukara's offices, even so late in the afternoon, but Jennifer had ordered the windows tightly closed, the thick cloth shades drawn, and the door shut, and had sent most of her clerks home. It was close and airless in the enormous room now, and though lamps and candles were lit, still gloomy. Better, she thought crossly, than the alternative—the Sikkreni farmers were burning fields west of the city now that the grain was harvested, and the wind had shifted to blow acrid smoke toward the city and the Thukar's palace only after it was too late to smother the fires.

"So what else is new?" she muttered and glared at the fat leather case centered on her desk, the surrounding stacks of papers and files. The deserted desks nearby were piled nearly as high; the ones across the chamber, where three of her clerks were readying the latest foreign trade contract for the printers, weren't much better—reasonably cleared only to make room for the immediate project, nothing more.

If she bothered to peer around the shade, she knew there wouldn't be anything to see outside except smoke and dust—lots of both.

Maddening. "I thought that was one of the good things I'd managed, leaving the smog behind in L.A.," she muttered under her breath. She sighed heavily, picked up the face cloth Siohan had brought her at midafternoon, dipped it in a deep bowl of cool herbed water, wrung it out, and patted her face and the back of her neck. It wasn't air-conditioning by a long shot, but it did help alleviate that sticky, stuporous hot feeling.

"If I weren't so fat—" She sighed again, ran a hand across the thin, loose red dress that was becoming less loose by the day.

6

The morning sickness had finally gone, but now her waist was going. "Ugh. Robyn was right. Pregnant in hot weather is *not* a good idea. Well, it can't be helped; think of something else."

She looked at the reasonably clear corner of her desk, at the chunk of machinery sitting in its midst, and smiled. "Typewriter. Genuine typing machine. I *told* that kid someone had to have come up with them."

She would probably go nuts trying to use the thing—the keys were in an odd order; it was a little like the first time she tried reading or writing in Rhadazi, brought it home that this wasn't her native language. Something nearer Spanish, perhaps, some polyglot Romance language, anyway—she'd long since given up trying to figure out the crossovers and even Chris didn't bother worrying about it much any more.

Too busy, he said, trying to find outside tech he could bring into a country only just beginning to emerge from a five-hundred-year isolation. And then trying to work the deals that would persuade the Mer Khani, English, French, and other outsiders to sell, and—most difficult of all—the ill and aging Rhadazi Emperor Shesseran XIV to let it in. *Keeps him off the streets and out of trouble. Edrith—Eddie, too.*

Typewriter. She ran a fond hand over dark-blue engraved metal. It was a very clunky manual, reminding her a little of the ancient machine her aunt and uncle had in their home back in southern California: Nearly a foot high, it must have weighed a ton; the space bar was actually polished ash instead of plastic and the tabs had to be set manually across the back of the machine; ribbons were damn near impossible to find. She'd typed school papers on the old monster, leaving her arms numb to the elbows sometimes, but her aunt had never seen the need for anything newer. "She can't really have said 'for anything newfangled.' I must have remembered it wrong later. They were country folks to start with, but they couldn't have been that hick." She dismissed that with ease of practice—school in Studio City all those years ago, fresh from the hills of Wyoming and most of her peers children of actors or somehow related to them, and much wealthier than she. Fifteen or more years back, plus the four-and-change she'd spent here in Rhadaz.

"You taught yourself how to type back in grade school," she said firmly. "You can do it again." One of the few clerks in the room glanced up; she shook her head and he went back to comparing several long sheets of thick paper.

Trade contracts—Chris's deal for that Mer Khani refrigerator, if she recalled; there had been half a dozen odd little things like that in this packet. And two large renewals of agreements, plus one she'd kept to go over herself: the English wanted to arrange a tour by a group of Rhadazi dancers, perhaps in exchange for a theater company of their own. Afronsan would be all for it, of course, and Shesseran had loved the string quartet that had come from London. *So did I, for that matter; bless Afronsan for getting them to come here when I was too morning-sick to go there.*

The Emperor still had a firm hand on imports, though, and if English theater in this place was anything like Victorian theater in her own world ... *Tact*, she thought. *Make sure he sees or reads the right things—nothing even remotely resembling Wilde. And wasn't Victoria "not amused" by Gilbert and Sullivan?* Whichever of them had written the lyrics she could never remember; the Queen had liked the music but found the words lacking in respect. Shesseran would've been able to give that old gal a lesson or two in arrogance, Jennifer thought, and bit the corner of her mouth to keep from laughing aloud. Then, if something like *The Mikado* were performed in English, he'd never catch a hundredth of it—probably wouldn't catch any more in Rhadazi, either. "My object all sublime, I shall achieve in time," she warbled softly. The clerk comparing documents was deep in his work and didn't look up this time. "To let the punishment fit the crime—heh, heh."

She went back to the stack of papers with a much lighter heart. And a stack there was: The Emperor's brother and Heir Afronsan had indeed given her the first couple months of her pregnancy completely off, just as he'd promised, but there was too much work for the vacation to last long and he was beginning to make up for lost time. "And next month when that darned telegraph line between the two of us is on-line—God." She blotted her throat once more, drew the typewriter across the desk, patted its squatty, heavy body fondly, and pulled the thick fold of paper from behind the platen.

A letter from Chris to brag up the gift and how he'd found it didn't surprise her; she'd heard from Robyn he was in Bez on his way to visit Duke's Fort and had half expected a fly-by-night visit after he rode up to Zelharri to see his mother, but he'd gone directly to Podhru and sent the box by Afronsan's courier. Her eyebrows went up; he'd actually typed the letter. "Forgot he knew how to use one of these things. Of course, he's—he *was*—

the computer-game kid, but that doesn't necessarily mean familiarity with a keyboard." She considered this, shook her head firmly. "Don't even think computer, either, Cray. Be grateful for low-tech goodies, it's definitely nine or ten up on ink pen and paper," she ordered herself.

The two pages were filled, front and back, liberally splattered with cross-outs, typos, and misspellings, and the spacing was creative, to say the least.

"Hey, lady, goody for you. It's a Mer Khani machine, why they don't want to spread the tech around to us poor Third Worlders is beyond me, but I only found out about them by weird accident (tell you some time, remind me) and actually had to go to the ENGLISH to find one I could buy.

"Good news is, the English will sell me as many as I want to buy—the guy I was dealing with has set up shop somewhere in their midlands, (I know, you don't care where, right?) and after I explained about the keyboard and how ours weren't set up in this order, he said if you wanted a bunch of 'em, we didn't actually get down to specific numbers, they could even change the arrangement of keys for you, make you a QWERTY special or something. I don't know, this was so goofy, using a typewriter AND doing it in Rhadazi at the same time, I wasn't as thrown by the order of keys thing, but you do more of this stuff than I do. Send word back to the Head Dude in Podhru; he and I are keeping in pretty close touch right now.

"The French are seriously tinkering with steam ships, did I tell you last time? Between that and the new canal through the New Gaelic Lake (Lake Nicaragua—I know, you don't care about the geography), we should be able to trim some serious time from these trips, and let me tell you, I am like heartily BORED with spending ten days to two weeks on a boat. Some of em are pretty with all the sails and brass and stuff, and the French speed ones are downright class, food and all, but they're still slow, and some of em—well, you don't want to know how the crews live, either, but it gets my hackles up, and it's hard keeping your mouth shut on a long trip. Ok, MY mouth. But I swear, I ever find someone hot to work on an airplane. . . . Okay, maybe a zeppelin, something with hot air and a propeller to guide it.

"Had to wait two days this last time through, spent some time on the right coast of New Gaul (Mexico to you) waiting for a ship to get me to French Jamaica, so I finally got to test the waters. As in, skin dive. Never thought I'd be diving that water—of course, I never thought I'd have to fake up my own fins and snorkle, I'm still trying to figure out a mask and burning my eyeballs out in salt water, but still, wow, I stayed under until I was one giant pink prune. The locals think I'm nuts, they sit on top of the water in hot, dry boats and sweat a lot, burn themselves black and fish with nets, go figure.

"I cut the Mom-visit short; sibs are both cute and ok but the whole Fort is just totally nuts right now. Isn't the old girl-pirate thing to plead your belly? Whatever, you better plan on being too preggers and sick to go visit if any of them ask you, it's cold and damp and has been all summer, and it's totally grim, Aletto's aching a lot and Mom's pissed about something and worried about Lizelle, who has to be sick cause she looks like death and hardly leaves her room and—well, plead your belly, stay home. The telegraph between you and them should be done by the time you get this, or not long after anyway, hey, it's almost as good as phone, right? So I'm almost out of paper and time and this thing is mangling my fingers, gotta go. Head Dude's putting a note in with this. If you don't get the typewriter, it's cause Afronsan has the hots for it so bad, he's almost drooling. I smell another super deal in the works for CEE-Tech, hope the English aren't pulling my leg about how many of these wristbreakers they can put out for us. Take care of yourself and don't let down your guard just because the rotten twins ate it and your old man offed their number-one pet brute, there's plenty more of 'em out there, believe me. Be as cautious as I am, you'll do fine, XXX, Chris."

Jennifer cast her eyes up, set the sheet aside and read the note Afronsan had put with it—typeset, fortunately. It was too gloomy in here with the shades drawn to read the Heir's writing, and he had a tendency to cover all bare paper, both sides, as though fearful of wasting the least inch. Worse than Chris—as bad, anyway.

"Thukara. I hope this finds you well. I thought you should know, the merchant Casimaffi has returned to Bezjeriad, and sent me a lengthy letter distancing himself from any illegal uses made, as he puts it, 'of my ships by my captains or others serving them—which uses I would never condone or permit if I knew of them.' In short, he claims innocence and has volunteered to come in person to assure me of his purity; unfortunately, we have no actual proof to link him with the illegal actions of the Thukar's twin brothers, or with any delivery of the substance Zero to anyone inside Rhadaz. I shall keep you apprised, Afronsan."

That rat. Jennifer glared at the letter with narrowed eyes, then pushed it aside. Casimaffi—Chuffles, as Chris's Bez partner Enardi called his father's old friend—had done his best to get them all killed. *Offer us a ship for transport, strand us on that high spit of land and then instead of a ship, send Dahven's brothers' men and Aletto's uncles' men . . . He only thinks I don't owe him for that one.*

She laid a hand on her stomach—not really that bowling-ball-shaped yet, she decided critically, but she'd have to let Afronsan get Casimaffi (if possible) and let that do her. *Humiliate the chubby little rat, that'll hurt him more than anything.* Probably the loss of the two or three ships the Emperor had confiscated when Zero was found on them—the ships and any future revenue they might have brought in—was hurting Casimaffi, whether or not he actually felt a financial pinch because of their loss.

She doubted he did; he had at least fifteen ships, or so Enardi said. Ernie, she reminded herself. Chris got shirty with her when she forgot the nickname he'd given his partner, just as he did when she called Edrith by his given name, instead of Eddie.

One more letter lay unopened on her desk, only one corner visible under the stack of official documents and papers from Afronsan. This one had come via caravan much earlier in the day. Jennifer unearthed it reluctantly, broke the seal, and unfolded it.

Damn Lialla anyway; if the Holmaddi don't kill her or Aletto doesn't strangle her, I'm going to. Back from the lovely, macho north one whole day and safe for the first time in weeks—and instead of heading home or coming to Sikkre to hide out until Aletto cooled off (*until I could cool him off*), she turned right around and went *back*? That much Jennifer already knew; the grandmother of the Gray Fishers had sent that message. Not why, just the flat, bare fact, along with Lialla's letter.

"Maybe she can explain herself. Damnit, she'd better." Jennifer groped for the damp cloth, dipped a corner in the water and sponged it across her face, blotted drips with her wrist, then began to read.

"Sin-Duchess Lialla to Thukara Jennifer:

"By the time you receive this message, I will doubtless be back in Holmaddan, somewhere deep within the city. Somehow, I am certain that even at such a great distance, I will feel the heat

of your—let us call it displeasure—that I have done something
so foolish." *You got that right in one, girlfriend,* Jennifer thought
grimly.

"I do apologize, Jen, for setting you between me and Aletto.
I know you understand how difficult my brother can often be—
stubborn, intractable and determined to swaddle all his women in
protective layers, wife, mother and sister alike. I admit he has a
little more cause to worry this time. I told everything to the Gray
Fishers' grandmother and my friend Sil who is one of her people; Sil promised to pass on to you what I told her if you send
for her. The grandmother tells me the caravan will stay in Sikkre
at least two days before moving on to Dro Pent. I fear that once
you hear Sil, you will agree with Aletto. Even during all my
years with my uncle and those days we spent together hiding
from him, I was never so near death so many times as I have
been in the north.

"In all honesty, a part of my mind tells me I must be mad. I
was cold and frightened most of these past days, in that village
and then in Holmaddan City. I was never certain—and still
not at all sure—that I accomplished anything, or that those
women are any better off than they were.

"But this time will be different." *Sure, lady, they all say that.*
"I have seen part of a shipment of the drug Zero. I know nothing
that can be proved but I cannot simply walk away and leave the
matter to others. And I think the city women can use me. Where
I stood out in a village, I might not in Holmaddan City. Also, I
left that stupid boy in danger—he is too proud, stubborn, and
young all at once to keep himself from trouble. Either he will
give away that he has learned to Wield or that he aided my escape, and they will kill him. He saved my life; I cannot let him
die because he is an arrogant young Holmaddi male and so not
worth the effort—or because I was too afraid to go back."

Jennifer read this paragraph twice, finally shook her head,
swore under her breath and went on. Hardly any of it made
sense. Boy? What problems in that village? This Sil had better
be ready to talk. She drew a pad over, scribbled herself a note—
*Get someone to locate that caravan this afternoon, get the
woman Sil here right away.* She glared at the note, transferred the
glare to Lialla's letter.

"Also, the boy knows the Duke's armsmen—his father after
all was one—and I think I can persuade him to help me learn

more about the traffic in Zero. If only for the mercenary reason that I will teach him more Thread.

"There is a last matter: The Duke has a Triad, which he has kept as close a secret from all outsiders as my uncle did his. Since it is no longer a crime to maintain one, I wonder why he does it, and if there is some secret purpose to it. If so, knowing Vuhlem as I now do, he has no good purpose in mind. But I also wonder about the Triad itself; Jadek's vanished from Duke's Fort before we ever came there, you will recall, and has not been heard of since." *Oh, great. It keeps getting better.*

"The grandmother told me what things have happened while I was out of contact with the rest of Rhadaz: A pity Dahven's wretched brothers could not have left well enough alone, and stayed away once they fled the lands. I am glad for you both, though, that you carry Dahven's child. Take care of yourself, and the baby. If you will, please, when you write to Aletto, send word to Mother that all is well. I hear she has taken a turn for the worse and I fear it is some dread disease she keeps from all of us. But—if she is taking Zero, as the grandmother said Robyn thinks she is . . .

"I see the son of the grandmother coming to warn me. I must leave Hushar Oasis shortly and go north with the Silver Hawk clan. Jen, give my love to my brother—and of course, to Chris when you next see him. I know he will laugh at the very notion, but warn him to be careful around those who traffic in this Zero; if the foreigners are anything like Duke Vuhlem, they are indeed deadly.

"Lialla."

Jennifer set the letter down and stared at it moodily. Finally she shoved it as far away from her as her arm would reach, planted her elbows on the desk and let her head fall into her hands. "I'll murder her. Twice. Her and Chris both. Telling me to be careful while they go out and tiptoe through the bear-traps, they're both nuts." She groaned and gripped her hair with both hands, tugged at it furiously. "And I'm nuts, letting them both use me as a switchboard. God." She stared blankly through her fingers for several moments, then sat up and pulled the typewriter over to the edge of the desk and threaded a sheet of thick Rhadazi paper into it. The letters were every bit as hard to find as Chris had warned—really strange for someone who'd been a touch-typist more of her life than not—and the action was more like using a ten-pound axe on cordwood than the electronic wonders she'd used most recently. *Better than ink pens, keep that firmly in mind,* she reminded herself.

Robyn had always griped about her handwriting; well, this time she might cuss at the content of the letter, but at least she'd be able to read it.

IT was barely past midday in Zelharri, but all along the second-floor hall of the fort, lamps were lit to counter the gloom of yet another heavily overcast, damp day. The stone walls smelled damp, even under the thickly scented incense burning in pots at both ends. Thick wads of cloth had been laid across the deep windowsill at the stair end of the hall to block the chill wind that whistled through the ill-fitted casing and to catch the water that puddled there when it rained.

Men's voices from the courtyard filtered into the silent hall. The hush was broken by the creak of hinges, the par-Duchess's glass-cutting shrill voice echoing in the hallway, immediately and blessedly muffled by the slam of her door. Robyn glared at the door she'd just hauled shut behind her and stalked down the hall to the Ducal apartments.

But at the double doors to the rooms Lizelle had once shared with Aletto's father and then with Jadek, she hesitated. Her right hand gripped the latch so hard her knuckles stood out white. "Damn. No, she isn't going to pull this on me again. And who knows when Aletto will be tied up halfway across the fort again?" How many times—Robyn had long since lost track how many times she had fought her own discomfort at prying and hysterical scenes both and tried to confront Aletto's mother—to get the woman to let her find a healer, an herbalist, or anyway to *talk* about what was wrong with her. "And each time, she goes into hysterics, or Aletto comes in and shoos me away. Or I back off." She looked at the crumpled sheet in her left hand: She hadn't even had time to tell Lizelle where her only daughter was, what Lialla was doing. Even that she was safe. "Yeah, right; safe like I used to be hitchhiking on Sunset Strip. Safe like a chicken playing with the foxes." She turned her head to look back down the dark, empty hall and sighed; her shoulders sagged. "Yeah, right, I love this crap. Jen, damnit, you owe me for this one. Go on, girl, before she quits squawking long enough to bolt the door."

She'd waited too long: Lizelle *had* bolted the door. It was just enough to tip Robyn's mood from tentative to furious. She slammed the side of her fist against thick wood. "Lizelle! If you don't let me in, *right now!*" Another echoing slam. "I am going to stand *out* here, *in* the hall, and let the whole fort hear me!" She stepped back a pace, folded her arms and waited.

A muffled, teary voice answered her. "Go away, Robyn. I won't listen to you."

Slam! "Well, everyone else on this side of the fort sure will! You really want that?" A long silence, enough for Robyn, who was panting slightly, to catch her breath. A faint click; the door opened just a crack and one dark, accusing eye looked out at her. "I'm serious, Lizelle." Robyn lowered her voice. "If it were just you—but it's not."

"Go away," Lizelle sniffed discreetly; she would have closed the door, but Robyn had the tip of her low boot shoved into the opening. She held up Jen's letter, by now badly crumpled.

"I have a message for you, from Lialla." Lizelle eyed her warily, then stepped back, letting the door swing free. She blotted her eyes against the back of her hand, walked to the center of the spacious sitting room and stopped just short of the hearth, her back stiff and unforgiving.

"Where—is she coming home?"

"She's been in Holmaddan—"

"I *know* that!" Lizelle snapped. "In that coastal village, pretending to be a common Thread novice and talking to women. Why she would ever go—" She made an impatient gesture, fell silent.

"Yes, well. You wouldn't have gone and neither would I, but Lialla did. She sent Jennifer a note—"

"Jen?" Like so many Rhadazi, Lizelle hadn't been able to manage Jennifer's full name; she still used the nickname. "She writes notes to Jen but not to her mother?"

"She apparently didn't have much time. She—"

"Why not?" Lizelle whirled around, sending her skirts dangerously close to the fire. Robyn eyed it warily.

"Because she had something important to tell the Emperor, and she went back. No, wait." Robyn held up a hand, silencing the older woman. "Just let me finish. I don't know any more answers to why than you do. She went back, she's in the city now. She told Jen to send you her love, and to tell you she's safe where she is for now."

"Safe." Lizelle blotted her nose on a gauzy little square of embroidered lace, and tucked it back in her sleeve. "She isn't safe in Vuhlem's city, she's mad to think it."

"I happen to agree with you on that point," Robyn said. "But she went back for you, in a way. Because she wasn't just there to help women, she was watching for outside drugs being brought into Rhadaz." She was watching Lizelle closely. "And she found them."

"I—" The par-Duchess opened her mouth, closed it without saying anything, and turned away. Robyn waited her out. After a very long, uncomfortable silence, she laughed and said, "What has that to do with me?"

"You know best what, Lizelle. Drugs like Zero aren't common here, not like they are where I come from. I used to take some of them, I've told you that, haven't I? So I know a little about what they do to people—"

"Zero?"

It was Robyn's turn to laugh. "If you're trying to fake me, don't bother. Everyone in Duke's Fort knows about it, Aletto's got border guards watching for smugglers—I'll bet damned near everyone in Rhadaz knows *about* it, or at least has heard the name." Another silence. "I think you're taking it, Lizelle. Not just for the fun of it, like I took things, but because you're hurting, and it helps the pain."

Lizelle started convulsively, then stood very still. Her back was still to her son's wife but Robyn had caught the sudden movement of her head, the direction of her anxious eyes. She swallowed the last of her compunctions and strode past the woman, caught hold of the small chest Lizelle had looked at, and yanked at the lid. With a shrill "No!" the par-Duchess threw herself on Robyn and clawed at her outstretched arm. "How dare you come into my rooms and touch my things? *Get out!*"

"Not until you explain this," Robyn shouted her down. A ring of thin, yellowish rope dangled from her far hand. "Who's bringing it to you, your girls? Because no one else has such freedom to go where they like and come back to you, Aletto's had nearly every place and every *one* around here searched at odd times, but never them, you'd never stand for that, would you?"

"Give that to me—!"

"Damnit, woman, don't you know what this stuff can do to you?"

"It's not—I don't—" Lizelle burst into tears again. Robyn gritted her teeth and raised her voice once more.

"It's-not-I-don't what? It isn't a drug, it isn't dangerous, you don't use it, you don't care? Your daughter's out there somewhere risking her hide to stop this stuff from taking over your country—*our* country!—and keep you from killing yourself with it. All right, let that go, what do you care about Lialla?"

"You can't—"

"Shut up and listen to me," Robyn hissed furiously. Startled, Lizelle fell silent and stared at her with wide, teary, smudged eyes. Robyn fought the urge to shake the woman until her teeth rattled. She looked like a spoiled child caught breaking the rules. *Like a damned victim, like Jen once said about me. No wonder she used to get so pissed.* Was that what all her own men had seen—what Chris had seen when he came down on her for using drugs? Some of his arguments came back to her, and inwardly she cringed, but her face stayed hard. "Have you looked at yourself lately, Lizelle? My God, you're a beautiful woman—you *were*, except you've aged twenty years over the past year. You look like a hag. How do you think that makes Aletto feel? You hide out in your rooms, you won't talk to us, you won't let us do anything to help you—hell, we don't even know what's wrong!"

"It's not," Lizelle began sullenly. Sounds from the doorway, someone shuffling booted feet on bare stone; she broke off and turned to look, then ran past Robyn and across the room.

"Oh, *hell*," Robyn mumbled. She knew it was Aletto before she turned. Aletto was holding his mother tightly while she wept into his shirt, glaring over her head at his wife. "How long have you been there?"

"I just came. One of Mother's maids came to get me; she said the whole fort could hear you screaming at her."

"Aletto—"

"Shhh, it's all right, Mother." He patted her hair. Robyn scowled at them both, then held up the rope ring where he could see it.

"You know what this is," she said crisply. He stared at it. Lizelle, sensing some change in him, pushed back to look at his face, then laid her own against his shirt once more. One accusing eye met Robyn's; she let it close and clung to Aletto's sleeve. "It's Zero; she's been taking it for God knows how long. And it comes from Holmaddan, unless I'm very mistaken." Robyn held up the letter. "At least, that's what Lialla thinks."

"Lialla," Aletto echoed blankly. He blinked; his mouth tightened. "What does Lialla know about this?"

Robyn told him, held out the letter. "Read it yourself, there's more. That's the important stuff, though."

"She—she went back, to try and prove *Vuhlem* is involved in that stuff? He'll kill her!"

"She's not totally helpless," Robyn snapped.

"She's a damned stubborn fool," Aletto growled. "But we can talk about that later. What were you doing going through Mother's things in the first place?"

Robyn rolled her eyes. "Why am I defending Lialla to you, and why are we fighting about this? Aletto, damnit, do you think I would snoop in Lizelle's room if I didn't have a damned good reason? *You* know what this stuff is, and what is does; she's killing herself with it! And by letting it come into the fort, she's undoing all the hard work you've put into keeping it out of Zelharri!"

"You can't—"

"Oh, yes, I can," Robyn said sharply. "I know about drugs. You've had my input on a lot of the stuff you've done to keep the Duchy free of it; you *know* I know about them."

Lizelle was eyeing her sidelong once again. "My *real* daughter would never—"

"Don't," Robyn implored her. "Your real daughter wouldn't say boo to you, all right? I know that. She's up north instead, risking her stubborn, stupid neck to cut off your supply, and leaving me to hold the baby instead. When she comes home, I think I'll wring her neck for doing this to me."

Aletto put Lizelle from him and stalked across the room; his shoulder was too high and his leg was clearly hurting him once more. Robyn compressed her lips and kept her concerns behind them. "Mother's not well, you have no business—" He stopped; Robyn had begun to laugh.

"Oh, hell, Aletto. Why are we arguing? I know your mother isn't well; I also know she's drugged to her hind teeth. And I *also* know that this stuff is dangerous." She dangled the rope ring under his nose. "And so do you. But if you won't put any pressure on her to admit she's sick and get a healer, do something *right*, I'm going to do what I have to. I don't want to fight with you, not over something we really both agree on." Silence. Aletto's face lost its angry set; all at once he looked worn and tired. Almost old. And when he finally spoke, he sounded old and tired; his voice was so soft, Lizelle over by the door couldn't have heard him.

"I—Robyn, what do you want me to do? I can't just—"

Robyn lowered her own voice. "You can put your mother in the guest rooms across the hall, have this apartment thoroughly searched, and have the guard keep an eye on those twins from now on." He looked at her unhappily. "But you won't, will you?"

He was silent for a very long time. He finally took the bit of rope from her and turned to face Lizelle. She looked back at him, her eyes wide and fearful, then threw herself at him—too late. Aletto took the two steps to the hearth and threw the ring into the flames. He caught Lizelle's hands before she could burn herself trying to retrieve it, held her until it had burned to ash and the fire settled down once more. "Robyn. Are there any others in the box?"

"No. Wait—a bottle of liquid, under her embroidery thread."

"Bring it over, pour it out. Mother, please, don't."

"Take her across the hall," Robyn said firmly. But Aletto shook his head, and once Robyn had poured the contents of the small brown bottle out the window onto rain-soaked slate tiles, he let go of Lizelle, took Robyn by the arm and led her into the hall, shutting the door behind them. Robyn's knees were beginning to tremble.

Once the door was closed, Aletto pressed her onto the low bench next to it and said quietly, "I left a meeting; I'm going back. I'll see you tonight at dinner." Robyn nodded; she wasn't certain she wanted to see his face just now. Aletto limped off in the direction of the kitchens; as the sound of his footsteps faded, she let her head sink into her hands.

I don't believe I did that. I don't believe it. What Aletto thought of her right now— *He's not stupid. He knows I had to, he's known it all along.* He wouldn't admit it, of course. Any more than he'd have Lizelle's rooms searched, or those of her girls. *I'll have to stay tough, and keep an eye on all three of them. God. I hate this. I really am gonna kill that Lialla.*

If Vuhlem, or his Triad, didn't beat her to it.

2

T was warm, even for the time of year, along the southern coast
of French Jamaica. Humid, too—particularly for so late at night.
Of course, there was hardly ever any breeze in lower Philippe-sur-
Mer, and anyway, the windows in this club were all shut tight.
Chris blotted his forehead cautiously on a finely woven, snowy
white sleeve, gave the man seated across from him at the oval table
a faint smile and shrug, then scooped up the cards the other had
dealt out, fanned them open long enough to see what was there—
Hey, not so bad—and flipped them shut again.

Several other men sat around the table, most of them simply
watching now as the second son of the Duc D'Orlean, Henri
Dupret, peered at his own cards by tipping up the ends with very
long, pale fingers. He smiled, too, a movement of thin, mobile
lips under a thickly drooping black moustache that didn't quite
reach his eyes; Chris scooped up two of the silver-colored metal
chips and tossed them into the center of the table.

"Out." The man on Chris's left sighed heavily, shoved the
chair back, scooped up his few remaining tokens and left the circle of lamplight. "Me, too." Another, halfway between Chris and
Dupret, leaned back in his chair and folded his arms across his
chest—like the men on both sides of him and on both sides of
Dupret, simply watching.

"Card?" Dupret inquired. Chris made a show of considering
this, finally glanced at his hand once more, smiled faintly and
shook his head. "I will take—one." The accent was only just
there, the man's English impeccable.

Cannot even believe I am doing this, Chris thought as Dupret
made a show of his own, discarding one, dealing the new card
with exaggerated care from the top, squaring the deck and setting

it in the exact center of the table before adding the card to his hand and picking it up. He moved one card, a second. Shifted the first one back; frowned at the cards, and then at the lamp. Chris suddenly felt faintly ridiculous. *Acting without cameras—or the other guys in the D&D game.* But poker *was* acting, after all. So one of Robyn's boyfriends had said. Chris leaned back in his chair and rubbed his shoulders against the padded surface, and kept his eyes on the man opposite him.

There wasn't much to see around them, anyway: Like most of the private clubs in French Jamaica, this one was quite plainly done up inside, nothing like Vegas or Reno—just a steep, narrow flight of uncarpeted steps leading to a single large room of dark walls, a discreet bar set against one of them, a few deep and high-backed chairs and tiny tables set close to the bar for men who wanted to sit and drink and watch the card games but still be able to converse without bothering the gamblers; anywhere from one table (as this place had) to four. It was only the third time Chris had been in such a club in his four-plus years of trading in this end of the world, but then, it took an invitation from a member, and members were ordinarily men like Henri Dupret: second and third sons of the wealthy or noble back in France or Spain or the Italiate Confederation of States, now and again a Balt or even more rarely, an Englishman. Men who had what was called Family, or Class, who kept to their own company, made what Chris considered to be disgraceful profits from their plantations and trading operations and shipped most of it back home, spending the great portion of what they kept—still notable wealth—on gambling, fine carriages and finer houses, expensive horses and the like. So far as he could tell, the word "charity" wasn't part of the language in this end of the world.

Ordinarily a trader—even the head of a highly profitable company like CEE-Tech, which sought out recent developments like the telegraph, typewriters, mechanized milling and spinning equipment, whose three owners had the ear of the heir to the Rhadazi throne and who paid very well for what they bought—ordinarily such a man would never cross the paths with the upper crust anywhere in this end of the world, particularly not in French Jamaica.

But Henri Dupret was a rarity: Known for his "hands on" approach to his business ventures, rather than leaving matters to the agents, he often came to the docks to meet with people, or to see his ships loaded and unloaded. It was said he even went into the fields to see how his sugar did and that he talked personally with his workers, something that would have branded a lesser noble-man as slightly mad, or Not One of Us. With his family connec-tions and his wealth, and his otherwise orthodox behavior, Dupret was instead looked upon as a community leader. He had twice been chosen as Governor by his peers.

Chris had been in port less than an hour this last trip out when Henri Dupret approached him, calling him by name and speaking with a familiarity that in anyone else would have left Chris wary at least. With Dupret—Chris had mentally shrugged, brought up the matter of the new French steamers; Dupret had smiled, though his onyxlike eyes remained flat and expressionless, dep-recatingly denied any knowledge of these matters, and instead mentioned a possible deal on sugar. Chris, never one to turn down a bargain on sugar since Jen still preferred it to the honey used throughout Rhadaz, had casually bargained price with him as Dupret watched crates of rum distilled from his sugar and boxes of exotic desert brandies being loaded onto the sleek *Le Chat* for shipment to his father's estates on the Mediterranean.

And then Dupret had casually made mention of machinery he used for harvesting; Chris had expressed interest, and Dupret suggested a visit later to his plantation to watch the equipment in use. He had finished up with an invitation to his club. "You are staying where—at the Parrot? An excellent establishment, I know the owner quite well. So, I will send my carriage for you, this evening at—ah, do you have a watch? Good. At nine, then."

Chris glanced at his cards once more and frowned, tapped one finger on the table and glanced at Dupret, who was busily shift-ing cards from one side of his hand to the other. *Actually, the dude's price on sugar isn't that good; besides, I already have a line on as much Cuban sugar as Jennifer could use. Gotta see if we can't expand the Rhadazi market, Mom would argue it, but honey isn't any better for you than sugar anyway. Bee poop, didn't someone call it that? Bad for babies, I remember reading that.* He picked up his own cards, raised his eyebrows and moved one from the center of his hand to the left—didn't mean anything, of course, but Dupret's fiddling probably didn't, either.

This guy only just thinks I'm gonna deal in booze. All those years living with Mom and a wine bottle—forget it. Not that he intended to tell Dupret that.

Because Eddie had mentioned Henri Dupret once or twice of late: as one of those to watch. One of those on French Jamaica who might well be involved in the trafficking of Zero—and who was high enough in rank to possibly know more than those Eddie talked to. *God knows the stuff is thick on the ground here; and man, talk about rumor mill— If I had a grain of truth for a hundredth of the gossip, I'd be able to go home, tell the Chief Dude who's trying to hook his country and retire to the country, right?* But there was a frustrating lack of fact about the shipment of Zero into Rhadaz as well as the darker powers and their intent behind the substance. *Well, sure. Where I come from, don't the cartels mangle people just to make sure the secrets stay kept?*

It wasn't hard to figure out the interest someone like old Casimaffi had: money. He'd lost a little ground recently, all those ships confiscated, and a major dose of humiliation when he'd turned up on the wrong side of a coup attempt by Dahven's brothers against him.

But even if he could find the nasty little man, old Chuffles was still small potatoes, Chris thought; it was unlikely anyone who knew the first thing about the man, or had dealt with him, would ever trust him with any major secrets.

Time to move up a notch, Chris had told himself this last trip out—and carefully kept that from his mother and his aunt. But it was time: With Deehar and Dayher out of action and a tight coast watch all up and down Rhadaz, things would slow down a while, but the upper hierarchy was still in place. *And I got a personal motive: It was probably the twins and their buddy Eprian who tried to murder Jen and Dahven with poisoned wine, but I'm the guy who drank it and damned near took their place. Yeah, someone's gonna pay me back for that little party.*

Eddie hadn't been terribly pleased with Chris when they had hooked back up, a few days earlier, and had argued long and hard the whole journey from the new Mer Khani Canal through the Gaelic States Peninsular Lake here to Philippe-sur-Mer. He was frankly horrified when Chris brought news of his meeting with Dupret on the docks, and the invitation. "You're not—you are taking it, aren't you? Chris, you're mad! I would plan on a good sick headache, if I were you. You know? You're the one always warning me not to fool around with the whole Zero business, yelling at me for talking to men on the streets and in the dives and now you're going to a private club like that? They could kill you, dump the body out the back door, who would ever know?"

Chris had laughed as he climbed into his one set of fancy dress—sleek black trousers, a fine-woven white shirt with frills, a bright blue embroidered silk vest and darker blue sash, and low black boots. "No one's going to mess up the carpet in a private club; you know what some of that stuff costs? When the revolution comes, and they string up guys like that by their bloated capitalistic thumbs from the nearest lamppost . . ."

"Yah. *Really* funny. Noble, not capitalistic."

"It's all money stolen from the proletariat, right? Hey, don't worry, they know we hang out together, I'll make certain this rich pig knows *you* know where I am this evening, okay? Cool?"

"Right," Eddie had grumbled. "Put *my* head on the block, too, why don't you?"

"Don't sweat the small stuff," Chris had assured him cheerfully. "A few hands of cards, lose a little cash, gain his confidence, maybe get a chance to talk to him alone, or set up something for later, like he said, out at his sugar plantation, talk about machinery and hostile takeovers—"

"You're nuts. I mean, *rully*. You want the body shipped home to Robyn, or just burned and the ashes dumped out to sea?"

"Burn it; it would be, like, totally gross by the time it got back to Sehfi. Mom would curse me forever." A discreet tap at the door. Chris had glanced at his pocket watch, tugged self-consciously at the frilled white shirt cuffs and gone.

THE shirt was sticking to his back now, and the high collar and matching white cravat were threatening to choke him. The embroidered silk vest might as well have been made of ripstop and filled with polyester foofing, the way it held in extra warmth. *Well, at least I didn't have to go with a jacket, or a real honest-to-God suit, that would have been the utter end.* This wasn't much better, so far as comfort was concerned. For looks, though—actually, he was rather pleased with the overall effect, though he was careful not to let Eddie catch him preening in front of a mirror. Swashbuckly stuff, particularly the way he wore his hair these days—longer (it was a lighter blond than it had been in L.A. and bore a wave, probably from so much sun and sea air) and with a long, narrow tail he tied back in black ribbon. This small, dark room and the card table were all it took: He felt like somebody in a classy pirate movie.

But so far, he hadn't had much chance to talk to Dupret, other than a few pleasantries in the carriage about the weather, the streets, about his trip through the new canal across what he'd once known as Lake Nicaragua. Once inside the club, they'd gone directly to this table, where Dupret was well known, had been brought an unopened deck, and other men had gradually drifted over to join the game.

It wasn't one of the fancy casino games—nothing really like the poker he'd known from old television westerns—and from the little he'd played with a few of his mother's old boyfriends, off and on. Similar—like the cards—and just enough off that Chris found himself glad he hadn't played much back in L.A.; a real card hound might well have been lost at the differences. *More likely crazy to learn a whole new way to lose money. Of course, how much poker is a seventeen-year-old gonna get to play?* Hard to remember sometimes, that was all he'd been when that old wart Merrida had caught them with a Night-Thread drawing spell and hauled him from a pleasant, if poor, life in L.A. to *this* world.

He put all thought of Merrida aside with no effort at all; it had been nearly five years, and if a guy couldn't adjust by now ... After all, he thought as he ran a finger along the edge of his cards and watched Henri Dupret thoughtfully considering his options, he hadn't done so bad, thus far. None of them had, really: His mother had been married all this time and to the same guy, she'd given Duke Aletto an heir and a daughter—and himself a couple really cute half-siblings in the process. In Jen's last letter, she said she and Dahven were working on a baby. *Wonder how she's gonna fit a kid into her schedule?* Between clearing contracts for the Heir, working on the Sikkreni market, running the household, just running ...

Dupret glanced down at his pile of silver tokens, then let his eye rest on Chris's stack. The piles had seesawed for hours, and were once again about even. *Wonder what time it is?* Chris thought suddenly. He didn't dare fish for his watch, though—didn't want to take his eye off Dupret, who just might be one of those guys who kept high cards up his sleeve; besides, the man would certainly interpret the move as a desire on Chris's part to be gone. *Which I would like, yeah. Never. But I really think I need to get close to this guy, I think I could learn stuff from him—and looking bored with his favorite playpen and his pet game sure won't do it.* He eased himself down a little lower in the chair, stretched long legs out in front of him.

The waiter came over with a tray: another cut-glass snifter of plain orange juice for Chris, a tall glass of something dark and mostly rum for Dupret. Chris sipped cautiously—*check for booze, they don't always remember and I don't want to pass out here.* Not, as he'd told Jennifer his last trip home, that he *couldn't* drink if he had to—he just truly didn't like to. Particularly rum, which tasted purely gross. But realistically, one drink of anything was enough to put a serious dent in his ability to concentrate. This tasted of nothing but orange: very cold, probably fresh squeezed, a little too much sugar, maybe, but otherwise all right. *I could do without the sugar, but they never remember that.* He took another sip, put the glass aside as Dupret tossed half a dozen tokens onto the table and blandly smiled at him.

He won that hand; Dupret the next; Chris the next four. He was vaguely aware now of different men sitting at the table, though no one else played. Of men standing around in the dimmer light of the main room, watching the game.

Dupret had been drinking steadily since breaking open the pack of cards, and the French accent which had been scarcely obvious became more noticeable. The men sitting around the table began to leave, one here, another there; no one else sat down and finally the two of them had it to themselves. There were fewer men standing around watching; it must, Chris thought wearily, be getting terribly late. And he was hungry. But a glance at Dupret told him it wouldn't be a good idea to try to quit now—not with most of Dupret's money in front of him. *So how do I lose most of this? Fast?*

He drank another snifter of orange, this not sweet at all; Dupret drank down two more rums in quick order and lost all but three tokens. He looked up as a man in a bright blue jacket leaned over him. "Sir, M. Dupret, it's nearly five, we must close the doors soon." Dupret bared his teeth and for a moment his eyes were blackly furious, but he turned the threatening look into a smile so quickly Chris wondered if he'd seen it at all. *Five! Whoa, no wonder I'm half starved!* He was light-headed, too. *Yeah, but that's lack of food, a rully late hour, God I must be getting old, I don't do that stuff any more these days.* He drained the last of his orange, set it aside. The room blurred a little; Chris blinked rapidly, blotted his forehead on his sleeve again.

"We could—we could finish this tomorrow," he suggested; he had to think, hard, to get the words out, to decide what he wanted to say. *Glad Dupret has his carriage waiting; I'd hate to walk back to the inn this tired. Jeez, I bet I couldn't even find it from here.* Sobering thought. He tried to blink his vision clear, chose the next words with care. "You know, let them hold the stakes, everything as it is? I'd be willing—"

Dupret turned that black gaze on him; his eyes focused and he relaxed. "We can—yes, we could do that. If you wish. Most gentlemanly sugg-suggestion." He glanced at the manager. "But for now—one last bet," he said, the question implicit. The manager spread his arms wide and sighed rather dramatically, but nodded and went away. "One last bet," Dupret turned back to Chris. "One more hand. All that—what you have of your own and what you won from me, now. All that if I win."

"Right. And if you lose?" Chris thought rapidly—or tried to. Probably wanted to give him a note of some kind, pay him back later when his bank opened. *Good thing I only drank orange juice tonight, I feel half plotzed anyway.* But the guy was wealthy, he had land and both a country house and a town apartment. A father to back him who was second only to the King of France for position and money. An I.O.U. might be tough to collect if Dupret wanted to stiff him, but then, noblemen usually didn't do that with gambling debts, something to do with honor and all. Might even be a good way to arrange another meeting, actually spend some time talking with the guy—

Dupret smiled, gestured broadly with his hands to take in the pile of tokens, his own few remaining bits, the deck of cards and the table between them. "If I lose, you keep all that—and I give you also my daughter."

His jaw must have dropped a foot; Chris simply stared and Dupret laughed. "Your—I can't do that!"

"Bah. Of course you can!"

"But—you can't just—you can't—!"

"I can! She is mine, my blood, my child to do with as I will! As any father in French Jamaica can do with his child." He scowled. "Do not look at me in such offense, it is not as though I offered you a—a servant in payment!"

"I can't—" Chris clutched at the table edge; Dupret receded behind a gray fog. When he came back to himself, the man was calmly dealing out cards, and the proper number of tokens were in the center of the table, his own fingers on the first two cards. A chill ran down his back. *Oh, jeez, I lost it. I really lost it, I can't remember, did I actually go along with what he said just now? But I must have, the cards, the ante— Oh, man? I know I didn't drink anything but orange—!* He couldn't think that through, couldn't remember anything of the last few minutes, and just trying to logic the situation out set the room moving, fading in and out in an alarming fashion. *Concentrate on the cards*, he ordered himself angrily.

Fixing his eyes on his fingers helped, a little. *And lose this one*, he told himself. But he suddenly couldn't remember why that was so desperately important.

Clink. He looked up. Dupret had just tossed two of his remaining tokens onto the table and was waiting patiently. Chris looked at the cards, shrugged and tossed out two. It was a gruesome hand, not much there. He thought about just holding it; no good. Dupret would know his opponent hadn't even tried, and he'd probably be deeply offended. *Careful about how you discard, too*, he reminded himself. Dupret frequently checked the discards once a hand was over. He stared at the cards, braced his back hard against the back of the chair, finally nodded and freed two at random, tossed them to the table, face down. Dupret, intensely onyx pebble-eyes fixed on him, dealt two, pushed them across the table, then took three for himself.

"What have you, my friend?" It seemed forever since anyone had spoken.

"Hey." It was a terrible effort, getting the words out, and it seemed dreadfully important to him not to let Dupret know he was losing it. "It's—um. It's your hairy bet. Why don't you show *me*?"

"Why not set them down together, since the bet itself is already agreed upon?" Dupret countered softly. He laid his face up, spread them with a deft gesture; Chris put his cards down and spread them with fingers that wanted to tremble. *Oh, jeez.* He couldn't think! Couldn't decipher his own hand, didn't stand a chance of figuring out Dupret's. *I've been Mickeyed. Jeez, but I can't have been! But—but who doctored that last glass of orange?* Not Dupret, at least; the man had been right here, and he hadn't so much as moved a finger that might have been suspicious. *Eddie, I swear I'll never laugh at your advice again, I gotta get out of here!*

Dupret smiled, turned his hand palm up and gestured across the center of the table rather grandly before gathering together the last tokens and dropping them with a clink atop Chris's cards. "Five of a kind against two pairs—my friend, fortune beams upon you, indeed she does. Come—yes, yes, Francois, we are just leaving, thank you for your patience in this, will you send one of your servants to make certain my carriage is downstairs?"

Somehow, Chris found himself in possession of an outrageous

fold of paper money in exchange for the tokens, on his feet, and being led down a flight of stairs to the street by Dupret—who was not terribly steady himself. Chris clutched at the railing and concentrated on his footing, breathed a sigh of relief as they reached the street.

It was light enough, easily, to make out the carriage waiting across the street; Dupret's man holding the door for them. Chris cleared his throat, glanced at the sky. "Whoa. You know, it's really late; my man is going to wonder where I am."

"Not so late as all that," Dupret mumbled. "Only half past six."

"Um, well—actually," Chris said, "why don't I just walk from here, save you the trouble—?"

He stopped abruptly as Dupret turned on him, his eyes gleaming with a truly murderous light, his teeth bared. There was no mistaking the look this time. *Wow. Dude's fifty bytes short of a meg.* They still fought duels in this part of the world. Chris swallowed, tried and somehow managed to keep to his feet and not retreat from the Frenchman. "You will come with me, M. Cray! Or do you forget the rest of your winnings?"

"Um. Well, no, I didn't forget, sir, and you know, I really, truly appreciate the honor, sir, don't think I don't. But maybe if you, ah, went and talked to her first, broke the news to her, then I could come over later in the day, maybe you introduce us—?"

"I said you will take her, marry her! Did you think I meant later? Tonight—now, this hour!" Dupret snarled. "Maurice, come aid the gentleman into the coach!" The servant—who, Chris noted unhappily, topped him by half a head at least, to say nothing of a foot of shoulder—came over and took hold of his arm, neatly escorted him the last few steps to the carriage and pressed him inside, closing the door behind both men. "We will talk, now," Dupret added grimly.

But for a moment or so, he was still. The carriage moved off down the street. Chris slumped back into the cushions as it turned a corner. He couldn't remember ever wanting so badly to just curl up and sleep; definitely couldn't remember too many times when it would have been more dangerous to do so. But Dupret smiled pleasantly, in a distinct and unnerving change of mood. Suddenly, he began to talk, pulling out his watch and opening the case as he leaned forward. "There. That is my Marie. I met her, oh, when I first came here—more years ago than you have entirely, I think. And I bought her contract from the house where she worked as soon as I was able, and she gave me Ariadne."

The inner face of the watch case held a miniature painting—a rather dark woman with a pile of gleaming black curled hair, high cheekbones, a slightly distorted and overly broad mouth. There were tears in the corners of the Frenchman's eyes as he looked down at it before closing it and putting the watch back into his pocket. He sniffed once, loudly, and his voice turned maudlin.

"I regret only one thing, after all these years, that I never wed Marie and made a wife of her—but the difficulties when you are French, and noble, and of the house which is mine. And a leader of your own class in a backward and barbaric part of the world such as this. So very much I loved that woman. Beautiful, gentle—ah, well." He took out a handkerchief and wiped his eyes, vigorously blew his nose, and went on, much more briskly and all business. "Ariadne—yes, you will take her with you, but you will marry her first; that much at least I can do for her. You are not a French nobleman—but she is not noble except by half, and not—not legitimate," he added distastefully.

Well, cool, so we got something in common, Chris thought irreverently. *Bastards the both of us.* His head cleared very briefly. *God, am I drunk or drugged—or just nuts? I can't let him do this to some poor girl!* He must have moved or spoken; Dupret looked at him inquiringly.

"You do not—do not dare refuse my only child? You do not insult me and her so? She is not legitimate, but she is still a Dupret, and the daughter of the son of the Duc D'Orlean! Whom do you think King Louis keeps by his side and consults upon the least matter of state? The Duc D'Orlean, my father—Ariadne's grandsire! You do not dare insult her by refusing her hand?"

"Oh—hey," Chris mumbled, "never crossed my mind. Swear." Swords and single-shot pistols—every bad duel scene from the movies came back to haunt him; one or two fencing sessions with Dahven, four years ago on the road, would be less than useful. Dupret would laugh at his bo and simply shoot him dead. He couldn't hit the broad side of a barn from the inside with one of those dueling pistols—most men couldn't, but Chris had a sneaking suspicion the man who shared the carriage with him was probably dead accurate with one. Dupret eyed him suspiciously; Chris managed a smile, but the fog had wrapped around him once again, and he couldn't get any more words out. He nodded cautiously; the interior of the carriage swam, and Dupret faded. He couldn't be certain whether he'd lost any time or not; the carriage had stopped before a stylish town house when he next glanced out the window.

"Go, put the coach away," Dupret ordered the driver as a uniformed houseman came out to open the carriage door. "But hold ready, should the merchant and my daughter need you. Come with me, M. Cray." The hallway was all white and palest blue, marble floor, well lit despite the early hour. Dupret turned to sketch a brief bow, then turned to tell the houseman, "Elonzo, this is M. Cray, a Rhadazi merchant and a wealthy trader, who is also my friend. Take him into the parlor and see to his wants. Send Peronne at once for Ariadne's confessor; she and M. Cray are to be wed this morning. M. Cray, a few moments only, I know how eager you must be to meet my daughter. I will bring her."

Before Chris could say anything, he was gone; the houseman had gone away also, but he came back before Dupret finished climbing the stairs to the landing. Another man in servant's clothing hurried out the front door. Elonzo eyed Chris without curiosity and bowed him into the next room. Chris closed his eyes briefly, then followed.

The parlor was all done up in the excess of poor taste he hated most: gilt and crystal chandeliers, heavy velvet drapes swagged back from tall windows, statues, paintings, hideous and hideously expensive carpets scattered throughout the room. *Gruesome waste of money that could probably feed a small Third World country for the next two years.* At least the chair the man put him in was high-backed and comfortable. He let his head fall back and sighed faintly. Now that he was sitting, the sick feeling faded, but the dizziness didn't. *Gotta get out of this*, he told himself firmly, but he couldn't seem to find the effort to move. "M. Cray." It took him a moment to remember who that was. Elonzo leaned toward him. "You look quite tired, sir. Will you have something to drink?"

"Drink—" *More orange? Who did that to me?* He wouldn't chance it. "Um—how about plain water, cold?"

"I can provide that, sir. Or perhaps coffee?"

Caffeine. Not a bad idea, maybe. "Sounds good. Both, if you don't mind. And thanks." The last time he'd drunk coffee was a cup with Jennifer, back in Sikkre a couple trips ago, and more to keep her company than anything else. Better than any of the other possibilities. *Don't think I'll ever drink orange juice again.*

The houseman went away. Chris leaned forward and rubbed the back of his neck, trying to get some blood circulating, maybe kick that sick, smothered-brain feeling. Overhead, a series of loud thumps, a woman's voice shrill, cursing inventively in

French. A loud *smack*! followed by a shriek, and then Dupret's voice, forceful and furious, words not quite clear.

And then, all too clear, as though someone had opened a door or Chris's ears had begun to properly function: "You will do as I say, or I will beat you so no man ever can look upon you with pleasure again! *Dieu*, but it makes me angry! What, that a mere girl shall say who she will and who not marry? That a child shall say *no* to her father? Where did you learn such arrogance, Ariadne? Well, I tell you this: You will speak the words when the papa puts them to you, and you will go with this trader when he leaves this house, or I swear it, Ariadne, the next beggar who comes to the back door seeking a meal will leave with you! And how do you think you will fare with such a man, eh?"

A high, furious, and very thickly accented voice answered him immediately. "I would cut out the heart of such a man, my *loving* father! Who wished first to sell me to a man his own age and of known perverse practices, and then to another even worse, and now what? To a commoner? And should I refuse him, and you cannot find me a beggar, then what, beloved papa? A brothel?"

Another loud slap. Chris clenched his teeth and shut his eyes hard, yelped as a hand touched his shoulder. The houseman stood next to him, a maid at his elbow with a silver coffee service and thin porcelain cups, a tall, bedewed, stemmed crystal glass of water. "Sir, your coffee," Elonzo said quietly. *Hey, I can't believe they don't hear that. But look at them both, you'd think they were deaf. How could anyone be* used *to a scene like this? God, I thought some of Mom's old boyfriends were total jerks!* Chris sat up as straight as he could, squared his shoulders and took the cup, let the man drop a square of sugar into it, and sipped cautiously.

One thing certain—after what he'd just heard, he couldn't possibly leave that girl here. He wouldn't dare, he'd never be able to live with himself. If only he could think of some way to simply slide out the door with her— But it was difficult, trying to concentrate with this dreadful rich-pig room all around him, two servants bending over his chair, his head reeling, all that dreadful screaming still going on upstairs. Before he could even try to form any more coherent thought, Elonzo refilled his cup, added another square of sugar to it, and asked softly, "Sir, would you like me to straighten your shirt and vest for you, perhaps a basin of water to wash your face?" *Hey. Not a bad idea. I must look like—well, we won't think about that, okay, Cray?* He nodded, set the cup aside and stood cautiously so the man could fuss with his clothing; the maid disappeared and came back with cloths and a basin. Chris splashed water on his face. *So the first thing she sees is this glassy-eyed, slack-jawed, staggery dude who looks like he's been up all night playing cards with the dudes at Dupret's club and matching the old man rum for rum. Great first impression, right.* It didn't really matter, though: He was going to find a way out of this. Somehow.

He resumed the chair with a sigh of relief. A moment later, Peronne hurried into the room with a diminutive, dark little man in green priest's robes and he heard Dupret partway down the stairs shouting, "Lucette will pack you one satchel, enough for today; I will send the rest of your things as quickly as possible to this hotel the Parrot. Ready yourself, Ariadne! If I must come back for you—!" He left the rest of the threat unspoken; there was no response as he came down the stairs. As the nobleman's boots clicked across the hallway, Chris heard a ferocious echo from a distant slammed door.

He blinked and tried to bring himself back to the moment; the priest was bent over him, apparently waiting for the answer to some question. "Sorry, didn't quite hear that," he replied cautiously.

"I ask, my son, are you Catholic?"

Straw. Take it; didn't they use to frown on mixed marriages, the Mackerel Snappers and the Great Unwashed? It wasn't much to clutch at, but it might be enough to call the whole thing off; maybe Dupret was that hooked on his Church, or at least the appearance of things. Chris pulled up an offended scowl and replied as angrily as he could manage, "Catholic? Me? Not damned likely!" The priest straightened and began muttering vexedly to himself, but before Chris could congratulate himself, Dupret broke in loudly and flatly: "It does not matter in the least. *She* is Catholic, and you will pronounce the words over them; what else should count?"

"But I—but, she—" The priest turned to wave his arms angrily at Dupret, but a look at the man's suffused and furious face changed his mind; he went abruptly and prudently still.

Dupret, in another of those frightening changes of mood, smiled blandly all around and snapped his fingers at Elonzo. "Bring champagne, the best glasses; we must toast the happy couple."

Happy couple, my feet, Chris thought and was unnerved to hear this thought echoed in an angry woman's voice behind him. "Happy couple, God's feet!"

Dupret whirled around and crossed the room in a bound, growling furiously all the while. A woman's hiss of pain, immediately silenced. Chris got cautiously to his feet, turned slowly as Dupret came back across the room. He held a young woman clad in black and emerald by one elbow, as though leading her, but Chris doubted that. The man's knuckles were white, the girl's lips tightly compressed. And then Dupret stopped and thrust the girl forward.

Ariadne Dupret was a full head shorter than he, though he was taller than most of the local men. At first all he could see of her was a deep green lace scarf draped across the cloud of tightly curled blue-black hair that escaped in fine tendrils from under the lace and floated in all directions. She was extremely slender, her shoulders and collarbones almost fragile against the wide, heavy, dark green velvet neckline and elbow-length green velvet sleeves; a deep spill of lace covered thin, dark forearms and stopped just short of impossibly small hands—more a child's hands than a grown woman's. Chris dug his nails into the palms of his hands to try to bring himself properly back to the moment: Dupret was speaking, his voice warm, pleasant—*scary. The dude's a regular Jekyll and Hyde.* Another thought struck him. *I'm dying of heat in what I've got on. How does she do that? Because she probably has another ten layers on under that thick furry stuff.* "M. Cray, my daughter Ariadne. Ariadne, the Rhadazi merchant captain, Cray." *He says, bless you my children, and I'll pop him one myself,* Chris thought confusedly, but then Ariadne looked up into his face and he forgot everything else.

She was no classical beauty; her face was too dark for that, especially in this end of the world, in this time and place. She was pale honey brown, though, as opposed to true unmixed black; her mouth was like her mother's—wide for that narrow chin. Her eyes were a very deep brown, at the moment mostly pupil, her nose rather surprisingly tipped up at the end. She held herself quite stiffly; Chris did not dare touch her and doubted that at the moment she would welcome any contact whatever. He inclined his head, managed what he hoped was a decent, reassuring smile. It slipped when his gaze moved across her face. Both high cheekbones were splotchily red, but the left bore the unmistakable print of her father's fingers, and a tiny cut from one of his rings. "Miss Ariadne," he managed.

"M. Cray." She gave him a very graceful and creditable curtsey, but her voice held no expression whatever. Henri Dupret put her fingers into Chris's near hand and propelled them toward the priest.

The ceremony was extremely brief, all in Latin or French or some mix of both—Chris was lost entirely, spoke where and when told to speak. There was a glass of champagne he did not want but could not somehow refuse, and then the priest was gone, Dupret holding the front door for them, the driver stacking a large chest atop the coach and Elonzo holding the door for them.

The dizziness had returned, or perhaps events had simply overwhelmed him. He thought later he remembered entering the coach, but could never be certain of it.

He came back to himself with a jolt as the carriage started down the street. Swallowed, cleared his throat. "Um. Listen."

"No," Ariadne Dupret Cray replied softly; her accent was much more obvious than her father's. "You listen. What my father has done, that cannot be readily undone. Not in Philippe-sur-Mer. But I tell you this, only once, and you will pay heed. Do you listen? Good. Touch me, in any fashion, at any time—*ever*—and I will kill you. Do you hear me?"

Chris blinked at her, then stared wide-eyed, as Ariadne drew up her skirt and thrust out her right leg, touched the leather strap just above her knee and drew the long dagger just enough for him to see metal, then let it back into the sheath and let her skirts down.

"I hear you," Chris said very softly. He drew a ragged breath. "It's—hot in here, isn't it?"

"You are drunk," Ariadne said scornfully.

"Not," Christ retorted, stung. He shook his head, flailed out with both hands to catch at the sides of the coach. "I'm not drunk; I never drink. I just—" He licked his upper lip, let his eyelids sag closed. The coach jolted on.

"Ah, Dieu, no! What has he done?" He was suddenly aware of a flat hard little hand slapping his cheek. He pried his eyes open to see at least two of Ariadne Dupret—Ariadne Dupret Cray, he reminded himself dizzily—on her knees, staring up at him anxiously, or perhaps furiously. Her face seemed paler than when he'd first seen her.

She pushed his eyelid up, felt his face and pressed her hand against the pulse in his throat, then caught at her hair with both hands. "I see it all. Loving, adoring father, my curse upon you!" She swore in French, then was abruptly silent. "Pull yourself together, M. Cray—as much as you can; we near the inn my *beloved* father named to his coachman. You must walk or you will never see a second day, do you understand me?"

"Walk," Chris muttered, and after a moment nodded. "I can do that, if I have to. I think. Why?"

"Why? Because, you great fool, otherwise he has already killed us both!"

3

𝖼

JENNIFER stood at the window of her office, eyes fixed on the
curved pattern of raked white stone in her Japanese-style garden. Behind her, Chris's voice droned on, his monotone at wild
contrast with his outrageous story. Better, she decided, to keep
her face averted until she was certain she could keep the shock
from showing. *Call it surprise; sounds better.* The exercise in se-
mantics didn't help much. Whatever, it would of course help
Chris get the words out, not having to meet her eye. *The useful
stuff you pick up in a law office.* Last time she'd used this tech-
nique, she'd been trying to pry the truth from a wealthy corpo-
rate client's teenage son who'd been picked up on a DUI. *Nice
comparison. Chris would love it—not, as he'd say himself.*

She bit the corners of her mouth, fought the sudden urge to
laugh out loud. Chris wouldn't see the humor—the very black
humor—in the situation.

Movement along the shaded north edge caught her eye: a flash
of deep green, visible and then gone into shadow once more.
That is Ariadne; Ariadne, Chris's wife. That was sobering. By itself, that would take some getting used to, the mere concept of
Chris as anyone's husband, let alone this—*Granddaughter to the
second most powerful man in France? A genuine royal? My
God*, she thought reverently. The rest of it—everything he'd told
her thus far—really—was going to weigh heavily on her re-
nowned ability to stay calm under trying circumstances.

It was certainly telling on Chris. "God, I can't believe I passed
out on her. Really gross, you know? Even if it wasn't 'cause I
was soused. Actually, I lost time all over the place, I think I remember most of the stuff at Dupret's house, but it's more like it
was an old TV movie of the week or one of those rich-pig night-

time soap operas one of my girlfriends got hung up on. And then
the ceremony. I *knew* it was gonna come back to haunt me, but
at the time I couldn't do thing one except go along with whatever Dupret and that poor spooked priest said. Did I mention he
was probably gonna kill me and dump the body in the harbor if
I just said no?" Jennifer glanced at him, turned away again. After
a moment she nodded. "Right. Look, I'm aware how insane all
this sounds, even for me. I guess you had to be there, see his
face, listen to him, the guy's a nut-case, okay? Unfortunately, he
isn't just your average island-hopping guy who owns one
busted-up ship, he's like Somebody. He can get away with damn
near anything, including probably killing people. *She* says he
can, and I believe her."

He cleared his throat. "*She* says we drank champagne after
the whole thing was over with—the mmm—oh, hell, *you* know,
the priest thing." His voice sounded suddenly strangled, and
Jennifer felt a smile tug at the corners of her mouth. Chris hadn't
ever had a problem with the "m" word, that she'd known; under
present circumstances, though . . . "Well, I guess that's what he
put the stuff in," her nephew went on flatly. "The Zero. In the
champagne. Because, next thing I know, we're in Dupret's fancy
carriage cruising along one of the streets down by the waterfront,
on our way to Eddie's and my hotel, and she's on her knees on
the seat, slapping me around and calling me every kind of
damned fool there is." He considered this briefly, then laughed.
"Whoa, you thought some of mom's old boyfriends could cuss!"

"I'm so pleased to hear she has unique talents," Jennifer said
dryly.

"Yeah, right, thanks Jen. Chill, okay? Eddie says he never saw
anyone so scared in his life as what *she* was—except him, when
she told him what her old man did. He says I was like utterly
gray all over and my eyes were going three different directions
at once."

"How's he doing?" Jennifer asked.

"Eddie? Oh, *he's* just fine. Down in Podhru chinning with
Afronsan, and Ernie's supposed to get in the next day or so, so
we can all get together, meeting of the board, *you* know." He
laughed, rather self-consciously. "Yeah, right. Anyway, Eddie's a
fat lot of help, he just says it served me right for ignoring him,
and at least I—urgh—won a wife with brains."

"And has she?"

"Hey, ask Eddie, he's the one who was there; I was trashed,

remember? But he said she was like rully impressive. Like, she got me outa the coach just like everything was okay and I was a little drunk maybe but God's gift to women anyway—that was to get rid of her old man's driver, make him think everything was how they wanted it." Jennifer turned and frowned at him. Chris waved a hand. "I know, clear as mud. Hang in there, it gets worse. Anyway, she gets Eddie aside, tells him what's up, chases him up to pack our stuff while she goes in to butter up our hard-nosed old landlord. Time he gets back, she's got the old booger nearly cooing, ready to do anything for her—including send Dupret the bill for our room at the Parrot and forward her trunks to the ritziest hotel on the main road, when they show up. That's classic misdirection, okay? In case you hadn't figured. Dupret apparently didn't, anyway, that's later.

"Somewhere after that, we're in this public carriage, and she's got some really disgusting stuff from a druggist—Eddie says, anyway, I think it tasted like gutter water—and she's cussing me out for a stubborn whatchit and pouring the stuff down my throat.

"Somewhere after that, Eddie had to haul me out into an alley to puke—I do remember that part, damnit, I *hate* tossing my cookies, you know?" he added feelingly. "Next thing I know af-ter *that*, Eddie's sitting next to me in this filthy little hole of a cabin on a ship halfway back to the mainland. And Ariadne's next door, trunks and all, and we're on our way home. Um, here. Rhadaz. And I was so seasick the whole way through the isth-mus and up the left coast, I thought I would *die*."

Jennifer stirred, glanced at him. Chris sprawled in her chair, long legs crossed, feet propped on the corner of her desk; he spread his arms wide and looked up at her as if to say, end of story. His face was utterly expressionless. *Give me strength*, she thought tiredly. "Chris, have you been reading Rafael Sabatini—or his this-world ilk?

"Ilk? Saba—say who?"

"Scaramouche. One of your favorite old swashbuckler mov-ies? Based on a book, if you know what they are . . ."

"Didn't this lecture wear out years ago?" he demanded of the ceiling. "I know it's a book, I even read it, I just forgot the guy's name. Compared to the movie—*bor*ing."

"Never mind. You're right, the lecture wore out years ago. But you swear you didn't just—make this up from whole cloth?"

"Hey," he growled. "I *have* a life, remember? Do I need to make up stuff? Did I ever?"

"All right." She sighed. "Chris, damnit! This is insane! You cannot wager at poker for young women, under any circumstances! Don't you know——?"

He snorted, silencing her. "Hey, come *on*! This is me, remember? You think I haven't been beating myself over the head ever since the whole mess went down? And weren't you listening? It was *not* my idea! But you think it's the done thing even in French Jamaica? Well, for your information, it isn't, all right? And you want to guess what she's been thinking, all the way from her house to here? It's like—what'd the Spaniard in that movie say? 'Humiliations galore.' The poor girl barely speaks to me, and I really cannot blame her!"

"But she still saved your life—I don't understand."

"Makes two of us who don't figure; all she had to do was let me croak and split before the old man's goons showed up. Hey, I've given up trying to sort it out, I got enough problems."

"If you croaked, where could she go? Try sorting again, just for aunty," Jennifer cooed. Chris cast her a dirty look; the fingers of one hand drummed the surface of her desk.

"All right. I was trying to get in Dupret's good graces. Mistake, don't bother to tell me, okay? And apparently somebody from the bar slipped me something in my orange juice while we were playing; Dupret obviously arranged that ahead of time." Jennifer simply gazed at him. Chris's mouth quirked, and he cast his eyes ceilingward. "Jen. Gimme a break, this is me, okay? I was *not* boozing, not in a spot like that, but I don't chug anyway, and that night I was not drinking anything but squished oranges. Besides, would I get drunk, pull a trick like that with *her*, and then come here first thing and try to pull a line like this on *you*?"

Jennifer sighed. "All right, point taken. You weren't drinking, and of course I really do know you wouldn't have accepted a bet like that if you were clear-headed at the time. So now what?"

"Hey, why do you think I came here instead of taking her home to meet Mom?"

"That one's easy. You got in way too deep and need me to pull you out—and think for you while I'm at it. In other words; what else is new?"

"You're so nice, Jen, thank you *very* much," Chris retorted sourly. "Lookit. She isn't talking to me much, but what little she's said, way she figures it is Dupret probably had Eddie

tagged from day one, so I got tarred with the same brush when
I showed. I think he knew about me, and that marked Eddie.
Whatever. We haven't exactly been strangers in that part of the
world, last few years, and gossip about what new people are up
to gets around fast. And all those questions Eddie asks . . ."

"And you don't exactly blend in, Mr. Cray," Jennifer pointed
out.

"Tell me another. You know, I warned Eddie," Chris added
peevishly. "I said, don't get down on the docks, don't ask all the
pointy questions and damnit, don't get too close to this drug-
running stuff. I told him it wasn't safe!"

"I'll bet he knows now, doesn't he? You notice how much restraint I'm using not tarring you with this same brush?"

"Okay, I got cocky. So I paid, in major spades." He considered
this, made a wry face. "Sorry, I rully didn't plan that. Anyway,
um, Ari—Ariadne. I guess she was already in heavy dutch with
the old man for a buncha stuff."

"Such as—?"

"Oh, like, girls in that class are supposed to be—nice, submis-
sive, foo-foo-girl stuff, you know. And she's got this temper, she
doesn't just say, 'Oui, Daddikins, as you wish.' And then he's
picked her out a husband little while back, pal of his, the dude's
noble but he's also three times her age *and* size, and she said
like, 'Death first.' But she says she already had found out stuff
about the Zero trade. Well, it ain't illegal out there, and who'd
try to put a Duke's kid in jail? But it's this ego thing for him,
he's supposed to be filthy rich, Daddy's money and his plantation, and she says he's really pretty cash-poor. So he's keeping
up the illusion of Daddy's money and wealthy plantations by
doing the Zero thing." He stretched, folded his hands behind his
neck, and resettled his feet on the corner of her desk. "Boy, you
think I pull dumb stunts, what d'you think she did? Only goes up
to her old man and says, like, 'Cancel the ancient fat boy for a
husband bit and I won't drop a dime to your buddies about
where the bucks come from.' You know, any girl back home
who'd ever seen any TV at all would never pull that, even on her
own dad, it's just begging to get offed, you know?"

"You—wait, let me think about this a minute." Jennifer turned
back to the window, rolled her eyes ceilingward, then closed
them. *God, what a can of worms!* No other thought came. "You
think he'd what—have forced her to marry this friend anyway?
Or just tossed her out a high window and said, 'Oopsie!'?"

"Probably the latter. Or drugged her lunch, shoved her in a crate and sent her out to sea for a trip halfway to France. I *know* he can do the weepy bit, he was crying over her mom, did I tell you that?" Jennifer nodded. "And Ariadne says the woman spent half her time applying cosmetics to cover the bruises. *You* figure. But, you know what?" Chris went on in an even more aggrieved voice. "All Mom's hairball boyfriends back in L.A., and all the creepy dudes I've seen since we came here, I've never seen anything like Dupret, he totally floors me. I mean, he just isn't real. No one can be that goofy, I swear."

"Sure they can. Ever heard of schizophrenia?"

"Isn't that. He's too in control. It isn't multiple personality, either."

"When did you take psych?"

"Hey, *I* used to watch the TV movies, you know? Get bored enough, you'll watch damn near anything."

"Really."

"Really. Chill, okay? I tried to figure him. I sure had enough time on the trip home, what Eddie got us for passage out of Philippe-sur-Mer was the slowest, dumpiest Dutch tub you *ever* saw. And then I thought we'd never find anything going west out of the lake, and they'd be fishing all three of us out of the drink—where was I?"

"Dupret," Jennifer reminded him mildly.

"Yeah, Dupret." Chris sighed. "*You* try. Real tears, I swear, but he didn't marry Ari's mother. I mean, even if she was so-called inferior stock because of being indentured and from Africa, who's gonna tell someone like that he can't marry whatever girl he likes? Even if daddy said forget it, he's clear across the Atlantic, how'd he know?"

"His ships aren't, are they? Daddy could've threatened to cut off the money, or maybe Dupret's cronies wouldn't ever play cards with him again, you already said he'd lose status if they found out he was making his fortune selling drugs."

"I guess. Hell, some such crap. Bottom line is, he didn't marry her. Okay, the woman was black and she came over on one of those five-year things where you have to work off the cost of passage, and he paid the indenture off, took her out of the fields or his factory or whatever. So Ariadne's illegitimate." Jennifer glanced at him sharply; Chris was staring at his hands and didn't notice. After a moment he sighed and went on. "He cried all over *her* after the—the priest bit." Jennifer cleared her throat.

"All right," he stirred and cast her an irritated glance, "the *marriage ceremony*, you like that better? Like he really cared. And then, I'm downstairs and I can hear him slapping her around up there—jeez, it was bad."

"Chris—"

"Let me finish, get it out, okay? Then you can yell at me all at once. The whole time he was so weird, one minute he's acting like we're both wild to do this married thing, the next it's like he's gonna strangle me on the spot or throw her down the stairs, and the servants are acting like nothing at all is out of the ordinary."

"It probably wasn't. But what he feels for a daughter might not have much to do with whether he married her mother or not, Chris," Jennifer said mildly.

"Oh, sure. Did I tell you he threatened to give her to—never mind. But trying to fix her up with his best buddy, the guy'd crush her first night." Chris swallowed and went red to his hairline. "Anyway," he muttered. "It wasn't—wasn't the virgin thing or the my-little-girl crap. Just—just weird, okay? And all I could think is, the guy has to have pistols in fancy wood cases, half a dozen sets, he openly wears a dueling sword and I bet he keeps daggers in his boots. And his manservants are the size of some of those guys on TV wrestling, or the guy that *was* the brute squad in that movie you and I went to see just before we—ah—came here? We are talking three times my size, thank you, his coach driver coulda broke me in half without working up a sweat. This is not something *I* come up against very often; even if I'd been totally straight, I would not have been any better off."

Jennifer looked over her nephew—all six-foot, superbly muscled-plus of him, and nodded. "I don't suppose you do find that often. But you sure don't look like anybody's victim."

"Sure I don't. *Never*." He drove his hands through his hair, stopped suddenly and carefully combed it back into place with his fingers. "Jeez. You should have seen her face, first look at her I got. My God, I never saw anything so gorgeous, not even magazine models or—remember that cute little thing I used to watch on that beach TV series? I forget her name," he added in mild surprise. "What could I say, though? He's lurking over our shoulders, all those servants and that priest right there. And it was like she was the Queen of France herself. She didn't meet my eyes, not once, she didn't say a word except what they made her say. God, I felt so *low*.

"Anyway, the whole time Dupret's weeping over his baby and glaring threats at me, babbling over the happy couple, and making certain the priest does a solid job of it, and at the same time he's worked out this absolutely *Gothic*, convoluted plot to make it look like she poisoned me on our wedding night rather than sleep with me, then killed herself so they wouldn't execute her for murder—or have to go back to daddy, even she isn't sure which, but she says probably Dupret's goons were gonna break into our room at the Parrot once I was safely dead or at least out of it, then hang her from the rafters."

"They assumed she wouldn't notice what was wrong with you, and just tamely go with you—?"

"She was supposed to think I was dead drunk; I looked dead drunk, and I sure felt it. So? She's a *girl*; they aren't expected to think in Dupret's end of the world. He probably figures if she's dumb enough to threaten him about his Zero traffic, she isn't bright enough to figure out what he's doing, okay? Also, that's what the coach driver was for, the brute to 'help' her help me upstairs, he'd probably have done us both right then if she'd looked suspicious. What mere innkeeper's gonna argue with a nobleman's servant, especially one the size of Detroit?"

"Too many Errol Flynn movies, kid."

"Yeah, I'm so sure, right. Shaddup and let me finish, okay? After that, of course, they'd find Eddie and dump him in the harbor. *You* figure someone like that. And you figure how much chance I had of walking once the dude found me on the docks and made his offer on sugar, okay?"

"Which meeting we won't talk about because I think we've covered that ground before. Chris, all the things you tell Eddie about drug trafficking. Do you ever listen to yourself?"

"Hey. Chill, lady, I'm where I gotta be, doing what I gotta, okay? You want Rhadaz to wind up the new China at the end of the opium wars with England? Forget it, okay? Also, end of story."

"You aren't the only person who could—oh, all right, we've chewed this cabbage enough times, and neither one of us shifts an inch, end of story."

She glared at him; no use. Chris grinned and relaxed back into the chair. "C'mon, Jen, pick your grouches, all right? You can't be pissed at me for everything, all at once—"

"Bets?" Jennifer demanded sweetly. He waved that aside.

"Who else in this chunk of dirt has any notion of what might be going on out there? After five hundred years of isolation, they don't even know about guns, safe milk, steam engines, freezers . . . all right, don't look at me like that. But this isn't twentieth-century L.A., lady; where else are you gonna find someone with the all-American hair to nail a Duke *here*? Long as he's been hanging out with me, Eddie still can't do that. And Dupret, hey there he is, offspring of the Duc D'Orlean, *a la lanterne*, and all that, except they haven't done the Bastille bit and the followup over there in *this* world, worse luck for me. You know, nobles still run things, so does the King. I guess, too many Moors hanging around the Spanish-French border for too many years. Well, if I got it right, anyway." He glanced at Jennifer, grinned again. 'Put the stone face away, I know, you don't *care* about the history, right?"

"To quote someone, I *have* a life. And no spare time for playing with world history with everything else I'm doing."

"Trust me. I could not leave Ariadne there with the old bastard, and once the priest did the man-and-wife bit, I couldn't have left her behind at all, even if I'd been running things when we split from Philippe-sur-Mer. Half the ports along the left coast of the New Gaelic State are rotten with Zero, probably with Dupret's agents, too. And—well—there's this—this other thing—"

"You married her," Jennifer said flatly. Chris made a strangled little noise, then sighed heavily. "All right, kiddo. End of lecture, you met your match and then some. So you couldn't leave her, and I can't see you dropping this in your mother's lap, or her handling it. I'm just not certain what you want me to do about it." She tugged at a long, loose strand of hair and thought for some time. "What could I possibly do to make anything better?" Chris sat and watched her, and kept his peace. "Hmmm. All right. How Catholic is she, and how strong a deal is it to be Catholic in French Jamaica?"

"Married to the death, near as I can figure," Chris replied gloomily. "*And* beyond."

"What about an annulment? You—haven't slept with her—"

"Jeez!" Chris slapped the chair arms, then looked up at her. "You better be kidding, and even then, you're in hot water, lady."

"Yah. Scare me again. Well?"

"All right. Ask *you* for help, see what I get. Jen, rully! You think I can talk to her about things like that? I mean, she barely talks to me at all, she already thinks I'm a jerk, you want me to be an even bigger jerk? Forget it, I just can't—how can I bring *that* up?"

"Open your mouth and say the word 'annulment,' and see what she says. But you'd rather have me to talk to her for you, that about it?"

He fell back in the chair, pounded one enormous fist against his thigh. "Oh, hell, Jen! I don't know what I want! And you know what? Maybe if I'd just somehow met her, got to know her like a friend, done it the right way, all that—it might have worked, for me at least. Well, Dupret put that right out of the picture, like, for life."

"Maybe not. Are you just throwing in your hand at this point, after what—three weeks aboard a dumpy ship in separate cabins?"

"Hey!"

"Well, then. And how old is she?"

He spread his hands, scowled at the desk. "Not quite twenty—I think. It didn't really come up, but she looks about twenty. Old enough to be considered past it in her dad's class, except Dupret has all these buddies who like 'em young." He considered this, made a face. "God! That is so totally disgusting!"

"Never mind. It happens in our own world, too; think about who buys time with all those teenage hookers." Chris glanced up at her and if possible went even redder. "Well, you spared her that, didn't you? One to you. Is she intelligent?"

Chris ran both hands through his hair. "Jeez, how should I know? Hey, don't look at me like that, okay? She's literate, anyway, and a lot of the women down there aren't. She thinks on her feet, way she got us out of that inn, got the right crud down into me, got all three of us off the island without getting caught by her old man."

"I'd call that at least clever. So tell me, why would an intelligent woman with most of her life before her hold a grudge against you forever, when she knows what her father is like?"

"Because she's got a block of pride that weighs more than *I* do, okay? And—sure, if I were her, I'd be royally insulted, too. Getting traded at poker, for God's sake." He shifted impatiently. "Look, this is all beside the point. Which is, Eddie and I need to get back to the Caribbean, you know?"

"*I* think she didn't feed you the nasty goo in time, kid; you must have urfed up all your brains along with her antidote."

He snorted. "Yeah, sure, really cute, lady. I gotta go back, okay? Take the argument, loop it on the tape one more time. Never mind I'm the best choice for the Zero-watch, I have a lot of loose ends left out there, real business stuff. The Chief Dude's typewriters, for one thing. And I have a last bunch of paperwork to run through with the guy in Florida before we can even think about refrigeration, which in case you forgot means freezers, fridges, maybe even air-conditioning—well, maybe." He considered this, shrugged. "And—"

Jennifer waved both hands wildly. "Spare me. Your business is worse than the history lessons; I get enough of it from the contract end."

"Yah. Look, one of these days, when I know enough of the people I trade with well enough, *and* I'm bored with spending half my life on ships and the other half in grubby port cities, I'll be able to set up branch offices, hire dudes I trust and run things from that place in the mountains. Particularly after we get telegraph between us and the Mer Khani and the French run it down through the Gaelic States. You notice how much restraint I'm using not mentioning *railroad*? Anyway, for now, if I don't get my backside out there soon, deals are gonna start falling through; it's tricky, remember?"

"You tell me often enough."

"Well, it is. Trust me. Don't look at me like that, okay? But we can't take Ariadne with us. You think I feel bad now, being the guy who got sucked into Dupret's little plot, think about if she gets murdered 'cause she was with us and we got rousted by her old man."

"I remind myself that I have promised not to lecture you any more on the subject of getting rousted by anyone," Jennifer said mildly. She turned away from the window to look at him. Chris gazed back at her rather anxiously. She sighed finally and sat on the corner of the desk, shoving aside papers and his large, booted feet to make room for herself. "Tell you what. I'll talk to her. I don't guarantee anything, though."

"That's enough, I know it. Hey. Thanks."

Silence. Jennifer finally broke it. "Have you even thought about what you're going to tell Robyn?"

"I'm going to pretend I never even heard of anyone named Robyn, okay? You want to stay my pal, you won't bring up anyone named Robyn, either." He sighed, let his feet down with two floor-shaking clomps, stood up and gave her a crooked grin. "All right. So, hey, Jen, come on down to your fancy Oriental rock garden, I, uh, I'd like to have you meet my—wife."

ARIADNE had discovered Jennifer's hammock in the shade under flowering bushes and a tree, and was a slender, still shape in its shadows. But as footsteps scrunched in the nearby gravel, she came swiftly to her feet, and was smoothing her dark green velvet skirts when Jennifer and Chris came around the small fountain. Jennifer smiled, held out her hands as Chris rather nervously performed the introductions. Ariadne gazed at the proffered fingers with visible doubt, then took them in her own. She would have curtseyed but Jennifer shook her head and said in English, "I don't need that. Not from family." She glanced beyond the girl's shoulder to meet Chris's eyes. He cleared his throat.

"Well, okay. I'll—uh—I've got to—" He shrugged, smiled at Jennifer, sent his eyes sideways helplessly, then turned and practically ran back inside.

"Family," Ariadne said thoughtfully. Her English was French-accented but understandable. "You are the sister of the mother—the aunt of Chris?"

"His aunt, yes."

And—this is your home? Your Duchy, Chris says?" Jennifer nodded. "You live here, you rule this hot and dry place? I would go mad."

"It gets to me—bothers me, sometimes. That's one reason for this garden. But you might do better in a dress that isn't quite so, ah—heavy," Jennifer said doubtfully. Ariadne freed her hands and smoothed the velvet.

"But this is the best my—my father"—she nearly spat the word—"ever had sewn for me. What less would I wear to meet the *tante* of Chris?"

"Of course." Chris was right; the girl had a towering pride. Jennifer thought it was at least half insecurity, and understandably so, if Dupret was a third of what Chris made him. She smiled. "It looks lovely on you, that shade of green and that style. But if you stay in Sikkre very long, you might prefer the local fashion." She indicated her own dress, a blue gauzy cotton that fell nearly to her ankles from a high and intricately embroidered waistband.

Ariadne studied the garment rather doubtfully. Probably it resembled what she wore to bed, nothing for mixed company or daylight hours outside her rooms. "But—do we stay here for so long?"

"You haven't asked Chris?"

The girl spread her arms wide; her mouth twisted. "How do I ask him such things?"

Jennifer smiled. "He's not that difficult to talk to. But why don't we go indoors, find something for you to drink, and get out of the heat?"

"As it pleases you," Ariadne said and inclined her head.

SHE was polite but distant as they walked into the palace and down stuffy, overly warm halls, but clapped her hands together and exclaimed in delight over the family dining room with its fountains and pools.

"It's probably my favorite room in this whole oversized barn of a place," Jennifer said. "We spent most of our time in here, in this kind of weather—or in that garden where you just were." To her eye, Ariadne was scarcely a beauty; Chris must see something she did not. She was a striking type: high cheekbones, dark eyes, thick blue-black hair with a natural tight wave that Jennifer envied. But her face was too thin, her mouth too prominent and overly wide, her chin too pointed and her nose too broad for classic beauty. She was truly a small young woman, much shorter and finer-boned than Jennifer; her hands and feet were extremely small. *Barbie doll*, Jennifer thought; she put the thought aside as unworthy, the tall and gawky envious of the small and perfectly formed. She wouldn't dare ever let the "B" word slip to Chris. Jennifer considered this, bit the corners of her mouth and carefully stifled a grin.

Ariadne walked around the dining hall, let her fingers trail in the water, peered curiously at the wall of water that cascaded near the main entry while Jennifer rang for a cool drink and for some of the plain little cakes the kitchen made in an attempt at cookies. Ariadne came and sat rather gingerly when the serving woman returned with a tray; she took the offered cup, accepted a plate and a square of linen to protect her velvet skirts. "Well," Jennifer said finally and raised her cup. "To new family." The girl gave her a blank look. "Well—or not, if you'd rather not be considered family."

"I do not understand." Ariadne had picked up the cup and gazed doubtfully at it. Now she set it down with a clink and the set of her shoulders was wary and tight.

"All this, these past days," Jennifer said evenly. "Including Chris. Particularly Chris, in fact." Ariadne firmed her lips together and shook her head. Jennifer made an inelegant little noise and leaned forward on her elbows. "Look, I don't doubt you've had it tough, what Chris has told me about your father. But that's behind you now, isn't it? One way or another?" Silence. "Believe me, I'd be ready to kill if I'd been bought and sold over a card game; you aren't the only one. But Chris didn't do that to you on purpose."

"You cannot—"

"Can't what?" Jennifer asked pointedly. Ariadne shrugged and let her eyes drop to the full cup in front of her. "Ariadne, you've misjudged the boy. Though, God knows, I can't blame you under the circumstances."

"He's told you—what?" Ariadne whispered.

"Everything he knows. Still, I can see that wouldn't tell me what you think." Silence. Jennifer cleared her throat and tried again. "I know Dupret is abusive and the marriage wasn't your idea. And that you don't dare go home, and why. Like it or not, you're either on your own or you're stuck with us—for now, anyway." She waited. The girl nodded once, sharply. Her eyes remained fixed on her lap. "I don't envy you the situation one bit. I can at least listen if you want to talk."

"Talk," Ariadne said scornfully. "What use is talk? When everything has already happened? What does talk change?"

"What use? Who knows? Maybe it might be there's nothing I can say or do to help you, but I can't do one damned thing if you won't talk to me at all." Silence. "I don't say that just because I'm also a woman, I'll be easier to talk to than either Chris or Eddie. But it's worth a try, isn't it?" She sat back, folded her arms and waited. The girl turned her head and gazed thoughtfully at the pool on her left, tipped it the other way and stared at—or more likely beyond—Dahven's empty chair. The silence stretched.

Finally she picked up the cup and sipped cautiously, then set it aside once more. "All right, yes. To speak to someone, I—I have had no one, not even the priest—my *father's* man!—all these days. The words are a lump, here." She struck just below her ribs with one small fist; her eyes were furious. "And I think perhaps you—I heard those two, you know, Chris and his friend. They spoke often of you on the journey here; both of them were certain you could make the problems better. Mine, theirs—I do not know which they meant. But Chris said to me that you have sense—are sensible," she amended carefully. She gazed at Jennifer searchingly for some moments. "You look like such a woman, a sensible woman, now that I myself see you."

"Well, I try to be. Keep in mind that sometimes it's easier to be sensible when you aren't personally involved in events."

Ariadne let her refill the cup and took a sip, considered this, then nodded again.

LATER, while Ariadne was dressing for the evening meal, Jennifer sent for Chris and met him in the large garden beyond the family apartments and the old parade ground, next to the fish pool where she'd nearly been drowned. "You had one thing right, kiddo; she is a proud young woman—but it's not family pride; she called her father a few choice things that—well, I'm glad my French is high-school textbook stuff."

"Told you she could cuss," Chris said.

"Sound proud of it, why don't you? She says the old Duc is a pirate and she hopes he fries."

"You're paraphrasing, right?"

"You listening, junior?" Jennifer crossed her arms.

"What, you getting auntly or just surly in your old age? Must be this kid you're building, turning you into a grownup or something." She aimed a swing at his ear; he grinned and ducked with the ease of long practice. "So—what do I do?"

"You go slow with her, act like you're acquaintances with a chance of becoming friends, take it one slow step at a time."

"*Rully*, Ann Landers," Chris said sarcastically. "So, look, does she know I'm going without her?"

"You can tell her that part; I didn't get a chance. We talked about Dupret and about you and that whole mess and it took a lot of time; the kitchen staff finally had to chase us out so they could ready the place for dinner. She didn't say much directly about you or the marriage, but she's truly troubled by how *you* view the whole situation, what you think about her personally."

"Wait." Chris got to his feet and paced back and forth. "You mean—she's pissed at *me* because I was the guy her old man picked on? He loaded my hand while I was goofy! Didn't you tell her?"

"You think that matters?"

"It does to me! But what, she's pissed because I know she's got an old man who'd use his kid for an ante?"

"Not pissed. She *is* upset. Wouldn't you be?"

"How should I know? No one's staked me on a hand of draw lately, you know!"

Jennifer shook her head. "Try it this way: Remember when the Cholani nomads grabbed you and beat your feet to twin pulps?"

"Oh, thanks very much for reminding me about that happy little Kodak moment, like I could ever—" He stopped abruptly, turned to stare at her. "Hang on. You mean, like, *she's* ashamed? Like it was her fault that happened?"

"Well, weren't you embarrassed to have anyone know?" Jennifer asked reasonably. "It's a common enough reaction. Think about it. Something she did say, though; about Dupret's temper. She says one of his personal servants told her the man has the Moorish disease. Now, unless I'm very mistaken—" Chris frowned as her voice trailed off; he snapped his fingers then.

"You mean, like Shakespeare's French disease?" Jennifer nodded. "Yeah—wild temper and mood swings the size of Baltimore? Second-stage syphilis? I don't—but I do believe it, it fits. At least—"

"She only knows what this Peronne told her. It's not exactly a dinner topic in this world, either."

"Sure," Chris growled. "You pass it on or pick it up, but you don't talk about it. Nice." He stared blankly toward the center of the fish pond, finally shook himself. "I don't know. I mean, he's got the mood swings like they say Henry VIII had, and the temper; and I read some horse-race murder mystery back when, the bad guy had it—Dupret's a lot like that guy was, but that was fiction, you know? All the magic in this world, you don't find a lot of that kind of disease going around—not where the French run things, at least; they have ways to cure it. I really don't know the local STD's—of course, Eddie might."

"Spare me," Jennifer said dryly, "discussions of your sex life, or Eddie's. Please. About the other thing, Chris. She's strongly Catholic, or so she says. She wanted to know if you had put me up to broaching her beliefs, preliminary to getting rid of her." She looked at him; Chris sighed and looked back. "Kid, you have *got* to talk to her. I told her you don't bite, that you aren't just going to dump her on a back road and run, or anything like that. I also assured her that you don't rape nice young women, even those you have a church-given right to jump."

Chris groaned and buried his face in his hands. "Oh, hey.
Thanks for everything. Can I just die now?"

"I'm serious. You think she hasn't expected you to assert your
so-called conjugal rights since the first night? Any man where
she comes from automatically would assume—oh, hell, Chris,
say something to her, damnit! Just plain old sit down and talk to
her, why don't you? It's not like you to skirt issues."

"This isn't issues," he mumbled between his hands. "This is
Ariadne and—and—"

"Chris, don't you dare start off on the wrong foot with this
young woman, it'll ruin both of you on each other for life." He
shook his head; blond hair flew. "I am serious. You said something earlier about having no chance with her. Well, you won't
have if you don't talk to her—and listen to her."

"Sure. Right. No, really." Chris sighed. "I know you're right.
It's just—well, never mind. I don't suppose we're eating any
time tonight, are we?"

"I'm glad to hear the drugs didn't completely mangle you,
kid." Jennifer pulled out her watch. "In not quite an hour, the
staff is fixing something special, in honor of, as they say. I still
haven't changed, and you reek from here. Go rinse off, pretty up.
Even Dahven's dressing up tonight; he'd never do that for
merely me."

"Yeah, sure." Chris cleared his throat. "Hey, look. Thanks. I
shouldn't have put you in a spot like that, I guess—"

"What I'm for, kid. And you know damned well you intended
to do just that all along." She gave him a shove, then flapped her
hands at him. "Go on, shoo, *in*. You haven't got that long before
they start bringing the food up."

ARIADNE now wore a plain emerald green skirt of something that
moved like silk when she walked, and a low-throated white shirt-
waist neatly edged in a thin band of simple lace; her hair was
caught back in a narrow green and gold ribbon, and plain pearl
and gold drops hung from her ears. Dahven bowed low over her
hand but otherwise made no great fuss, which seemed to please
her. Chris appeared right behind her, in the narrow trousers, vest
and white ruffled shirt. Jennifer winked gravely as he passed her
and murmured, "Errol *who*?"

He flushed right to his hairline, though he looked pleased as
he held out a chair for Ariadne. But he mumbled out of the corner of his mouth, "Yeah, right, really cute, lady. Shut up, okay?"

Ariadne eyed him sidelong as he dropped into the chair next to her, then turned her attention to her food.

Her appetite was healthy, Jennifer thought, and was glad to see it. It couldn't be usual in a woman of her breeding—it wouldn't have been in her own world a hundred years earlier, or even in her own time. Chris was politeness itself at the table, unusual for him within a family setting; his manners were impeccable. He helped her to various things, said please and thank you at all possible proper moments, refilled her wineglass. Using manners to keep his distance, Jennifer decided. His appetite hadn't suffered at all, but nothing ever seemed to harm Chris's ability to put away a huge meal. The kitchen staff would be delighted.

Two of the women came to clear what was left of the cold meats and bread; two others brought bowls of cool fruit and cake, a flask of pale apricot sweet wine to go with the dessert. Ariadne sampled this doubtfully, then smiled and dug in. Chris picked up his own spoon. Dahven swallowed a bite of dessert, washed it down with wine and said, "So, Chris. Are you going straight back to sea from here, or were you planning on a trip to Zelharri first? Robyn is expecting you, isn't she?"

Chris snorted. "Jeez, dude, practice your English on another subject, will you?" Ariadne cast him a startled glance, transferred it to Dahven. Both men were grinning. She shrugged and went back to her food. "She's not. So, I don't know. But I haven't heard anything since I was there last time, when Lialla was futzing around in that village and the whole fort was utterly nuts. If it's still that bad we're staying right here, keep Jen off the streets and out of trouble for a while."

Dahven set his cup aside. "You haven't heard—you didn't tell him the latest news, Jen?" Jennifer shook her head.

"There hasn't exactly been time."

"Latest?" Chris asked warily. Jennifer shook her head again, very firmly, and sipped at the spoonful of dessert wine Siohan and the midwife allowed her, washed it down with water. Dahven gave a brief, succinct outline of the latest letters and telegrams, including Lialla's note to Jen. Chris groaned and set his spoon down with a hard clink.

"God. I'll murder that girl."

"You have to stand in line, Chris."

"No doubt. That settles it, Mom can come visit here before I go back to sea. Uh," he added hastily as Ariadne set her spoon aside with elaborate care and turned to look squarely at him.

"Um, that is, I told you about my mother, right? But I don't remember if I mentioned Lialla—"

Ariadne merely looked at him expressionlessly for some moments; his voice trailed off. The silence stretched. But as Chris opened his mouth, she held up a hand. "Be still and let me think of this—think *on* this." Another deadly little silence between them; Dahven, his forehead creased in confusion, looked to Jennifer; she shrugged and cast her eyes up. "I see it now! You mean to leave me here—this place or that one where your mother lives. In this Rhadaz, somewhere. And then you will than go back to French Jamaica, possibly even to Philippe-sur-Mer?"

"I didn't say that!"

"You did not have to say so, I can see it. You are mad," she said flatly. "Completely mad."

Chris spread his arms wide, nearly knocking over his glass and hers. "Hey, give me a break! I got caught out one time, ever, in four years, it was an accident!"

"My Father is not an accident! He is a fiend from Hell, and you are a madman or a fool or both!"

"Look, lady!" Chris replied, topping her but not by much. She closed her mouth, folded her arms, and glared at him. Chris flushed. "I mean—Ariadne, lookit!"

"I am looking! And all I see is a fool!"

"I don't have any choice, okay? I have to go, I just happen to have this business that's gonna fall apart and die if I don't get back to that end of the world and finish some deals. I'm not going within a long mile of your old man, okay? And you'll be safe here—"

She beat on the table with a small fist; her spoon rattled in the empty porcelain dessert bowl. Chris stared at her. "After so many years of my father, do you think this is a thing I must have—*safety*? And do you think I cannot tell you lie to me? Business—I know men conduct business by agents; you do not go back there for business, unless revenge is business! And I shall be a widow at not yet twenty!"

"Hey, I am *not* going after Henri Dupret! You don't understand that much English all of a sudden? But so what if he takes me out? You'll be rid of me, won't you?"

"I do not wish to be a widow at not yet twenty!" Ariadne shouted and pounded the table with both small fists. "I do not at all look well in black!" The glared at each other; Chris ended the moment by tipping back his head and breaking into a raucous laugh. "How dare you mock me!"

"Hey, I swear." Chris got his mirth under control with a visible effort. "Ariadne. Really and truly, I do *not* mock you. I don't look so good in blood red, you know? Especially when it's my blood." She compressed her lips once more and waited him out. "Look, no one's gonna take me out, I'm not gonna do any more parties with your old man and I'm not drinking anything with anyone in French Jamaica 'cause I—am—not—going—there. Okay? I have business in Cuba and points north, and I don't use agents yet because I'm the only guy who knows what I'm looking for, and how to get it. Look, I can explain that to you another time. But I can take care of myself."

"Do you say," she replied in a silken and dangerously soft voice, "that I cannot do this? Take care of myself?"

"How should I know? Lookit, your old man fights duels, I know his kind, why would I go looking for someone like that? And what could you do if you came along, grab a sword and run him through for me?"

"Yes, I could do that. If you laugh," she added warningly.

"Hey, I remember the pig-sticker you wore next to your knee first time I met you; I wouldn't dare laugh at you."

"You know," Dahven put in quietly, before either of them could say anything else, "he does have a point, Ariadne. Chris does run his business the way he says, and for the reasons he told you. Also, he's doing our Emperor a service, and it's one that could put him in extreme danger without much warning—as it did with your father. If he has to protect someone besides himself—"

"Protect *me*? When in all my life have I ever looked to *men* for protection? Men where I come from are the thing a woman protects *against*." She laughed mirthlessly and leaped to her feet. "How can I prove to you that I have enough sense to avoid peril? That I can survive in places where a lesser woman might not? I have lived nineteen years in my father's house, and my wits and my bones are intact. I have better sense for my own skin than *he* has for his." Chris stirred indignantly, but as Ariadne glanced his way he twisted his lips into a tight knot and rolled his eyes. She nodded once in Chris's direction; her eyes fixed on Dahven. "*He* tells me you can use a sword. Is this so?"

Dahven shrugged and said diffidently, "I know a little about them."

Ariadne smiled and sketched him a curtsey. "Yes. And so do I—a little. Of course you have here swords?"

"This is—or was—a garrison, as well as an overlarge and drafty nobleman's house," Dahven replied dryly. "Yes, there are swords. Why?"

"Send for them, if you will. I shall prove to you, here and now, that I do not need *his* protecting."

"Here and now what?" Chris demanded suspiciously. She chopped a hand in his direction for silence; her eyes remained fixed on Dahven's face. Dahven gazed back at her thoughtfully, then got to his feet.

"It will answer some things, certainly. All right, why not? Chris, go out to the hall; someone should be there. Have the rack of plain blades brought from the lower hall near the kitchens—do you mind if we go outside, Ariadne?" he went on blandly. "I prefer not to duel among the furniture; Jennifer fusses so when I slice up the chairs." His eyes were alight, one eyebrow raised. Ariadne seemed to be fighting laughter. She nodded, leaned against the table and looked at Chris; he swore under his breath and went. Dahven cast Jennifer a warning glance over the girl's dark head; Jen merely rolled her eyes expressively and kept her mouth shut. This had gone completely beyond her. *I swear he started the whole mess on purpose.* That would be like him, to precipitate a situation and get it over with. Well, it was out of *her* hands; let him handle it. Settle the girl. But Ariadne showed no signs of having had her bluff called. *And why am I suddenly reminded of myself four odd years ago, ankle-deep in sand, a nasty long dagger in my belt, a six-foot ash staff in my hands and murder in my eyes? Daring a brute at least twice my size to come at me so I could wipe him out? You did okay, girlfriend, give her a break.* She turned her face away to hide a sudden grin. Robyn was going to absolutely adore her new daughter-in-law. Right.

"If you want to change from that skirt," Dahven suggested; it broke a long but not uncomfortable silence. Ariadne glanced at him, at the folds of fabric that fell to within a finger's width of the floor, then shook her head.

"In a real fight—not a duel but a real fight—you make do with what you have."

"True enough. Well, then—ah, here we are. Pick what you like; I can use any of them." Ariadne was already walking around the rack and the bemused young armsman who held it steady. She drew one fancy basket-hilted blade partway from its resting place, then another, finally settled on a very slender rapier with a plain hilt and leather-wrapped crosspiece. "Good. I like those, too," Dahven said cheerfully. Chris mumbled something, fell silent as Jennifer stepped on his foot and scowled at him. Dahven ran his eye over the rack, drew a similar sword from near the end, and bowed rather grandly. "After you, my dear young woman. Out the door and to your right, and then to your left and down the steps into the courtyard." He followed her, leaving Chris and Jennifer to come after.

Chris grabbed Jennifer's shoulder when she would have walked out and hissed, "Look, this is real nuttiness, she's goofy, okay? Dupret's insane, and she inherited it!"

"Maybe not. Leave this to Dahven, why don't you? He's the family diplomat—not either of us. Remember who pulled Aletto down off his high horse on the subject of swords?"

"I—"

"He won't hurt her, you know."

"Jen! You think that's the point?"

"You dropped the gauntlet, kid, and she picked it up. What did you want her to do, bat her eyelashes at you and coo, 'Whatever you want, sweetie'?" Chris sighed heavily.

"Lookit. If she's just gassing, and she loses, she'll be grim death to be around. Worse than she already is, which is bad enough!" He ran a hand across his forehead, pushing hair aside. "And if that's the family diplomat, we're in trouble—who brought up this whole mess over dinner? Wasn't me, remember?"

"You were planning on pinning a note to her pillow?" Jennifer asked sweetly. "No, it goes on the pincushion, along with a lock of your hair—don't you take a swipe at me, kiddo; remember my delicate condition."

He snorted. "Yah. Delicate. You and a rhino, lady."

"Dahven won't make her look foolish, whatever happens."

"Sure. Me, too. So what if she's half as good as she thinks she is? I'll never hear the end of it, you know? And she'll rip my ears off if I try to leave her here." He bowed her broadly into the hall. "Pincushion, my—"

"Language, child," Jennifer admonished lightly. She laughed as he made a very sour face at her. "But she may have a point, if she's as good as she thinks she is. Keep in mind she knows that end of the world better than you do. She might prove useful to you."

"Oh, thank you very much," he replied bitterly. "Just whose side are you on?"

"Mine and Dahven's; has that ever been a secret?" She walked into the still-hot early evening and settled on one of the low stone walls flanking the shallow steps that led to the old parade ground. "I am also remembering a woman who used to hate having men make a big deal out of holding doors and elevators for her, and some boy or other who threw fits when anyone tried to coddle him—and one was me, and the other was you."

"Just swell." Chris threw up his hands, settled onto the opposite wall and drew up his feet.

A few feet away, Ariadne walked back and forth, testing the sword. She turned back finally and asked, "Are you ready?"

"Whenever you are."

"Then—I am ready." She bent suddenly sideways and spun the back of her skirts around her left arm, away from her heels, then brought up the sword and waited. Somewhere she'd shed shoes or sandals, and was now barefoot.

Dahven brought his blade to ready, touched hers, and quite suddenly lunged. Ariadne parried, retreated two paces, parried once more, lunged in turn.

Chris stared, rubbed his eyes in an exaggerated fashion and groaned. "Oh, jeez. I am just gonna *hate* this!"

The girl was undoubtedly good; small but precise in all her movements, fast and extremely light-footed. Jennifer watched a dazzling display of swordplay with pleasure, and ignored Chris's muttered running commentary. Dahven couldn't possibly be pulling his punches, not much, anyway, because his blade was slicing the air and the tip was a blur. But Ariadne was giving back as good as she got. After several minutes, she nodded, then stepped back, released her skirts and held out the sword, point down. Dahven took it from her and bowed gravely. "Quite impressive, young woman. I hope you don't feel I insulted you earlier."

"There was no insult," Ariadne said calmly. She didn't even sound particularly winded. "It is a most rare thing for women to do this in French Jamaica, particularly among Father's class. His man Peronne taught me in secret—" She smiled widely, her eyes alight with malice. "It was that, or have Father learn he was stealing from the cellars." She turned to Chris, and the smile vanished. "I will tell you this all at one time, you will do me the courtesy to listen. I do not *need* you to take care of me. I can take care of myself; that I still lived when you took me from Father's house says as much. You say you go to manage your businesses, but my father also has business in many of these places you name. I know his friends and many of his agents by sight, and you do not. Also, I know something about my father's trade in the yellow powder, and I speak French from childhood. Your French is dreadful, your friend's worse, and you have no *entrée* to the higher classes of society without someone such as me." She paused expectantly.

Chris laughed shortly. "Swell. But what if your old man's agents and his off-island buddies already know you left with me—and why? What if you're a mark the minute you set foot ashore anywhere down there? You want him to finish the job he started—on both of us? Because I'd really rather not, okay?"

"You can take care of yourself and avoid him; remember, you said so? If I am with you, we both avoid him, yes? Remember, please, that my father is an important person in French Jamaica, but that does not make him God, elsewhere; he is simply a rich man whose father is noble. But if our paths cross, his and mine, I owe him for this shameful thing he did to me. And to you."

"I second that," Chris growled. "I don't like being used—" He stopped abruptly and flushed. "I mean—"

"It was not your choice to wed, you have said so," Ariadne broke in flatly. "I will not remain here in this desert, among people I do not know, while you go to get yourself killed."

"Thanks for the vote of confidence."

"It is nothing." She must have heard the sarcasm in his voice; she ignored it. "I do not stay here. I go with you, or after you. And if the chance comes, then Father is *mine*, whatever you do to his business or his friends."

"One question," Jennifer said mildly, "before we get completely emotionally out of hand. Who is paying Dupret to raise the drug—or process it or ship it, or whatever it is he does?"

Ariadne shrugged. "It comes in by foreign ship and it is powder in clay pots or gourds when he gets it. He has things done to some of it in the place where he distills brandy, and most of that is shipped out, some I think to France, but there are many places his ships stop between Philippe-sur-Mer and Orlean."

Chris snapped his fingers. "In boxes of flavored brandies?"

"Or rum. Some, I think, to my grandfather's estate. Where it goes from there, I do not know. I think I remember something, though, my father arguing with one of his brother's agents, that they are trying to take more land to the east."

"Swell." Chris rubbed his chin, thought for a moment. "I'm awfully tired of this attitude," he added in a mildly aggrieved voice. "You want land, you don't fight for it; you get everybody on the other side wasted and hooked on drugs, then waltz in and take over. Terrific."

"But my father is not the one sending it here, to Rhadaz. Because none of his ships come here."

"But he could be supplying the English or the Mer Khani, who *do* come here. Great. Terrific. It's still anyone's Zero, and I'm back at square one."

"A suggestion," Dahven said. "If we have proven whatever various points needed proving, I left a cup of very nice wine inside, and it's considerably cooler in there."

Chris sighed heavily. "You are all in league; I swear this isn't fair."

"Life isn't fair, remember, kid?" Jennifer said.

"When do I ever get a chance to forget? All right, all *right*." He flung his arms wide, let them drop. "You come, too, Ariadne. You can hang around and be like totally bored while I do deals, okay? Tomorrow we'll go down to the market and I'll buy you a couple nice skinny swords for a wedding present. And if Dupret gets you after all, I'll put roses on your grave."

Ariadne smiled sweetly; the smile fell short of dark, angry eyes. "There will be no need. But I will put them on yours." Chris threw up his hands, swore under his breath, and stalked back into the hall.

4

THE Gray Fishers caravan reached Holmaddan City at daybreak, just as a pale yellow sun rose in a rare, clear blue autumn sky. The breeze was cool, but with a hint of the even more rare heat to come. The last wagons cleared the gates, and Vuhlem's guard; moments later the grandmother's cart pulled into the shade of two low, spreading oaks fronting an enormously squat two-story stone building. Her son leaped from the seat to open double doors, then took the harness to lead the horses as they balked at the darkness inside.

"Get someone in here to make light," he shouted to the next wagon in line. "Or at least open some shutters; you know what the beasts are like!" Two slender young women in bright billowing britches and flying scarves scrambled from the back of the grandmother's cart, each with a fading blue-light, and sprinted into stale-aired blackness. Moments later, clear northern light flooded the far end of the area as they undid weatherbeaten shutters, revealing an enormous single room used for storage and stabling. The grandmother eased herself from the seat as her son stopped the wagon and began undoing the harness; she stretched cautiously, then crossed the chamber. Near the open windows, a broad stone staircase went up to more heavy doors.

"You two, come with me," she called out as she wrapped her skirts around one hand and slowly climbed. One of the young women pressed past her and drew an enormous key from her pocket as she reached the doors. It went in easily, but turned hard and with a loud and horrid screeching of metal on metal. The double doors separated in the center with another loud squawk; the grandmother shoved them open, then turned to call down, "Anbresar, bring oil for the wards when you come! Sil"—she

61

turned back to the young woman who still held the key—"go
and light the fires, but make certain the flues are clear this
time—no more scorched pigeons in the hearth, thank you!" Sil
wrinkled her nose and nodded once sharply, set the key on the
grandmother's outstretched palm, and hurried off across a dim
cavern of a room.

The grandmother took the other woman's arm and felt her way
to the right wall, then along it. "There, sin-Duchess, do you feel
the window ledge? I can find the shutters, but the bars are too
heavy for me to work any more. Can you? Up, hard, and to the
right." For answer, Lialla walked her fingers along the deep, cool
stone sill and then cautiously up dry, splintery wood until she located the metal pivot-bolt. The bar turned reluctantly, finally
gave and moved shriekingly from horizontal to upright. The
shutters fell open, enough to permit a narrow but brilliant shaft
of sun; Lialla blinked furiously, threw a hand across her face,
and shoved the shutters back as far as they would go, then turned
quickly away, rubbing her eyes. She could see nothing but light:
flashes of it, and an enormously glaring window-shaped rectangle overall. The grandmother dogged the shutters open and drew
her away. Cool air flowed into the chamber. "A little better," the
old woman said. "At least one can see. Bah, the whole place
reeks of damp; that comes of not using it very often. We should
have had fires here most of the summer. Or at least the shutters
opened now and again."

Lialla blotted brightness-tears from her eyelashes, blinked rapidly until she could finally see something besides sun-flashes.
There wasn't much to see: Like the chamber below, this was
mostly one large room; unlike that lower area, there were no
boxes, bales and other goods stored here. More windows were
opened; now she could see several small plain alcoves, bare
metal or wood bars where a blanket would be hung to close them
off from the central chamber. There were one or two narrow
doors along the windowless west wall. No murals, no pictures,
no tapestries—nothing but plain whitewashed stone, plain windows flanked by dark wood shutters, and, at either end of
the massive room, vast hearths of dark stone around deep fireplaces. One of the older women knelt well inside the nearest of
these, peering up the chimney; as Lialla and the grandmother
passed, she backed out and stood, dusting soot from the knees of
her heavy travel britches. "Clear," she said briefly. Two boys
who had been waiting nearby dropped double armloads of kin-

dling and small logs and began building a pyramid of wood deep inside the fireplace. The older woman stood watching, nodding from time to time.

More caravaners came from below, bags, bundles and piles of bedding in their arms or piled on slings carried between two. Some were already setting out individual family carpets at intervals arm's length or so apart, as close to the fireplaces as possible—or sensible. Voices echoed as they bounced off the high ceiling, filled the room. Hard to make out individual words unless you were right next to someone. *Privacy of a sort in that*, Lialla decided. But caravaners were by nature gregarious.

Sil was crouched before the farthest fireplace, working a bellows. One of the boys knelt next to her, stacking wood against the wall. Smoke puffed out into the room; Sil coughed, rubbed her nose vigorously against one sleeve, and swore. But the fire was crackling now, and a shaft of bright flame soared up the chimney.

People were still coming from the stables, some of the women setting out food on a trestle under the windows. Two of the taller men pinned a long piece of dark blue cloth over the entrance to one alcove; a young girl settled the grandmother's small carpet before it. Lialla rubbed the last yellow-orange flares from her eyes. "There is a separate chamber for you, of course," the grandmother said, and pointed toward the closed doors. "We reserve the alcoves and doored rooms for those who need privacy, mostly the recently mated. It seemed to me you would be more comfortable."

"If I take space from someone else," Lialla began uncertainly, but the grandmother waved that away.

"Don't be foolishly polite, child; we are caravaners from birth, and most of us prefer the camaraderie the open space provides. Since the Duke insists we maintain these quarters in the city . . ." She shook her head. "Poor old Vuhlem. Sil has finished her work, I see; you and she had better go, hadn't you?" She eyed Sil critically, then pulled a dark cloth from her belt and rubbed soot from the tip of the younger woman's nose. "Go, both of you. Remember, Sil, which shops I told you."

"Of course," Sil competently turned down fingers as she repeated a list of fifteen or so names—Lialla, who had been in on both planning sessions with the grandmother, her council, and her niece Sil, couldn't have remembered even one of those names at the moment. *Be easy on yourself, you swore you would, this time.* Sil came here several times a year and dealt with this market and these shopkeepers regularly, after all. *I do remember names in Sehfi, and people, and about their families.* She'd have to begin doing that here, right away, if she wanted to make any headway. People liked it when she remembered who they were— not just their names, but things about them, important to them. She came back to the moment; Sil and the grandmother were debating one additional shop—a potter's, Lialla recalled after a moment's hard thought. She bit back a yawn; there hadn't been much sleep the night before, and precious little all the days before that. *It can't be—but I really did only leave this city twelve days ago.* Two in Hushar Oasis; the rest traveling back to Vuhlem's duchy and then on the caravan's usual roundabout route to his city.

Poor old Vuhlem. Lialla cast the grandmother a sharp glance; the woman hadn't been smiling when she said it. *He'll think poor old Vuhlem when I've done with him,* she promised herself.

The grandmother was speaking again, Lialla set aside inner distraction and tried to pay attention. "Well, use your best judgment, girl. If the husband is in, don't you say anything, to him or to her. Have Lialla see if she can't find a pot, something special, say it's to hold a gift for one of the Dukes or some such. If that distracts him sufficiently that you dare pass the message to that poor floorboard of a woman—why am I telling you all this?" She shrugged broadly. Sil grinned and shook her head. "You know what to do. Go on, go, there's plenty for me to take care of here without tending to *you* two children." For answer, Sil simply nodded once, caught hold of Lialla's wrist, and drew her across the room toward the fireplace she'd just left. "Another door and stairs over here; we'd never make it down the inner ones right now."

As they passed the hearth, she raised her voice to be heard over the chatter. "Petronn, don't you dare let my fire go out!" The boy stacking the wood glanced up, startled, and a cascade of small logs rolled down to clatter loudly on the tiled hearth; one smacked into his legs. "And don't go making a mess, either!" she shouted, and laughed as the boy made a face at her. "The inner door better not be locked," she said as she pulled open one of the narrow doors and drew Lialla behind her. "If I have to fight back through that mob to get a key, I'll—oh, good."

She interrupted herself as they fetched up against a solid wooden barrier at the bottom of the steps; it was gloomy, but

Lialla could see the hasp and the open lock dangling from it. The latch was as bad as the locks at the other end of the building, and the hinges protested loudly as she shoved the door open. "Goddess of gaudy baubles, that's awful!" She spoke through clenched teeth. Lialla laughed and Sil glanced at her. "How can you not let that kind of noise *bother* you?"

"It does bother me; I don't show it, that's all. But the faces you make—"

"I'm good at them," Sil replied solemnly as she led the way down a narrow flight of stone steps and into a small, high-walled courtyard. "It's my best talent, I think." She glanced sidelong at her companion, then laughed merrily. "You thought I meant that, didn't you?"

Lialla grinned. "I never *can* tell when you're not serious."

"Serious is for someone like the grandmother, or her thundercloud of a son. Come, help me with the gate; as wet as the summer was here, it's going to be *hideously* tight."

It was; it took book of them to shift the swollen wooden bar, and then both of them with backs pressed against the thick slab of oak to get it to move enough to let them out. "Another day or so of this dry weather, it should move easier," Lialla said as she caught up to Sil, who was walking rapidly down a narrow dirt track. Brush and the backs of several older buildings lined the right-hand side; the tall, dressed stone wall of the caravaner's building was on the left.

"Hah. Wet as it's been, it'll be stiff for utterly days." They reached the end of the building; Sil turned right onto a slightly wider, smoothly cobbled street.

"It gets wet in Zelharri, too: I know these things."

"You don't get fog at night, and ocean damp year round," Sil said gloomily. "I truly loathe Holmaddan—and that's leaving aside the prevailing attitude and the present Duke." Lialla shushed her hastily; Sil merely laughed and shook her head. "Oh, come on, look at us," she said cheerfully. "Couple of young caravaner women—they'd think something was wrong with us if we weren't rude! Here," she added and pulled Lialla to a halt, mid-street, to adjust the scarf that lay across her hair. "Ends tucked in—like that. Now it won't fall off."

Several men working on a wall had stopped what they were doing to stare, deliberately and openly rude. One of them muttered something Lialla couldn't hear, but his face made the comment clear enough; the other men laughed. Sil smiled at them radiantly; the speaker blinked and turned away. The others looked at each other as if uncertain what to do next, then finally went back to work. Lialla sighed as she and Sil went on. "I really do wish you wouldn't do things like that; after this last trip—"

"Yes, well, this is what you need," Sil broke in vigorously, but her fingers gripped Lialla's wrist and her smile was warm. "A dose of caravaner backbone. They'll never look for *you* under the Gray Fishers' clothing, and if you act as if you're sword-proof, you'll begin to feel that way. Vuhlem might be stupid enough to hold a sin-Duchess hostage, but he'd never dare attack a caravaner woman. The caravans would boycott him, and Shesseran himself could back us all the way." She let go of the other's arm. "And with the caravans still Vuhlem's best source of goods for his outlying villages, and sometimes his only way of bringing food to the city, he knows full well he'd better not anger us."

"Yes. All the same. He's got his own fleet of ships these days, you know."

"I also know the Emperor's interdiction against outside things coming to anywhere but Bez and Podhru."

"So does Vuhlem," Lialla said dryly. "And it hasn't stopped him bringing in at least one outside substance." She hesitated; the grandmother had told her the last time she'd come to Holmaddan to keep the entire matter of Zero to herself. But Sil merely nodded.

"Yes, I know about the drugs; the grandmother told me. Since you and I are going to be spending so much time together."

It was Lialla's turn to eye Sil sidelong. "We are?" she asked finally.

"She's leaving me here; didn't I say last night?" The caravaner hesitated, glanced at Lialla. *Is she worried I won't want her?* But why should Sil expect friendship? They'd known each other, casual aquaintances, since Lialla was very young and Sil hardly more than a baby. They didn't know each other very well, though. *She's probably heard all the stories: that I'm unfriendly, that I don't accept help with any grace. My face doesn't show much because I never really dared to let it, all those years with Jadek.* Sil was still eyeing her in cautious, swift little sidelong glances as they walked. *Say something.*

What Sil had said suddenly sank in. *I'm not going to be here alone this time.* Lialla smiled. "You're staying? That's wonderful!"

"You—don't mind?"

"Mind? I'm delighted! Now I can blame half my mistakes on you."

Sil laughed, the bell-like giggle that was extremely infectious. "Make that three-fourths; I'm supposed to know these people and this duchy, after all. But—really, you swear you don't mind?"

"Believe it. I wish you *had* said something last night; I might have slept better." Lialla craned her neck; the avenue had suddenly doubled in width, and there were people everywhere, filling the broad open space between low, broad shop fronts. "Where are we going?"

"You didn't listen? I can see why the grandmother wants you to have a guardian." Sil grinned, erasing any possible sting from her words.

"Yah. All those northern names. And at such an early hour, too."

"Early? The sun was up already! What, do you sleep until midday back—uh, back south?" The caravaner clapped a hand over her mouth and glanced quickly around; no one was paying them any attention. "Oops," she added.

It reminded Lialla of Chris, suddenly; so did Sil's impudent grin. "Oops, yourself. At least I don't crawl into my blankets with the hens, like certain caravaners I could name. Like, all of them."

Sil laughed aloud once more, and several people turned to stare. One older man frowned and twisted his mouth in an elaborate pantomime of distaste, then turned away. Sil blew a kiss at his back, and Lialla clapped both hands over her mouth, stifling sudden laughter. "Not *with* the hens," the caravaner said finally. "It's those sharp, pointy noses, you know." She considered this. "Still, they'd be better than Anbresar, I'd wager. All right, once more, from the top: Emios the baker, we've got nuts and flour for him. Then Bowdli at the tanner's, and Ortos and his wife, who—"

"If you dare to recite that entire list again, Sil—"

"Those three for a start," Sil replied hastily. "They're all in this section of the market. After that, across the square and down nearer the docks."

"The docks." Lialla shook her head. "I'm turned around."

The other woman pointed down the avenue. "Sun comes up in

the east, remember? Docks are north—so, that way." She lowered
her voice. "Does any of this look familiar? From the last time?"

"I don't think I could remember where I was to save myself,"
Lialla replied gloomily. "It was dark—and I was awfully afraid."

"I'd have been. But you've no idea at all where the boy's barracks might be? He didn't say?"

"I don't think he said anything. If I could recall the captain's
name, though . . ." Lialla thought, finally shook her head.

"Don't give up. We can send a couple of the boys to look for
him; they always like it when you find them errands."

"That's if we don't get anywhere this morning," Lialla reminded her.

"True. Are we making wagers on it?"

"You *think* I'd bet anything at all on that boy?" Lialla retorted
darkly. Sil merely laughed, threaded her way between several
small empty tables and benches, and plunged into the shop behind them. The sin-Duchess followed.

The room was broader than deep, lit in patches by high,
glassed windows in the back of the shop and by the open doorway. A high counter ran the length of the back wall. There were
piles of breads on this, stacked according to shape and size, and
racks behind the counter that held long skinny breads and baskets of rolls; a brightly colored curtain hung across a doorway
near the right wall, and a bear of a man leaned on his elbows between two tall piles of pale, flat bread at the other end of the
small room. The air was warm and fragrant: yeasty and spicy. He
looked up and smiled as the women entered; the smile faded as
he took in the bright caravaner colors and wide-legged britches.

Lialla's stomach grumbled; Sil glanced at her and smothered a
laugh behind a square, capable hand. She fumbled in the small
patchwork leather bag dangling from her belt and pressed two
copper ceris into Lialla's fingers. "Here," she murmured. "Buy
us rolls from Emios; distract him while I try to get a quiet word
with his wife. Something with fruit in it for me."

Distract him—right, Lialla thought sourly. If that was Emios,
she would have her hands full; he was openly scowling at the
pair of them, arms folded and eyes narrowed. There wasn't anyone else in the shop. She hoped Sil wasn't planning on trying to
walk through the curtain; Emios looked capable of strangling her
for even thinking about it. *Maybe he simply doesn't like mornings either.* But his eyes followed Sil as the women separated,
and he kept them in a fixed, flatly rude stare on her all the time

he dealt with Lialla, answering her questions about the various rolls and breads with one or two clipped words, finding what she finally decided upon by feel; he brought the coin up to look at it, without taking his level gaze from Sil, before dropping it in the small basket behind him. Lialla turned away, glanced at Sil, who came back to smile at the merchant, as if unaware of his plainly uncivil behavior. "You've none of the dark bread this time?" Emios shook his head, but some of the tension seemed to leave him. Sil waited.

"No flour for it," he volunteered finally.

Sil's smile widened. "Ah. Then we come in good time. Gray Fishers, just in this morning. And we have what you need."

"You've rye?" His eyes narrowed, and one heavy hand tugged at his beard. "How much a sack?"

"I was to tell you this: The grandmother of Gray Fishers sends Master Emios her greetings," Sil replied formally. "Tell the baker we have twenty large sacks of rye flour still unpromised, but the Duke's kitchens have taken all the rest we had and left call upon the twenty, if they are not sold by midday. The price is four silver."

"Four silver—bah." Emios tilted his head back to glare at the ceiling, then sighed heavily. "All right. Four silver ceris a bag. But only if the grind is good!"

"The Duke's chief cook thinks it is," Sil replied mildly.

"Bah; the Duke eats rye bread that's half hull, and poorly made at that; Flirin may be a cook but he's no baker. All right, I'll take all you have left. You're still not delivering?"

She spread her hands wide, shrugged. "The grandmother's regrets. But that's your Duke's ruling, not our choice, sir."

He sighed again, even more heavily. "I know it. No large wagons on the streets in daylight hours, more bother for men like me with a business to run and bread to make—and no real improvement to the crowding, either." He grinned, a flash of teeth that didn't reach pale blue eyes. "So, tell me, caravaner, how many Gray Fisher women are out right now, hawking those twenty bags?" He held up a hand, strode across the small chamber and thrust aside the curtain. "Mertis! Have you not finished in there yet?" A woman's high voice replied; neither Lialla nor Sil could make out the answer but moments later a woman emerged, one hand smoothing down her skirts, the other rubbing flour from a thin, pale cheek. "These women just brought word, there's rye flour, finally—it's at the compound?" he demanded of Sil, who nodded. "I'll give you the coin for it, wife, you'll have to go—ah, blast, you're not any good with the new team, I'll do it, and you watch the counter. Can you manage that much?" Mertis nodded. "It won't be for long, you only need to watch the counter, and not let anyone cheat you, or steal the bread."

"Of course, husband." She glanced at him as if asking permission, then looked beyond him and smiled. "Thank you for bringing us word. Do you want the rolls wrapped? You could have them here, perhaps something to drink with them?"

"If you have hot tea, we'll have them here," Sil said. "If not, you can wrap them and we'll go. We've plenty of stops to make before midday." Emios hesitated, looked at her and Lialla, then back at his wife. He shrugged finally.

"Plenty of stops—to get more competition for that flour, eh? There's tea," he added and turned to scowl at his wife again. "Well, woman? Cups and a pot—that's an extra seri, for the tea," he added. Sil dug out a coin, but he had already pressed past her and disappeared behind the cloth hanging.

Mertis sent her eyes toward the cloth, then came into the room. "There's also orange, if you prefer it." She brought her hand edgewise to her lips, glanced warningly toward the cloth-draped doorway once more. Boots clomped on a wooden floor: Emios came into the shop a breath later. He ignored the women, dropped Sil's coin into the cash basket, and disappeared below the counter; Lialla could hear him cursing and mumbling but couldn't catch the words. His color was high, his lips tightly compressed by the time he came back into view, two deep baskets clutched in one hand. Still mumbling to himself, he counted something on the fingers of his other hand, then began tossing round loaves, braided loaves, and stick loaves into one basket. A double handful of plain rolls went into the other. He draped a cloth over each, caught them up rather awkwardly by the handles, and gave his wife a sharp look.

"I may as well make the deliveries now, save harnessing up a second time. Can you handle matters here by yourself for once?" The woman merely nodded and held the curtain for him; she followed but came back a moment later with a small tray that held a steaming dark clay pot and cups.

"The table inside might be better," Mertis said, indicating a small, plain rectangle fronted by a low bench next to the door leading to the street; it sat in shadow and was hardly visible to Lialla, even though her eyes were used to the mostly dim shop interior. "The breeze outside can be quite chill, especially so early in the day."

"Inside," Lialla said firmly. Mertis led the way and set the pot down, poured tea into the two cups and put a flat dish of honey and a damp cloth between them. She held up a hand as Sil would have spoken, took one step back and cautiously gazed out the door; she smiled then.

"It's all right; he's truly gone."

"Leaving you alone with a pair of caravaner women." Sil laughed as she dribbled honey into her tea. "He's gone trusting in his old age, hasn't he?" She glanced at Lialla and winked. "I thought of warning you, but after that village, I didn't think you'd find old Emios very odd. Mertis, we won't stay long."

"Thank you. He's got Bronten from the potters' cooperative across the avenue to watch over me when he's gone out." She gave them an apologetic smile and a small shrug. "He's no worse than most. Better than he was when I was first wed to him. Any news from the grandmother, besides the flour?"

Sil bit into her roll, chewed rapidly and washed it down with tea. "Yes. Spread the word as best you can, Mertis; Gray will be in the city for at least five days. There will be a meeting tonight, and another in two days, same hour as usual."

"Good. I'll come, unless he's wakeful tonight. He shouldn't be."

"You've still powder to dose his wine?"

Mertis sighed. "As much as he drinks these days, I haven't needed it often. But yes, I still have some."

"Good. Don't chance not using the stuff, Mertis; a drunkard can waken at the damn-most awful moment. But I have other news for you." Sil tucked the last bite of roll into her cheek. "When Gray Fishers goes on, at least two of us will stay behind."

"Good. We need someone who can keep us focused. There's too much infighting of late; we'll get nowhere like that."

"I know it. Tonight, fourth hour from sunset, the small door." Sil drained her cup, blotted her lips on the damp cloth, and got to her feet. Lialla tucked the last bite of roll into her cheek, swallowed the last of her now tepid tea, and followed.

Sil wove a light-footed path through slower-moving men, around a snarl of small carts blocking the entry to a narrow alley. Past more of the little two-wheeled carts lined along the main avenue, men and an occasional older woman selling vegetables and fruits here. She turned down another of the innumerable alleys, edged sideways through a tight snarl of foot traffic and finally into a clear space. Behind them, a rooster crowed and chickens squawked, the sound echoing between high, narrow stone alley walls. "Nasty brute, isn't he?"

Lialla caught up with her; her ears were ringing. "Who— Emios?"

"Suspicious, grasping, rude—he's one of the worst old-liners around," Sil replied cheerfully. "I thought you should first see the lower end of what you'll be up against. Some of the men around here actually believe their women can think—well, almost, anyway."

"Suspicious, fine," Lialla replied sourly. "But why of a caravaner? After all, you were bringing him an offer on something he needed, not openly subverting his wife."

"He needs the flour, and other things we bring in," Sil replied. She skirted a foul-smelling puddle and emerged into a street bordered on their side by prosperous-looking two- and three-story buildings and on the other side by a very tall hedge. Beyond the hedge, Lialla could see nothing but the tops of trees and sky. "He doesn't like or trust caravaner women; most of them don't. Nasty, independent creatures, have their males underfoot, completely opposite of how things should be. So, of course, the thought that his wife might have dealings with us and pick up any stray attitudes—certainly he's suspicious."

Chris and the things he's told me over the years, Lialla thought, and grinned. "Of course. It rubs off, right?" Sil considered this, then laughed.

"Like warts? Exactly! Now." She led the way, left and along the south edge of the street. "No more nasty surprises for you this morning, all right? Well—no one like Emios, anyway. Next stop Bowdli and the tanner's, he's all right. He does saddles and things for some of the Duke's men, and we can leave the message about the boy."

Lialla hesitated, finally shrugged. She'd gone along with the grandmother's idea for locating Kepron without calling the wrong kind of attention to him (if he was still alive and free, of course) but just now, in the Duke's own city, it sounded unlikely to get her anywhere—except noticed by Vuhlem. *Paranoia,* she decided firmly. *Remember what the grandmother said: It's a huge city, and the Duke can't have an eye everywhere.* Especially when so much of his attention was elsewhere—on foreign ships, village women, and illegal trade. *And a Triad.* Well, but she wouldn't think about that.

Bowdli the tanner. Lialla wrinkled her nose. She'd prefer facing ten worse than Emios if it meant not breathing air that reeked of rock salt and long-dead hides.

The tanner fortunately kept his shop apart from the tannery itself; the only smells in the little building were finished leather, wax, and dyes—a familiar and rather pleasant combination. The tanner himself eyed the women warily, but not as suspiciously as had Emios. Of course, his wife was safely across the shop, measuring a small boy for boots. He even managed a smile for Sil as she came over to his work bench. "Gray Fishers, aren't you?" He laid a broad-bladed tool and a mallet on a thick leather strap he was working and dug his knuckles into the small of his back. "Got any of that southern wax this time?"

"The grandmother's greetings," Sil replied. "There's a small crate of wax, all we could get in Bez at a decent price."

"Small crate—how many boxes?" Lialla stood back and let her eyes wander back to the woman, who was now showing leather samples to what must be the boy's father. The boy sat near the door, wiggling small bare toes in a patch of sunshine. Sil and Bowdli talked price and delivery; Lialla gazed past the boy, into the sunlit street. It all seemed very strange and foreign—not as strange or foreign as had her first day in that coastal village, but strange enough. The same early hour, cool air, unfamiliar smells, food that was not quite what she was used to, an accent not like Zelharri's. The attitudes of shopkeepers. *In Sehfi, men have let their women run shops and keep a share of the profits for years; even under my uncle that was common practice. Plenty of men accept their women as partners, and only a few treat them like children or idiots. Or property.*

Somewhere out there, across that street, past that hedge—not nearly far enough away—Duke Vuhlem's castle stood on a high cliff overlooking the sea. Had he missed her yet? Doubtless he had. Had he fixed blame—had his Triad returned to help him with that? She blinked, turned away from the door. *You weren't going to think about Vuhlem or his Triad out here.* Besides, Sil and the tanner had settled on a deal for the wax and they were talking casually now, Sil picking up a little local gossip, finding out what else a local tanner might like from outside, the tanner hearing about new English splitting machinery that would speed processing; he was extremely interested in her description of the Mer Khani-cut boot currently popular in Bez and Podhru.

The customer left, hauling the boy up by the wrist and leading

him out. The woman gathered up her samples and measurements
and came back to join them. Sil smiled a vague greeting, turned
her attention back to the tanner and brought up the second reason
for their visit. "We have a message—a letter, really—for a local
boy, he's said to be in one of the Duke's companies, the grandmother thought you might be able to help us get it to the right
company and the proper boy."

Bowdli tipped his head to one side. "What name?"

"Kepron," Sil replied promptly.

The tanner shook his head, as quickly. His wife volunteered,
"It's such a common name, my brother's son is named Kepron,
and so is the paper-maker two doors down. You haven't the
name of his company, or that of the boy's father?"

Sil smiled faintly, shrugged. "The grandmother was given only
that much information by the woman who sent the message. It's
some wealthy distant relative of the boy's mother, down in
Sikkre or Dro Pent, I don't really recall. I *do* remember the
grandmother saying what the southern woman called the boy's
father was *quite* impolite. And not at all what one would put on
the face of a message."

The woman smiled blankly. Bowdli tipped his head back and
roared with laughter. Lialla smiled at the woman; Sil grinned and
waited for the tanner to get himself under control. "Impolite!" he
managed finally; this set him off a second time. "Ah, that's a
good one, I'll remember that. I know of two other Keprons, but
one's an old man. The other, now, he's young but he may not be
your Kepron, you know, and last time I saw him he wasn't in the
Duke's guard. But I can find out. What do you want passed on?"

"Just that there's a letter for him. He can come to the caravaner's quarters near the east gates and claim it."

"You'll have more Keprons there than you know how to manage," Bowdli said. He considered this, laughed briefly. "Perhaps
not. An impolite name of a father might narrow the search some,
eh? Here," he added, easing himself off the bench, "let me get
a sample of that leather; if your people can match the quality, I
have a customer who'll pay well for it." He was still chuckling
as he dug through a cabinet against the back wall.

Sil met the woman's eyes, glanced at the tanner's back and
quickly murmured, "Fourth hour from sunset, tonight, same
place." The woman sent her own eyes sideways; Bowdli dropped
his handful of scraps and knelt to pick them up, and she nodded

once, a scant movement of her chin. She walked over to the cabinet then, touched his shoulder.

"Let me sort that, husband." She bent over and began piling bits of leather back in order. He drew one from her fingers and brought it back with him.

"Soft and very thin, d'you see?" He handed it to Sil, who turned it over and stroked it. "Can't do that with much of what's raised around here."

"It's not something I know, hidework," Sil replied. "It's very nice work."

"Nice skin to begin with, really."

"I'll give it to the grandmother; when you come for the wax you can speak to her about it. Or her brother; he knows leather." She tucked the leather swatch into her sash.

"You'll be in the city how long?"

"Five days. I wouldn't wait until the last, though; it'll be mad around the compound."

"I won't; I'll be there late today or early tomorrow." Sil nodded and left; Lialla followed.

Four more shops in rapid succession; Lialla lost track of streets and alleys almost at once, and kept her sense of direction only because she could see the sun, still short of midday and riding rather low in the southern sky. Faces began to blur; too many people on the streets and byways, crowded into shops and around carts. Too many people Sil spoke to. *How does she ever remember so many faces?* Sil didn't always have a name but she knew people by face and could attach a trade, a child, some accomplishment to the face and speak about that. *I thought I was good at this kind of thing; what, I know thirty or so families in Sehfi? She's talked to probably a hundred people this morning, and that's in one city.*

Sil did all the talking in the various shops: offering goods to the merchants, sneaking a word with the wives or daughters whenever possible, passing on the message about—and for—young Kepron now and again.

"One last stop," Sil said as they emerged from a cloth dyer's shop. There was a smudge of deep red running from ear to chin where she'd walked into a hanging bundle of drying cloth.

Lialla tugged her to a stop once they were safely out of view of the shop owner; Moderbas had been nearly as unpleasant as Emios the baker, and if possible even more suspicious of caravan women. Angry, too, that the grandmother had not been able to obtain any of the Zelharri blue for him; Sil hadn't even bothered to offer him finished denim blue cloth. "Here, you've got a stripe of color."

"Ah, I thought that stuff felt wet. Drat." Sil tugged a cloth from her sash, poked the end into her mouth and rubbed at her cheek with the dampened fabric. "I can't see what I'm doing; here, you try."

Lialla rubbed, finally handed the cloth back. "It's better, I think, but it's not coming right off; you'll need soap."

"How bad?"

"Visible—not awful."

Sil stuffed the cloth back into her sash and sighed. "Could have been worse, I suppose."

"Could have been Zelharri blue," Lialla agreed. "Do you still want to make that last stop?"

"Might as well, it's between us and the caravan compound. Besides, I want to make certain for myself Ibys gets word about tonight." She rubbed at her face with the end of a sleeve, sighed and shook her head. "Come on. We can be back in time for mid-day meal, and I wager you'd like some time off your feet after that. Maybe some of that sleep you missed last night, hmmm?" She plunged across a narrow, crowded little street and into an even narrower way leading off at an angle. There was mud everywhere; Sil swore and moved off to one side, gesturing Lialla to say close behind her.

"Lead me to it. What do we have to get through to reach the compound?"

"Mud like this," Sil grumbled. "A few side alleys and one main avenue where they're probably selling cattle today, with any luck. And—"

"I meant, how bad's the man?"

"Oh." Sil considered this, laughed and shook her head. "He's not what you'd expect: no temper like Emios, none of the cooper's jealous clinging—"

"As hugely muscled as that cooper is, does he really think someone would dare try to steal his wife?"

"No. That she'll leave him."

"Sounds like my brother. Without the charm," Lialla said dryly. They emerged from the alley and Sil hung back to let Lialla catch up with her.

"Yes, there were rumors all over the Sehfi market this spring; how he wouldn't let his fair-haired outlander Duchess out of his sight, and how unhappy she was about it."

"Market gossip," Lialla replied gloomily. "But that's not fair of me. Aletto wasn't being nasty, he just didn't realize what he was doing. And he's eased up a lot since Robyn told him."

"They should all be so agreeable. No, Chiros isn't like any of those, he's, well, you'll see. Here—" They came out onto a neat little green square of park; Sil led the way across it, past a small pool, skirted a grove of dark-leaved trees. Two young women with babies sat on the stone lip of the pool, talking quietly; there was no one else about. "This is quite popular late in the afternoon on a hot day, and the men take it over evenings for some kind of ball game. I've never been interested enough to watch—of course, *women* can only watch from the boundaries, so there isn't much to see. And who'd want to only watch, anyway?" Lialla shrugged. They crossed a pool of shade, emerged onto another street. Sil skipped nimbly between two small carts and vanished into another shop. Lialla followed.

Serviceable, plain britches and shirts were neatly piled on two trestle tables, a sample of each stack hanging against the wall behind it. A tall, rangy woman came down between the trestles. "Ah," she said, then called over her shoulder, "Husband! Gray Fishers is back!"

"What of the cloth?" A deep voice came from the back of the shop; the owner was somewhere behind a precariously balanced pile of dark, wadded fabric.

"We have five medium crates of the blue." Sil held her arms apart, indicating the size of the boxes. "All we could get."

"About three stanchet each, husband," the woman translated over her shoulder.

"Medium crates, hmmm. That's not much cloth. How much is already gone?"

"You know what the grandmother said, since it's so scarce: No one can prepay for a shipment, or any part of one, it's whoever comes first with the coin when we have denim in reasonable quantity, by straws when we have less."

"Five crates. Same price as the last batch?"

"Same."

"I'd better—" Wood creaked alarmingly; Lialla's eyes widened as Chiros came into sight for the first time. *Don't stare*, she admonished herself, and turned away to finger the nearest pile of shirts. Jadek's horrid cousin Carolan had been soft and fat; Chiros would have made three of Carolan. She glanced up as he stopped at the end of the trestle, one enormous hand braced against the wall for balance; he was already breathing hard. But he actually smiled in a friendly fashion as she met his eyes. "I'll have to go."

Ibys came over to take his free arm. "Husband, five medium crates, it'll be gone in no time at all, and look where the sun is, there's no shadow left in front of the shop. You'd have to run all the way. Let me go. It's not bargaining, after all, or luck of the draw, it's simple paying for a share of the cloth. I can manage that much."

"I—well, yes." He expelled his breath in a loud gust. "Take forty ceris from the coin box, that's ten ceris more than they let us have last time. In case, *you* know." Ibys nodded, let go his arm and hurried into the back of the shop. He turned to Lialla. "You'll let her leave the cloth until I can arrange to have it moved?"

"Of course," Sil put in smoothly as Lialla was trying to decide what to say. Ibys came back, a pile of coins in her outstretched hand; Chiros merely glanced at it and nodded.

"All they'll let us have, woman." She nodded in turn and hurried out of the shop. "I suppose you can still get the britches themselves?"

Sil spread her arms in a wide shrug. "The Mer Khani are doing just what you thought they might, Chiros; buying the cloth and making their own clothing with it. The Sikkreni have more britches than they can use, all at once."

He laughed. "Serve them right, trying to keep a monopoly. That desert cloth guild, let me tell you, young woman—" Sil simply shook her head and smiled. "Well, never mind. The cost is still high, I'd wager."

"Let them sit on stock for a moon or two, it'll come down."

"Aye. And meantime someone else here decides to purchase and establish himself with those tight-fisted sons of weavers, so that when the price does come down he's first in line for the reduction, eh? Ridiculous price. Still, the Duke likes them for his shipmen, he'll buy from me once at least. Take word to your grandmother, Chiros will purchase whatever she can pry away from the Sikkreni."

"I'll take word to her. And send someone back who can set the terms with you." She glanced over her shoulder as three men came into the shop. "Your wife was right, there's no sun on the street, and I said we'd return to the compound around midday. Gray will be here five days at least, Chiros; someone will come to work out a bargain before then."

"Good." He turned to deal with the customers; one, Lialla

would have sworn, was the same narrow-eyed wall-mender from early in the morning. The look he gave her was certainly the same. She found it easier to ignore this time; she turned and left the shop, Sil on her heels.

Outside, Sil took the lead again, across the park the way they had come, right and down a tree-lined path, onto a roughly cobbled street Lialla found vaguely familiar. Sil pointed. "Compound's just over there."

"You might have warned me," Lialla said rather breathlessly.

"What—Chiros? You did fine. He knows people will stare, seeing him the first time; why d'you think he sits back in the corner and lets Ibys manage? You can see why he'd be possessive of her, though."

"Why's she—Sil, for pity sakes, slow down a little!—why does she need these meetings?"

"He's better than some here; that doesn't mean perfect, you know. And there are other men. Mostly so she can talk to other women in this area who don't get a chance to even leave the household, and believe me, there are some who haven't so much as been outdoors in years. There, see? Compound, and probably we're in time for midday soup. No, poor old Chiros isn't so bad; I worry about Ibys, though, if he dies before she does and she has to fight his brothers for the business. They'd make a mess of it in no time; she'd be successful, but she's not strong enough to stand up to both local custom and her brothers-by-wedding. The grandmother's probably already given her the message about tonight, along with a receipt for the denim." They crossed a street at least twice as busy as it had been earlier; it still took the two of them to open the outer gate, but someone had oiled the hinges and those on the door. Sil enumerated on her fingertips as they climbed. "All right, we made the stops; we passed your message, we—"

"Wore out my slippers," Lialla grumbled.

"Yah. They said you were tough; anyone who walked a circuit of lower Rhadaz *should* be tough."

"There aren't cobblestone streets most of the places I walked, not like here. So, now what?"

"Now what? Sil dragged the upper door open, paused and leaned back against the jamb. "Now we have some soup, you have a rest so you're at least braced for tonight—and if you mean the boy, we simply wait."

5

㋡

Most of Duke's Fort was bedded down for the night; in the kitchens, one young apprentice checked the ovens and replenished the wood supply under them, while a journey cook turned meat marinading in a deep dish of brown liquid. Two men stood on the outer wall just above the main gates, heavily cloaked, hands held to a small brazier. Oil lamps burned at each end of the upper hall and a blue-light in the nursery window, visible through the open door. In the Duke and Duchess's bedchamber, another blue-light above the deep window seat; in the fireplace, wood popped and flared, then settled back to burn low, fading to red coals and clinkers. The large chamber was quite warm.

A dark cloth had been stretched from the edge of the window seat to the floor, weighted down at the corners by two of the Duke's boots and a pair of heavy stone bookends; it formed a triangle with wall and floor. Just visible under this makeshift tent, one dark curly head, and at the other end, a small foot.

Robyn sat on the edge of the massive Ducal bed, legs crossed, head and arms dangling loose, eyes closed; Aletto knelt behind her, his fingers digging into her shoulder muscles. She winced; he relaxed his grip and edged around to look at her face.

"I'm sorry, Robyn. I didn't mean to be so rough."

"No, it's all right. It feels good, don't stop." He slid back where he had been and laid his hands on either side of her neck so he could work his thumbs along the sides of her spine.

"Poor Robyn; I'm the one usually this tight. Is that any better? Really?"

"Mmmm—wonderful." She sighed faintly, reached up to move his right hand to one side. "There, a little more to that side—that's just right. It's been a bad few days, that's all. I'm sorry I've been such a screeching monster, Aletto."

"You haven't—well," he considered this, laughed quietly. "Well, all right, you have been louder than usual, for you, certainly. But hardly a monster. And you've had reason to be upset. My mother, Iana's nurse—"

"It wasn't Frisa's fault; her mother's ill, of course she had to go. Poor thing, after the way I carried on when she told me, she probably won't want to come back."

"Oh, I think she will. She's very fond of Iana, after all." He glanced over his shoulder, to where Iana and her brother slept under the tent Robyn had rigged up for them.

"Frisa, Lizelle, those wretched twins of hers," Robyn's voice droned. "Lialla—I think I could have handled all of that, even Lialla pulling that stunt, going back north without even *talking* to you first! And then getting Jennifer to send you a message, that's pretty darned rude."

"It's also very much Lialla," Aletto reminded her. "She wouldn't have come back home, she'd be afraid I'd find a way to keep her here. And what could she possibly have found to say to either of us directly? I'm just sorry Jen got caught in the middle of things again."

"Yah. Poor woman, she'd better be used to it by now. Well, I think I could have handled all that, even with your mother and her damned Zero, and throwing shrieking fits all over the place; the servants must absolutely *hate* it around here."

"You weren't here when my uncle was," Aletto said mildly. "Trust me, it's not nearly as hard on them as it used to be. And there can't be anyone in the fort who doesn't realize you were trying to help her. Don't be harsh on yourself, Robyn."

"Yeah, sure. Me, too. I'll tell you, though, Jen's last letter was *it*. I swear I'm gonna murder that kid of mine."

"It may not be so bad," Aletto said soothingly. His thumbs described circles below her ears, his fingers rubbing her jawbones.

"Says you," Robyn retorted. "This is Chris, remember? It's probably worse. The more I think about it; he nearly gets himself *killed*! This after he pulls a stunt right out of an old folk song." Aletto let his hands fall to her shoulders; he edged around to look at her inquiringly. Robyn cleared her throat and in a thin, soft voice sang, "I won my wife in a card game, to hell with those Spanish grandees."

He frowned. "Pretty. My English isn't what it should be, probably, but I thought the girl was French, not Spanish?"

Robyn laughed faintly, leaned back into him as he began rubbing the base of her throat on both sides. "Poetic license. Tragic song, too; I can remember when I'd have cussed Jen out for hitting me with a song that tracked something happening to me and it ended sad. Sure, she's French. And Chris's daddy sure as hell wasn't a Spanish grandee." She closed her eyes, hummed the melody line very quietly as he ran his fingers along her collarbones. "I think I'll murder him anyway, scaring me like that, and pulling a stunt like that on some poor girl. You know how many times I've told him what he's doing is dangerous?"

"Lots," Aletto said promptly. Silence again.

Robyn sighed finally. "Yeah. And he always says he has to, he's the only one who knows what to do; then he goes off and scares me into early gray hairs. I guess I ought to be glad Jen wrote, because I'll bet you anything you like, Chris doesn't say a word about the cards."

"At least she did warn you."

"I tell myself that's good; at least I have a few days to brace myself. God. I remember when I used to think he ought to get himself a girl, settle down—"

"Well, he has the first part of that now, hasn't he?"

"I guess," Robyn said doubtfully. "Especially if she's really Catholic, like Jen says. That's for life." She considered this, reached back to find his hands. "Of course, a person doesn't need that kind of excuse." He kissed the back of her hand, shifted his grip to her shoulders and began working them back and forth.

"Don't let the situation upset you, please, Robyn. Not until Chris gets here and you can talk to him."

"I'll try not." She laughed, very quietly. "Talk. I'll give that kid *talk*." She considered this, laughed again. "It sounds funny, you advising me to cool off and relax; doesn't it usually go the other way?"

"You've got cause right now. There's so much business going on right now with the council and Afronsan's men, I don't have any time or thought to spare for gnawing on myself over Mother. And everything going on with that—the smuggling business, the new telegraph, the additional roads, more guards—it all seems so far over my head, it's gone beyond me worrying about it."

"It is not over your head," Robyn said firmly. "It's just—there's a lot going on, but you're managing it. If you weren't, Afronsan would've said so by now. Or we'd be up to our back teeth in bandits, instead of having them pushed back to the Cornekkan border. Or—"

"All right." Aletto laughed in turn. Behind him, one of the children moaned, then settled back to sleep. He lowered his voice. "Thank you for the vote of confidence. I don't always remember to say so, but you know I feel it."

"I know. I don't always need things in words, you should know that by now." She ran a hand through her hair, hesitated, then said, "Aletto? I—have something to tell you. A—about Iana."

"Iana?" She nodded. His fingers tightened on hers; his voice, when it came, was very soft and totally without expression. "If it's what I think—"

Robyn drew a deep breath, said flatly, "She's got my—my talent, Aletto."

Silence. His hands worked absently at her shoulders. The fire popped and both of them jumped. "I know."

"You know? And you didn't say anything?" She turned her head to look at him. His face was nearly as expressionless as his voice had been; she couldn't tell what he might be thinking. He nodded then, managed a very faint smile. Enough. She fetched a little sigh and turned back to stare across the room.

"What could I have said? I didn't know if *you* were aware of it. How long have you known?"

"A month or so—just before I went to Sikkre and those men attacked Jennifer. You remember how Iana was acting about then."

"I know. She—it was while you were gone, she got angry and—well, there it was."

Another silence; his hands continued to rub her shoulders, almost as though he'd forgotten about them. She couldn't look at him. Robyn let her head drop to her hands. "God," she mumbled finally. "I'm sorry."

"It's not anything you did on purpose—remember that's what I told you four years ago, out in the middle of the Sikkreni desert? It's not something you did to Iana deliberately, after all."

"No. I'm sorry anyway, though." She sighed, sat up a little straighter. Aletto pulled her back against him and kissed her hair. "I suppose the whole fort knows about it?"

"Not that I've heard. My man would have said something; he hears all the gossip and sees I get it right away." He laughed. "I'm never certain if he means well or he's just got a malicious streak. But I hear things you don't."

"Yah. I don't think I want to hear half of what goes on around here, considering how great I feel right now. Better for my stomach." She shook her head. "Damn. I've been putting it off, and I can't. I'll have to talk to Iana, let her know that this isn't something to bring out in the open. Somehow do that without making her feel she's got a dirty secret to hide."

"You can do it."

"Yeah. I guess." She turned her head a little, eyed him sidelong. "I'll have to teach her more than that, once she's a little older. She'll have to know how to control it, and how to use it safely." He went quite still; Robyn waited. He nodded. "It's not like I would have been at her age; I'd have learned how *not* to use it, it would have scared me half silly. Iana, though—"

He laughed, glanced over his shoulder at the makeshift tent. "I know. Tough little girl, she'd be up on the outer wall first thing, testing her limits, and she probably wouldn't care if half of Sehfi saw her at it."

Robyn groaned. "That's right, make me feel better, why don't you?" He laughed again and rumpled her hair. "I'll manage. I guess." Another silence, this one more comfortable than the last. Robyn broke it after a long while. "Aletto, what are we going to do about your mother?"

His hands went limp on her shoulders. She slewed around to look at him. "I wish I knew." Robyn waited, watching him. Aletto stared into his upturned palms. "She's sick, terribly ill, or she'd never have done it. Started using that stuff, I mean. Look at all the years with—with Jadek, she could've done like I did, drunk herself into a stupor and stayed there, but she never did. Now, I don't know what to say and after all, what *can* we do? Lock her in her rooms, take her girls away from her? Robyn, I can't do that!"

"I know. Maybe a few days ago I would have argued that with you, but honestly, now I don't know. If she were my mother, I couldn't bully her any more than you can. But, if we don't do something, if those girls have free run of the fort and the outside, if they can get her whatever she wants—"

"She's so dependent on them, Robyn. But they'll be watched

from now on when they go out. And searched when they come back."

"If I thought it would do any good to *talk* to them—! But I've done it so many times, I've lost count; they cry and swear they're not doing anything wrong, and I can't prove they are. And then your mother throws a fit because we're picking on her darling little maids."

"You don't have to convince me, I think like you do; they're somehow getting the stuff in the market, somewhere nearby, and bringing it back for her. What their reasoning is—you know," he went on as she shook her head. "If they meant it to help her, or if someone's got them to try to open up Sehfi and the fort for the stuff—"

"You only *think* I haven't tried to pry that out of them," Robyn said darkly.

"I know you have. We won't give up, all right? If they're bringing Mother drugs, we'll catch them at it, and then the fort guards can ask that question; with maybe a better chance of scaring an answer out of them."

Robyn sighed. "And won't that be a fun scene, the twins hysterical, your mother upset—don't look at me like that, Aletto, I've said all along we had to cut off her source; that's more important than me avoiding another screaming match with her. Things like this are never simple, or easy; they weren't in my world, either. But, you know what's so hard for me is that my own feeling is, if she weren't breaking security having the stuff smuggled into the fort and if the stuff wasn't a danger to other people, I'd say hey, let her have it. If she's using it to feel better, or if it takes the pain away, if she's really that ill. There's nothing noble about having to suffer." She scowled at her hands. "Damn the woman, anyway," she added irritably. "Arbitrary, secretive, stubborn—If she'd only let us get her a healer, find out what's wrong with her. Aletto, what if she isn't as ill as she obviously thinks? Or if she is, but there's another way to deal with it?"

"I know. I agree with you, remember?"

"Of course. Damn. If only Lialla—"

"Lialla didn't get any farther with her than we did; Mother wouldn't let Li do anything for her."

"Right. I'm grasping at straws, can't you tell? I wish Lialla were here anyway; she could take some of the pressure off both of us."

"I'd feel better if she were at least two days' ride away from

Vuhlem, instead of back within his reach," Aletto said flatly. Out in the courtyard a bell rang. "It's late; we'd better try to get some sleep. I've got messages to put together for Afronsan first thing in the morning before council, so the pouch can go back to Podhru. And if Chris and his wife are coming the day after—"

"Shhh," Robyn said hastily. "I'll never get any sleep at all if you bring that up."

THE Ducal palace in Sikkre was still well lit at this hour; the Thukar had only just dismissed the last of his councilors, and in the Thukara's offices a pair of lamps flanked the long table where two of her clerks checked final revisions on a long and particularly involved contract which needed to go to the printers before sunset the next day. Lights shone from the guest apartment, from the back entry to the kitchens, from the blue hall where serving women were collecting used cups and empty wine flasks left after the Thukar's evening hearings.

Lights also burned in the Thukar's apartments. Jennifer, still damp from her bath and wrapped in a pale blue robe, sprawled in her favorite chair, one bare foot hooked on the edge of the cushions, the other braced on the cool tile floor, arms dangling loose over the arms, her legs bared and robe twisted to spill between them. A thin leather envelope was propped between one leg and the chair, still unopened. *More things from Afronsan; possibly the last hand-delivered messages.* The telegraph was nearly finished, Podhru to Sikkre; at least in the beginning, the Emperor's Heir was bound to use it for everything but contracts and any other things that absolutely had to be sent on as hard copy. *Kid with a new toy.*

She brought her arms up, flexed her fingers and winced. *Yeah, whose arms ache all the way to her biceps from using that wretched typewriter? Even when longhand would be faster and easier? What kid with a new toy, I wonder?* She started to shake her head. "Ouch." Siohan's comb caught a snarl.

"Sorry, Thukara. If you would hold still while I'm doing this, though."

"I know. I try." She transferred the scowl to her reflection in the hand-blown and slightly wavy mirror. Hair slicked back, no makeup—"I swear my face is half again as fat as it was," she mumbled.

"Now, Thukara. It isn't, you know," Siohan laid the comb on

the back of the chair, separated out a finger-thick strand of hair and began working it into a skinny three-part plait.

"It *feels* like it."

"The midwife said it's common to feel that way, especially for a first pregnancy." Jennifer sighed heavily, said nothing. Siohan completed one braid and bound it with a bit of ribbon, began another. "Thukara. This young woman, Ariadne."

"Chris's wife," Jennifer reminded her sourly.

"Yes, of course. Somehow, it doesn't seem—" Siohan sought a word, shrugged and fell silent. Jennifer laughed.

"I know. It doesn't seem. What about her?"

"I can understand there wasn't time to provide for her when they came north. But she's a noblewoman, Thukara. She's not used to shifting for herself, we can all see it. And, well, I suppose it's proper in one sense for her to travel with him, you know, together, alone—but in another way, it's simply not right." She frowned, finished her braid off and separated our hair for another. "I'm not expressing myself well, I'm sorry."

"No—that's all right. And you're correct, of course. It isn't proper for her to travel without a woman companion, even if she *is* married. I wasn't thinking. But then, I'm not used to the idea that it's right to have someone take care of me, even yet. Not that I don't appreciate everything you do for me, Siohan, don't think that."

"I know."

"She said as much herself; no one to talk to. Even if she and Chris were truly close, not just getting to know each other, she'd need a woman, wouldn't she? Someone to share girl-talk with, make certain she doesn't look ragged the way I did when Dahven and I first came home. Lord knows I was concerned enough about first impressions around here; but to Ariadne, these things really matter."

Siohan nodded, drew more hair into another plait. "My thought. It would be better, I think, to find her a woman in Sikkre—there's a better chance to locate someone at least willing to travel as far as Podhru than she'd have in Sehfi. Or better yet, to find someone who can be spared for that long from the household here; someone who at least knows how to deal with a noblewoman. Once they reach Podhru, they should be able to find someone who would go overseas with them and tend to her needs. It is," Siohan went on severely as she tied off the plait and began another, "a much better marriage gift than matched duelling swords."

Jennifer laughed. "Ah. Heard about that, did you?"

"The entire staff talks of nothing else."

"Yes, well. If she's going off to play with the big boys, it's a good idea for her to know how to use their toys, don't you think?" Siohan shook her head, more dismissive of the subject than in disagreement. Silence; Jennifer stared past the mirror while Siohan finished the last braid and tied the lot at the back of her neck in a wide ribbon. In the Thukar's dressing room, she could hear his new manservant puttering; probably finding where things were, what Dahven had and how it was arranged. *It hasn't been that long since Anselm—* She put Anselm from her mind at once; no good thinking about poor dead Anselm, she'd had enough dreams those first days, that dreadful shriek, blood everywhere. . . . She resettled in the chair, glanced in the mirror. Siohan still had a broad red mourning band tacked to the sleeve of her dress; Jennifer had always suspected her woman never much liked Anselm, but Siohan wasn't the type to say such things; and Anselm had frankly been a hard man to like. The new man, Widric, was quiet, self-effacing; she couldn't remember five words he'd spoken directly to her.

Yah, what an act to follow, though. Stepping into the shoes of a man dead by violence, right inside the Thukar's halls. *I'm surprised Dahven got anyone to come here, after that.* Even though the man responsible for Anselm was dead himself.

But there had been another death that night: the girl from the kitchens. And both of her sisters were still in the household. She sighed, very faintly. This wasn't a good time of night to worry about household matters. Maybe Afronsan's messages would take her mind out of this pointless rut. But as she pulled the envelope into her lap, footsteps came up the hall, hesitated at the doorway.

Chris's inevitable shave-and-a-haircut tap on the outer wall; his voice came around the partly closed door. "Yo, lady, you decent?"

She sat up a little straighter, pulled the robe down over her knees as Siohan made a vexed little noise at her. "And hard-working, and God-fearing—also covered, c'mon in, kid." Siohan gathered up the comb, Jennifer's day slippers and the dinner dress she'd shed earlier and carried them into the Thukara's dressing room as Chris stuck his head around the corner. He looked harassed.

"Hey, lady, I need your help, okay? Red Sonya—the swordswoman down the hall, you know?—she says she's cutting her hair off," he slashed his hand meaningfully across the nape of his neck. "Like, by herself, right now."

"She's—she *what*?"

"Hey, it's not my fault this time, okay? Just come talk to her, she won't listen to *me*."

"Siohan!" Jennifer jumped to her feet; Siohan came out, a half-folded shift in one hand. "Need your help," Jennifer said tersely. "Come on." She pushed past Chris; he stepped aside to let Siohan follow and brought up the rear.

"Thukara, your feet—!"

"Bother 'em, I won't die of cool floors this time of year." Chris slowed, stopped and leaned against the wall as the two women hurried down the corridor and vanished around the corner, heading purposefully toward the guest apartments. Let them handle it entirely, he decided. At least, give them long enough to get Miss Hot-with-a-Sword calmed down enough to listen to reason.

"Yah," he growled under his breath. "Like she's capable of it." He settled his shoulders against rough stone and gazed at the ceiling. "Somebody tell me what I did to deserve this, huh?"

JENNIFER rapped the door panel sharply with her knuckles, then shoved the door open. Ariadne, still in the green skirt and white blouse, looked up from the dressing table, visibly startled; one hand clutched her throat, the other gripped a pair of ornate silver scissors. She stared, wide-eyed, at the finger Jennifer leveled at her nose. "Don't you *dare* cut that hair! Don't you even think about it!"

"I—"

"All that gorgeous, black, curly stuff—"

"But, I—" Ariadne blinked rapidly, set the scissors down, pulled her mouth shut, and wrapped hair around the fingers and tugged it out sideways. Her eyes were mutinous. "It is hair, it grows again."

"It won't if I murder you here and now for cutting it off," Jennifer said flatly.

"What are you thinking of, madam?" Siohan came into the room. Her English was nearly as heavily accented as Ariadne's. "It is such beautiful hair—"

"It is impossible hair," Ariadne replied stiffly. "Also, it is very visible; men of my father's who do not know me by face could know me by this."

"Pin it up, then," Jennifer began. Ariadne shook her head; hair
flew.

"If my maid Lucette or Honoria before her could not put in
the pins to hold hair up, so"—she wrapped both hands in it and
held a wad of curls to the back of her neck—"even while I do
nothing more vigorous than read a book in my bedchamber, how
shall I manage it? While riding a horse, or aboard a ship?"

"Well, then braid it," Jennifer replied. It took a huge effort to
keep the exasperation out of her voice.

The girl wrinkled her nose. "To wear a child's plait other than
for sleep?" Jennifer turned her head and held out a handful of
tiny braids.

"This is for bed; but I often wear a braid when it's warm and
I'm busy. When I run, I always braid it; that isn't childish, it's
sense. But if you're afraid all that hair makes you visible, what
do you think hair cut shorter than Chris's is going to do for you?
It's not as if that will change your face—or his looks. He's
highly visible, remember? And what other young woman is going to be traveling with him?" Ariadne looked at her; her mouth
was set, her eyes still mutinous. "Ariadne, you can't do this.
Please. All that wonderful hair. I know," she added hastily as the
girl scowled and opened her mouth to speak, "it grows. I know!
But not *that* quickly."

Siohan gently freed hair from Ariadne's grip, ran her fingers
through it. "Wonderful hair. It *is* very heavy. But I think the
Thukara has pins that would hold it. If you'd permit, madam—"
She looked up; Jennifer nodded, and Siohan went back into the
hall.

Silence for some moments; Jennifer could hear Siohan's slippers pattering crisply down the hallway, then nothing. Ariadne
was watching her. "Why do you do this?" she asked finally.

Jennifer managed a smile. "What, bully you?"

"No—this with your hair, so many little plaits."

"Because it doesn't curl like yours does naturally."

"But mine will not, either; it makes a mess that is not curl and
not straight." She eyed Jennifer, less wary now, eyes speculative.
"There is a powder, a French one, my maid put it into the soap
once in summer and once just before the Jesu-fest, to make the
curl." She turned away, slammed both hands flat on the counter
before her; the scissors jumped and skittered along the slick surface. "What use is all this *talk*? What good are pins?"

"You might at least give them a try before you give yourself a crewcut," Jennifer said crisply. Before Ariadne could stop her, she snatched the scissors and shoved them in one of the deep robe pockets. "Of course, if you're just trying to pull everyone's chain—creating a lot of uproar and noise to upset Chris, and everyone else—then pins aren't any good to you, are they?" The girl stared at her blankly.

"How dare you speak to me this way?" she whispered finally.

"Because you deserve it, that's why. Look, I don't doubt for one minute you've had a hard life to this point, but now you have the chance to *do* something with yourself, make some of your own decisions—why not start by *not* trying to alienate everyone around you?" She looked up, past Ariadne, as the door to the dressing room opened. Chris poked his head around the corner, indicated the door bolt with a broad gesture, retreated into the smaller chamber and closed the door with an audible click. Ariadne started, whirled around. "That was Chris, by the way," Jennifer said. "Locking himself into the other room for the night, and letting you know it."

"*Dieu*, what a mess." Ariadne turned back to gaze at her reflection in the mirror, drove both hands into her hair and burst into tears. Jennifer sent her eyes heavenward, then went to one knee and put her arms around the other's shoulders. For a moment, she thought the girl would shove her away; her shoulders remained stiff, her whole body unyielding.

"It's a mess, all right," Jennifer agreed. "You don't have to make it more of one, though. But things are bound to get better, don't you think?" Ariadne shook her head fiercely; hair flew, temporarily blinding Jennifer. She freed a hand, shoved the stuff out of her eyes. Ariadne swallowed hard, rubbed her eyes with the heels of her hands, swallowed again.

"I am sorry," she whispered. "You must begin to hate me—"

"I could frankly live without the dramatics—the scenes," Jennifer said. "I'm not used to them, frankly. I'll hate you only if you cut that hair." A light tap at the entry brought her around. Siohan came into the room with a small basket in her hands, and at her heels, hair in a loose plait under a neat white kerchief, still blinking sleep from her eyes, stood one of the kitchen girls. Jennifer got to feet; Siohan inclined her head and set the basket on the dressing table, then motioned the girl forward. "Madam Ariadne, this is Dija. She knows something of hair and clothing. She has agreed to care for your needs while you are here, if you will have her."

Dija bent one knee and bowed deeply. "I speak a little of English," she murmured shyly. "Siohan says the lady wished her hair combed for the night?" Ariadne blotted her eyes on the back of one hand, looked from Jennifer to Siohan, finally at Dija, who could not have been any older than she, and was visibly much less sure of herself. *Surely, she won't sent a nervous child like Dija packing,* Jennifer thought. Ariadne sat very still, eyes still fixed on Dija, who looked steadily back. Wordlessly, then, the Frenchwoman held out a comb. Dija took it, glanced at Siohan for reassurance, and tucked it into her sash so she could hand-separate the hair first.

"Well. I'll leave you, then," Jennifer said after a moment. Dija looked up, startled; Siohan nodded her approval, then turned and left. Jennifer followed. But as she reached the hall, Ariadne came running out.

"Jennifer." Her eyes were wary; she glanced back toward the open door and lowered her voice. "This—this girl is not to spy upon me, is she?"

"To—to what? To *spy* on you? Why? Ariadne, for heaven's sake! She's in there to serve you as a lady's maid; Siohan already told me you were probably used to one, and obviously you needed someone to comb your hair tonight, if nothing else. Dija is there to fix your hair, hang up your skirts, and sleep in your dressing room on that couch, if you want the company, or the chaperone. If not, let her untangle your hair and braid it for the night and go back to her own room, same as Siohan does. Why would she spy on you?"

Ariadne opened her mouth, closed it again and shook her head, spun on one heel and started back inside. At the doorway she turned. "Because Honoria did, and Lucette I think did, for my father. That is why." She was gone. Jennifer remained where she was for a long moment, then slumped against the outer wall. *If she's going to screech at poor little Dija and chase her off, I'd better be here to pick up the pieces.* But she could hear a low murmur of voices, Dija's pleasant alto and Ariadne's lower response. *No one's going to kill anyone else in the near future,* she decided.

She started back down the hall; Siohan was right, the floors *were* decidedly cold at this hour. So was the air, for that matter. She shoved her hands into the deep pockets, and her right encountered Ariadne's fancy scissors. "God," she mumbled. "I used to think I *wanted* a girl!"

A faint click; she slowed as Chris stuck his head into the hall. "Hey," he said.

"Hey yourself, kid," Jennifer replied gloomily. "You wanna talk to me, you've got as long as it takes me to reach my bed, all right?"

He came into the hall, still dressed but barefoot. "You got through to her?" In answer, Jennifer pulled the scissors from her pocket and held them under his nose.

"Siohan brought Dija up to tend to her. You'd better factor a maid's salary into your family expenses from now on, kiddo."

"Well, yeah—Okay. Dija. Isn't she the one whose sister—?"

"Same one. I'm not sure why Siohan brought her up, except she does speak enough English that they won't need to resort to charades. But so do some of the other women."

"Well, yeah. If she speaks some English, that's a big help, cause I don't think Ariadne's gonna bother picking up any Rhadazi, except maybe 'no.' "

"Big surprise," Jennifer said. She felt tired all over. "You owe me one for this, kid. And in exchange for keeping your young woman from looking like a skinhead for the next year, and for lending you Dija as long as they *both* want the arrangement, you find out what that stuff is Ariadne uses on her hair, and get me some."

"Stuff?"

"Think permanents, think very curly hair. I don't know what it is; it obviously doesn't hurt the stuff it curls, because just look at *her* hair. Find out, and get me some, you got that?"

"Hair stuff—got it."

"Good." Jennifer stopped outside the Thukar's apartments, grabbed his hand and slapped the scissors onto his palm. "Give these back to her in the morning. I'm going to go get myself some sleep."

"Yah. You seen the size of that couch?"

"Good for you, kiddo. But you can always use the room next to it."

"Too late to bug anyone for blankets," he said gloomily. "Besides, maybe this way she'll feel sorry for me, stuffed in the servant's room and all. And she won't stab me dead with these when I give them to her." He tossed the scissors high, caught them deftly and left her. Jennifer sighed.

"Give me strength. I don't want a boy, either!"

6

~

ONE hour after sunset of a very foggy day, well into an extremely foggy twilight, the north coast of Holmaddan lay muffled, cold and utterly still. Inland, if anything it was even more gloomy and chill than near the water; in hollows and against the inner cliffs, it was impossible to see anything beyond arm's length. Here and there, a child brought in stray geese, another penned sheep. A few women and older girls were out feeding and watering fowl or milking goats, but by and large village Gray Haven was indoors and already bedded down for the night. In a rare pool of nearly clear air, the men's long hut was briefly visible as a dark and uncertain shape; ruddy light flickered around the edges of improperly fitted shutters; the muted sound of coarse laughter filtered out to a deserted main road.

Only a few of the older boys and the unmarried men were still in the hut, drinking and waiting for one of the older women to bring food. The married men had gone home before full dark.

Even the headman, this particular night.

Ryselle leaned against the outer wall of her father's house, eyes closed and jaw set, cloak pulled close around thoroughly chilled arms and hands. Her father's outraged, intimidating bellow was scarcely dampened at all by the heavy shutters. She listened intently, holding her breath as he finally paused—for air, likely; he wouldn't expect or welcome comment from her mother.

Her lips twisted; she turned her head slightly, freed a hand and blew a sardonic kiss toward the goat shed. If she hadn't been out there preparing extra rounds of herbed cheese for her father to trade when the next caravan came through, she'd have been in the house long since; she'd have been facing the brunt of the old

94

man's hot fury, and probably the back of his hand. *Instead of Mother, who's taking it for both of us.* The faint smile slipped. *Thank you, goats, thank you, Mother—no, it really isn't at all amusing, is it?*

She jumped convulsively; her father was shouting once more. "She wasn't where she belonged this morning, nor yesterday evening, but that's nothing new, is it? Wandering about, what's she up to these days? Time she was wed once more, spending her hours properly, caring for her man and babes! She's had her time of mourning, wife! More than a year, nearly two! You've indulged her, and I've let you. And it isn't as if she were wed to that South Branch fool long enough to warrant full mourning— she wasn't with him long enough to be properly wed, I'd wager."

If Dronic had dared to touched me, I'd have cut his throat while he slept, and he knew it. Ryselle reminded herself grimly. It had been a strange, short, wedded life; she and Dronic had come almost at once to a kind of truce. She suspected he didn't care much for women, anyway. *Poor creature; he had no more choice about wedding and producing sons that I did.* She shrugged him aside; two years, after all, since he'd drowned, and she'd only known him something less than a moon-season. She shook her head sharply, laid her ear against the damp outer wall.

Her mother was saying something—she couldn't tell what, her father's bellowed response overrode everything, as it always did. "Did she quicken? No! Two strings of dower silver his kin wouldn't give back, and she didn't even prove her worth with a son! If she's capable of sons! Look at her sister, wed for six years and four sons already. *She* cost me a mere half string of silver, and has she been any problem, ever? Detta knows her place, and keeps it properly. But Ryselle, oh, no!" A faint, distressed murmur, too low for Ryselle to catch her mother's response.

"Yes, well, all right, I'll grant that much, she's good with the goats, she's been useful about the place. Her cheeses sell for good coin, why do you think I tolerate her attitudes, her arrogant ways and her backtalk? Another man would beat her senseless for daring to open her mouth! But I'll tell you this, woman, when our Nyel weds the Wielder's sister, they'll need that bed Ryselle has now. We'll have Emalya to muck the beasts and milk them, and there will be Emalya's money to pay a dowry for Ryselle. Emalya isn't so simple as she seems; she can learn to make a cheese worth good coin. Those girls of hers will prove useful— they'd better! But Ryselle is getting above herself; I won't toler-

ate that in this house, and I won't take lip from her much longer,
I'll tell you, woman!"

"But, husband—" Ryselle wasn't totally certain she heard her
mother's faint protest right; a ringing slap and a shriek covered
the words.

"Dare to argue with me? I was right, Ryselle has no place in
this house, she's giving you airs now! I'll tell you, woman, the
headman at village East Bluff has been asking about her of late;
he'll take a smaller dowry because it's not his first wife and she's
used goods, after all. And he's willing to have the woman now,
the coin when it comes, so as soon as I have the first part of the
dowry in hand for her, she's gone to East Bluff. The headman
there will teach her to curb that tongue—she'll learn, or he'll cut
it out of her head. What? What's that? Don't you *dare* mumble
at my back and look at me in that fashion, woman, I'll black
your other eye!"

Ryselle swallowed hard, caught her lower lip between her
teeth. *If I were half as brave as I pretend, I'd go in there, right
now; I'd stop him somehow—I wouldn't let him shout at her like
that; I wouldn't let him beat her. He's not so big or so strong any
more, he's half drunk all the time, he's old, and no taller than I.
I do more heavy work here than he ever did, my hands and arms
are strong enough. And his sons—my beloved brothers—are
down at the men's hut, drinking or passed out, they're no use to
him tonight.*

One drunken, furious old man, alone. She could hit him—one
quick blow, use one of the long, heavy gate pins from the goat
shed, he'd be down and out for the rest of the night at the very
least, long enough for her to convince her mother to leave. . . .

Her shoulders sagged. *To try to convince her. Hah. As if she
would ever leave him. I've tried—once, ten times, twenty, I've
lost count. But I've never struck anyone. I—I don't think I could,
not out of cold purpose. And if I did, then what? I've dared to
raise my hand against father, elder, headman—we'd both be
dead, Mother and I.*

Wed to East Bluff's headman. There was a living death. She'd
be—what? His third wife? Or was it already his fourth? *One in
childbirth, a second who took ill from trying to quicken with a son
for him, after three daughters. His new wife will share the household with the last wife but one, they say she doesn't talk well since
the last time he beat her, she only sees clearly in one eye and she
can't remember anyone's name, but she still can cook for him and*

his sons. Her future narrowed, spiraled in around her, encompassing and thick as the fog. "I'll die first," Ryselle promised herself flatly. She clapped a hand across her mouth, sent her eyes sideways toward the door. It was quiet in there; he might hear her. She pushed away from the wall, walked steadily back through the goat pens and out onto the main road. A chill drop of dew trembled on the tip of her nose. She blotted it; another fell from the hood and slid down to take its place. The Wielder. Sretha had promised to help her before. She'd have to, now.

SRETHA took one look at the headman's younger daughter shivering on the doorstep and drew her through the dark and empty main room, into the little back chamber. A fire burned hot on the small hearth, making it overly warm and even stuffy in the Wielder's combination workroom and kitchen, after outside; the lamp gave off a mixed scent, pine oil trying to cover the rather unpleasant smell of the tallow Emalya insisted on rendering herself. For once, Ryselle scarcely noticed the pungent and cloying mix of odors; she clutched the cloak tightly around her throat, hands gripping the thick fabric close to her body from inside its warmth, and fought to keep her teeth from chattering.

The Wielder said nothing; she settled the younger woman at the plain, well-polished table, marked her place in a thin book with a wad of red string and shoved the remains of her own meal and an empty mug to one side. She turned up the lamp until the dark bare walls were visible to the low ceiling, and moved away to fuss with cups, kettle, and cloth herb-bags.

"Here. Ryselle, here's tea, I sweetened it, drink it now, while it's hot." Sretha wrapped the girl's trembling hands around the thick clay mug and pressed it toward her lips. The fingers were icy. "Drink it, I say."

"I'm not—n-not cold," Ryselle protested. She was shivering violently.

"I know. Shhh. Drink it."

She let her eyes sag shut, shook her head faintly, but the Wielder's hands held her fingers and kept the mug in place; warmth spread to her palms, her chin. She finally nodded and drank, draining the cup. The warmth eased tremors, loosened a painfully overly tight throat. She drew a deep, shuddering breath, let it slowly out. When she looked up, the Wielder was watching her, her face made visibly older, more heavily wrinkled, by the bright lamp in the middle of the table. Her arms were folded

across the breast of her faded Blacks. A rustling sound and footsteps almost directly overhead; Ryselle started and nearly
dropped the cup.

Sretha snatched it up, set it on the table, sent her eyes toward
the ladder. "Emalya," she murmured softly. Ryselle looked that
way; Emalya was descending cautiously and heavily from the
loft, a blue-light clutched in one hand. She glanced at Sretha,
then eyed Ryselle sidelong, and with that blank lack of curiosity
that was either Emalya being cautious, or just as dull-witted as
she looked; none of the village women were certain which it
was, and Ryselle didn't ordinarily care. Emalya blinked, rubbed
vigorously at the tip of her nose, snuffled loudly once, then
crossed to her blankets. Ryselle and Sretha watched; Emalya appeared unaware of their sudden silence as much as their regard.
She eased her way carefully to her knees, one hand clutching the
blue-light, the other clinging to the rough wall for balance. She
finally sat with a pleased grunt, stayed there for several moments, breathing heavily, then set the blue-light next to her pillow so she could work her way out of her low shoes.

A look passed between headman's daughter and village
Wielder. Ryselle compressed her lips. *Damn it all, how is it possible to forget that woman is here? After what she did to Lialla,
sending for the Duke's guards—Look at her, pretending she
hasn't seen me, or doesn't care. She remembers the things I've
said to her, all right.* She blinked rapidly, remembered what little
Wielder sign Lialla had been able to teach her in her brief stay.
Sretha. Sister—safe?

Safe. Sretha's sign was firm indeed; she glanced toward her
sister, who seemed fully occupied with undoing her foot wrap-
pings, then nodded once, very briefly. But her eyes, the faint line
between them that usually wasn't there—Ryselle's lips twisted.
*She isn't certain—but who can be, after what Emalya did? If I'd
let Sretha teach me Wielder sign, as she wanted—it should be re-
quired for all village women, any slave who has to keep secrets
from a master—or a master's filthy snitch. Like Lialla said about
her uncle, and his personal armsmen.* Too late now—for the moment, anyway. She considered, found alternate signs that would
pretty much cover what she wanted to say.

Safe, Sretha, worried, why?

Sretha cast her a wicked, bright-eyed grin before she bent to
take the tea cup and refill it. One hand moved. *Yes. Worried. Sister stupid.*

It was unexpected, almost too much; Ryselle clapped both hands over her mouth and covered laughter with a fit of coughing. Sretha slid the tea mug between the younger woman's elbows and shoved the honey dish after. Her eyes were still bright, but they shifted warningly toward the main room and the single blue-light against the far wall. Ryselle blinked, got control of herself, spooned honey into her cup and drank.

To all appearances, Emalya was blissfully unaware of both the tension in the small house and the silent conversation going on across the gloomy central room; she set her shoes and foot wraps aside, leaned back against the wall and began to massage one foot; her lips moved constantly and a very faint drone of one-sided conversation reached Ryselle's ears. *How does Sretha bear it? I'd have murdered the woman two days after she came home.*

Of course, Ryselle's hearing was phenomenal, Sretha's not nearly as sharp, especially the past year or so. *It's her sister, after all; maybe she's really fond of the woman, like I am of my mother. Or poor sweet Detta, before Father sold her to a tanner two days' ride to the south.* Her brothers—Ryselle drank more tea. She didn't want to think about her brothers. The youngest—mean-tempered and stupid Benaret—was on some errand for her father and not due back until at least midday the next day. *Probably bargaining me off to East Bluff's headman right now.* She shivered. The other two—this time of night it was a near certainty both her elder brothers were in the men's hut, full of sweet wine or more likely that fruited stuff they'd taken from the Lasanachi ship. If the latter, they'd be long since passed out. She'd scarcely seen them since that ship ran aground, them or any of their friends. Just as well. Nyel had trashed the milking area in a drunken rage last time he was home, and supposedly grown Fronek still liked to pinch her hard when she got too close to him—just as he'd done when he was six and she five. Anything to make a bruise, or cause pain. *What Holmaddi woman would be fond of any brother past his first beard hairs?*

Her mind went blank; impossible to remember enough Wielder handsign to say what she must. By now, her father would certainly know she wasn't in the goat pens. If he was tired and hungry enough, if the fog held, he might simply bar the doors on her for the night; but he might be angry enough to send for older boys from the long house to seek her out, or go looking himself. In that event, they'd surely come here. . . .

She licked her lips, swallowed. "I can't stay any longer." She eyed Emalya narrowly; Emalya sniffed, rubbed her nose vigorously with the back of one hand, and ignored sister and sister's guest both. "I heard him tonight, Wielder. Bullying Mother. Beating her. He's—promised me to East Bluff."

"To the headman?" Sretha asked quietly. Ryselle nodded; the Wielder steepled her fingers and studied them. She finally nodded in turn, settled one hip on the edge of the table. "Yes. It's long since time for you to leave, Ryselle."

"Mother, though—"

"She won't go. You know that."

Another silence. Emalya shifted her weight with a low grunt and massaged her other foot. Sretha waited; Ryselle finally sighed and nodded. "I know. I wish—"

"I wish, too," Sretha said flatly. "For many things. I wish your father and so many of the other men here were not fools and brutes."

"He'll kill her, one of these days."

"Perhaps. He can do that whether you go or not; it's the danger each Holmaddi woman faces, Ryselle. Even the village Wielder isn't exempt. Maybe your father will mellow with age, with three sons and a son's wife to ease his way; men do, you know. Or he may die of alcohol and exposure before the end of winter, as his father did. This new drink he and the others salvaged from that wreck may kill all of them."

"I—I've heard. It must be very strong; Petras said the men lie about half-asleep for hours, and yet they actually drink very little of it, there are boxes and boxes unopened, she said."

The Wielder shook her head. "There's something about that stuff I don't like. It's—well, that's no matter to talk over now. You can't stay here for long."

"I know. If they come looking—"

"They might well come here," Sretha said. She sounded calm; she didn't look it. She gave the darkened main room a very casual once-over look. Emalya sat now with her eyes closed; she had bent forward and was starting to free her hair from its complex plaits, a turn at a time, combing her fingers through the ends. Sretha seemed satisfied. She drew a shallow, long box from under a jumble of black cloth and opened it, squinted at the contents. "We'll see you gone before that."

"But Mother . . ." Ryselle fell silent. Sretha turned, box in her hands, and simply waited. Ryselle stared down at her hands, then sighed very softly. "I heard her, in there, tonight," she whispered.

"Trying to turn him from selling me to East Bluff. She was standing up to him, Sretha—trying to. If only I could—"

"That was brave of her. But she won't go with you, Ryselle, not now, not ever. Stay for her, and you've lost your own chance. Face that. The best thing you can do for all the women here is to go, at once. Save yourself." She tipped her head to one side, studied the girl thoughtfully. Ryselle gazed back, her mouth set and her eyes mutinous. "You're ready for this; hardly any other Gray Haven woman is—or ever will be. Do the brave thing yourself, now. Take that first step: Go to the city, learn how to survive there. Make a path others can follow, if they will."

The anger was draining from her; Ryselle was all at once acutely aware of the vast gulf of the outside world. "You're trying to frighten me, Wielder," she whispered.

"No. It's an unsweetened truth, nothing more. Remember you won't be truly alone; the caravaners will aid you, of course. The sin-Duchess is sure to. And so will I." Sretha took Ryselle's hand in hers and pressed a small cloth bag against the palm, closed the girl's fingers over it. "You'll need that."

Ryselle rubbed the bag between her hands. Coins—five of them. Very likely all the coin the Wielder had. "I can't take—" Sretha shot a quick glance toward her sister, who was running a comb through long, plait-waved hair and humming tunelessly.

"You will need that," Sretha repeated firmly. She rummaged in the box once more and drew out a single large three-sided copper. "That for your boot," she said very softly. "Not under your toes, high on the side, if there's a place to settle it that won't raise blisters. The rest—keep that bag under your skirts, only one small copper piece in a pocket or where you can easily get to it, for food or drink. Not so accessible that someone can take it from you. Don't show more coin than one, ever."

"*I* know—" Ryselle began indignantly. Sretha shook her head.

"Remember a city is not just a village grown large. You won't know the people, and many of them aren't honest. Or otherwise trustworthy. What's the day today?"

The question momentarily threw Ryselle; she blinked, considered. "Tomorrow's full moon, it must be the seventh tonight."

"Good. Red Hawk sent four carts north from the Dro Pent cut-off, they're lodging at East Bluff one night each side of the full moon, then going on to Gull's Face and the city."

The breath stopped in her throat. "East Bluff—?"

"East Bluff is like Gray Haven; the caravans are kept outside the village when they visit. Besides, who'd think to look for you there?" Sretha turned away, box in her hands; she paused in midturn, walked over to the small window and pressed the quilted cover aside. "The fog's shifting; I thought I felt north wind under the door just now. You'd better—"

A loud clatter of shod hooves on the road outside brought the two women around, and Ryselle halfway to her feet. Sretha caught the girl's arm and drew her toward the back door, but the horses were already gone, heading with purpose toward the center of the village. Ryselle's skin prickled; she spun around and clung to the edge of the table with one hand; the other leveled at Emalya. "If you've done anything . . ." she began furiously.

"The children." Emalya said anxiously; she shoved her hair over her shoulder and worked to her feet. "They'll wake the children—" She hurried across the room and caught hold of the ladder. Sretha clutched Ryselle's wrist, hard.

"Let her go. She's not been out of my sight or hearing; whatever that was about, it wasn't Emalya's doing. Let's go and see."

"See—"

"You need to leave, and soon, but not with such a question on your shoulder. It's dark; we can stay in shadow and on the fringes of whatever's afoot. Come." The Wielder caught up the black bundle of cloth that had covered her coin box, drew it around her throat and shoulders and started for the main door. Ryselle followed. But halfway across the larger room, she turned, settled her fists at her waist and glared at Emalya, who had paused partway up the ladder.

"If you've done anything—said anything, snitched to anyone, Emalya. If that trouble riding up the road is your doing in any way—"

"It wasn't me. It may not be trouble," Emalya protested faintly.

Ryselle laughed sourly. "A company of horsed men at this hour? In this village? Of course it's trouble! And if I learn you've had any part in it, you'll pay dearly." Emalya stared at her, mouth sagging. "If they've come to behead *me*, I swear my shade will haunt you all your days, Emalya."

"But, but, I didn't—!"

Ryselle shook her head. "Don't bother. You'd say anything. Just remember what I said." Emalya was still staring as she hauled the outer door shut with a bang and ran after the Wielder.

*   *   *

Fog still drifted across the road and lay pooled in low areas; it filled the ditch on both sides of the road. But Ryselle could already see horses and men grouped in front of the men's longhouse. Armed men and a dark, flapping banner which must be Duke Vuhlem's. Moonlight seeped through high, thin clouds, turning the road blue-white, glinting off metal helms and drawn blades.

Sretha had gone ahead; she was waiting three houses short of the Duke's company. When Ryselle would have gone on, the Wielder caught hold of her elbow and drew her into shadow and against the nearest wall. "Don't," she whispered. "There's trouble down there, stay clear. We'll be safe right here, we can see, and deaf old Nissa will never hear anything—us or them down there." She kept her hand tight around the younger woman's arm even after Ryselle nodded.

Men's voices rose sharply, muted by the walls of the longhouse, the words indecipherable from where the two women stood. The mounted guardsmen with the banner shouted back, "You have it?" More shouting, mixed with angry and frightened yells. "Bring it! And get those worthless men out here!"

Someone inside the building shouted a brief reply; total silence followed. Ryselle shifted her weight, craned her neck so she could see the door of her father's house. A thin line of light shone where someone had pushed a shutter partway open, but there was no other sign of life. There were no villagers in the street—whoever watched did so from behind shutters, within darkened rooms—or stood in shadow, as she and Sretha did. The main street and the paths leading from it were deserted. *Duke's men, coming late at night. No one with sense would be out here; it couldn't be anything but trouble.*

Two of the Duke's guards emerged into the bright light of a nearly full moon, both carrying wooden crates. They set them on the edge of the porch and went back inside. Someone in there was protesting in a furious, reedy, whining voice—her middle brother Fronek, Ryselle thought; no one else of a male sex could make that much shrill noise. Two of the village men were pulled onto the porch, down the shallow steps; the Duke's men had to hold them upright. *My brothers; my drunken, disgusting, worthless brothers.*

More shouting. Sretha put her mouth close to Ryselle's ear and murmured, "It's about that fruited stuff; I think those are the boxes. Can you make out what's being said?" The younger woman shook her head. Sretha let go her arm and began moving her fingers—drawing in Thread. "Ah. I hear them now. Fool men. The captain says those boxes were meant for the Duke's cellars, that liquor is rare and costly. What's left of that foreign ship was spotted off our shore a few days ago, they apparently couldn't even draw it far enough back to sea to sink it properly. The captain wants to know why the wreck wasn't reported at once and why the villagers dared steal boxes with Vuhlem's mark." The two guards were still bringing out crates of liquor, and now the rest of the local men came unwilling into the open, one of the Duke's guard behind them with a drawn sword. They huddled unhappily against the back wall.

One of Ryselle's brothers waved his arms wildly and fell into the other; both went down, nearly taking their guards with them. More shouting, lost in laughter; even the Duke's captain seemed to be laughing as one thin, shrill voice rose above all others.

"Your brother Fronek is trying to put blame on Nyel, who swears he saw no mark—and now he says they were holding the cargo until someone could carry a message to the Duke, to retrieve it."

"He'll blame my mother next," Ryselle said bitterly.

"He's already tried that—all us women, actually. Didn't you hear the captain laughing?"

"Silence! All of you!" The captain's voice topped the babble, his bellow so loud and sharp-edged even Sretha could clearly understand him. Silence he got. The guards dragged the fallen men to their feet. "Take them up there, apart from the rest. You, go fetch the headman. You and you—get some of these worthless men to help you bring out the rest of the Duke's property, now!"

For some moments the only sounds were the jingle of harness as horses shifted, and the heavy, echoing clomp of booted men carrying heavy crates across a poorly constructed plank floor. The captain slung one leg across the saddlebow, and waited.

The guardsman came back down the street at a run. "Sir! We can't find him!"

"You searched the hut?"

"Yes, sir! No one there but his woman; she says he's not been home all the night but she's nursing fresh bruises."

"Bah! Well, never mind; it's dark, it's late, and I want out of this impoverished sty as soon as possible. The Duke expects us before midday, you know! Go find a wagon for the Duke's belongings, then. And hurry it up!" The guard turned and ran. The captain sat and watched boxes being brought from the longhouse. Silence for a long time, save the creak of boards as men walked back and forth, the muted *clonk* as the stack of crates grew higher. The captain finally resettled himself on the horse and stood in his stirrups. "Is everything out of there yet? Good." He turned to look back up the main street as the guard came running back. "Where's that wagon?"

"We found one, sir, hut next to the headman's; the man's not there, but his woman is harnessing—"

"He's one of these fellows, doubtless. Someone's with her, to bring it once the thing's ready? I suppose the horse is on its last feet?"

"I left a man, sir. It's an ass, elderly but not dead yet."

"Good enough." He turned to look at the huddle of village men on the porch. "You all heard; whoever owns that cart and beast can either take the Duke's compensation now, come forward to drive the cart to the city and bring it back, or come to fetch it at the barracks later. Your choice." Shifting among the men, low mumbling. Ryselle couldn't see or hear what was going on, but the captain's voice remained at parade-ground pitch. "You? All right. If you can keep the beast moving and stay with us. You! Any sign of the headman yet?"

"No, sir!"

"Keep—is that the last of the wine?" The captain turned to look up the street. One of his guards was leading the ass and swearing furiously; the beast was shaking its head and prancing sideways, trying to shy away from him or perhaps the small, two-wheeled wagon it pulled. "Get that thing up here, hurry it! You men, start loading, get the cargo settled so nothing breaks. Duke Vuhlem will have my head and all yours, too, if he loses what's left of this stuff!" The owner came forward to hold his beast's bridle and calm it as best he could; the other men were lined up to shift the boxes from porch to wagon bed.

Ryselle's brothers stayed where they were, braced against the wall; one of Vuhlem's guards stood close by, leaning against a long sword.

The captain gestured sharply; guards herded the village men back against the cart, while two others clambered onto the porch to retrieve the brothers. Fronek was still weaving, and without help would have slid to the wooden planks; Nyel was just able to stand without aid. Their faces were white in the moonlight, and to Ryselle they suddenly looked very young and foolish.

More noise up the street; Ryselle started convulsively as her father's outraged roar topped all other sounds. Two guards came up, the headman firmly held between them, he blustering furiously all the way. The captain stared down at him. The headman stuttered, mumbled something, and was abruptly silent.

"Where did you find him?"

"Sir, hiding in the barn where the ass was!"

"How fitting. You, Ninro. You know the Duke's laws. It was just possible for him to overlook your possible complicity in the presence here of the Zelharri noblewoman. But boxes bearing the Duke's seal, found breached and inside the men's hut, in your village—Ninro, the Duke will not be pleased at all to hear of *this*." He stared down once more. Ryselle could no longer see her father; the captain's horse blocked her view of him, his two guards, the cart, and most of the men.

Nyel fought his way to the edge of the porch. "Father—!"

"Be silent, you!" the captain thundered. "You have said everything you will be permitted to say! You and the other!" He gestured. The guards holding the two younger men jumped down from the edge of the porch, pulling their prisoners down and out of Ryselle's sight. Sretha caught her breath, took the younger woman's shoulders and spun her around, pulling her close.

"Don't look!" she hissed.

Ryselle stared at her, bewildered. "But, I didn't—" Sretha's hands shifted, and one clapped against the back of the younger woman's head. Ryselle's mouth was full of black scarf; she couldn't see.

Sretha's breath tickled her ear. "*Don't look*! No one should see such a thing!"

She turned her own head, burying it in Ryselle's shoulder as Nyel's voice rose in a towering shriek, suddenly cut off. Ryselle heard the unmistakable sound of a heavy metal edge burying itself in the planking. Her father was cursing in a high, horrible wail that didn't sound like him at all; Fronek's scream topped him, echoing across the village for what seemed forever. Then he, too, was still, and there was no sound save the headman's sobbing.

Ryselle was trembling violently; Sretha clung to her and shook. *She was right; no one should see that. Just to have heard it—I'll hear them in my sleep. Forever.*

"You men, mount up!" The captain snapped. "You, Ninro! Be grateful I do not listen to you too closely just now. Your Duke has until now been satisfied with your rule in Gray Haven. I would continue to please him, if I were you! He's left you one son, and your own head; a sensible man would be grateful for so much. You—old man, if you want to bring your ass and cart back, get up on that seat and ready yourself!"

Sretha let go of Ryselle's arms and leaned back against the wall of the hut behind them. Ryselle opened her eyes as the small armed company of Duke's men rode up the road at a canter, old Jefne and his cart in their midst. Behind them, a huddle of frightened village men and somewhere in their midst, her father. She could still hear him, cursing and weeping, wailing for his dead sons.

The Duke's company was gone; the sound faded, was suddenly gone as the horses topped a hill and rode down the other side. The only sound now came from in front of the men's long hut. Sretha looked skyward, then touched her companion's arm. "The moon will take the last of the shadow here very shortly; you'd better go at once, Ryselle." She couldn't speak; she nodded. The Wielder peered at her closely. "You're all right?"

"Fine," she managed. "Mother—"

"I said I'd look out for her, didn't I? You remember she lied for him tonight, though. Go, out the back way, girl, now—onto the high path. You'll make East Bluff and reach the caravaners before they retire if you hurry. Go!" She turned to ease her way around the back of the hut, came back and hugged Ryselle close. "Go! Send word as soon as you can!" Ryselle nodded. Sretha edged along the thin line of shadow and was gone.

Ryselle drew a deep breath, cast one last look at the men's hut, and followed. She could hear deaf old Nissa snoring on the other side of the wall. *Probably the only person in Gray Haven who didn't hear—that.* She swallowed, shook her head fiercely.

The men were still in a tight huddle at the edge of the porch; she could just hear her father's voice, but couldn't make out what he was saying any more. No one paid the least heed as she hurried across open ground and down into the hollow behind the long hut. Sretha had suggested the high trail; Ryselle knew the low one much better. Down between the hills, she wouldn't be visible in the moonlight, should anyone happen to be looking. If Benaret should happen to be on his way back from East Bluff, she'd hear him long before he could see her. *He won't be out at this hour. He'll be in the headman's house or the men's hut.* This way was sure, though.

Her hands were still shaking. She stuffed them in the fold of her cloak, and with her right, felt for the Wielder's coin pouch, presently tucked inside the broad, green-and-yellow patterned belt every

Gray Haven woman wore. She'd have to find another place to keep
it safe. *Because once I reach that caravan, I'm burning the sash.*

SRETHA regained her own small house without being seen, and
shut the door quietly behind her. Emalya, who was once again on
her blankets, this time weaving her hair into one thick braid for
the night, looked at her sidelong.

"What was the noise about? I thought it would wake the dead,
all that shouting."

"Not quite," Sretha replied flatly. She drew the scarves off her
hair and neck as she walked across the main room.

"It *was* the Duke's guard, wasn't it?" Emalya asked. Sretha
nodded. "I don't know why you act so—so—it wasn't me, I
didn't have anything to do with them this time."

"I know. No one blames you, Emalya." Sretha dropped her
scarves on the table, drew her book over in front of the chair by
the small hearth. The fire had burned low, but two or three small
sticks would remedy that. She turned the lantern down. *Wasteful,
not to have done it before Ryselle and I went out.* Emalya
wouldn't have done it for her, of course.

Back in the main room, Emalya was droning on in that sullen
tone Sretha disliked most—whining about the local women not
liking her or trusting her, most likely. *Twenty-seven days.* Sretha
thought as she sank into her chair and opened the book. *Nyel
won't be claiming her, of course. As if she'll care greatly which
of them takes her and her girls in, so long as some man does.
Fool. I wonder if the headman will put Benaret forward, to make
certain of her dowry? He's not much older than her Kepron, but
after tonight, the other men won't deny him much—for a while,
anyway.* She dismissed Emalya from her thoughts, began wrapping the red string around her fingers in a complex cat's cradle
as she read. In the main room, Emalya finished with her hair and
rolled into her blankets; she was still grumbling, but Sretha no
longer heard her. *Twenty-seven days. I can last that long without
strangling her. I think I can.*

LIALLA's head ached—combination, she decided, of the constant
noise level in the caravaners' vast barn of a building, the contin-
uous smoke from two fireplaces kept constantly alight and neither drawing as well as it might, the smoke from too many
sour-smelling pipes. It was strange, too, trying to sleep with so
many people awake at all hours: the family wing at Duke's Fort

was extremely quiet once night fell, and stayed that way until midmorning. *One good night's sleep—is that too much to ask?* She hadn't had one yet.

There were city women about most hours of the day; always someone for her to talk to. Unfortunately, most of those who wound up in the same place at the same time were women who couldn't agree on much of anything—and who disagreed at top volume. Typical of northern city women, Sil said.

The main Red Hawk grandmother had been able to subdue them; she had a voice that could etch pottery. But Red Hawk had left two mornings before; for a day and a half Sil and Lialla had the vast, echoing chamber to themselves—and the women who came whenever they could find enough time, or an excuse to leave husband and family. Late this morning, a small family group from Green Arrow Clan arrived—five wagons which plied the route between Holmaddan City and Cornekka. Their grandmother was a woman scarcely older than Robyn, with five children of her own; the small group had more children than all of Red Hawk (or so it seemed to Lialla). The grandmother had barely found time to speak to her and Sil between setting up and clan duties.

Sil had been subdued since her clan left: She wasn't used to being separated from her people, and Lialla wondered if the caravaner woman was having second thoughts about staying with her. *I hope not. Sil isn't good at settling arguments or shutting those women down once they start shouting at each other, but she's good company, and she always manages to make me feel I'm doing the right thing.*

Just now, the two women had the far end of the second floor all to themselves; the Green Arrow Clan was feeding its people down around the other hearth, and even the children were blessedly quiet for the moment. Sil knelt before the west hearth, blowing on the small struggling fire under a pot of soup. She flapped her hand in front of her face, coughed discreetly into her sleeve, then sat back and dipped a long-handled spoon into the broth. Lialla blew on it, drank it down and nodded.

"Wonderful. I'd probably have starved, left to my own devices."

Sil glanced at her, drank down a spoonful of soup herself. "Yes. Anyone can tell just by looking, you don't eat much." She spooned soup into two deep bowls and handed Lialla one, then set her own aside to rake a packet of flat bread from the edge of the coals.

"That's not fair," Lialla protested mildly. "I'm not anywhere near as thin as I was. And that wasn't not enough food, that was—" She sighed faintly, shook her head and dipped a piece of the tough bread in soup, sucked broth from it and ate it.

"Yes, I know," Sil said. "All the same—a soup like this isn't difficult to make. But I forget, noblewomen don't cook."

"Hah. You've met my brother's wife. Robyn—"

"Duchess Robyn is not quite representative of the class."

"True." Lialla ate more broth, spooned some of the vegetables from the bottom of the bowl and spread them across a bite of bread. "You'd have to poke me hard these days, to find ribs."

Sil laughed. "Which I won't. I've seen you swing that long stick of yours, and I've heard about some of the other things those outlanders taught you. Why don't you use that stick on the local women, next time they get out of hand?"

Lialla rolled her eyes. "Don't tempt me." She drank the last of the broth from her bowl, shook her head when Sil held out a hand for it. "Not yet. Save the rest of my share for later. Or will we have to fight for time at the fire later?"

"Don't think so. Gray Fishers' southern carts aren't due in until tomorrow and Green Arrow will be gone by then." She was silent for some moments, her hands busy tearing up a last bite of bread and rolling it into tiny pellets. "About that boy—"

"I wish I knew. But we told—what?—at least five shopkeepers, and most of the women who've come through here. And it's been four days? I'd think that by now he'd have heard about the message or someone would have passed it on to him, and he'd have come here if he could."

"Well—remember what the tinker's wife said this morning, two or three of the horse companies are outside the city on Duke's business and I heard rumor last night about a raid on one of the coastal villages. Could be he's gone with them. Don't worry about him."

"I don't, really," Lialla replied gloomily. "I'd just like to know."

"Maybe he's even gone south to Dro Pent. Were I him, I'd find a way to stay behind when the company returned to Holmaddan."

"Probably has."

"In which case," Sil said cheerfully, "you can wring his neck when you finally *do* find him."

A male voice interrupted them: abnormally deep, as though the speaker were young enough that it still cracked on him. "Bah! You send this fool's message from every corner of the market, you call the attention of my captain and possibly the

Duke himself, and then *you* would wring *my* neck?" Lialla set her bowl down with extreme care and turned her head. Kepron stood just behind her, arms folded across his chest, eyes narrowed. "How typical of women, that," he finished sourly. Sil stirred indignantly; Lialla laid a restraining hand on her friend's arm, then got to her feet.

"Never mind, Sil," she said, then scowled at the young Holmaddi. "I forgot what an arrogant little mutt he is."

"I wonder how you possibly could," Sil replied cheerfully.

Kepron's eyes darted her direction, came back to Lialla. "Arrogant." He snorted. "What are you doing in the city once again, after I risked my life twice to rescue you?"

I am not letting him get to me this time. Lialla unclenched her jaw and tried to match Sil's tone. "Besides calling attention to you, of course? I'm working with the local women and keeping an eye on your Duke's drug traffic; remember why I came north in the first place?"

"You left because of his Triad. Do you think it less powerful now, that you return?"

Lialla sighed. "Why am I arguing with a know-everything kid? Never mind my motives, boy."

"I have been watching and listening both; there is no need for you here. Did I not tell you I would send word when I found anything? The Duke knows you have gone—"

"Yes. Of course he does. And that someone helped me get out of that particular cell."

"*I* know this. It's all the talk in my company. He's still quite angry; he won't like it if he finds you here."

"You won't like it if he finds out you helped me, kid. Look, it's done, all right? I'm here, and for now I'm staying. Also, I wanted to make certain Vuhlem wasn't in the process of taking you apart."

"I don't need your protection—"

Lialla snorted, silencing him. "I'm not trying to baby you, like your mother did. Sensible grown people watch each other's backs."

"My company—"

"Your company! Tell me they would never hand you over to Vuhlem tomorrow if they figured out what you did," Sil put in sharply. Kepron glanced at her, bit his lip and fell silent.

"Right," Lialla said crisply. "Sensible grown people, remember? I'm here anyway. You did me a big service, I'm grateful to you for that. And I'm offering you something extra, because of it. You continue to keep your eyes open, bring me news or send it, I'll teach you more Thread-magic." Silence.

"You ask me to—"

"To do just as much as you planned to anyway, and nothing more. You want to die of old age in this city? Live with men like that all your life? Never dare Wield where any of them might catch you at it? Maybe you like being in your father's old company?"

Kepron scowled at the wall behind her. His shoulders sagged, and he shook his head. "No. They are better than those village men. But not much better. Not enough."

"Fine. Learn what I can teach you while I'm here, kid, and you can go south when I do, get yourself a proper apprenticeship. Help me track down Vuhlem's drug shipments; I help you get out of Holmaddan. Deal?"

He turned away from them. Lialla glanced at Sil, who cast her eyes ceilingward. He was quiet for some time. Finally, he turned back; his mouth was tight and his eyes unfriendly, but he held out a hand and said, "Deal."

Lialla knelt before the fire once more and made a place for the boy next to her. She could hear loud voices at the far end of the open room; Sil got back to her feet and craned her neck, finally shrugged and sat down. "It's Red Hawk coming in; I forgot about the four carts that take the west road loop. Better finish the soup while it's hot, we might get crowded off the hearth after all."

"Sounds good to me. Don't glare, Kepron, I can talk and eat, you'll be out of here in no time. What we need—"

"Where did *that* come from?" Lialla looked up, startled; Kepron slewed around. Ryselle, her skirts wrinkled as though she'd slept in them for several days and her short red hair all anyhow, loomed over them, arms folded and a very disapproving scowl fixed on Kepron. Lialla simply stared.

A long, tense silence; then Sil began to laugh. The others turned to gaze at her in mild surprise—and in Kepron's case, visible irritation. She flapped a hand at them, finally gained control of herself. "Ah! I'm sorry, it's nothing! I'm just remembering how *dull* I thought it was going to be around here!"

7

🜨

ENARDI was smiling as he made his way down a very crowded Podhru street. *And why not?* he thought expansively. *Who would ever have thought when I first met Chris and Eddie, how well things would turn out for all of us—and particularly for me?* Years of working under his father's thumb had loomed ahead of him, before Chris. Not that Fedthyr was grudging with his money, or a slavedriver, or harder on his sons than his other workers—Enardi knew plenty of merchants like that—but after all, Fedthyr and his fellow ex-Zelharrians had been on *their* own at his age. So had his eldest sister Marseli, with her charm shop. It was nice, being able to live up to such a high family standard.

It was particularly nice to be so well known in Bez and Podhru both, and to have a heavy gold chain fixed to his out-lander watch and the fine foreign vest. Like most of the younger Rhadazi merchants, Enardi had adapted quickly to the outsider fashion of britches, boots, shirt and vest or jacket, keeping the long robes (like his father and the other old men wore all the time) for after hours. There wasn't any doubt it was more com-fortable to stride around Podhru or Bez in a single loose bag of cloth. *But who wants to be marked as one of the old men, in times like these?*

All his family—even his father's friends and business acquaintances—were quite proud of Enardi, these days: a man scarcely beyond boy's state and already on personal terms with the Emperor's Heir. *And all of this in four years; when I was a boy, who would even have thought there would be travel between the outside world and Rhadaz?*

He squeezed between a long table piled high with fruit and a ribbon merchant's, turned down one of the many side streets.

Fewer people away from the market and shops, at least this early
in the afternoon; he could walk and think, both at once, without
worrying about stepping on anyone or having his pocket picked.

And there was plenty to think about just now: He patted the
inner breast pocket where Afronsan's signed and sealed permit
for the import of ice machines rested. *There* was a nice gift for
Chris, when he arrived; Chris had worked long and hard at both
ends to make certain the machines would be available, and be
permitted entry when the ships brought them here. And the profit
should be—well! Enardi slowed to a complacent saunter and began to work out on his fingers where Chris might be right now.
Twelve days ago—wasn't it that long ago?—he'd just missed
them when they docked in Bez; two—three?—days after that, a
message sent south from Sikkre, then three days in Sikkre, three
more in Duke's Fort, allow for travel between those two cities,
then down to here . . . Chris and company—including Eddie's
boyhood friend Vey thief turned guard, *there* was an odd shift—
should arrive no later than tomorrow night, unless he was somehow detained. Eddie might have picked up a message with a
definite arrival time, though; when they left the civil service
building just now, Eddie'd said he would go by the south city
public telegraph shop they normally used, to see if Chris had
sent word, and if so, he'd leave word at Kamahl's before going
down to the docks to find them passage.

Fortunately, the telegraph was already in place on the rela-
tively short hop between Zelharri and the capitol. *I hope Chris
has telegraphed a message, it's nice knowing these things.
Funny, I can barely remember how things were before the wire.*
Two and three days for handwritten messages to travel between
Duchies, a mail service that was slow and not always depend-
able; the mirror-messages ordinarily reserved for Dukes and
emergencies, but no one in his proper senses used the mirrors because whatever message was sent, after passing through ten or
fifteen stations, was never the same when it arrived. *Garble-
graph*, Chris said his mother called it.

*I wonder how his mother took it—a new wife and acquired in
such a fashion?* Robyn was such a nice woman, she wouldn't be
as openly difficult as some, but it would surely be a surprise to
her. Enardi still wasn't entirely certain Eddie hadn't been pulling
his chain, as Chris would say, about this bride. *But Chris—if
such a mad thing happened to any of us, it would be Chris. As
if we haven't warned him to be careful outside Rhadaz. They*

aren't all civilized, those people—haven't we told him often enough?

Chris should know, of course, since he came from a world no more civilized than some of the places out there. The stories he and Eddie brought back—Enardi listened to all of them in fascination at the time, and invariably swore to himself afterward he'd *never* travel beyond the borders of his own land.

It seemed odd, all the same. Chris married; first of the three of them. *He's said so often he wasn't ready for that. We always thought I'd be first, particularly once I knew for certain Chris had no desire to wed the noble weaver's first daughter and I had the opportunity to present myself. After all, I've been courting Meriyas three years now; with any other woman, I probably would already be long since wed. But Meriyas still teases me with Eddie, and I swear Lord Evany encourages her. He probably has hopes of lowering the dowry my father insists upon.*

It was funny in a way: His father Fedthyr and Lord Evany had both once been native Zelharrians, but of vastly different ranks. That a Sehfi merchant could ask, man to man, for a nobleman's daughter was something, but that *Lord* Evany should even consider Eddie as a mate for his eldest daughter—! The daughter of a high-ranking (if exiled) nobleman and one (ex) market thief. *Who of course happens to be in a much more legal business these days, to say nothing of extremely well placed and rich to boot.* Like himself. *I'll win out in the end.* Eddie was having too much fun with all those foreign girls, anyway. And like Chris, he had been intrigued at once by Meriyas's pretty face and all that wondrous hair—spooked, as Chris would say of them both, by the woman herself. But beneath that flirtatious facade was the girl herself, and Enardi liked what was there: the real, sweet Meriyas. *She's flirting because it's the last time she can—married women can't tease the same way. She'll have me, in the end.* It was maddening, all the same.

He thought about going past the weaver's shop, perhaps even taking flowers. Decided against it at once. Halfway across town at an hour when the market was its busiest; it would take him forever even if he could find decent blooms, this time of the year. Besides, her father would see the gift as desperation on his part, and Evany would be on the wire to Bez, trying to lower the dowry again. *And Father would never let me live it down.*

Besides, if he went straight back to the small apartment above Kamahl's shop where CEE-Tech's Podhru office was presently (and very temporarily) quartered, he might have time to change out of his best britches and boots before Eddie came and they went in search of evening meal and wine. The boots were brand-new and still pinched, even though his father's man had fitted them with care and chosen fine, soft skins. The trous were nearly new but had become too snug in the waist, all at once. *Too much rich living for you, my lad; you'll resemble your stout old grandfer before long, if you aren't careful.*

Part of that was the constant traveling, living part-time in his father's house, part-time in various inns and spare-room apartments in Podhru or down in Fahlia, eating in inns and shops. A firm as prestigious as CEE-Tech should have proper offices, and employees to manage the day-to-day business; the principals should have a place to entertain clients and discuss deals in private. *Less strain on my waistband if I have control over what is fed them and myself,* he thought ruefully, and tugged at his sash.

And clients had more faith in a company that had permanent local housing. It was something he'd have to discuss with Chris and Eddie. *One of us, most likely me, is going to have to take initiative on this.* At least for Podhru; whatever quarters might be needed in the places Chris went most often, he could manage. Edrith had no intention of traveling outside his own country for any reason whatever.

And once that telegraph was fully run between Podhru and Bez, he could find himself a house in Podhru, hire servants and purchase furniture. Perhaps even hire agents to handle the travel between Bez and Podhru for him, so he didn't need to bounce back and forth—and that was the word for it: The road wasn't much better than it had been four years earlier, though these days he drove a small, one-horse carriage much nicer than his father's old wagon. Springs made an enormous difference, but they didn't mend that road. And ships really did make him ill, even when the sea was calm. *When Chris comes, I'll show him that vacant shop on the Street of the Blind Muse; it's been empty long enough that I can talk down the price. It would do for now: It's cheap, a short walk to the civil service, not so far from the port and the main west road, and only two streets from where they're putting the north telegraph shop*—He was busily planning his attack on Chris when someone ran into him.

He blinked, stepped back and brought up a rueful smile that would have to serve until he could catch his breath enough to apologize for not watching where he was going. Even though the other man was clearly at fault; he'd been almost running when they had collided.

But he was also half again Enardi's size: He stepped back and stared, round-eyed, and his mouth sagged wide; his booming voice made Enardi's ears hurt and raised echoes up and down the narrow, high-walled alley. "Enardi—it *is* Enardi, isn't it? Of all the small wonders, meeting you here and like this!"

It was Enardi's turn to stare. "Choran? Well, but I would know you anywhere! What a surprise!" His smile widened; inwardly he sighed. Of all the people to run into—literally or otherwise— why must it be this overgrown fool? Casimaffi's second son was a bore; he always had been, from the earliest days Enardi could remember: *I was five and he at least two, only just walking at that age and howling whenever he fell—that voice was enough to shatter pottery.* The wretched man must be about twenty now, and as huge as his early height and girth had promised. Of course, his mother's kin were all hulking brutes, too. His voice was lower in pitch than his baby whine but it still rang off the surrounding walls. He still looked thrown together, Enardi thought fastidiously: His hair seemed to have been cut by some-one aboard ship, in a storm, *with* a dull blade, and by the smell of him he hadn't washed the hair or any of himself since that last cut. His heavy shirt was stiff and reeked of salt water. Enardi fought the urge to brush at his own clothing where the man had slammed into him. "But, Choran, I thought you were at sea these days ..."

Choran smiled expansively; enormous white teeth gleamed behind very heavy dark beard. "Most often I am. Father's given me mastery of the *Whelk*, you know. We've just come in from trading down the far south coast." He laughed and slapped Enardi on the shoulder, then caught him as he staggered. "Taking up some of your slack, you and those partners of yours! Here, come and have some ale with me, I've some messages for you from Bez."

"Ah—do you know, I'd like that, I never hear what my old friends are up to these days." Enardi glanced overhead to check the position of the sun, drew out his watch and sighed— convincingly, he hoped. "But I fear events are against us. I have to meet Edrith very shortly, there's a contract we've—"

"Ah, well, another time." If Choran knew he was being put off with a polite lie, if he sensed that Enardi had no intention of get-ting stuck in his company, he didn't show it. But as Enardi was trying to find a way to say good-bye, Choran smiled, took a good hold on his elbow and began piloting him down the street in the direction he'd already been heading. "Why, then, I may as well walk with you, pass on my messages, eh?" The smile stayed on his lips; it didn't reach his flat, expressionless brown eyes.

"That's a sensible thought." Enardi smiled in turn but his heart sank. Choran had an excellent grip on his arm; he'd never get free without a scene—and there was no one about to come to his aid if he *did* create a scene. *Let him talk, and then leave him—he's a fool but not stupid, and after all, this is the Emperor's city, not one of those southern ports.*

They walked in silence for some ways. "My father tells me, Enardi, that your father is upset by the class of men you deal with these days."

Enardi shook his head. "My father? He says nothing to me. But I don't understand what you mean, my friend."

Choran laughed unpleasantly. "Oh, come now! You're in partnership with two commoners: an outlander and a Sikkreni market thief—oh, they say he's reformed, but what thief ever is? I'd not let that watch and chain out of my hands at night when he's about were I you, Enardi. And this outlander—my father brought me to your father's house, remember? When these outlanders first came with young Duke Aletto. Those shoes, that voice; the things he said and the way he said them. My father was shocked to his soul and so was yours—and you know it. Now, Enardi, people like that—"

Enardi snorted loudly; Choran turned to look at him. "Choran, really! Is there a purpose behind this unpleasant gossip about two men I like and trust, I may say, very much? Chris and Edrith are not 'people like that,' they are my friends and business associates." He scowled up at the much taller Choran. "If that is all you have to say to me—"

Choran stopped mid-street. Enardi resisted the urge to tug at a collar suddenly much too snug; he couldn't breathe properly with Choran staring at him like that. But his companion burst out laughing, all at once, and started down the street once more; Enardi, still clutched tightly by one arm, went with him perforce.

"Ah, yes! I well remember how loyal you are to friends, Enardi! But it will get you into trouble this time—and that is what my father told me to say to you. He said, remind Enardi that true loyalty would never demand you lower yourself in such fashion, and he reminds you, on your father's account, of your own class and kind."

"And he thinks—what, my friend Choran? Shall I return to my father's house this moment? Shall I give up a lucrative business—of which my father is highly approving, mind you!—so that Casimaffi's sense of honor—?" He couldn't finish; it was exasperating, ludicrous at the same time.

But Choran seemed to actually consider this. He shrugged. "You wouldn't have to actually *leave* those men. My father suggested—" He cast Enardi a swift, sharp glance. "Now, my father's business is growing at least as fast as this little venture of yours. If the Emperor has a choice between your outlander friend and this thief—and an old and established family like ours—well, which way do you think he'll lean?" He stopped mid-street and waited. Enardi waited him out, and hoped his face showed nothing; inwardly, he was going all to pieces. *Is he actually making threats? What is he trying to say? And—gods of high profit, there is no one else in this narrow little alleyway; Choran might strangle me and bestow the body where he chose, and who would know?* Unpleasant thought: It would probably haunt his dreams for days to come—if he lived to have any.

He licked his lips, glanced sidelong at his companion; Choran was still watching him closely, waiting. "Well," he managed finally. "You know—about the Emperor. You're certainly right about that much. And—well, I suppose I *have* thought about it. Tell your father—tell him I'll consider your message." He faltered to silence; Choran said nothing. "I—I couldn't just leave them, they'd wonder why—"

Choran smiled suddenly. "Oh. We don't expect you to do that. After all, Father only gave me that message in case I should run into you—and I did, didn't I?" He tipped back his head and laughed ringingly. Enardi laughed, too, but to his ears, he sounded simply scared. Choran stopped laughing abruptly and leveled a finger at his companion's nose. "All the same, see you think hard, Enardi. You weren't born and trained to become a lower-class traveling merchant."

I never could act, Enardi thought gloomily. *I can only hope Choran's no better at reading people.* He tried to look thoughtful, finally nodded. "Well—that's so."

To his surprise, the ship's captain finally let go of his shirt. "And if not for men like my father and yours keeping to their own class and kind in Bez, where would Duke Aletto be today?"

"You're right." Enardi said at once. "Please tell your father I hadn't thought of it that way. I'll talk to him, as soon as we can meet."

"Good," Choran replied. "But remember, it's a dangerous world of late; a man's safest when he sticks with his own sort." Without warning or further word, he let go of his companion's arm completely, turned and strode back up the street. Enardi stood where he was and managed somehow to stay on his feet; Choran's heavy footsteps echoed from the walls around him for what seemed forever, but when he finally dared look, the man was nowhere in sight.

"Gods of easy coin and quick profit, what was all that to mean?" No answer—except that he still walked in the direction he'd been going, and still breathed. He brushed at his sleeve; Choran's enormous hand had set creases in the fabric and there was a grayish, dirty streak where none had been before. Suddenly, he was utterly shaking with fury. "Grubby, filthy-handed, wretched—he *threatened* me! He wants me to spy on Chris and Eddie for old Chuffles! My own class and kind, indeed!" He spat on the cobbles.

The anger left him as suddenly as it had come, and now he was simply shaking. He swallowed, shoved trembling hands deep in his pockets and began to walk as quickly as the uncomfortable new boots would allow; Eddie might be back at the apartment, Eddie would know what he should do. There might even be word from Chris; suddenly he wanted to see Chris very badly indeed.

*   *   *

CHRIS urged his horse onto the high plateau meadow, then drew him to one side. He sighed happily. "Man, I just do love this place. This whole area. You know?"

Vey gazed across the nearly level ground before them, straight across to open sky. He was relieved to be out of thick forest—trees and limited visibility made him nervous. "Well. It's nothing like Sikkre, of course."

"Not any. Nothing against Sikkre, you understand, but it's flat, hot and dry. I guess I'm just a mountain kind of guy."

"Oh." Vey freed a hand from the reins to shield his eyes against a winter-low sun. "It's better than that place where we spent last night. All those trees . . ." His voice trailed away. Chris grinned.

"Says you. I'm crazy for trees, never had enough trees around when I was a kid, a whole forest like that really does me. I'm surprised you didn't like that, growing up in Sikkre and all."

"Anyone could be hiding out there—or anything."

Chris shrugged. "I guess so. But bears don't go looking for people, and no person would hang out in the middle of a forest, waiting for maybe someone to come along. Zelharri's got bandits but there's nothing like that down this way. City's worse, you ask me: buildings, narrow streets—"

Vey shook his head. "I *know* where to look in a city, and what to look for."

Chris scratched his head. "You do have a point there: The trouble's in the cities. Bet you'll feel right at home in Podhru."

Vey eyed him sidelong. "Like I did in Sehfi?"

"Yah. Sehfi's not a city, it's an overgrown village in the middle of a forest. Besides, Podhru—we'll get there in plenty of time for the Emperor's birthday, and there's supposed to be real partying in the streets this year. Should be fun."

"Fun." Vey considered this. He could hear the clink and creak of harness behind them, Dija's smothered giggle. He cast a quick glance over his shoulder and smiled, very briefly.

"She's good company, isn't she?" Chris asked; he'd noticed the look.

"What a time to discover it," Vey said. "As she leaves Sikkre."

"She still may not go south with us, you know."

"Oh—I think she will. She and Madame Ariadne are like good friends, and she is very fond of the lady." Vey sighed faintly. "It is a good position for her, of course, much better than the palace kitchens."

"Gives her a chance to get away from all that—mess with her sister and all. And I'll—we'll be back in Sikkre for sure before the end of the year." Behind them, Dija murmured something, and Ariadne laughed delightedly.

Chris went momentarily blank-faced, then shook himself and smiled as he became aware of Vey's interest. *Yeah, everyone wonders about her and me, even him.* "So, hey, if we keep up this pace, we could actually make the city right around full dark. You know, first time I rode from Podhru to Zelharri, it took two days to get just to here. Of course, we had a wagon and we came *up* the hill. This time—"

"Up?" Vey asked warily.

Chris pointed down the road toward the long expanse of frost-

seared grass stubble and stone and blue sky beyond it. "I forget,
you're a flatlander." He grinned wickedly. "You'll like this."

"Oh, yes?" Vey eyed the road as far ahead as he could see.
What had Eddie said about this place? He couldn't remember.
Unless—"Is this where Duchess Robyn nearly fell?"

"One way to put it. Yeah, this is it."

"Oh. There is a long slope, Eddie said."

"You could call it that."

"Oh." Vey looked over his shoulder. "I think I will go back to
Dija. Warn her about this."

"Sure. And—uh, ah—if you'd ask the lady if she'd mind join-
ing me for a few minutes—"

A cool alto broke in from his other side. "I am here. I just saw
you point that way, and I see road vanishes into sky. There is
something I should know of this?"

"Depends. How're you for heights?"

"High places?" She shrugged, guided the horse into place next
to his. "All I have seen are in French Jamaica but they do not
bother me. Why?"

"There's something of a downhill coming up."

"Oh. The horse is well behaved, I can manage this." She
turned and stood in her stirrups to look behind them, then stared
out ahead before dropping neatly back in the saddle. *Boy. And I
thought the local version of jeans didn't do much for anyone.*
Chris bit back a sigh. *Who'd have figured she'd even wear them,
let alone look that good in them?* Even with one of the blankets
wrapped shawl-like over her own inadequate jacket—she swam
in Chris's and wouldn't wear it—Ariadne looked taller, trimmer
and—well—great in denim. Sleek. *Hands off.* Chris reminded
himself gloomily. *Don't even look like you'd want to touch.*

He dragged his attention back to the moment. Ariadne was
talking to him, just chatting—something she was starting to do
more often of late. "You would really like to live in that place
you showed me this morning?" He nodded. "All those trees, the
cool air—it would be a very fine house, but you would need
more warm clothing."

"Thick wool and lots of firewood," he agreed. "And a helicopter." Ariadne frowned; Chris spread his arms wide. "Old joke between me and my mom: a way to get back to civilization in an
hour or so, instead of a couple days. I really hate fighting
through snow on horseback."

"Snow—?"

He was hard put not to laugh; Ariadne had suddenly reminded him of the Calgary Olympics he'd watched on TV way back when—rooting, like so many, for the bobsled team that had come from his world and her home island. *Snow? Right.* "You've heard about it, right? Gets so cold the rain turns to bits of white fluff, piles up on the ground?"

"Ah. Snow. They have this in France and even in the north mountains of the Gallic state on my uncle's ranch also. Mostly it makes mud of the roads, though my uncle Philippe who runs the Orlean estates wrote once to say it fell so thick in the hills below the mountains, one could not pass."

"Yeah, it does that around here, gets deep as your nose. You'd probably hate it, it gets *cold*. Water freezes solid, the whole bit."

"I might not like it to live in," Ariadne said thoughtfully. "But I would like to see it." She drew a deep breath, smiled as she let it out. "So much clean, fresh air that does not smell of fish, and so far one can see to things that are not ocean."

"I agree with you. Last time I was in Philippe-sur-Mer the whole place reeked of dead fish and you could've drunk the air."

"Storm air." Ariadne nodded. She gave him a swift rather shy smile. "I do not care at all for storm season." He studied what he could see of her face; Ariadne was gazing across the plateau, her face flushed with the cool air and exercise, taking visible pleasure in her surroundings. *Wow. Neat. We're actually just talking, like real people, and we agree on something besides her old man's dead meat.* It made him nervous, though, now that he realized what they were doing; how did he keep this up?

C'mon, guy. Talk about what you like, the way you would with Eddie or Vey. He licked his lips. "Of course, it could get lonely up here, no one else around. But I grew up in a big city, so it would make a nice change—sometimes, anyway."

"I can understand that; not to have to bother with people. I too would like that, some of the time."

"It *is* kinda dry up here on the plateau just now; but you should have seen it during the summer. Even before first freeze, last month the grass was up to your waist and there were purple and yellow spiky flowers everywhere."

"I would like—yes, I want to see that. Tell me, then—what is this helicopter?"

Chris laughed. "It's a joke—here anyway. Flying machine. There's nothing even close in this world and probably won't be while I'm alive, so I'm thinking maybe a hot-air balloon—"

"Oh, I know of those. They have had them in Paris for a long time, my father once had a ride for pleasure when he was a small child. And my uncle Philippe, he has such a balloon of his own, so he can oversee Grandpere's estate because it is so huge, and my grandpere so fussy about his lands."

"Yeah. Even the Mer Khani and the English have 'em these days. Most of the ones I've found, you can't steer, though."

"Ah. Like the one my father tells of. But my uncle can put his in the direction he wishes to go, he says. And he says also there is a carriage he has now, which goes by steam—"

"Whoa!" Chris turned to stare at her. "You're kidding—I mean, you're making a joke, right?"

She shook her head, plainly bewildered. "Why does that make a joke? They are very new, he says, but Orlean is the most vast estate in all France, by horse he was never able to manage properly. Though he says the balloon is still better for seeing."

"Wow. I know there's steam trains, nearly everywhere but here, anyway. But there's actually a car ... Oh, jeez. Lemme think." He was quiet for a long moment, muttering soundlessly to himself and unaware of Ariadne curiously watching him. "Hmmm. Car. Really. Tell me: Are you on better terms with Uncle Philippe than with your father? I mean—if you asked, would he talk to *me* about these machines? Because if he knows who makes them, and he'd be willing to get me in to talk to them, and I could do a deal to buy cars, he'd get a cut of the profits."

"Well—I think he would do this. After all, I am his only niece, even if not by proper means as they say; he has now and again sent me a small gift on my birthday. But since I was, oh, fifteen years, he and I have made a small correspondence." She considered this, finally nodded. "I will ask him."

"That's great. Thanks." *As if ol' Shesseran would ever let cars into the country. Good luck. But I bet Afronsan would. Funny, if it was because of her that I could finally work out a way to have that house up here. Of course, she's stuck with me, I guess she'd rather I made a lot of money.*

"I—am glad to be useful." She sounded stiff but not unfriendly. "I like your mother."

He glanced at her; Ariadne was fiddling with her gloves, eyes fixed on her hands. "She's a good lady, my mom. She likes you, too."

"You think so? I surprised her, I fear. Not—what she desired for a son's wife, perhaps?"

"I know she likes you, she told me so. You didn't disappoint her, she's just got a lot on her mind with Aletto's mom being so sick." He sighed faintly. "Then my little half-sister—" Well, no point in telling her about that. But it figured Iana would be able to shift; she had Robyn's temper. At least Aletto was being cool about it—or so Robyn said. *I can't believe she came out and told him. Bet Jen was behind that idea.*

"They are nice children, those two. I seldom am around any."

"Oh." Was that supposed to *mean* something? He decided to let it slide. "Me, either. It surprises me, really; Mom never was much into marrying herself. Of course, that was all a different world."

"Oh." Ariadne still wasn't certain she believed him about this other-world stuff, he could tell. "She was kind to me; that was nice of her, since I was the surprise to her."

"She's always been good at that; all those years raising me helped, of course. It's always been a joke between us, whether I'd ever get married—uh, I mean—" He could feel his face heating. "Look, I'm *sorry*." Somehow, he managed to keep most of his exasperation with himself out of his voice; she'd think he was angry with her. "I swear I don't mean to keep hitting you with that, and I swear it is not personal—"

"I know that." She glanced up at him, then away, studying the plateau around them. "You do not need to say so always, I can understand that one might not wish to marry. I did not, though as a girl in French Jamaica has little hope of avoiding it. And with my father—" She compressed her lips, shook her head. "I know why I chose not to wed. But, why would you not?"

He shrugged. "Well, hey. I'm only twenty, you know."

"This is young for a man of your class to marry?"

"There aren't any classes back home, or rules about marriage. Most people figured you get some job success first, make money, think about marriage and kids later. Men and women both." He sighed, very faintly. "I was still in school, not even thinking about what I'd do when I left. And my mom—well, she's all right now, but back then, she drank a lot and hung out with guys that yelled at her and hit her and stuff. It just gave me a bad outlook on things like wine and being hooked up to one person." He was staring at the horse's mane. His face was burning, and Ariadne had gone very still and was watching him. Silence. He forced a laugh. "Well, yeah. Anyway. She's fine now, *you* saw.

But now you know why I don't do wine, anyway. And I never could see a reason to hook up with one chick for life."

"Chick. Chick?"

"Woman—girl. Sorry."

She frowned at her hands. "Girl or woman is all right, but chick is not?" She considered this briefly, shrugged it aside.

Chris stood in his stirrups, shaded his eyes against the low sun. "Ah—we're just about at the cut. You sure high places don't bother you?"

"I said they do not." Ariadne dismissed heights with a wave of her hand. "That was kind of the Duke—your mother's husband, I mean—" Whatever else she meant to say went unsaid; Ariadne was staring ahead, wide-eyed; she caught her breath in a shrill little squeak.

Chris's skin crawled; he stood in the stirrups and looked where she was gazing. Nothing but the edge of the plateau and the very distant forest beyond—and well below it. "Well, I did warn you." The road itself suddenly dropped off at a nasty angle; it must look to her as though it dropped off the edge of the earth. *Looks like that to me, too.* He swallowed. Heights didn't bother him at all, but this place now and again got him right under the ribs. *They just got to do something about this chunk of road.* Shortest route between Duke's Fort and the sea—and this lousy pass.

"Oh!" Ariadne's voice was faint, her face pale. "You do not mean we go down *that*?" She dragged the horse to a halt and leveled one trembling hand at him. "You said high places! Not a—a—"

"It's not so bad as all that, really," he urged reasonably as she faltered to silence. "Once you get past the first long drop—"

"Do *not*, for the sake of God, say *drop*!" Her voice soared.

"Sorry. Anyway, just a little ways down, around the bend there, it levels out kind of, and the outer edge isn't quite as steep a dr—a fall—a—oh, hell! Anyway, all you have to do is stay close to the inner edge and keep your eyes away from the other side and it's no big deal at all—" He was cut off by an utterly terrified shriek from behind.

Ariadne gave him a narrow-eyed glare, pursed her lips and turned her horse; just behind them, Dija was panicking, big time, and if Vey hadn't grabbed the reins of her horse, she would probably have been halfway back across the plateau by now. The bright red tassles on her Zelharri-made winter scarf flew wildly around her, upsetting her mount.

Chris couldn't make out what any of them were saying: Dija's voice was shrill, the words spilling over each other, and Ariadne's French was much too fast for him. For Dija, too—she spoke less of it than he did, even if her accent was better. Neither of them could possibly hear low-voiced Vey. But Ariadne's voice was soothing, and though she was quite pale, she otherwise managed to look calm and capable. The hysterics abated—a little. Vey dismounted, handed Dija's reins to Ari and walked over to join Chris, who slid to the ground and dug his fists into the small of his back. He looked down the road for several long moments, then shook his head.

"You rode up that four years ago? On a horse, all the way? And with a wagon? You're mad!"

"Yeah, everyone says so, and not just about this road. So?"

Vey gazed out across open air. "My apologies to Duchess Robyn, when you next speak to her."

Chris grinned. "Right. But now you know how come I didn't warn you what was coming; you'd never have believed me, right?"

"Well—sure. You know?" Vey managed a smile but he looked worried and his hands were wrapped in the horse's mane, possibly to keep them from trembling.

"Hey—guy. You okay?"

"I won't like this, but I can manage. But Dija—"

"Dija can also manage," Ariadne said coolly as she came up. "Is this horse as placid as it seems?" She brought her maid's mount ambling forward with a tug at the reins. Dija clung to the saddlebow, eyes tightly closed, her face utterly white. A tear made its way down an already wet cheek.

Time: all the time this trip had already taken him. *If I'd been alone, I could've done the whole circuit in three or four days, max. Now we're gonna have to go back and around the long way and it's gonna be my fault she's scared—because I do this all the time, so why should I think this spot would totally freak someone? Oh, man?* But if Dija absolutely refused, he really couldn't insist. *She'd hate me. I'd hate myself. Ariadne'd hate me for life. Hey. It's already been a few extra days, what's out there that's so urgent you gotta yell at Dija for being scared of heights?* Poor kid. Chris managed a smile. "Mom told me she likes that gelding because he's so easy to ride; she's pretty nervous around horses. Why?"

In answer, Ariadne turned and spoke to Dija for a long time, her voice so low Chris couldn't catch any of it. Dija shook her head frantically at first; Ariadne continued to talk, quietly persuasive. The girl sighed very faintly, then finally, reluctantly, nodded. She dismounted and stood very still while Ariadne pulled the blanket from her shoulders and tossed it across the saddle, then handed Vey the reins of her own horse. She wrapped an arm around the girl's shoulders then and started walking toward the drop-off, well to the inside, with Dija's horse between them and the drop-off. Dija's eyes were tightly closed, her hands over them. "All right," Ariadne said softly over her shoulder. "We manage, we two. Let us get this done with, and quickly, please!"

"You got it," Chris replied. He mounted and urged his horse forward, around and just ahead of the women. Vey took another wary look at the steep road and decided he would walk also; he put himself right behind Dija, where she could hear him—and where he couldn't see the edge, either. Aletto's men rode single file, bringing up the rear.

It took time; Chris reminded himself frequently that they'd have had to bring the horses down this particular incline at a slow walk whether everyone rode or not. *At least we're moving forward and headed in the right direction. Don't sweat the small stuff, okay?* By the time they were halfway down, Ariadne—who had been talking in a nonstop soft-voiced monologue—managed to get Dija back on her horse so she and it could be led down the rest of the way.

Chris consulted the sky at that point, then his watch. "No point in rushing things," he said. "There's a good place to camp not far from the base of this hill; we'll stay there the night."

"Hill." Vey laughed; there wasn't much humor in the sound, and Ariadne gave him a sidelong look.

"Hill," she scoffed. "And my father is your *cher ami*, with whom you cannot wait to again play cards." Her eyes were very bright; Chris laughed, but he couldn't begin to guess if Ariadne was laughing with—or at—him.

*   *   *

THE apartment above Kamahl's weaving shop was small and crowded with excess stock and stacks of cushions. A huge bed filled one entire wall side to side; a table clearly used as a desk and currently piled high with papers, a chair pulled so whoever sat at the table could look out the room's single window, a pile of pillows against the wall next to the door, and a series of pegs for clothing completed the meager furnishings. The single room seemed even smaller with two medium-sized men in it, particularly with one pacing it in long-legged strides. Edrith worked his shoulders into the too-soft cushions and waited; his head turned to watch Enardi stride back and forth. Enardi was still suffering a reaction from his meeting with Choran; he was all but wringing his hands, and sweat beaded his brow. "It is all very well for you and Chris," he finished. "You travel; you go to lands where any kind of man might deal in whatever goods, including this Zero. One becomes used to uncouth and dangerous men, or so it seems to me."

Edrith considered this, turned a hand over and shrugged. "I suspect we do; I hadn't really thought about it, but—"

Enardi overrode him. "Eddie, this is Podhru! Not one of the filthy waterfront places you and Chris talk of! This is the Emperor's very capitol, a clean and—and *decent* city, and that man *dared* threaten me right on the street, I tell you!"

He paused, hands clenched tightly together, and stared at his companion, who shrugged. "I don't doubt you, Ernie. I don't even doubt that he was following you and arranged the collision. But men like Choran travel to Ucayali, they absorb the way things are there. Threats are a way of life to them. But there've always been rough men in Rhadaz anyway."

"Well. Yes, but—"

"You warned us about Casimaffi, remember? Four years ago. And I have been in the same waters as Choran, though I don't recall the man, you know? But there are stories—"

"—which I do not wish to hear, thank you," Enardi said sharply. Edrith smiled, shrugged.

"Choran had a hard reputation even before his father gave him that ship."

"I know. I grew up around him and even as a boy five years his elder, he frightened me at times. And now! Well, you would remember him if you had met him, he's a bear of a man, all hair and beard and hard, huge, grubby hands—"

"You would be astonished, Ernie, how many men out there match such a description." Enardi rolled his eyes, let his hands slap against his legs. "Well. I'm surprised only that it's taken them so long to choose you as the mark, as Chris would say."

"You—it is? I mean, it has? I mean—why?" Enardi flung his arms wide. "But why? Because of my family, their money, my connections? Or perhaps for my father—?"

"It could be any of that; you're easier to reach through those connections, you know. I don't have anyone to use against me—no one except my mother, and even I don't know where she is this past year. But I think it's that they know you don't see violence, like we do. *You* might be swayed by threats to your person; Chris or I ignore them when possible and retaliate if not. And these days Chris is what he calls 'bulletproof'; his only kin are in highly protected places, particularly since the attack on Dahven. Casimaffi thinks he can use you because he can threaten you and your family, but even Casimaffi would never be fool enough to threaten the Thukara or Duchess Robyn. The Heir wouldn't stand for it." He considered this. "I doubt even the Emperor would."

Enardi laughed dryly. "I'd wager you on *that*. Particularly as unwell as Shesseran has been this past year and more. But I know all too well about Chris and bulletproof. That didn't protect him against one Henri Dupret."

"Well, we have warned him, you and I," Edrith said mildly. "You can be tough, and Chris is; there can still be one tougher."

"Ah, yes," Enardi said gloomily. "And what a price to pay for his foolishness."

"Mmmm. He's fortunate he isn't long dead; the lady has wits, at least. And, I suppose she's attractive in her own way, but not what I would choose. But you know Chris: This won't change anything. You know he's already making plans for how to deal with Dupret when we go south again?"

"I could tell him how to deal with the man: Avoid him!" Enardi began pacing once more. "Eddie—what am I to do? If Choran—"

"Well. Yes, Choran." Edrith sighed faintly and began maneuvering himself up from the pillows. "First of all, be sensible, and don't walk around the city alone. Old Casimaffi is cautious, didn't you say? He wouldn't want anyone to overhear his son threatening you, and he'd never chance having you killed around witnesses." He looked up; Enardi closed his eyes and shook his head. "You heard, I suppose, about the letter he wrote the Heir?"

"Heard? Afronsan let me read it." Enardi snorted. "The nerve of that man! To lay blame upon the Thukar's brothers and evil-minded outlanders, painting himself a mere innocent caught in the middle—as if anyone could believe that! And let me tell you, Afronsan was not at all pleased that he could not prove otherwise. But, do you know what I find worse? That men like my father will believe old Chuffles!"

"It does not surprise *me*. So—no, he won't want any witness to any—unpleasantness he intends upon you, wouldn't you think?"

"I will not even think about unpleasantnesses upon myself," Enardi replied firmly.

"You had better. My early years in Sikkre taught me, and being out there with Chris reinforces it: You *must* think about real danger to yourself, if only to plan how best to avoid it." He looked at Enardi, whose mouth was set in a stubborn line. "I suppose it is no good to suggest you carry a knife? Or your bo?"

"And what would I do with a knife? Choran could take it from me and use it upon me!" Enardi shuddered. "And that bo—what good have I ever become with it?"

"Ernie, you just don't practice. Even Duchess Robyn can use one." Enardi shook his head and waved a dismissive hand. Edrith shrugged. It was an old argument, and it wouldn't be resolved today, either. He sighed. "Well, then. I wouldn't—but you could talk to the city guard."

"And tell them what? Choran broke no law, and I have no witness. The guard would wonder why I report such a thing, with no proof. They might even think we planned this to smirch Casimaffi's repute, and—"

"I know. I said I wouldn't go to the guard, but, then, I carry a knife and a bo both when I go into supposedly empty alleys. If we could get some kind of proof—"

"No. I have nothing to do with this, not if it means confronting Choran *or* Chuffles. Certainly not if the proof is my body," Enardi said firmly.

"For that, who would blame you? Well, you stick with me, friend. Men like Choran know me, by repute if not by sight; they know I can take care of myself. And my friends." He thought about this a moment, chuckled softly. "Did I tell you about the tavern in Juitata? When three men set upon me and I was—"

"You told me." Enardi abruptly sat on the edge of the room's only chair and let his breath out in a gust. "I'm sorry, friend, I'm tedious today. But—"

"You have a right. Just stick with me, or Chris after he gets in, and you'll be all right."

"And when you both go south? I cannot hide in Kamahl's apartment all the time!"

"No." Edrith rubbed his chin. "But when we go, you can hire a bodyguard."

Enardi blinked. "Do you know what that would cost?"

"I couldn't guess. But not as much as your funeral."

8

᠗

CHRIS'S party camped in the woods near the place Aletto's company had stopped four years earlier, only a few miles outside Podhru's north gates. The evening passed quite pleasantly, if too cool and foggy for Ariadne's tastes and clothing; the Zelharri armsmen were used to weather of this sort, but Dija and Vey were nearly as unhappy as Ariadne. Chris disliked damp, foggy weather but thought it better than Sikkre any time of year—or Zelharri, where it was probably cold, damp and snowing in the higher villages already. *But, it's eighty and sunny in the Caribbean; that beats anything Rhadaz has this time of year. Can't wait.* Maybe he'd have a chance to skin-dive again, once his most immediate problems were taken care of. Ariadne would really think he'd slipped a cog.

Just now she was wrapped in two blankets, huddled with Dija under a third as close to the fire as the two dared sit. Good thing Robyn had insisted on his taking all those extra blankets, even though they made an awkward additional bundle to fasten onto the pack horse. Just as fortunate Ariadne had left most of her luggage in Bez, to be picked up on the way back, of course. *Shoulda got her something fur-lined or quilted in Sehfi, definitely warm gloves. Of course, Podhru won't be chilly like this and we'll be inside at night. Astonishing, how much warmer it is once you get out of these woods and next to the sea. And we're leaving this climate almost at once.*

But if they came back in mid-November, even Sikkre would be chilly in the morning and there would be snow in the mountains. Chris grinned. It would be very interesting to see what she *really* thought about snow once she got her feet and hands in it. *We come back this way in winter, I will definitely have to get her something warm to wear.* It made him uncomfortable—*providing* for someone. Not just buying gifts for a mother or an aunt, but the supporting thing. Ariadne was accustomed to men providing for their women, of course. But provided for by Chris? He had no idea how she felt about being beholden to him.

Far's I know, she doesn't even like me, even though she's talking to me like real people. Right, I can hear you, Jen, just ask her. Sure. Me, too. Just now they were getting along quite well, thank you, and he wasn't about to rock that boat. *Great relationship.*

The evening passed quietly, almost pleasantly; the two women crawled into their shelter as soon as dinner was over and Chris rolled into his blankets once he'd helped clean up and banked the fire.

But by the time they were on the road the next morning, not long after daybreak, he and Ariadne had already snarled at each other and she wasn't speaking to him again. He urged his mount ahead of the rest of the company. "Not my fault," he grumbled. The horse turned to eye him. He scowled at it. "Jen's right, you critters have an attitude. You watch the road, not me, okay? It was not my fault! I get the usual headache from sleeping on the damp ground—yeah, right, like she's supposed to know that. But how was I to know something as simple as 'You want a second cup of coffee, or is it all right if we break camp?' was gonna set *her* off?"

"Just as well," he mumbled under his breath. She and Dija were so far behind the pack horse, he couldn't hear them at all, though when he risked a glance over his shoulder they had their heads close together and seemed to be earnestly discussing something. *Probably how lousy all men are.* "Yah. I bet Mom and Jen both got a massive twitch when I thought *that*. Well, it ain't my prejudice." All men this, all women that ... Chris sighed, shook his head, which set his temples to pounding again.

Vey was back there, too, leading the laden pack horse and talking to Aletto's men. Of course, Vey knew him well enough to stay clear this early in the day. *Weird—I never used to be like this. 'Course, I'm not sixteen, either—but twenty isn't exactly ancient. Guess I'm just more like Aunt Jen than I thought, not madly verbal before noon. Maybe I should learn how to drink coffee. Might even come in handy with some of the guys I do business with, being able to make sense just after sunrise.*

He glanced back at Ariadne again; she and Dija were giggling over something. *Damn.* Part of him wanted to shake her until her teeth rattled; another part was scared half silly he'd even *think* that. The rest—*jeez, why can't she just chill out and give me half a chance?* "Good luck," he mumbled. "Forget that, okay? Forget her. Use the time while everyone's avoiding you and figure out some stuff."

And there was plenty for him to work out before they got into the city: He hadn't done up a written list of things to go over with Ernie, like he usually did, and they weren't going to have very long to talk, this trip. With any luck, Eddie'd already found them decent passage south, something fairly fast and leaving in the next couple of days. If Ariadne—hell, she'd never stay behind. *Forget that, she's right; who'd wanna stay with people they don't know in a strange country? Wasn't for her old man and old Chuffles out to get me and probably her, too, I wouldn't even suggest it. Well—maybe not.* Of course, who was to say she'd be safe here?

"Yeah. Fine. Forget that, too." He was talking to himself out loud. "Well, so what?" No one around here thought only loonies talked out loud to themselves. Eddie laughed at him for it, mostly because he turned red when someone caught him. But with no tape recorder, and with his handwriting so crummy—particularly on a moving horse, or a ship—it was about the only way he could take notes (and remember them). "Iceboxes. Gotta get Ernie on the boxes themselves, if Afronsan's finally okayed the deal, and get him pushing the deal harder, if the Heir hasn't sanctioned the import yet. Local cabinetmaker—then again, someone out of Bez might be better 'cause it's closer to the Pacific. Maybe one there and one in Podhru, from the start, but only if Ernie's talked to enough people to have some good presale numbers. Need someone who can build solid, classy-looking boxes and won't balk at my input about the metal lining and the insulation. Classy-looking 'cause Afronsan is gonna want to pass judgment on the design, bet anything, and he'll never go for something that looks like junk. Or is totally plain. Besides, they'll sell better if they look like cabinets people already buy around here. Guess I'll have to sketch out the interior basics before I leave." That wouldn't be too tough: just a box with a tight seal on the door, insulated somehow and lined with tin or whatever. "Make sure Ernie remembers we need someone who can follow my plans and make them pretty and for sure handle volume. Last thing we need now is a mess like the first blue jeans."

That could be the real problem. Generally, it was the most frequent problem he had any more (leaving aside a stubborn, aging and insular Emperor who thought anything new was Pure Evil, and a father-in-law with all the emotional stability of a schizo hamster). CEE-Tech was absolutely going to have to assemble a pool of craftsmen who could deal in volume. "There's a job for Ernie—in his 'spare' time."

But Ernie was good at that kind of thing, finding the right people for the job—and it was something he liked doing, fortunately. "It would drive me nuts." But Ernie had neatly resolved the jeans problem. (One of Fedthyr's buddies was reportedly still pissed off over his lost deal on the "blue trous." One of Ernie's contemporaries figured out mass production just fine; he was presently building a genuine assembly-line type factory to replace his old one-room operation.)

But jeans were going to be nothing at all, compared to iceboxes. Not everyone would wear jeans; people like Fedthyr wouldn't be caught dead in them. But ice on demand . . . Chris was just about willing to bet his shirt every owner of a cafe, coffee shop, or meat market, and every housekeeper in Bez and Podhru was going to line up for the means to keep food fresh and drinks cold.

He dug in his pocket for his watch: At this speed, they probably had another hour before they reached the city gates, which would get them to Kamahl's about noon. Ariadne and Dija were just behind him now; he could hear them giggling over something. Well, so what? he demanded of himself. *It isn't necessarily you, you know. They're girls; Ariadne couldn't walk in a bar back home, and Dija wouldn't even be old enough to vote, I'll bet. Probably the most giggling Ariadne's done in her whole life; figure on Dupret putting up with that, huh? Give her a break; at least she's enjoying herself, even if it isn't with you.*

He could still get silly as anyone, under the right circumstances; early morning with a lot on his mind and plenty to accomplish in the next two days just wasn't the best time for it.

The road was deserted except for them, though there was never much traffic between Podhru and Zelharri—not by this direct route, anyway; the surface was hard on carts and no one liked the cliff face. The new road from Bez to Duke's Fort connected with the old Podhru–Sikkre road; it was nicely surfaced, fairly level, and even with the extra miles out west and back east, it often took less travel time.

"Yah. You got to go through the mountains and camp on your future ranch. Forget the road." Behind him, Ariadne's laugh pealed out. He hunched his shoulders a little higher and held up his left hand, level with his nose, ring finger turned in to touch his palm. "Okay. Ernie, the icebox contracts, in case they aren't done yet." Middle finger down. "Ernie, cabinetmakers." Little finger turned in. "Eddie, the ship thing, three decent cabins on something soon and fast." He considered this and sighed. Not many fast ships came as far as Podhru; few of them had decent passenger space, and often late in the year it was hard to even find a ship with any kind of separate cabins. They might have to rough it as far as Bez and wait for another ship there. "Still. He's arranged something like the trip home, he changes it. That was gross." He ticked the fingers one at a time against his palm. "Contracts, passage, cabinetmaker, check. *Ho*-kay!" Index finger. "Eddie, find passage that won't leave for a day or two so maybe I can meet with the Heir about Zero and Jamaica—"

"What of Jamaica?" Ariadne had ridden up beside him; he jumped as she spoke almost directly into his ear.

His voice came out shrill and breathy, nothing like normal. "Yeek! Don't *do* that!" She tipped her head to one side and simply waited. Chris drew a deep breath and waited for his heartbeat to drop back to something near normal. "Sorry, I was thinking. Ah—Jamaica, right. The drug thing, this Zero? I told you someone's trying to sneak the stuff into Rhadaz, get people hooked on it. Emperor's Heir is going to want to know what I've found out, and I like to talk to him personally about stuff like that whenever I can. And there's some business deals he has to approve, I want to make sure he knows what's going on with those." Ariadne rode in silence for some moments, her eyes fixed on the distance. Her face was grave when she looked up once more. "Shall I—do you wish for me also to speak with this Heir?"

"You don't have to. It's your father, after all. I remember the stuff you told us back in Sikkre."

"Yes. But there is more I know—a little, at least." She frowned at her hands. "I have seen enough men and poor women who use it—it is shameful that any of my blood deal in such a thing. Perhaps the priests are right, that God will punish them when they die—but that means nothing to a man like my father. Or my grandpere." Her face was suddenly flushed; she gave him a sidelong look, shook her head. "I speak too much."

"No—hey. I feel the same way about it. Guys getting rich on

other people's misery—that's sick. And using the stuff deliberately to weaken people and take over a country—that's disgusting. I saw enough drugs and stuff back home, I don't want that
crap getting started here. So if I can do anything to slow it down
or stop it—"

"Just so."

"Yeah." He laughed. "Couple of happy crusaders, right? But if
you'd talk to Afronsan, tell him what you know? That would be
great. Maybe we can nail some of these jerks—I mean—"

"Jerks?" She considered this. "I will be pleased to 'nail' my
father—and any who aid him."

Sure. For revenge, he thought gloomily. Well, whatever
worked. He wondered what else she knew. *Could be anything.
Had to crowbar the little I do know out of her, and that was Jen
and Dahven, not me.* He put on a smile. "Great. Hey—thanks,
lady."

"Lady." She gazed at her gloves, then eyed him from under
her lashes. "Do you not understand by this long a time? My father is noble; by law I, however, am not—"

Chris shrugged. "Lady. It doesn't mean noblewoman when I
say 'lady,' okay? It's—ah—well, okay, it's like 'chick.' Except,
my mom would utterly kill me dead if I called her a chick, and
she doesn't mind being called 'lady.' "

"Oh." Ariadne was silent for some moments. "You know,
there is clearly too much time and too little for people to do in
your world, that they play so with words and what they mean."
She sat up straight, and pointed down the road. "Is this the city?"

Chris looked; he could just see pale walls between the trees
and the first few outlying houses. "That's it. Almost there."

"Good. And we go where? Because I could not possibly go
like this to meet an Heir—"

"We have a room above the shop of a local weaver, and you'll
have plenty of time enough to clean up. Don't worry about the
Heir, though; he's no more formal than Dahven. Puts up with
me, doesn't he? But I'll have to get us an appointment, and even
I need a bath and a clean shirt."

ALETTO's three men left them not far inside the city gates, at the
nearest inn. "No sense getting ourselves lost in all this city, sir."

"Tell *me,*" Chris replied feelingly. He fished in his pocket and
drew out four silver ceris, which he pressed into the man's hand.
"Yeah, I know, the Duke gave you enough for two nights' room

at least. Take it anyway, my thanks for the company and for riding all the way down here with us, all right?"

"Well—thank you, sir." The man smiled. "It was certainly better than patrolling the road to Cornekka." He sketched a bow in Ariadne's direction. "A pleasant journey to you, madam."

"*Merci.*" Ariadne's thanks were warm, and so was her smile, but her attention shifted at once to the city around them: The main street was already draped in bright banners for the Emperor's birthday fete; there were people and stands everywhere.

Vey caught up with Chris, who murmured, "I hope those guys weren't too insulted; I couldn't remember which name went with which of them, even after three days on the road."

"That was Drolen, but he won't expect you to recall that. You had other things to think about, after all."

"I guess." Chris waved a hand at their surroundings. "This suit you better than Sehfi?"

"Interesting." Vey glanced over his shoulder to make certain Dija was still with them and taking the city all right; but she was close to Ariadne, the two talking animatedly and pointing things out to each other. "Much more a city, yes. But, perhaps a little confined."

"The old outer walls up at this end are pretty high, yeah. The Street of the Blind Muse isn't close to the walls, though; it's more out in the open."

Vey grinned. "Yes. Harder to locate; I heard."

"Yah. Wasn't my fault we got lost. Besides, that was four years ago, ancient history."

KAMAHL himself greeted them at the entrance to his shop, and Enardi came down right on his heels. Chris gripped his arms; Enardi embraced him extravagantly and pounded on his back.

"Hey, Chris! You know? You look great! And this—clearly this is Madam Ariadne!" He crossed the small chamber and pounced on her hand. Ariadne's cheekbones were suddenly quite pink; her eyes very bright. "Dear lady, welcome to the Emperor's city."

Chris tapped his shoulder. "Ahem. Taking lessons from your dad? Kamahl, thanks again for letting the guys use your spare room. This is Madam Cray." It helped, all the times he'd had to introduce her in Bez, in Sikkre and Zelharri; the name and title came out without the least stutter or blush. "And her maid, Dija.

And a friend of ours from Sikkre, Vey, he's one of the Thukar's personal guard. Ernie, where's Eddie?"

"At the telegraph offices, checking for messages from Bez; he won't be long." Enardi extended both hands to grip Vey's and inclined his head politely to Dija, who smiled rather shyly and kept close to Ariadne's side.

"Good." Chris turned to the merchant. "You know, Kamahl, no offense or anything, but I didn't mean to land so many of us on you. Why don't I get the ladies a room at your cousin's inn—?"

He stopped perforce; Ariadne had discreetly taken hold of his elbow and was exerting an unpleasant amount of pressure on the nerve. "But no!" she said sweetly. "I would not dream of staying so far from you." She tugged at his arm and as he bent down, she hissed furiously against his ear: "You cannot leave me behind so easily as that!"

"But I will not hear of the ladies staying at an inn," Kamahl put in smoothly. He took Ariadne's hand and, like Enardi, bowed low over it. Chris freed his arm and backed away from her; somehow he managed to keep a straight face as Kamahl looked up. "There is my guest chamber; I would be honored if you and your new wife took it for as long as you stay in Podhru." He smiled; Chris could feel his face heating. Ariadne simply blinked.

"Hey, that's great," he managed finally. "Tell you what, though; I have a lot of business to work out in the next couple of days, and I shouldn't short the lady on sleep. But if she and Dija can have the room, I'll pay you—"

"Pay." Kamahl snorted. "What is this, pay? Find me more of that silk the southerners bring in from across the western sea at any price whatever, and I will buy, that is payment enough."

"Chinese silk? I imagine the Peruvians are still selling. Do what I can for you. And thanks." He turned to Ariadne, whose cheekbones were still quite red. "You'll like Kamahl's guest room; it's on the main floor here, I have to walk past it to get in or out, so you won't have to worry about *losing* me."

It would be like her, he thought anxiously, to ignore the broad hint that he couldn't go anywhere without her knowing; like her to start shouting at him. But she was once more on company manners, as she'd been at Duke's Fort: She gave Kamahl a radiant smile and a curtsey, and said, "But how very kind of you, to do this for Chris." Kamahl sketched a neat bow and kissed her fingers, then went to the back door to his shop to bellow down the hall. One of his weavers came running.

"Take this lady, and her servant, and her baggage—my good madam, that is all of your luggage, two small bags?—take them into the guest chamber, and see she has all she needs, then tell my son to tend the horses and send for Lasenya to have the tub brought to the downstairs guest room, and water for bathing. Also make certain there is bathing water in back for my good friend Chris."

Ariadne raised one eyebrow. Chris managed a crooked grin. "Hey. You'd probably like to see where I'm sleeping—if I get to, that is?" He winked at Kamahl; the merchant would never know what it cost him. "Gotta make sure the lady knows where I am, right?" He leaned down and murmured against her ear: "Grab my crazy bone again and I swear you're dead meat, okay?"

Ariadne didn't understand L.A. slang translated into Rhadazi via her own French but there was no doubting she was quick: She gave him a radiant smile that fell far short of her snapping black eyes and neatly folded her hands together at her waist. "But, of course. You must show to me, please, where you will be these next many long, dull hours." Kamahl's face cleared, and he beamed at them both impartially before he strode into the family quarters, shouting out orders as he went. Chris bowed Dija and Ariadne ahead of him so they could follow the apprentice weaver; Enardi followed them along the narrow passage, Vey right behind him. They could still hear Kamahl shouting at someone behind a closed door, some distance away.

The boy opened a door near the base of a narrow flight of steps and set Ariadne's bag just inside; Ariadne signaled Dija to go on in and handed over her small bag. The boy went on down the narrow hallway; Chris pointed Ariadne toward the stairs and followed her up. "So, Ernie, how come you're hanging around here at this hour, instead of breaking bread with Meriyas?" Enardi cast up his eyes and shrugged.

"She's getting a little of the medicine—you know? Her father tried to raise the dowry once more, and mine is howling. Besides, we have things to discuss, and Afronsan—"

"I need to see him, me and the lady both, actually. Think he'll mind?" Ariadne hesitated on the little landing, where three sets of narrow stairs branched; Chris touched her shoulder and pointed right.

"Mind? He sent a message early this morning, I have it up-

stairs, but basically it says he will keep open a little time today
at fifth hour if you are here, and if not, the same hour tomorrow.
Certainly he'll be delighted to meet the lady."

Chris's eyebrows rose. "Wow. Holding time open? For me?"

Enardi chuckled. "If you ask me, it's these infernal machines
for typing. His chief clerk said only the fact that no one in the
building knew how to use one kept him honest about sending the
Thukara's to Sikkre."

"Yah. Bet he was more worried about how the Thukara would
get even if he kept her typewriter," Chris said.

"You think? Perhaps. All the same, he mentions them every
time I see him, and I have never seen the man so pleased with
one of your findings—not even when he signed the papers for
the telegraph. You'd better obtain at least one and send it to the
man for his personal use, this next trip. You'll have a friend for
life."

"Works for me. That's one reason I have to get back to Cuba,
fast: Remember the paperwork from last trip, raw cotton to the
British in exchange for sneaker canvas? The guy with the typewriters is the brother-in-law of the milliner dude, there's some
kind of family politics going on with those two that I, like, do
not *even* want to know about. Bottom line is, the canvas deal
only works if the typewriter dude cuts a deal." Ariadne turned
and gave him a long look. Chris smiled blandly and opened the
door for her; Enardi edged past Ariadne to scoop up cushions
and stack them on the edge of the bed. She looked around in visible surprise at the size and plainness of the little room, then sat.
Vey wandered over to the window and gazed out across the
strange city.

"I am reminded." Enardi crossed to the table and fished out a
tied, flat packet of paper. "Signed two days ago."

"Ice contracts, right? All *right*!" Chris clapped his hands together. "Hey, that's great, Ernie, I knew I could count on you.
Remind me later, we gotta work on the cabinets end of things before I leave. First thing, though, I gotta get some laundry
washed; Afronsan's city guard wouldn't let me past the front
door like I am now, and I only have three shirts with me. And
I think Ariadne might—"

"Dija and I will manage the washing for me," Ariadne said
firmly as he hesitated. Her color was rather high. Oops, Chris realized. Not polite to bring up a lady's undies in public.

Or even between the two of them. "Sure, whatever you want.

But Ernie sends his to a couple of old ladies down the street. They do good work, they're fast—and they're poor."

"Oh." She tipped her head to one side, studied him for a long moment. "So you give them the business and pay them for it and they are no longer quite so poor. Does such a thing really matter to you?"

"I've been poor."

"Ah." She nodded. "Then as you please."

Enardi set the contract back down. "Your trunks and all are still in Bez, at my father's house. But Eddie said he brought a bag with clothes for both of you. It's against the wall, over there." He pointed to a stack of blankets, small rolled carpets and faded cushions.

"Buried, right? Like everything in this closet of a room. I'll dig it out in a bit. But that helps; maybe we can do the Heir this afternoon." He walked over to the window and picked up the packet of contracts. "Anything in here I should know about?"

Enardi laughed. "Like, you can only import the ice-making machinery if he first gets a typing machine? I don't doubt he thought of it—but it's not in there." He considered this, raised his eyebrows. "I don't think it is."

Ariadne got to her feet. "I leave you to your business; Dija will worry where I am."

Chris set down the contracts. "Sure. Want me to get that bag out now?"

"No. The gentleman spoke of a tub and bathing." She drew a loose strand of hair out where she could see it and wrinkled her nose. "No hurry at all. I will see Dija readies laundry."

Enardi hurried over to open the door for her and again bow over her fingers. Ariadne eyed Chris over the Bezanti's dark head; her smile was ironic, but warmed immediately as Enardi straightened.

"Thank you—it is Ernie, I think Chris said?"

"Ernie," he replied gravely. Ariadne inclined her head, turned and ran lightfooted down the stairs.

"Hey," Chris growled. "You got one of your own, okay?"

"But she is enchanting! Who would have thought the blue jeans could look so fine on a lady? And such an exotic! That hair, that dark skin and such eyes!"

"Well, her father's French and dark as a Bezanti, and her mother was black." Chris frowned. "African. You know."

"I know. They came to Bez in one of those elaborate ships this summer."

"The deal for medicines, sure. I forgot about that." He stroked his chin thoughtfully. "They didn't have any problems in Bez, did they?"

"Problems? How problems?"

"Because of—no one cared they're dark?"

"Why should anyone care about that? Marseli says the medicines they brew from their plants are fine ones and well made; what else should matter? They were different—but so? So are the English and the Mer Khani."

"You don't think people will treat Ariadne—different?"

"Why? But did they treat her different when you landed in Bez?"

"This last time? Who knows? I wasn't watching, but I had other stuff to worry about, if you remember."

"Like being wed and nearly killed all in one day?"

"Yah. Thanks for reminding me."

Enardi spread his arms in a wide shrug. "You are very light-skinned and blue-eyed and yellow-haired. Quite unlike most Bezanti. Has anyone given you trouble for that?"

"Mmmm—gotta point. Don't think so. I just don't want her getting hassled, she's had a pretty rough life so far, everything else and then—well, then me."

"Yes, Eddie told me all about this marriage. This is Rhadaz, Chris; we are civilized people. And she is a pretty lady with a warm smile; that will take her far."

"Yah. Doesn't she just." Chris made a face; Enardi raised his eyebrows. "Never mind."

Ernie always had a good ear for gossip, he remembered bleakly; no doubt he'd pried all the dirt out of Eddie, who of course didn't have any reason to not spill the whole mess. Enardi broke the silence. "I suppose she goes with you?"

"You kidding?" Chris asked gloomily. "Can't wait to get back down there and get her neck wrung by daddy's men, right alongside me. Except she's planning to pull his card instead." He grinned. "You better watch out for her, dude; she wears a knife next to her knee."

'But she—I mean, I would certainly not—" Enardi stopped and stared at him as Chris's last words sank in. "Knife? Eddie did not tell me about that!"

"Ask Vey, you don't believe me. She swings a mean sword,

too, ask Dahven." A tap on the door; the weaver's apprentice stuck his head in.

"Sir, a message from the Prince's offices for you." He held out a folded and sealed sheet. "And the master said to tell you, the tub in the wool storage is ready if you would bathe."

Chris looked up from the unfolded message, pulled the watch from his shirt pocket, and frowned at it. "Ernie, dig out that bag for me, will you? I gotta get my stuff out, take the rest down to Ariadne. There's just time to get clean and eat something—hope Afronsan doesn't mind a few wrinkles."

"Here, give me your shirt and whatever else; Kamahl's wife hangs mine in the dye room over the steam."

Chris ruffled through the bag, fished out a dark blue shirt, a silver-buttoned vest and a pair of Bez-denim pants. "The new pants and socks, too—great. Gold star for Eddie's forehead. I won't ask how he knew what of *her* stuff to bring."

Enardi picked up the bag. "He asked my sister Lasinay to pack the clothes for her, of course. Here, let me deliver this bag—and the message for you."

"Yeah, like I trust *you*." Chris grinned to take the sting from his rude words, and snatched the bag back. "You keep that knife in mind."

"Knife."

"I see Eddie," Vey said suddenly. He tapped sharply on the glass with his knuckle, waved enthusiastically.

"Great. You guys go ahead and catch up, I'll go bathe and take Romeo here with me. C'mon, Ernie, you can tell me things while I'm scraping the Sehfi–Podhru road off my hide."

DIJA peered anxiously through a very small opening when Chris tapped on the door, took the satchel and closed the door almost on his fingers; he had to knock again to pass on the message. "There isn't time for her to have a long soak, but she can catch up on hot water tonight, Kamahl always has plenty around." Dija nodded once and the door shut. "She's not used to so many people in such a small household, I guess, and it's all pretty strange to her," Chris said as he and Enardi headed toward the back of the house. "Never been out of Sikkre in her life."

"More likely your lady's in the bath already; Kamahl needs a privacy screen in his guest room for times like this."

"Yeah." Chris's voice trailed away. He blinked. "Anyway," he said in a determined change of subject. He opened the door into the room where Kamahl, his sons, and his apprentices bathed. The air was warm, very humid, and fragrant with lanolin from the bundles of raw wool stacked floor to ceiling along the far wall. Enardi went on down the hall with Chris's wrinkled shirt, then came back and settled on the nearby bench. Chris had already stripped out of smoke-scented clothes and was chin-deep in warm water. "Yeah. I was dreaming about *this* last night. I hate damp ground, you know?"

"For sure." Chris scrubbed down with a fat sponge, slid down until only his head and knees were above water. Enardi drew a deep breath. "Casimaffi—"

"Yeah, I heard he got off. For now, anyway. Creep."

"There is other you didn't hear," Enardi said flatly, and told him about his encounter with Choran. Chris eased partway back up to rest his elbows on the sides of the tub; his eyebrows drew together as the Bezanti finished his story.

"He actually said that?"

"Every word."

"I heard the dude wasn't too bright, but jeez. So, what did the city guard tell you?"

Enardi spread his hands wide. "I didn't go to the guard."

"You didn't—Ernie, damnit! You're the law and order guy around here; are you *serious*?"

"But—what good will it do? I talked with Eddie about it, we both agreed, the guard would think I made up the whole thing, to smirch Casimaffi—"

"Ernie," Chris broke in, his voice heavily patient. "You can't talk to Eddie about the guard; he grew up picking pockets and stealing stuff. To him, any city guard is The Enemy, and he's got no reason to love the Podhru guard after our first trip through here. Remember?" He shook his head. "Anyway, the city guard can think whatever it wants, including that you're out to get the old dude. Afronsan is running the show and he knows better, okay? Just because he had to let Chuffles slide this last time, the mess in Sikkre—"

"Chris, I have no proof, nothing but my word!"

"But it's *your* word, Ernie. Not like you're just some jerk off the street, you're Enardi son of Fedthyr, and the Heir knows you. Also, this is something for Afronsan to add to his list. Hell, Ernie, you know how the Heir works! He's methodical; betcha he's got a file on Chuffles and his bunch and it's probably half the size of the bay out there! So you got to keep him up to date on these things; you and I don't know what's going to be the key that tips things, but Afronsan does. Tell you what." Chris sat up the rest of the way, scooped soap from a curved pink shell on the floor next to the tub and vigorously rubbed it into his hair. "We go see him this afternoon, you come along. That way I know you won't talk yourself out of it again."

"I wouldn't—I mean—" Enardi spread his hands wide. Chris shook his head. Enardi sighed, got up to fill one of the large ewers with fresh water. Chris poured it over his head.

"You would so. Hey, guy, this is me, remember? I know you don't like making waves, but the Heir's not going to catch old Chuffles pulling something right out in the open where Rhadazi law can nail him, it's going to have to be what Jen would call preponderance of evidence—which means—"

"I know what it means." Enardi sighed again. "My father will never forgive me for doing this."

"Well, he's got to hear about it first, and he won't from me. He'd be a little less forgiving if you got killed, right? Come with us, damnit, talk to Afronsan. And then we'll get you your own personal rent-a-brute, keep you nice and safe."

"Yes. All right." Enardi sighed and went back to his bench, was quiet as Chris finished rinsing and dried off, then wrapped himself in one of Kamahl's enormous drying sheets.

"Oh, fritch, I forgot to bring clothes down. Guess I'll have to climb back into—"

"I'll fetch one of my robes."

"Yah. Ariadne sees me in a blue and purple stripy dress with my legs hanging out, she'll never stop laughing. Guess it's better than being caught by one of Kamahl's customers hanging out of a bath towel." He spread his arms wide, grabbed at the bathing sheet as it slipped. "You know, Ernie, this is ridiculous! We gotta get permanent CEE-Tech housing, here and in Bez at the very least. What's so funny?"

"Nothing much." Enardi was laughing as he opened the door. "Merely parallel thoughts. I have a house to show you, just down the street." He started out, then came back and shut the door behind him. "You know, I just remembered—what you said about knives, it reminds me. There is a tale I was told, back in Bez, when I was on the docks for some reason—I can't remember, maybe last summer, when the Africans were there? About a secret society of women, witches of some kind who live across the other sea, and then—what?—foreign women in the warm southern waters, one of the islands. A secret society of women assassins—"

"Sewing circle and terrorist society, no doubt," Chris said sardonically. "Or lady ninjas. You and your dockside gossip, Ernie, *rully*!"

"Well, some of it is true, you know," Enardi replied. "And this wasn't sewing—I'll remember, maybe. But your talk of Madam Ariadne and this knife, that reminded me."

"Yah. Likely assassin *she* is, there's nothing sneaky about Ari. She's more the stomp-right-up-and-clean-your-clock type."

"That sweet tiny lady! I don't believe it, you are trying to keep me from her. As if I would try anything, Chris! All the same, a little harmless flirting—"

"Yeah. Tell me that when Meriyas starts on *me* again."

"Why not you?" Enardi said gloomily. "She flirts with everyone else. I will bring the robe." Chris's laughter followed him into the hall.

Back in the washroom, Chris gathered up his dirty clothes and boots, and set them by the door. He walked back across the chamber to where he could catch a little sunlight from the partly open shutter and began vigorously toweling his hair dry. "Ladies' sewing circle and terrorist society—just like that button Juan's goofy girlfriend picked up at the gaming convention." He sobered momentarily, sighed. "Hey, Juan, bet you finally got that black belt." He finished toweling his hair, rubbed down his chest and laughed quietly. "Ernie—I swear, they see you coming and pull out the biggest whoppers they got. Island women assassins—yeah. I can just see her now, sneaking around the parlor and slipping arsenic in someone's tea." *Get real. Henri Dupret would've been dead years ago.* Chris shook himself. "Sure. Arsenic in the tea and a knitting needle right through the heart." He was still laughing when Enardi came back with the robe.

9

ROBYN stared out the window, sighed heavily and pulled the drapes. There wasn't anything to see anyway: gloomy, dead garden just beyond the small family dining room—even at ground level, she could barely make out the courtyard with its bare and weedy-looking shrubs, the black leaves and a few frost-blackened buds clinging to her favorite yellow rose bush. The central pool and fountain were nothing more than a blocky shape in the early gloom and fog. Down in Podhru there might be citywide celebration for the Emperor's sixty-fourth birthday. Here— "Can't even see Lialla's tower," she grumbled. "Hate this. Just hate it."

"You're not supposed to say you hate stuff, Mommy," Iana remarked virtuously. She was still nurseless with Frisa gone north, and had spent most of the afternoon trailing around Duke's Fort with her mother. Robyn smiled.

"Mom was bad, wasn't she? Let's go over and sit by the fire until your father comes down with Amarni, all right?"

"All right." It tickled Robyn, how sophisticatedly verbal Iana was for her age. Chris had been a very quiet child—*probably because of all the weird shit going on around him*, she thought glumly. But Chris had remained a quiet kid right through junior high, only really breaking out in high school. Not even then: He'd pretty much come into his own when they arrived here. *Makes a good big fish in a small pond. Hey, whatever works, he's doing real good.*

Iana was sitting primly on the hearth, feet dangling, skirts smoothed neatly over her knees and hands folded. *Little faker, she learned that look from her nurse; she's about as prim as a—a—* Nothing came to mind. She dropped down next to her daughter and slewed around to warm her hands at the fire.

"Mommy?"

"What, sweetie?"

"Am I—does Daddy not like me?"

Robyn stared at her blankly. "I—of course he likes you! Why would you even have to ask?"

Iana was quiet for a long moment, clearly seeking the words. "Because Amarni gets to go with him a lot and I don't. And Frisa said Daddy was upset because I made feathers and—and—" she shook her head in frustration; the light brown plait slapped her shoulders.

"Oh, sweetie, Daddy would love you no matter what. That's part of being a daddy. *I* love you, don't I?"

"Ye-es. But, Frisa said—said Daddy doesn't like when people make feathers."

"Well, he doesn't like it when other people do, but he still likes you, all right? He didn't get mad at you that time when you got mad and made feathers, did he?"

"No-o." She was quiet for a moment, digesting this.

"I think what Frisa wanted to say to you was most people can't, ah, make feathers. And so it kind of scares them."

"Oh." Another silence. Robyn wasn't sure how much of that made sense to Iana; some of it, anyway. Enough to reassure the child, she hoped.

"That's why I said you shouldn't get so angry, so you won't scare people. Understand?" Iana gazed up at her mother solemnly, finally nodded. "That's why your mommy doesn't get really, really mad—so *she* won't make feathers."

Iana giggled. "Mommy-feathers!"

Robyn laughed with her, but her heart sank. *I told Jen; you simply can't spook this kid.* She gave her daughter a quick hug. "Besides, Iana, that's no fun way to make feathers. You wait until the weather's nice, and we'll go somewhere private, just you and me. And I'll teach you how to do it right."

"Promise?"

"Sure. Cross my heart." She suited gesture to words, then tapped her daughter on the tip of her freckled nose. "But only if you promise not to fly out of your bedroom window once you know how, all right?" Iana giggled delightedly, but nodded and crossed her own heart. "Good. Or any time without Mommy. Because you could get hurt, Iana. And you wouldn't want to scare people here, would you? Because when you scare people, they don't talk to you and when they see you they go the other way."

Robyn frowned. How to explain something as complex as prejudice to a three-year-old, however bright, without scaring her away from people. . . .

But Iana regarded her, suddenly very wide-eyed and serious indeed. "I know. Frisa said maybe Joras would be afraid to put me on my pony if he knew about the feathers. And then Daddy would have to send him away. She said people would point and whisper."

"Daddy won't send Joras away, Iana. Joras likes you too much." *Aletto's guard captain spoils her rotten is what.* "Frisa's right, though. Some people would point at you and whisper, and you wouldn't like that, would you?" Iana shook her head vigorously. "Good. I guess Mom will have to teach them it's not a bad thing, then they won't be afraid. But meantime, we won't tell anyone, okay? Since it's just you and me that can make feathers—"

"Oh, no," Iana said confidently. "Amarni can."

Robyn's hands went cold. "Oh?" Somehow, her voice managed to show nothing but mild interest. "Are you sure about that? Because *I* didn't know about it!"

"*I* did. 'Cause he told me so."

"Told you so? You didn't see him do it?"

"No, he just said, 'cause he was there when Frisa told me not to get mad and do that, and later when she went to get our dinner, he said he could make them, too."

"Oh." She wasn't certain what to think about that: Amarni was after all nearly a year younger than Iana, and his grasp of language still very iffy. *Probably just trying to make her feel better, or not feel alone, or maybe trying to one-up her. That would be like him.* She was trying to decide what to say in response to this rather unsettling revelation when the latch clicked and Aletto came in, Amarni clinging to his back and giggling.

"Me, too! Me, too!" Iana shouted. But Aletto was favoring his bad leg and his brow was furrowed, his lower lip caught between his teeth. Robyn pounced and caught hold of the boy as they passed, scooped him off his father's back, and swung him around in a circle. Amarni shrieked with delight.

"You, sir, sit," she ordered Aletto sternly. Aletto managed a breathy chuckle and bowed, then lowered himself rather cautiously into his high-backed chair.

"Yes, ma'am. But only if this handsome gentleman sits next to me—*and*," he added loudly as Iana jumped to her feet and flung herself at him, "if this fair young lady sits on my other side." He looked up at Robyn and grinned. "You're out of luck this evening."

Robyn raised one eyebrow. "Ah. But *I'll* have you later."

"Oh. Ah." Aletto tried to copy her gesture but as usual both his brows went up. He grinned sheepishly and wrapped an arm around each of the children. "I could use a good rubdown; everything aches tonight."

Robyn nodded feelingly as she took her seat across from him at the six-person plain oval table she'd insisted upon as a replacement for the banquet-sized monstrosity Jadek had kept in here; the smaller table was just right for quiet family nights like this one, light enough that it could be moved out for larger and more formal events—and both cheap and tough enough that the kids couldn't hurt it. "It's all this fog and damp. I can feel the nasty sprain I did to my ankle a few years ago, and that arm I broke way back in Wyoming is absolutely howling at me tonight. I'll trade you later, rub for rub."

"Ah—hem." Aletto colored. He glanced at Iana, who was watching his face eagerly; at Amarni, who had clambered onto his knees so he could grasp the water cup already set out. Robyn filled it partway for him and watched him drink. Iana pulled her cup over and pushed it into her father's hands.

"It's over their heads," Robyn said. "Relax."

"Relax," Aletto said gloomily. He poured water, handed the cup to Iana. One of the women came in with deep, two-handled cups of broth for the children and thin-cut bread. Aletto waited until the food was set out, the children drinking soup, the woman gone, then said, "I guess you must not have heard, then. The guard caught Minett on her way back from the market—found her around the back side of the household tower, actually. Getting ready to attach a packet to a line hanging from Mother's window, for Mosay to pull up."

Robyn glanced automatically at Iana, who might make sense of some of that; Aletto followed her look but Iana was intent upon sopping the most liquid possible into her bread, just short of the point when it would break and fall into the soup, then transferring it to her mouth and leaving a stream of dribbles across the table top. Ordinarily one of them would have reprimanded her for it; tonight Robyn merely shrugged and lowered her voice a little. "He—it's what I think it is? Zero?" Aletto nodded. "And?"

"They—talked to her, over an hour before anyone came to even tell me. It's not pretty."

"I didn't expect it would be. Why you had them do it that way, after all."

"She was in tears the whole time; good thing it wasn't either of us. But they got a little out of her. She says it comes south from Cornekka but not via the main road—"

"We know that—"

"Let me finish," Aletto broke in crisply. Robyn bit back an angry retort: He must really be hurting tonight; ordinarily nothing would make him so rude. "She said her family—their father and mother—were taken somewhere, they're being held so she and her sister will do what they've been ordered."

He paused, drank a little plain water. Robyn nodded. "Which is get Zero into Duke's Fort. You believe the girl? About her parents?"

"Joras does, that's good enough for me." He sighed. "Bring it into Duke's Fort, yes. And spread it around the market. They were given a list of contacts in the market, just a few people, but one or two names on that list surprised me. I left a copy in our room; you can look at it later."

"Anything about where or how it comes into Cornekka? All the trouble they've gone to up there to keep the Duchy clean, Misarla will need to know—"

"Of course. A messenger just went out; why I was late."

"Oh. Sorry."

He managed a faint smile, squeezed her fingers. "It's all right." He looked around. "We're eating tonight, you and I?"

"I hope so. I can go get—"

"It's all right, stay put. Minett admitted Mother isn't really ill—nothing as bad as we thought, anyway."

"Not ill—just hooked. Because of them and their rotten dope." Robyn could feel her face heating. "It didn't occur to them to *tell* someone—you, me, your mother?—about the hold these people have on them? Ask for help instead of turning your mother into a junky?"

"Robyn, be reasonable! They're girls, little backwoods commoners, they don't think that way!"

"Oh? I'm a little backwoods commoner myself, and I used to call *our* city guard pigs! But even I'd have—"

"I know you better than that; you'd never have taken a problem like theirs to people you don't trust."

Count five, Robyn ordered herself. *Make it twenty.* Iana looked up from her broth, wide-eyed, and she managed a smile. "'S okay, kid, finish your soup." Aletto poured himself water, hesitated, then took her cup and filled it. "All right, Aletto, leave that. What now?"

Aletto drank, set the cup aside carefully. He would no longer meet her eyes. "Gods of the Warm Silences, *I* don't know."

"You'll have to tell Afronsan right away."

"I—"

"Get a message to Jubelo and Misarla, once you've had the guard wring out of those girls who's backing them, they can find the parents, and then—"

"We tried that! The guard did! They don't know anything! Who'd trust them with a secret like that anyway?"

Robyn picked up her cup, set it down again, water untouched. Her stomach churned. "You're giving up, aren't you? You're tossing in the towel on this stuff—"

"Robyn, I *talked* to Mother just now! I tried! It was—she was about half mad, it was awful!"

"I bet it was. I know how addicts get when they're strung out." Sudden certainty tightened her throat. "Aletto? Let me guess, you told her she could have it—you gave her that box, didn't you?" Aletto stared at his hands; his lips twitched. "You did, you bailed on this! Damnitall, Aletto! How could you do that? All the—you know it's killing her! And you're letting the stuff into the fort! How's Afronsan ever going to keep it out of the country if people like you pull stunts like this?"

"It's not a—we can control what she gets, make certain it doesn't spread, control how much comes in, I can't just—!"

"I *knew* you'd fold! I just knew it!" Robyn pounded the table with both fists; Aletto and both children stared at her, wide-eyed. "All right, who's next? Let it in, sure! Let it walk right through the front door, and who's going to want to try it next, Aletto? You? Maybe your guard, sure, that would be terrific! Get them all stoned full-time, and who's out there to watch the borders? Play into their hands, why don't you?"

"Robyn, I—" Aletto held out a hand. She slapped it away and jumped up, caught up her cup and slammed it to the floor. Water splashed; the cup rolled into a corner.

"Get yourself hooked, those guys out there would *love* that! Probably what they wanted in the first place!"

"Robyn!" Aletto staggered to his feet, swore as his weak leg cracked into the heavy chair. He clung to the back, lips tightly compressed; involuntary tears sprang to his eyes. Amarni stared at him, then threw himself from the chair and around the table. Robyn knelt and caught hold of him; Amarni was screaming at her, swinging his arms and pummeling her as hard as he could.

"Don't you make my daddy cry!"

"Amarni, stop that—!" Aletto started after him, froze at the end of the table. Robyn was staring down at the boy's arms—and the line of dark, downy feathers forming there. She knelt and gripped his wrists, pulled him against her in a crushing embrace; stricken blue eyes met Aletto's over the boy's head.

Aletto's mouth sagged; his eyes were wide with shock. "You—what you did—"

"I did—?" she echoed blankly.

"Your blood—and—and—look at my son!"

If she'd been able to lay a hand on him—but Amarni clung to her now, sobbing. She patted his hair and said very softly, "Your *son*? Is that all that matters to you, Aletto? Not my shifting, not your daughter—your son, the boy, the male, the heir—!" Her voice was rising; another moment and she'd be beyond control. He looked at her without expression; he must hate her just now. Iana was trembling. "The children and I will eat in the nursery tonight, Aletto," she said quietly. She got to her feet and added, very formally, "You may tell the cook to serve us there. Iana, come with me. Now, Iana."

Ordinarily, Iana might have objected; this was visibly new and terrifying to her and, subdued, she slid from her chair, skirted the table and the puddle of water on the floor, took her brother's near hand and whispered against his ear. Amarni rubbed a fist in his eyes, sniffed loudly, and let himself be led away. Robyn stayed where she was for a very long moment, eyes fixed on Aletto, who hadn't moved so much as an eyelash. Iana's quavering little voice broke the silence. "Mommy? I can't make the door move by myself." Robyn brought her chin up, turned on her heel and walked across the room, worked the latch and let the children precede her. The door closed behind them with a faint click.

"Thank you, Iana. Let's go, children." Her voice was trembling nearly as much as Iana's suddenly. "We'll have a picnic in your nursery, all right?" Iana glanced back at her and nodded. Amarni clung to his sister's hand and quietly trailed along after her.

He can't leave it at that, Robyn thought unhappily. *He'll come after us and I'll apologize—God, did I really say all that to him?* But they reached the wide, carpeted stairs, climbed them, walked down the hall to the nursery in complete silence.

ALETTO watched the door close, bit his lip. "Oh, gods, no. Birdy—Birdy, I didn't mean that, you can't think I meant—" He started across the smooth tiled floor at a lurching run and stepped into Robyn's spilled water. Already off balance, he flailed for a chair, the wall, anything, then threw up both arms to shield his head as he went down. His elbow hit the floor with a wicked crack; the leg under him folded. For a very long moment, he couldn't remember how to breathe. Somehow, he forced himself partway back up, but he couldn't move any farther. Everything hurt, much worse than it had when he carried Amarni into the room; searing pain flared from his ankle. *That's—the bottom of my boot*, he thought dazedly. *My foot can't turn over that far.*

THE latch to the nursery door was stiff; Robyn needed both hands to work it. She looked down at two very subdued children. "Daddy will be up in a few minutes, it's all right, you two." She set her shoulder against the door and shoved, hard. The door gave way grudgingly and swung back with a ratcheting creak that set her teeth on edge. "I think we better get someone to oil this door, what do you think?" No answer. Iana tugged at her brother's hand and drew him into the room. Robyn sighed faintly and followed.

It was warm and close, though the fire had burned down to embers; the room itself was otherwise dark. "Iana?" The children were dark shapes well into the room, blocking the glow of the fireplace. "Do you know where the lamp is?" *I thought I left it lit when we came down. Out of oil, I guess.*

Iana moved away from the fire. "I can get it."

"That's okay, kiddo. I'll—" Robyn had taken two steps into the room; the door was torn from her hand and closed with a sharp click behind her. As she opened her mouth to shout a warning, two bulky shadows rose from behind Iana's bed. One caught hold of Iana, yanked her off her feet and out of sight; the other tossed something into the center of the room and dove for Amarni. Robyn threw herself frantically toward the boy; there was a loud "pop!" and a cloying, horrid smoke filled her mouth and nose. She was unconscious before she hit the floor.

*   *   *

SUNDOWN went unseen; the Podhru docks were heavily fogbound and all but deserted. The air hung heavy and wet; plank walkways were slick and treacherous. Men worked to bring boxes and crates of goods in or take them out to the waiting boats which ferried them to waiting ships. Water slapped heavily against pilings, splashed over the low platform where two rowboats were tied up and a line of men shifted heavy crates from the dock down a spindly-looking ladder. Five ships were due to leave the Emperor's city at the turn of the tide, bound for Fahlia, Bez and points beyond.

Ariadne sat by herself in the new waiting area, bags at her side and chin in hand, staring at the nearest wall. Her free hand felt for and closed on her personal satchel; she kept a grip on the strap, sent her eyes sideways. Over near the door, Chris and Enardi were still talking—more of the business that had occupied them so totally the past two and a half days, she decided drearily. *But who was to know he meant this, that he did all the business himself? All the things for which my fiend of a father employs agents. . . .*

To her left, much nearer the small stove, her maid sat in a low chair; Vey knelt beside her and held her hands. Neither of them was saying anything at all, just now. Dija was abnormally solemn and pale, Vey quiet even for him. *Poor child.* But Dija wouldn't stay behind. Ariadne was glad: She was as fond of the Rhadazi girl as the girl patently was of her. *Honoria—Lucette. I did like both of them but I could never dare be certain of either, nor dare confide in them. Because of my father. This girl—* It was comforting to be so fiercely protected and cared for by someone. *If I could have that with a man. They say it is possible.* Looking at Vey and Dija, she could almost believe it. She shook her head impatiently, dismissed that. Innocents, those two. Babes in the matter of men and women together. One knew better of romance and of men, whoever said what about either. Romance: So many sang of how wonderfully tragic it was to die for love— *how foolish. Better to live, I would think.* And men: This man of *hers* said one might fly in a machine that went about the entire world in an hour, so high one could not breathe without a glass bowl upon his head. Or her head, because both men and women did this. He must intend to pull the chain, as he himself would say.

As if he could pull mine. I have seen a thing or two and heard of others.

She sighed heavily, shifted her chin from left hand to right hand, and closed her eyes. Chris was talking loudly enough that she could make out what he was saying. *Wretched machinery for making ice. If I hear of this once more within the next day and a half . . .* Chris's short, sour laugh broke into her thought. "Now, lookit, Ernie. You know what Vemoris is like, he's a good guy but he's out of date, almost worse than your dad's buddies. You gotta be tough with him. You know?"

"I know tough," Enardi said wearily. "Vemoris wants a contract with us so badly, but he could never keep up with the need for cabinets. And the metal lining—he can't make that."

"That's no big deal, I don't mind if someone else does the tin box and the main guy puts it together. Hell, I don't care if one guy gets all the parts from different places and only assembles the iceboxes. Bottom line is, quantity and a look Afronsan will accept—and let us sell. You were there, you know what he said, a really class product. Emperor won't pass it otherwise."

"I was there. No contract for Vemoris."

"Hey, Ernie. Tell him we'll help him gear up for volume production, it he wants. Then we can do business with him. That should keep him from hating you for life, shouldn't it?"

"It should help."

Ariadne slewed partway around and eyed the two sidelong. Chris clapped his friend on the shoulder and laughed. "Sure, it will. He's no dummy, he just needs to get out from under his old man's thumb, like you did." He turned and Ariadne looked up as the door opened and a sailor leaned inside, bringing damp, chill air and the distant sounds of celebration with him.

"Sirs, madam—the *Galifrey* will depart on the tide, as planned, and the boat will come in for you and your luggage shortly." He was gone before anyone could thank him. Ariadne eyed the stack of cases, bags and parcels with resignation. And this was only a small portion of their goods: Her trunks were still somewhere in this Bezjeriad, her green velvet and all its accouterments left with Chris's mother in Zelharri. *And still, all of this. So much new I owe him for.* She wasn't certain she liked it, being in debt to Chris. *But this is how it is supposed to be, how you learned. For all he says of women in his world, women here cannot do work and receive pay for it, and live apart. Unfortunately. Whatever I have, and will ever have, has come from men—father,*

uncle, and now Chris. She sighed, picked up her personal satchel
and settled the strap over her head and across her chest, made
certain the bag itself was comfortably low on her hip.

Chris had suggested jeans for travel. *They are comfortable.
But I would never dare wear such trousers in the south. The
black breeks I wore in the back alleys of Philippe-sur-Mer would
be best of all, but they are for private, not for others to see.* Dija
had remarked on them—Ariadne had put her off with a tale, im-
probable to her own ears, about wearing them for exercise. Dija,
innocent that she was, had accepted that without remark. *But I
did after all walk in them; and run.* And kill. She brushed that
aside with no effort at all. Eliminated, say, rather. As one
squashed mosquitos.

The blacks: The upper garment was smooth-fitting and fully
concealing, the scarves obscured hair, face and throat. The trousers: Loose, lightweight, snug at the ankle, they allowed freedom
of movement women's skirts could never permit; even the jeans
Chris bought for her were constricting in comparison. And the
jeans were too snug at the ankle; even if she could fit the knife
and its sheath under the jeans, even if it could ride there unnoticed, she couldn't reach up and free it. *I do not plan to need the
knife, or the blacks, really. But then, this Ernie never planned to
be met in an alley by a thug; Chris did not expect drugs in his
champagne or his orange.* Ariadne ran a hand across her leg just
above the knee; the strap was snug, holding in place as it was
meant to do.

Chris was still giving Ernie last-minute instructions. "He does
not even pay heed I am here—not that I care for that." She
scowled at her hands. The rings on her left hand, now hidden
under warm black gloves, made a sizeable lump at the base of
her finger. *One my mother's band, that my father gave her when
I was born.* And that Henri Dupret gave Chris to put on her hand
when the priest spoke the words. *Forced upon him. At least it
came to me, however I got it.* The other, an intricately wrapped
silver surrounding a large fire opal. She'd seen it in the Sikkre
market when he took her out to purchase those swords (and her
jeans) and had exclaimed with delight at the fiery, dazzling
stone. *And he purchased it for me, like that. Only because I liked
it.* Married women in France and Philippe-sur-Mer normally
wore emeralds or rubies, very refined gems set in gold. But those
were *normal* married women—properly contracted for, not won
or lost at cards. *Any woman can wear emeralds, if her man is*

wealthy enough. Or rubies. They mean nothing if they are only bought because they are costly and so others know they are.

She turned a little and watched Chris from under her lashes; he was talking animatedly, waving his arms, moving his head so the long blond tail bounced. Not what she would call handsome, she thought judiciously. Attractive, in a foreign way. Much larger and stronger than men she'd thought attractive before. *What woman in my skin would wish a man so much bigger than she?* The muscles—those she liked. Men Henri's age generally had bellies instead of muscles; if not, they simply sagged. Those men nearer her own age were most often pale and thin. Dissipated. The rich, at least. The rest were already worn from bad food, too much drink, heavy work in the factories or fields.

Ernie spread his arms wide and said something; Chris clomped him on the shoulder with a large, capable-looking hand and laughed cheerfully. *The laugh—yes, it is a good laugh; no malice or ill will in it. And the hand is strong, but I have not yet seen him raise it angrily.* He'd laughed like that with her, on that trip down from his mother's Duchy—once or twice. *When we were not screaming at each other for some stupid no-reason reason. My mother was right; I must learn control of this temper. Now that my father no longer commands my life—*

"Madam Ariadne? *Vas tu bien?*" Dija had come up on her unnoticed, and knelt beside her.

Her French improved hourly, Ariadne thought. But she answered in Rhadazi: "I do well, thank you. Your friend, do not leave him for my account."

Dija's cheeks were pink. "*On* my account, madam."

"On. Do not, though. Since I cannot convince you to return to Sikkre—"

"No, madam," Dija said very firmly as Ariadne paused. "Too late in any event."

"Bah. Your Vey has three horses to lead back to Sikkre; one could readily hold you."

"*No*, madam. Shall Chris comb your hair? Look at the mess he makes of his own! And Vey—" She glanced over her shoulder; Vey was talking animatedly with Chris and Enardi. "I like Vey as a friend. But I told you what he was as a boy. Why his hand—" she held out her own, palm down, left-hand index finger turned under at the second knuckle. "He has changed, at least as much as the Thukar himself. But it's so sudden—I think it would be better for us both to think a while."

"Ah." Ariadne nodded. *The child is not so innocent and simple as I feared.* She got to her feet and pulled Dija up, gave her a smile, a half-turn and a gentle shove. "Go. Talk to your man. Whatever else he may become, he is a friend; one should take what time one can with a friend, no?"

Dija smiled gratefully. "Yes. *Oui, Madam Ariadne.*"

The door opened, letting in more cold air and fog; Edrith came into the waiting room and shut the door hastily behind him, hurried over to Chris. "Here. I thought I would never get through all those people, it's like one huge party all the way from here to the north walls—on the *lit* streets, at least. *This* was on the table, buried under Ernie's papers." He cast the Bezanti a narrow-eyed, sidelong look. "You owe me."

Enardi shrugged. "Oh? And which of us was scattering papers here, there and across the floor?" Both turned to look at Chris.

"Well, hey, man," Chris growled. "It's hardly my fault we got so much paper this time around, and nowhere to put it. Ernie, definitely do what you can to get us that house, okay?"

"For certain."

"Yeah. I know, dude, in your spare time. All the same—"

"I put it at the head of my list—with the cabinetmaker. But, you know—"

The door was flung wide; two common ship-hands came in, followed by a dark-haired, heavily bearded man in officer's jacket and hat. His English was accented; neither Mer Khani nor English, but something Chris couldn't quite mark. "I am second master of the *Galifrey*. Ladies, gentlemen." He removed the hat and bowed. "The tide turns shortly, if you will be so kind as to come with me now, these men will see to your bags and goods."

"Gotcha," Chris said. He strode over to join Ariadne. "How much of this you want me to carry?"

"I have the only bag I need for now." She touched the wide strap. Chris picked up two of the bags atop the stack, handed them to one of the seamen, took the one beneath that held his personal gear and bowed her ahead of him. Edrith picked up his personal bag, and went out behind him. Dija came after with Ariadne's cosmetic box; Vey took it from her and took her arm. Enardi looked at the remaining pile, shrugged and followed.

Ariadne shivered: The damp air seemed to seek her bones; it swirled across the dock, blurring the close-set light poles. She drew the black scarf over her hair, tucked the ends across her throat and shivered down into her thick shawl. Just behind her,

Chris was grumbling to Edrith, "Jeez, will I be glad to get away from this! I hate fog like nothing else."

"Yah. I wager it's just like this all the way down the Gallic left coast."

"Worse," Chris said gloomily. But the two laughed, and Ariadne smiled into her scarf. The laughter was infectious. The second mate was drawing away from them, now only a darker shadow on a too-dark pier. She lengthened her stride.

Behind her, Edrith tugged at Chris's sleeve and spoke close to his ear. "Something's not right. This guy—second master?"

"Yeah?"

"He looks—familiar."

"You arranged the passage. You maybe saw him then."

Edrith shook his head. "Not from here. Just—familiar. Not good familiar, either."

"Why?"

'Don't know."

"Probably jumped his last ship and signed onto the *Galifrey*. Guys do that, you know."

"I know. But—"

"Well, then," Chris began. He looked up as Ariadne slipped on the planks some distance ahead and swore.

Edrith smothered laughter. "Her Rhadazi improves."

"That's improvement? You know what my mother would do to me if *I* said that?" He stopped and turned; someone way back down the pier was urgently calling Enardi's name.

"What message?" Enardi shouted. Chris couldn't quite make out the reply. Enardi sighed. "All right—a moment! Chris, wait, will you? It sounds important."

"I'll try," Chris called back. Enardi ran back up the dock. Someone else was walking very quickly, coming toward them.

Edrith gripped Chris's upper arm suddenly. "Him!" Edrith hissed sharply. "Isadya harbor, last fall—that man of Casimaffi's, it's a trap!" The footsteps were suddenly right behind them, coming fast; Edrith's hand was torn from Chris's arm and he gasped as powerful hands took hold of his arms and clamped them to his sides; Chris was gone, running down the pier for Ariadne, who was already down the inclined gangway and almost at the boat.

"Ari! Stop, it's a trap!" he shouted. Ariadne let out a squawk; he heard a scuffle, the sound of a body falling. He couldn't see her or either of the men with her. Behind him, Dija screamed; someone swore in Rhadazi and someone else in English. Chris threw himself down the gangway. Ariadne lay at full length, the second master on his knees beside her. As gloomy as it was down here, there was enough light for Chris to see the long knife in his hand.

Her lips moved. "Go!" Before he could even draw in enough air to yell, one of the other men gripped his wrist and twisted it up between his shoulder blades; cold metal touched his jaw and settled against his throat.

"You do not move," a voice whispered against his ear, "and nothing bad happens. Indicate you understand." Chris sent his eyes sideways; the man who held him was just enough shorter that he couldn't see anything but a large hand and the heavy knife-hilt. He nodded, very cautiously. "Sensible. Step into the boat. Quietly. Or the lady—" The second master moved the knife a little; Ariadne bit her lower lip.

Chris was all but trembling with fury as he nodded a second time; he let himself be guided into the boat. Something slammed into the back of his head, and he fell. He could hear Ariadne's whispered protest, smell her familiar scent; her heavy skirt cradled his face. The boat rocked heavily as it was pushed away from the dock.

Behind them, Eddie's voice rose in an astonished yell; a loud splash followed. Then nothing.

"TRAP!" Enardi heard that much; he hesitated, then turned and ran back toward his friends. Men everywhere; he couldn't see much but there was plenty to hear: feet scuffling on smooth boards, oars slapping hastily into the water. Eddie's shout and an enormous splash.

Shapes loomed up ahead of him—not Eddie, but Vey and the maid, he trying to hold her, she fighting wildly to get away. "Dija, don't!"

"Vey, they've taken her! They've—!"

"What can you do? Dija, wait!"

Enardi plunged on past them. He couldn't see anything out here; the fog had grown thicker, and at least one of the lamps was gone, or burnt out. A tall, thin figure loomed up before him. "Eddie, thank goodness—!" he began, then stopped and caught his breath on a faint, frightened squeak. It wasn't Eddie. This man was one of the foreign sailors, and in his right hand, very steady indeed, was a long, broad-bladed sword. Enardi spread his hands wide and began to back away. The foreigner grinned, white teeth shining against a dark beard, and stalked after him, sword at the ready. "Now," Enardi said nervously. "Now, you don't want to start a scene on the Emperor's docks. . . ." The man only smiled more widely and began to edge to his right. *He's cutting me off, pushing me back toward the water!* A moment's panic. He swallowed it. *I can swim. Get me near enough to the edge of the pier, and filthy as this water is I'll jump before* . . . He could hear frantic splashing all at once. *Eddie. Gods of easy profit, they threw him in, and he can't swim, he'll drown!* He *had* to go in.

Someone behind the foreigner: Suddenly, Vey was there, his face grim and something long, thick and solid in his upraised hand. He slammed it down across the back of the man's neck; the sword fell, its owner groaned and collapsed onto it. Enardi dragged air into his lungs. "Eddie's out there; stay close, you'll have to help me get him out." He then turned and dove into the water.

It was dark, the water obscenely cold, the air seemingly even colder when he surfaced, and his new boots suddenly impossibly heavy. He trod water, sought direction and used the moment to bring his feet up and pull the boots off. Black on black on black—but Eddie wasn't far from the pier at all. Enardi followed the sound of splashing, of rapid and terrified panting and trod water again. "Eddie! Eddie? My friend, help me find you, say something!"

"Help—me—!" He'd never have known it for Eddie's voice. "I will!" He judged direction as best he could. His second long overarm stroke came in contact with a shock of wet hair just beneath the surface. He clutched hard, kicked furiously and got a better hold as Edrith came up whooping for air and flailing wildly. Enardi drew a deep breath and shouted, "Vey, lie flat on the dock and hold out your arms, I have him! Easy, Eddie—" His own head went under. He kicked hard and got them both to the surface, tightened his grip on Edrith's hair and backed away from him; his shoulder slammed into one of the pier uprights, and he swore. Then Vey's capable hands were there, gripping his arm and moving down it to find Edrith's wrist. "You're safe now!" Enardi shouted; a wave caught him full in the mouth. Edrith was coughing so heavily it was doubtful he heard. "Vey—wait, here's his other arm, hold him steady. I'll climb up and we can—" But he didn't have the strength for that, suddenly; his legs felt like iron weights and his hands were too cold to grasp anything.

"I have him," Vey said calmly. "Eddie, I have you, don't fight me. Ernie, you'll have to help me, I can't pull him in alone."

"I—I can do that." *I will have to*, Enardi thought tiredly.

"Here." Dija's tear-filled voice. "I can help you hold—"

"No," Vey said. "They've gone?"

"I—bastards!" Dija swore viciously. "They're gone, yes," she added flatly.

"Then we can't do anything for them, Dija. Eddie needs help. Walk along the edge, help Ernie find a low place so he can get out."

Without Dija talking to him, guiding him, he wasn't certain he'd have made it. Moments later, he lay flat on the low boat platform, trembling as chill air whispered across his wet clothing and bare feet, gasping for air, unable to move.

Somewhere out there, a rowboat had surely reached its destination. Somewhere in the fog, down the dock, he could hear Vey calmly talking to Eddie, who was still coughing. Then shouting from the head of the dock, and the unmistakable whistle of the city guard.

Help: but too late.

10

lost something there, Chris thought dazedly. Eddie's terrified yell and a splash were the last things he could remember— now he couldn't hear anything but the slap of waves against the side of the boat, the "ploosh" of oars. His ears rang, which didn't help. The scented lotion he'd bought for Ariadne in Sikkre's market teased his nostrils; her thighs cradled his head. *Probably have busted it open otherwise.* Not that that was going to save him. *Nasty thought. Chill, Cray.* He eased his right arm cautiously forward and something smacked hard against the back of an already sore head; a voice just behind him snarled a warning. Light flared behind his eyelids and everything went.

This time, he couldn't have been out for more than a breath or so, and he could suddenly hear Ariadne—her voice high, frightened and very unlike anything he'd heard out of her before now. "Please, do not—" She gasped and was suddenly quiet. A moment later, she shifted her leg cautiously; the man who'd held her down growled warningly. She cried out and her leg jerked. Chris's cheek was suddenly pressed hard against the inner edge of her thigh, just above the knee—against smooth, hard muscle and an even harder thing. *Knife. That nasty frog-sticker she was wearing in Jamaica. She's foxing them, has to be! Letting them think she's a scaredy-girl type and letting me know about the knife.* At least one of them was thinking. His spirits rose, but only briefly. *Great*, he decided sourly. *There's three of 'em here, and who knows how many waiting for us? And if she moves, they cut her throat. I* can't *move, but if I try they flatten my skull. Or—oh, hell, with my luck, she's really blowing it big time.*

At least the men hadn't simply batted them both over the head and dropped them in the harbor. Which could mean someone on

165

their ship wanted to talk to him first. *Hey. Thinking again yourself.* It wasn't much of a thought: The someone might want to do more than talk.

His head ached ferociously. Lialla's trick with Thread for fixing a crack like he'd just taken—yeah, he could probably still make that work, but not here: It took more peace and quiet than he was going to get here—more than he was likely to get from now until these guys—*Hey. Forget that kinda spook-yourself thinking.*

The boat was rocking more than it had been—farther out in the harbor, where tide or river surge could hit it, maybe turning from its original course. He kept his eyes closed and lay very still. Ariadne smelled good, he decided.

One of the men behind him suddenly stood; the boat rocked wildly, then steadied. Ariadne flailed for something to grab hold of; Chris heard someone snarl at her and she froze. Voices above them, low and urgent, speaking Rhadazi. But that didn't tell him anything; most of the Americans and English who came here spoke some Rhadazi. At least one of Dupret's men on that Philippe-sur-Mer dock had spoken unaccented Rhadazi. *Don't think Dupret, okay?* Dupret would be the absolute worst he could think of—here in Podhru harbor, yet.

Someone grabbed him by the collar and hoisted him to his feet. He swayed as everything around him tilted. What little he could see tilted: Out on the water it was dark and extremely foggy, the only really visible objects the boat he was in and the rowers holding it steady, the ship next to them. He could hear a ship moving past them; someone in its bow hammered on the enormous brass bell that would warn other ships away. The man who held him tightened his grasp, almost cutting off his air, and held up the knife where he could see it, then gestured. Chris nodded carefully, and shut his mouth. Tight. *As if yelling at a passing ship for help was useful.*

Two very large men were helping Ariadne up the thick mesh cargo net slung over the side; she looked like a limp doll between them. *Good kid, don't fight 'em.* He hadn't expected that many smarts of her. She vanished into the gloom, high above. "You next," his captor hissed into his ear; onion and tobacco engulfed him. "And try nothing. Remember where the lady is, and what I hold."

"Yeah," Chris muttered. "Hold me, too, why don't you? My balance is shot." The knife pressed into his collarbone. It hurt. "Hey," he growled. "Cool that, I'm serious. What d'you think I'm gonna pull on you anyway? I can't walk back to shore from here and the lady's up there, remember?" There were two men still in the rowboat, waiting for him and his knife-holding companion to go up. Both were suddenly visibly armed and watching him closely. *Either they're worse than those camel-dufusses who tried to murder my feet, or else I've got me one helluva rep these days.* It gave his spirits another small boost, but did absolutely nothing to help him up the net; in the end, his exasperated captor had to call for help, and two of them hauled him over the rail and dropped him on the deck.

Hell with them all. My head's screaming at me; I'm staying down. Silence, except for the creak of rigging and the sound of chain rattling—either the anchor or the boat coming up. Footsteps on the planking then; large boots stopped just short of his face. "This is the right man?" A low, very quiet and inflectionless voice—definitely one he didn't know. *Not Dupret. That's something, anyway.*

The man who'd hit him said, "The hair, the voice, the men on the dock who came with him and this woman—all tally."

"Good. Did you search him?"

"Well—"

"Do it now." Chris went limp and let hard hands poke at his ribs, his legs, check his boots, run over his pockets and his belt.

"No weapon, sir."

"The stick—I'm told he carries a stick—"

"If he had one, sir, it didn't make the boat with him."

"All right. Tie him. Securely, and I do mean securely."

Chris bit his lip, forced himself to remain limp. His arms were dragged behind his back, secured at elbow and wrist, his ankles tied but separately.

The boots moved away from his face, scraped to a halt a few paces away. "You, woman," the voice said crisply. "Your name, and his, at once, please." Ariadne made a strangled little noise. Silence. "We aren't going to hurt you, why should we? Someone wants to speak with your husband, nothing more."

"To speak—" Ariadne managed that much in a tremulous voice and unusually French-accented Rhadazi. She whimpered for some moments, apparently trying to gain control. The man the others called "sir" waited her out. "To speak—and for that, you do this to him, and to me? That—that man, upon the docks, I am cut at the throat, there is—is—there is b-b-blood . . ." She caught her breath on a sob and Chris could hear her weeping—trying to be quiet about it, not totally succeeding.

One of the other men spoke after a moment. "It's her, sir, the Frenchman's daughter. That's their accent."

"Mmmm—aye. Ariadne Dupret, aren't you? And this man the merchant Cray?" Silence again. She must have nodded. "All right. Tie her as well and put them down in the storage; all the noise you made, the city guard will be out here after us before we can get away." There was an edge to the voice now.

"Sir, I'm sorry. But that Sikkreni recognized me—"

"I know, all right. No one's fault."

"I didn't even know he'd seen me before," the man said resentfully. "And Nerlin didn't make it back with us."

"Bad luck, nothing more. Nerlin knows where to go, just as you did if you'd been stranded. Leave it, it's done."

Bare feet slapped the planks, someone came sprinting up. "Sir, we're passing the harbor entrance right now, we'll be in open water any moment."

"Well. Good. So much for the city guard. What of this fog?"

"There's enough breeze, we can manage. Steersman knows the north shoreline well enough, and he says the east wind will pick up around midnight."

"Good. You all know your tasks, get to them. I'll be in my quarters if I'm needed. Get these two off the deck and out of sight, just in case."

Feet—bare and booted, all running; the boards shook under Chris's cheek, setting his head to pounding worse than ever. He heard a gasp from Ariadne, then gasped himself as one of the men grabbed him by the elbows and hauled him to his feet; agony flared hot through both shoulders. He had a brief, confused glimpse of hurried activity all around him, sails being shifted in the gloom and fog, the mainsail just above and ahead of him billowing in a sudden breeze; then a dimly lit square of a doorway leading to a shallow flight of steps.

They'd hobbled him, and the rope between his feet wasn't long enough to properly manage the steps. He skipped down the last two, nearly overbalancing the guards and gaining him a hard blow across his ear.

"Leave off," the other guard growled. "Get them stowed, there's work topsides." A lantern hung from a hook beside the steps, the flame burning very low; he could make out the low-ceilinged passage and closed doors on both sides. The man who'd hit him kneed one of the doors open, let it slam against the inner wall and shoved him inside.

Chris staggered, took half a dozen short, quick steps; badly off balance, he slammed into the far wall, then fell hard, facedown, onto a low pile of sacks. Ariadne landed on him and the door slammed shut, throwing them into total darkness. Flour dust rose from the bags. Chris fought a sneeze. "Let me up, damnit!" Ariadne couldn't hear him: She was cursing under her breath in ripe, furious French. If she'd been terrified up there, she certainly showed no sign of it now.

He sneezed resoundingly; Ariadne jerked away from him, startled, and slid to the floor, where she landed with a loud and probably painful thump. When she got her breath back, she was cursing again, but now, Chris realized gloomily, she was cussing *him* out for scaring her. "Oh, the *hell* with it," he muttered sourly. And sneezed again.

*   *   *

"EDDIE, my good friend. Eddie?" Edrith could hear Enardi's panic-ridden voice over the soothing monolog Vey was using to try to keep him still. He tried once again to be still, to breathe normally; he coughed rackingly as a trickle of cold salt water slid down the back of his nose. They were talking up there, but he couldn't make out the words over the noise he was making, and the shrill ring in his ears. Hands fumbled at his wrists; Vey had him two-handed by one arm and now Enardi had the other in a surprisingly firm grip. "Eddie," he called urgently. "Listen, we're going to pull you out, but you have to help us. Use your feet against the piling, push up when I say—*now!*" It wasn't much of a push: He was utterly exhausted, trembling now as much from cold water and chill air as from reaction, and his feet slipped on the slimy piling. It must have been just enough, though; he felt himself almost flying into the air and then he slammed into the planks, face-down. The edge of the pier cut across his shins.

A soft bit of cloth was being rubbed vigorously over his face. He pried his eyes open. Enardi crouched beside him, one of his pale linen kerchiefs clutched in his fist, and stared anxiously into his face. "Gods of easy profit, but you *are* pale, Eddie. Did you swallow any of that?" Edrith let his eyes sag closed, nodded. "Don't move, and don't worry; you're ashore now, that's the most important thing. We'll get the water out of you in a moment." Edrith nodded again and listened without much interest to the conversation going on just above his head. "Vey, it's been forever since those men attacked us. Where possibly is the city guard—?"

Vey shoved to his feet. "The fog has slowed them, I wager. Or the fete. But it hasn't been as long as you think. Still—I'll go look." Edrith felt the dock sway slightly under him as Vey pounded back up the dock; he gasped and clutched at the boards. Enardi gripped his arm.

"That's just Vey, you're all right. We won't let you back in there, Eddie. Dija, take that scarf, please, and—"

"Not scarf." Dija sounded near tears. "It is madam's shawl."

"Yes, well, she'll understand if you use it to dry Eddie's face and hair and wrap it around him. It's cold out here, and he's soaked." Edrith sighed very faintly as warm, fragrant wool enveloped his arms and upper body. "All right, my friend." Enardi's weight came down on his back, and the Bezanti began working his arms over his head. Edrith shook his head suddenly and tapped at the Bezanti's arm. Capable hands stripped him of Ariadne's shawl, hauled him to his knees and around toward the water; Enardi held him while he was miserably and violently sick, then drew him back from the edge of the pier and wrapped Ariadne's thick shawl around him. Enardi's square, capable hands pulled him close and chafed his back. "Here, you'll be all right now."

"All right?" Edrith whispered peevishly. "I feel worse than I did, you know?"

"You'd feel worse if you kept that water inside you. Dija, why don't you go back into that waiting room and rouse the dockmaster? Find this poor man something to drink so he can wash the taste from his mouth." The girl's light footsteps pattered back up the dock. The two men could hear the rhythmic splashing of water hitting the pier, the more distant and confused creakings of ships leaving the harbor at the tide. Most, Enardi knew, would anchor beyond the bay once they'd taken advantage of the shift in current and higher water; they'd wait for the fog to lift and for good winds, which came around midnight most nights this time of year.

Suddenly, he could hear men shouting a good distance away, back toward the city. Edrith heard it too. "I think Vey—found the guard." His voice was extremely hoarse, hard to understand. Enardi pretended he didn't notice.

"I think so. Are you better?"

"Maybe a little. Mouth tastes awful and everything's—mmm. Yeah. Dizzy."

"I am not surprised. The things in that harbor—!"

"Don't tell me," Edrith replied sharply. He suddenly sounded much stronger, and he pushed Enardi away. "Did you see—?

Rully! That man threw me in there! Picked me up like a sack and threw me in that—that—on purpose, you know?"

"I saw. Frightening. I would have been terrified if I had been you. Of course, I'm Bezanti, so I swim." He leveled a finger at his companion's nose. "Eddie, you swore to me you would learn!"

Edrith sighed heavily, spread his hands in a wide shrug. "I—well—"

"I was thinking then," Enardi went on severely, "of boats and ships, and accidents which befall both, not men deliberately trying to drown you!"

"I- yeah. All right," Edrith replied gloomily. "So I messed up. So throw me back in. I—Ernie!" He stared wildly all around, then tried to scramble to his feet; partway up, he swayed and fell with a heavy thump onto his backside. Enardi caught hold of his arm. "They've got Chris and Ariadne!"

"I know they do."

"What're we gonna—?" Edrith dragged the shawl from his shoulders. The sounds of the guard were much closer; he still couldn't make out what they were shouting, or see them yet. "We need horses, fast ones. A couple of good lanterns. That lousy coast road—but if we can reach Bez before that ship hits the isthmus . . ."

"Eddie," Ernie broke in. "You and Chris have been entirely too long out there, you know? You sound like those kinds of men."

"You forget who I am—or was," Edrith replied flatly.

"No. You *were* a market thief. Now, you are a successful businessman; you have money and prestige—*and* the ear of the Emperor's Heir. This is serious, Eddie, it's not just boys picking pockets! Afronsan can manage this better than you or I." Edrith shook his head stubbornly. Enardi threw up his hands. "Damnitall, Eddie, even the Emperor won't stand for something like this! Kidnapping by violence upon his very docks? And even if we *could* reach Bezjeriad before that ship does—which I very much doubt—what could we do then? No. We go to Afronsan so he can wire to Bezjeriad. And then—"

"Hah. The line from here to Bez isn't complete yet, you know that!"

"It's near enough. There are horsemen at Duke Lehzin's palace and a hut at the nearest pole to carry messages those last miles. Do you think *Lehzin* will stand for such funny business as this, at his very doorstep?"

"I think it's a large sea, and a broad isthmus," Edrith said grimly. "And I think a ship can evade him—if they don't simply tie Chris and Ari in sacks and dump them in the middle of—" He shook his head violently.

Enardi closed his eyes and shuddered. "Yes. I know that's possible. And if so, they're already dead, for all we can do. But if they wanted only to kill Chris tonight, once there was no chance of doing it quietly as they clearly planned, why not simply murder them on the spot? Why bother to take them?"

"Maybe." Edrith swallowed.

"If they were taken as far as the ship, why delay the killing? With this fog, twenty strokes of the oars from here is as good as twenty leagues and in the very center of the sea, don't you think? But Vey swears he heard nothing save us, and the sound of oars. No cry, no splash—"

Edrith groaned and clutched at his head. "I don't know what to think. My brain is full of salt water, I can't think."

"Then let me. Lehzin is better equipped to block the isthmus from the north than you and I, he has good seamen, plenty of ships and barges—and he has a good relationship with the Gallic State on the south shore, I'd wager they'll help him." Silence. "For real, Eddie, we have to tell Afronsan. For anyone to pull such a stunt—that shows nerve, and I think great fear also. Why take them here? They could wait for the three of you to reach one of the foreign ports; who would miss you there?"

"Yeah. If they were in some hurry—but what could matter that much? What's today, besides Shesseran's birthday? And why us?"

"You stir wasp nests and ask that?" They could hear Dija's voice; the planks under them rattled as men came running.

Edrith sighed. "All right. Afronsan. Chris would kill me if we didn't. You had better be right, though, Ernie; I'll hate us both forever if we did this wrong."

*   *   *

CHRIS sneezed resoundingly. Ariadne snarled something in French and he snapped back in English, "Will you like, *shut up*?" Dead, rather nasty silence. He sniffed loudly and rubbed his nose on his sleeve. "I mean, jeez! Like I can help it my face is full of flour?"

"Are you done making justified of yourself?" Ariadne inquired flatly.

"Justi—oh, like it's *my* fault we're down here?"

"You say it is mine? Did I not try to tell you to run? Would anyone with *sense* not have run from that boat and those knives?"

"Well excuse *me* if I couldn't quite run off and leave you there to get mangled!" Chris replied huffily. He was testing the ropes that bound his arms—without any success. "I *hate* this," he mumbled. "It's totally as gross and uncomfortable as last time and I really, truly hate it!"

"They threatened me with the knife to make certain of *you*," Ariadne said sourly after a moment. "You had only to run—"

"Sure. Pardon me, but I don't operate that way. Besides, before I could even say boo, that clown had me in a hammerlock and that big ugly frog-sticker of his shoved up against my carotids, no way I was going anywhere." Another nasty silence. "I'm *sorry*," he added; he didn't sound it and probably Ariadne didn't care. But if she'd been able to decipher three words of that— He only just resisted the urge to slow his speech as if to the mentally slow. "All right, by the time I saw you were in trouble it was too late. They were ready and we weren't, and the guy had a knife at my throat. I try not to mess with guys that have a knife at my throat, and besides, I didn't think you wanted to take a bath in my blood, okay?"

Another silence. Chris managed to edge up onto one elbow and get his face out of the flour sack, which helped enormously. *Probably figuring how to get at that knife and take that bath*, he thought crossly. But when Ariadne finally spoke, she sounded wary or possibly curious: The hold was so dark, he could barely make out where she was, let alone see her face.

"You—would really not have simply left me?"

"Hey. I told you, didn't I? I don't lie about things, in case you still haven't figured that out—and my mother didn't raise me to run when things get tough. You, her, Jen—anybody I care for in a spot like that, I'd do what I could for 'em."

"Oh." She was moving down there, cloth shifting against him as she edged up the sacks slowly and carefully. Her scent was faint, nearly buried under the odor of rye flour, salt-soaked wood, and a few unpleasant things he preferred not to identify— still evident, part of her, really, and rather pleasant. "Here," she said quietly after a moment. Her hair brushed against his chin and then his ear; her breath tickled the hairs on the side of his neck. "My knife—they did not look for weapons on me, I still have it, but I cannot reach it. Can you free it for me?"

"Yeah. Hey, you really did that good, playing all scared like that."

"I thought it better. After all, if one keeps an eye to the main chance—"

"I know; get 'em off guard so you can wipe the floor with 'em

later on. Believe it or not, I usually take better care of myself
than this." He shifted his weight; flour tickled his nose. "Hold
still, okay? I'll try." It took some work, getting rolled over and
facing the other direction, with nothing but his knees and elbows
for leverage; he was panting when he finally got into position
and he'd scraped his chin on the sacking. It stung. Ariadne's hard
elbow thumped into his back a moment later, and he snarled,
"Ow! Hey! Watch those ribs, okay? I might get to use those!"

"Be silent!" she hissed sharply. Chris sighed and compressed
his lips. Ariadne's skirts slid along his thigh, then her soft, low
boot slipped into his left hand. "There. That is the leg."

"Hold still. This may take a minute." He was fighting giggles,
all of a sudden: both of them trussed like turkeys and rolling
around a dark hold, him groping his way up her leg. *Bad Fifties
horror movie love scene. Right. Where's the zipper monster?* He
bit back laughter; Ariadne would think he was laughing at her
and take offense. *Get the knife into your own hands before you
get her seriously pissed, okay?* His fingers slid along the back of
her knee; she jumped and he would have sworn she was fighting
giggles herself. *Tell me she isn't ticklish! God, all we'd need.* He
edged himself down a little farther and his right hand brushed the
lower strap; he gripped it, walked his left hand up and around
her leg. She edged toward him. His hands were getting numb;
hard to get them to grip the hilt. It proved impossible to raise his
arms enough to free it. He set his jaw, tried again. This would be
hard enough on anyone's shoulders, and his were miserably sore
from that clown hauling him up and hyperextending everything.
Payback's a bitch, guy, he thought in the direction of the deck.
"Try something," he whispered. He curled into a ball and the
knife moved a little; Ariadne edged down the bags. "Got it."

But before he could get a better grip on it, her fingers tugged
at his numb-prickly fingers and took the blade away from him.
"Hey!" he protested.

Ariadne's voice came right against his ear; it tickled. "Can you
cut ropes without seeing them, by feel, with a very sharp knife?
I *know* I can do this, and I wish not to lose skin to anything less
than my own skill. Do you object?"

"Lady," he assured her, "I don't like knives even with my
hands free and both feet under me. Just don't cut anything I'm
going to need to get us out of here, all right?"

"I know this knife very well and I know what I do—and I cut
nothing but rope," she replied stiffly. He felt cool fingers slide

between his forearms and down toward his wrists; the knife came right behind them. *Doing it by Braille. Swell.* He closed his eyes and swallowed.

She poked him once but not badly; he doubted he was even bleeding but he was too numb from the shoulder down to tell. Moments later, the ropes on his wrists parted. She edged up behind him and sawed at the ropes that held his elbows. The knife tugged at his sleeve; he bit his lip and kept quiet, put as much outward pressure on his elbows and the ropes as possible. When they finally came apart, he rolled onto his stomach and let them flop. "God, I think my shoulders are broken," he groaned.

"Never mind that, time may be short. Do your hands work yet?"

"Kind of," he admitted.

"Good. Take the knife, undo first your feet and give the fingers time to waken before you attempt my hands. I also prefer to lose nothing useful."

"Yeah—right." He groaned again as he rolled over and sat up. Ariadne hissed; he collapsed onto his side as someone clomped up the corridor. Heavy boots mounted the steps and ran onto the deck; the boards overhead groaned and dirt sifted down on them. Chris was already working his feet free; he flexed his hands, then ran his left over Ariadne's bonds to find a safe starting point, and slid the knife between turns with his right.

She fortunately wasn't tied anywhere near as tightly as he'd been. "Here," she whispered. "Hand it to me again, to free my feet." Before he could reply, she snatched it back from him and bent down to work on her ankles. "Good. Thank you."

"I—well, hey, why not?" He kept his voice light, but he was thinking as fast and hard as he ever had. Getting loose was a very small first step. Still . . . *If the fog's thick, we may have a chance of getting across that deck without anyone seeing us. And off the ship. Ask the lady if she can swim.* He could have laughed aloud, all at once. Great line, silly movie—and this wouldn't be nearly as nasty a first step as the cliff the two pirates and the girl had gone off. "You swim, right?"

"I swim," Ariadne replied calmly. "You plan to get us off this ship?"

"Think it might be a good idea. What with them in a hurry to get out of Rhadazi waters as fast as they can and with the fog as bad as it was, we might pull it off. There could be a guard up there at the hatch, though—and guys on the deck."

"We might evade men on the deck, if we are quiet and careful and they do not expect us there. You are right." She sounded entirely too calm for his liking: He already knew she could act. If she panicked at any point before they got into the water and away from the ship— He shook that off.

"Glad you approve. So, why don't you lend me that knife again, and I'll get us out of here." He laid his hand, palm up, against her knee.

Silence. She'd gone very still. "No," she said finally. "Not you." Chris swore under his breath and edged toward her; she backed away. "Wait and listen," she said softly. "This knife—I am familiar with it. With knives, not just this particular one. And you do not even carry a blade of any kind."

"So? I can use one if I have to."

"You have?"

"No. But if it's going to be him or me, he's gonna die every time—"

Ariadne's hand gripped his forearm. "No. Listen, let me say it all. It is not him or you in a place like this. He sees you and the knife and he has only to yell, the others come at once. And we have gained nothing."

"I know that. You gotta sneak—"

"Sneak is nothing; you stab in the wrong place and he yells, and again we have nothing."

"Yeah—well. Maybe I pick the right place." He reached again; she backed away from him.

"Listen to me! To come quietly behind an unsuspecting man and put the knife where he will be dead before he can cry out— can you do this?"

"Oh, sure," Chris replied sarcastically. "Can't everyone?"

"No—but I can." He couldn't see her face; her voice was without inflection and somehow all the more convincing for it. "Because I have done it before." Silence. Chris suddenly couldn't recall how to breathe. She seemed to come to some decision all at once. "In French Jamaica, upon the back streets of Philippe-sur-Mer, against noble and violent men who deserved far worse than the quick and painless death *I* gave them." She drew a harsh breath, then added flatly, "Five times."

* * *

THE dock was suddenly swarming with men—most visible through the fog as dark shapes, though one of the nearest held a lantern which shone on Shesseran's red and gold. Edrith got stiffly to his feet and helped Enardi up; he was keenly aware both of them were dripping harbor water and no doubt reeked. The look the nearest guards gave the two and then each other wasn't reassuring. Vey came forward. The guard with the lantern asked, "These are the men?"

"These are my friends," Vey said steadily. "The men who attacked us are gone—that way." He pointed down the dock and out toward the fogbound harbor.

"You say you are in the Thukar's guard?"

"I *am* one of Thukar Dahven's men," Vey replied. If he was irked by the other's patent suspicions, he didn't show it, and he cast Edrith a warning glance. Edrith bit his lip and sent his eyes heavenward. "I carry no papers because I was on a personal errand to Podhru, though I was also helping guard the merchant Chris Cray."

"Why should a merchant need a guard?" another of the guards asked sharply. "And where is this man you say you hit?"

Vey sent Edrith another warning look and Enardi's hand tightened on his friend's upper arm. "Sir. My friend here was in the water and in danger of drowning; I don't know when the man I hit got up and ran. As for the other matter, Lord Afronsan knows why the merchant needed protection. He knows the merchant—and these men—personally."

Enardi let go of Edrith so he could dig through his jacket pocket; he pulled out a thin, soaked leather wallet and turned to let what the lantern light fall on the contents as he tried to separate them, finally asked in an exasperated voice, "Is it not possible for us to go back into the waiting room, where there is decent light and warmth? We two are chilled right through."

Their interrogator shrugged, gestured for two of his men to bring up the rear and led the way. It was much warmer inside; the lights were turned up to full and Dija was talking to the harbormaster, arguing over the luggage still piled against the back wall. As Vey came into the room, she hurried over to him and wrapped her arms around his waist, burying her face in his shoulder. He slipped an arm across her shoulders and gathered her close, but his eyes were fixed on the chief guard's face. The guard in turn was watching Enardi sort through his wet papers.

"Here," he said suddenly, and held out a folded square of pale blue. The guard took it reluctantly, held it away from his uniform and carefully opened it. Enardi gave him time to read what he could of the water-streaked contents, then said, "I am Enardi, principal of CEE-Tech and Fedthyr's son. As you can see, that is a conduct to Lord Afronsan: I suggest you take us to him at once; we will certainly answer your questions, but I am deeply concerned for our friend Chris and his lady. The men who took them went out into the harbor; I fear the ship is already on its way west."

"Perhaps." The guard eyed him narrowly, then handed back the piece of paper. Enardi wrinkled his nose fastidiously, but folded it and returned it to his wallet. "All right!" he shouted. His men came to attention. "One of you, take these four to the Heir at once, and wait in case there's any orders. You, harbor-master! Get us boats—five of them, and men to row who will take orders. Men who can take care of themselves, if possible; there could be trouble out there if we find the right ship. Take lanterns and check all the ships in harbor." Someone was mutter- ing to himself. "I know, it's an impossible task, but the Heir would set us to it anyway, so start now! Once the harbor's checked, move out beyond the narrows and find any ships you can. Master, you have a manifest of who was here before the tide shifted? Get it, so we can see what of them might be missing."

Dija stirred in Vey's arms. "I won't go, I won't! If madam is there, if they bring her back—!"

"We'll both stay," Vey assured her calmly, and she subsided against him once more. He looked across her head, met the cap- tain's eyes. "I can tell you what happened, and you'll want a de- scription of the two they took."

"Good enough. We need a description of this ruffian you struck as well, see if we can't find him." The captain's lips thinned; he was clearly thinking of the crowds in all the major and most of the narrower streets, celebrating Shesseran's birthday. He finally led the way across to the windows and Vey went with him, taking Dija. One of the other guards tapped Edrith's shoulder.

"If you're ready, sir," he said.

Sir. Edrith bit back a rude retort, shed Ariadne's shawl, and shoved salt-water-spiky hair from his forehead. "More than ready. Let us go."

WITHIN steps away from the docks, the fog began to thin, sliding past them in pale ribbons. Cool air touched Enardi's right cheek and ear; he shivered. The east wind was coming down the Pod River Gorge; it must be later than he realized, or the wind was early. *At this rate, that ship will be halfway to the isthmus before we even find the Heir,* he thought gloomily. The guard who'd ordered them out spoke briefly to his companion, who sprinted up a narrow side alley. "He'll get word in, they'll be waiting for you, with any luck," the captain said. He sounded almost friendly. Edrith merely nodded; his mouth was still set and the looks he'd cast Enardi since they'd entered the waiting room all said, *Told you so*. In truth, Enardi was himself still put out by the suspicion that had greeted their story—*as if any man would make up such a foolishness to tease the city guard*, he thought indignantly. And if this was the treatment Eddie had received from Sikkre's guard all his life, no wonder he distrusted the guard. But there was no point to alienating this man. They were still far from Afronsan's ear.

"That was well thought, sir," he said politely. "Thank you." The guard merely nodded; they covered the rest of the distance quickly, via less crowded back ways, and in silence.

To Enardi's surprise, once the city guard turned them over to house guard at the massive civil service building, they were shown onto the second floor and to the right—the Heir's private apartments. The room they entered was a small one, low-ceilinged and extremely cozy. A fire burned in a small hearth at one end; several deep chairs were drawn in a half-circle around it. A long, polished table took up most of the opposite wall, with a narrow doorway in the corner leading to a hall that vanished into darkness. Two chairs were drawn up at the far end of the table, near the door, and a brass sconce of several candles lit the remains of a meal. It was close and wonderfully warm, and the faint smell of spiced meat still lingered. As the door closed behind them, Afronsan came through the opposite doorway. He stared, clearly shocked, at his two visitors.

"They didn't say you were wet! Wait." He turned and leaned through the doorway. "Alessya, my dear, please have wine brought, and towels!" He looked over his shoulder. "Unless you would prefer tea, or coffee?"

"Anything hot, I think, sir," Enardi said when it became clear Edrith was at a loss for words. Afronsan turned back to call down the passage and Enardi elbowed his companion.

"We interrupted his *dinner*!" Edrith whispered, aghast.

Afronsan came across the room. "Here, move over to the fire, warm yourselves. The guard said trouble and gave your names so of course I had them bring you at once—but he didn't say what trouble."

Edrith was persuaded to stand before the flames and heat his back; Enardi knelt on the heated flagstone hearth and held his hands to the fire and as Afronsan took a chair, he made as concise and quick a tale of the matter as he could.

He looked up. Afronsan's face was expressionless but his eyes were dark and, Enardi thought, quite furious. He caught hold of the ornate rope hanging next to the fireplace and yanked, hard, then jumped to his feet and crossed to the door, giving it such a tug it slammed into the wall; he beckoned to the house guard standing just outside. "Metripan, go down to the telegraph office, please; make certain it's switched on and the night operator there, then come right back, I'll have a message."

"Sir." They could hear the man's boots pounding down the hall. A woman came in from the other direction, carrying a tray. Steam rose from one of the pots. Enardi staggered to his feet, but Afronsan was already there, taking the tray from his Fahlian wife. Ash-colored hair tumbled over pink-clad shoulders—like Afronsan, she was dressed plainly, and even the small brooch pinned to her shoulder seemed to be there only to hold fabric together. "My dear, it wasn't necessary to bring this yourself."

"It's all right." Her voice was high and resonant. She smiled at him, and then at the two men by the fire, and if she was surprised to find two soaking wet men in the Heir's private dining chamber, it didn't show on her face. Edrith glanced in surprise at Enardi, who was momentarily at a loss for words. "Frolia's bringing the blankets and everyone else is eating, I didn't want to disturb them." She came across to the fire and held out her hands—small, soft hands. Enardi bowed low over them.

"An honor, Lady Alessya." He sent his eyes toward Edrith, who bent his head; he had to put out a hand to keep his balance.

"It's all right," she said quickly. "Don't stand on ceremony, I'm just going." She laid a hand against Afronsan's cheek in passing. "Don't be all night, if you please," she murmured and went back down the hall. They could hear her talking to someone just out of sight and moments later, an older woman came in, arms piled high with blankets. Afronsan made a move toward her but checked and turned as someone knocked at the outer door; Enardi went to take the stack, and set it on the nearest chair. He shook the top one out and draped it over his shoulders. Edrith eyed the blankets warily. Enardi hissed at him, handed him the shaken-out blanket and took another.

Edrith sighed as he wrapped himself in thick blue wool and leaned against the smooth black stone wall of the fireplace. "I didn't think I'd ever be warm again. But—"

Enardi shook his head and whispered rapidly, "My friend,

don't insult the Heir by refusing his hospitality. Blankets wash, you know."

"I—yeah, okay," Edrith whispered back hastily as Enardi hissed at him again. Afronsan was still in the doorway, talking to a small man who was gesturing emphatically down the hall. A thatch of black hair fell over his eyes; he shoved it back. Afronsan held up a hand for silence, turned away from him.

"He tells me the wire is down. Wait." He spoke to the boy in the hall once more, then closed the door and came back to the fire. "I've told him to send riders. Breaks do happen."

"There's been no wind. Someone might have—" Edrith hesitated. He was clasping and unclasping his hands.

"It may have been cut," Afronsan agreed. "I've also sent guards in case of that—and a man who knows how to tap into the wire beyond the break. The wire was working at midday; I received a message from Lehzin about then. We'll know soon enough." He was clearly aware of the tension over by the fireplace. "Messengers will go out by road also. Erdron just now said the fog has lifted; the wind's come. There was a French sloop in the harbor this afternoon. He's sent to find out if it could be persuaded to sail for Bez." He came across, sat and began pouring dark, steaming liquid into cups. The smell of very strong coffee filled the room. "Tell me what you can of these men."

Enardi moved cushions and forced himself to sit on one of the polished wood chairs. *Everything we could possibly do, he is doing,* he told himself firmly. Out of the corner of his eye, he could see Eddie's leg, jittering up and down under the blanket, the way Chris's did when he was fighting impatience or anger. Eddie's face, when he glanced up, showed very little. He gave his friend what he hoped was an encouraging smile, then obediently launched into a description of the man who'd tried to drive him into the water. Afronsan drank coffee and heard him out. "No one you knew? No recognizable features? Nothing to prove him ours, English, Mer Khani—?"

"I knew one of them," Edrith said suddenly. "From down south, the Incan Empire—he was drinking in a tavern, Isadya harbor, with one of Casimaffi's captains, but I've seen him frequently before that—and heard plenty about him. He uses several names. The Italians I know want him and they don't care if he's alive. He speaks English; I don't know if he's English or Mer Khani, or if he just speaks it." He turned to Enardi. "You saw him, Ernie. The one who came into the waiting room to call us out?"

"I saw him, and also heard him. Whatever else he may be, his English has a Mer Khani accent." He looked up at Edrith, who cast his eyes up. "You know I have a good ear for these things." He looked back at the Heir and shrugged. "But the man who had me at sword point was not a Mer Khani. He was very dark, like the Italians who came last spring, perhaps. He didn't speak."

"We'll find out," Edrith said grimly.

"Oh, yes," Afronsan replied mildly; his words carried all the more weight for that. "I think we will. Here," he added as he set his empty coffee cup aside. "This came a while ago, a gift from Duke Lehzin for my brother's birthday celebration. Some trade he made with the English, he says." He held up a flask: It was not very large, oblong, smooth clear glass with indentations for thumb and two fingers. The cork was fixed with red wax and an ornately looped silver ribbon. Afronsan gave the ribbon an expert twist, shattering the wax, and drew three tiny cups toward him so he could pour.

A startled sound interrupted him. Edrith was staring at the bottle. He dropped the blanket and caught hold of the Heir's wrist. "Don't, sir," he whispered. "Don't drink that." Afronsan looked at the hand gripping his for a very long moment. He shifted the bottle to his other hand and set it aside, and only then looked up; his face was utterly without expression. Edrith let him go at once. "I—I'm sorry, sir. I didn't mean—" Afronsan simply looked at him, and waited. Edrith picked up the bottle and turned it in one long-fingered hand. "That's an English seal, the red and silver, but this bottle isn't English, sir." He looked down at Afronsan, who was still watching him, perhaps waiting for him to make sense. "You couldn't mistake a bottle like this for any other. It's unusual."

"You recognize it, I assume?"

"It's French, sir—the bottle is, at least. Made over there. Chris told you about Henri Dupret—his lady's father? Bottles like this are shipped from France to French Jamaica by the hundreds, I've seen them. And the stuff in it—I wager it's fruited brandy, and it's also from Jamaica, sir. Because Chris and I've both seen it before—I watched crates of the stuff loaded onto a ship called *Le Chat*, bound from Philippe-sur-Mer for France."

"You think this is his?"

"I can't swear to it, sir. But it's the wrong kind of coincidence. And if it's Dupret's—then I'll wager anything you like, sir, that stuff is loaded with Zero."

11

IT was suddenly very warm in Afronsan's private dining chamber, and so quiet Enardi could hear his heart pulsing—much too fast. Afronsan studied Edrith for some moments, then held out his hand. Edrith handed him the bottle, watched him anxiously. The Heir's mouth turned in a very slight smile.

"I don't intend to drink it, friend; I take your word the stuff may not be as—wholesome as it looks. Pull the cord, please; three times." Enardi nodded and reached for the cord; Afronsan was already out of his chair, striding toward the inner hallway. He leaned through it, shouted, "Alessya! There is a second bottle of the brandy, have it brought here at once!" A pause; Enardi looked blankly at Edrith, who shrugged. "At once! It's—gone bad, I think!" He came back into the room, crossed to the other door. "I'd rather not frighten her." He flung the outer door open, leaned out and looked both ways. "Odd. No one."

Edrith came over to join him. "Sir—it's not—?"

Afronsan glanced at him. "The usual man is on an errand for me, of course, but normally there would be someone in the hall."

"If I might suggest, sir," Edrith said uncertainly, "given that bottle, you might close and bolt the door."

"Nonsense!" But Afronsan looked up and down the hall once again and now there was a deep groove between his brows. "I think—" he began, and now he sounded nearly as uncertain as Edrith.

"Better a little foolish but safe than the alternative, sir," Edrith suggested. "Don't you agree?"

"Mmmm." The Heir closed the door. "There's no bolt for this door, just the short privacy bar."

Edrith flipped the forearm-length piece of wood around and

into its rests. "It's enough for warning, anyway, sir. And for caution."

"Mmm." Afronsan nodded, then disappeared down the inner hallway. Edrith shivered and went back to the fire. "What the man must think of me, Ernie. Presumptuous—!"

"Eddie, you know him better than that. But—do you really think—?"

"I don't know—what, that someone poisoned the Heir's brandy, and might be planning to murder him, right here and now? It does sound pretty wild, doesn't it?" Edrith spread his hands wide and managed a rueful smile. "But over dinner tonight, wouldn't it have seemed equally wild, an attack on the Emperor's very docks?"

Afronsan came back at that moment, the unopened brandy gripped in one hand, four household men and a guard trailing behind him; he was talking in a low, rapid voice. "All right. You know where to go," he said. "Get someone back to me at once, the moment anything's known." The household men left, two back the way they'd come, the other two out the main entry and down the hall, pulling the door to behind them; it hit with a crash and creaked slowly open again. Afronsan and the guard stopped just short of it; Edrith edged around behind Enardi so he could see into the hall—empty. He met Enardi's eye, shook his head.

Afronsan was still talking rapidly. "As quickly as you can, first the Emperor's private house by the north wall; take three men with you, well armed. Tell him—here, wait." He strode over to the windows and sat on the low, long bench, drew over a block of paper and pen, flipped open the large ink pot. He scribbled noisily, then ripped off a square sheet of paper and blotted it deftly. He held out the sheet; the guard shoved it inside his tunic. "That will get you either to the Emperor, his first wife or his steward. Bring back any bottles like this one—wait. Let me think. Any bottles of liquor recently sent to my brother, or gifts that might contain drug. Find someone else in the guardroom before you go and send him and two others out to the Emperor's estates—just in case there was such a gift sent there. Any brandy—here, wait." He scribbled another note and handed it over. "And warn them what's happened here. Better to be safe than foolish." The guard nodded, turned and ran. Afronsan followed him to the door, closed it behind him. "There are two men watching the door," he said. He turned as someone tapped on it and an older man clad all in black stuck his head in.

"Sir—word just came, the men who rode out to test the telegraph? The line was deliberately dropped, they say. And they were attacked."

"Reinforcements—"

"Yes, sir, already attended to, before I was sent here with the message. To bring back a prisoner, I'm told, or more than one. Aubrion sent back word your message has been sent to Bez and confirmation received from Lehzin's man at the other end. Aubrion said they'll stay out there until day, in case of messages or more sabotage. And I've sent word down for the workmen to mend the wires once it's light."

"Good. And?"

"I just came from your wire office, sir. Your test message to the Thukara in Sikkre went through some hours ago—we had confirmation. But just now, I had them send word to Zelharri and the line to Duke's Fort isn't working. And immediately after, when we attempted Sikkre again, *it* didn't respond."

*   *   *

A small company of well-muffled and heavily armed horsemen rode through the gates of Duke's Fort—five of the Duke's special guard assigned to patrol the roads and borders and at their head, their commander, Gyrdan himself. Just behind him, surrounded and closely guarded, two more men, heavily shackled. Once inside the outer wall, Gyrdan beckoned to the boy who manned the gate and eased himself stiffly down from his saddle. "Close and bar the gates, Hesiom, we won't want these two wandering off. Once you've done that, fetch Joras if he's still about or Garret otherwise, tell them I've two men for them to question and a boxful of yellow rope rings for him to lock away." He looked up at the stone-faced prisoners. "Unless you think your Duke will object to our taking his property?" he asked; broad sarcasm edged the words.

The men simply gazed back at him—arrogantly, he thought. That would change before the night was over, if he had any say. Hesiom touched his sleeve tentatively; words poured out of him in a boy's tremulous, worried voice. "Sir, I daren't close the gate, or leave it, the healer's been sent for. The Duke's fallen—" He fell silent as Gyrdan chopped a hand, sent his eyes sideways to indicate the prisoners. "Sorry, sir."

"Don't be," Gyrdan said; his eyes went to the upper windows and his voice was rather absent. "I wondered at all the lights in the family wing. Well then, bar the gate against any fool's move by these two, but stay at it so you can let the healer in when she comes." He turned to his men—the pick of Aletto's fort guard. "You, Lysne, take charge out here. I'll go in, see what's amiss." He was already moving, his ground-eating stride taking him across the courtyard and into the fort.

It was unnervingly silent in the lower passage, nearly dark since only two lamps had been lit and one of those was guttering. Gyrdan took the stairs two at a time and emerged into bright light and chaos. Lights everywhere; most of the kitchen servants huddled at the top of the back stairs and the rest were halfway down the broad hall; the par-Duchess stood in the open doors to her apartments, her face yellowish against the black of her high-throated gown, the back of one hand pressed against her mouth. Everyone jumped as a sharp outcry came from the Duke's apartments.

Gyrdan shoved through the crowd, tapped at the ornate double doors, and pushed them inward without waiting for a response.

The room was no less bright than the hall; the fire had been built up, making it unbearably hot to one just coming in from the chill autumn night air. Aletto's man Zepiko bent over the enormous bed, a dripping cloth between his hands. One of the younger household men had been trying to ease the boot from Aletto's right foot; his hands were stiff, fingers splayed as if he'd just snatched them back from hot coals. His face was utterly white.

Aletto's was a greenish shade; eyes were screwed tightly shut, hands twisted in the cloth. His right leg had been propped on a stack of cushions. A black swelling ran down the right side of his face; the back of his right hand was badly scraped and still seeped a little blood. "Here!" Gyrdan said sharply as he strode over to the foot of the bed. "Let me deal with this!" The servants hastily retreated.

Aletto opened one eye at the familiar voice. "Gyr. Didn't expect you. Glad—to see you, though."

"What's wrong?"

"Foot. Turned—it." Aletto's voice was a pained whisper; Gyrdan had to lean close to hear him. "Wrong way."

"Doubt there's any right way, my Duke," Gyrdan replied. "How bad is it?" Aletto shook his head very cautiously, caught his lip between his teeth once more and let his eyes close. "Either of you—I know the healer's sent for but where's Yzakk meantime? He's no true healer but he's dealt with as bad as this for others in the guards."

Aletto's man set his wet cloth back in the bowl. "We sent for him when we brought the Duke upstairs; he's gone to his mother's house up north—"

"Ah, hells, he picked a time," Gyrdan growled. "The healer?"

"We sent at once, sir; the festivities in Sehfi, though—"

"All right, all right, I know. Emperor's birthday, worse luck, we had to go all the way around the town to get into the fort— never mind. Make certain someone's down at the doors to escort her up here at once when she's found. Meantime—clear the room, will you, Zepiko? You can stay if you'll keep quiet. Wager your Duke would like some of that." He moved up the bed, laid a hand on Aletto's forehead and let it slide down to his undamaged cheek. "What was injured—anything besides the foot?"

"Don't think—so. My face, the hand—that's just bruises. Fell—pretty hard." Aletto swallowed hard, tried to smile. "Boot's way too tight."

"Swollen, of course; wager your ankle would like a little fresh air and room, both." He drew his belt knife. "How fond of these boots are you, sir?"

Aletto laughed weakly, gasped and bit his lip again. "Like them—but not nearly as much as my foot."

"Good." Gyrdan was as gentle and careful as he could possibly be, easing the soft leather away from skin and cutting without sawing at the stuff; not that it mattered. Aletto turned paper-white and passed out as soon as he took hold of the foot. Just as well, Gyrdan thought grimly, and worked as quickly as he dared. He tossed aside the ruined boot and bunched the soft, already loose wool foot-wrap. On the outside of the Duke's ankle was a blood-dark knot half the size of his fist, and the whole foot was swollen. Gyrdan glanced at Aletto's face; reassured the man was still unconscious, he put his ear close to the joint and worked the foot cautiously back and forth. It didn't seem to be broken—painful, of course, but not as bad as a break at the joint would be. The healer should be able to get this under control in a matter of days. Gyrdan straightened, dug both fists into the small of his back as stiff, aching muscles protested, then moved up the bed to push dark, sweat-soaked hair from Aletto's face. He wrung out the wet cloth, laid it across his Duke's brow and went over to the door. Servants and housemen everywhere out there, nervous little clutches of them, all watching him anxiously.

"Duchess Robyn," he began. One of the cooks came running from the nursery, her hands knotting her apron.

"They're gone! The Duchess and the children—they came up here, I heard them, she said they'd take dinner in there tonight, but they're gone!" She was gasping for breath. Aletto's man caught her by the shoulders and gave her a shake.

"Talk sense, woman!"

She pulled loose and glared up at him. "I am, Zepiko! There's a—a dreadful mess in there, a strange and horrid smell, and they're all three gone!"

Gyrdan cast his eyes heavenward, then waved his arms as the cook's announcement seemed likely to cause full-blown hysteria.

"All right, all right! Some quiet out here, please! Your Duke's in a good deal of pain right now, I doubt he needs *this* sort of worry atop everything else! Especially when there's bound to be a sensible explanation. You and you"—he pointed at the trembling cook and the woman who had just come up to wrap an arm around her shoulders—"organize a search for them, they could just be somewhere else. You"—he turned to the servant who'd been trying to remove Aletto's boot—"go down to the courtyard, tell the men there they'll need to manage without me for now, bring me any new word on the healer." An idea occurred to him. "Check the stables, doesn't the Duchess sometimes take the babes down there of an evening?" He turned a full circle, eyed the men and women scattered along the hall. "The rest of you—I know you've tasks, better see to them!" He turned on his heel and walked up the hall to the nursery.

The cook was right—the room was a shambles, and not the kind children would make. There was indeed an odd smell to the air—but it was faint, nearly gone. "Idiot," he growled. "Leaving the door open, much aid that was!" Well, the lady wasn't here—anywhere in this end of the fort, surely, because she'd have heard the excitement. *They probably heard it out there on the curtain wall*, he thought sourly. Duchess Robyn, though: It was very odd, her and the children nowhere about, and on such a chill night. There'd be some explanation for it, no doubt. But the others could deal with that; he had enough to do at the moment. He started back to the Duke's apartments, turned as someone came pounding up the stairs. The boy he'd just sent outside came racing up to him.

"Sir, the healer's come, she's on her way up. But—the carriage, Duchess Robyn's carriage? Hesiom—at the gate?—he says she left some time ago. At least—"

"At least?"

"He thinks she did," the boy said doubtfully. "It was her carriage, you've seen it—"

"Yes? So?" Gyrdan longed to grab the boy and shake the words from him.

"When the top's drawn over as it usually is this time of year? You can't really see inside. He says—Hesiom says the carriage came out of the stables and he could see someone the right size in there, in a dark hood and heavy cloak. She—he thinks it was the Duchess, but she never spoke—just held up a hand and waved it at him as she went by."

"Went by—going which way?" If she'd just taken the children into Sehfi for some part of the festival, she'd be returning any time. The town wasn't that large, the celebration not that exciting, and this late in the evening there wouldn't be much for children. The boy caught his breath.

"She turned—right. Down the main road."

"Right?" Gyrdan frowned; the boy watched him warily. "There's nothing that way."

"She—takes them for rides sometimes, sir. When there's been—" The young face was even redder, all at once; he sent his eyes quickly toward the room where the Duke lay, then away again. "When they've argued."

"Ahhh." Gyrdan sighed heavily and cast his own eyes heavenward. So there had been a spat. "Well, no doubt she'll be back any time now, all three of them damp and half frozen from the fog." The boy hadn't thought of that, clearly; he suddenly looked relieved, and Gyrdan realized he'd been very worried. *What, does he think Lasanachi in the fort, running off with the women and children?* he wondered dryly. Well, if Robyn and Aletto had been spatting, it would be like her to absent herself for a while. All the same . . . "Do me a favor, will you, lad? Tell Hesiom to find a replacement for his watch and send him up to me." The boy nodded, turned and ran.

* * *

ROBYN cautiously opened her eyes; she couldn't tell anything about her surroundings save that she was indoors somewhere. There was an underlying feel of neglect, dust everywhere and too much quiet. It was very dark, and whatever she was lying on was rough and scratchy. Carpet, but not very clean. The leg under her had gone to pins and needles. She moved it and the other came with it: Both were wrapped in several turns of thick, harsh rope. Her arms—the same. Something lay across her throat, some kind of flat bit of smooth metal. A chain? Something dangling from it that had slipped inside her bodice. *I don't wear necklaces; where did it come from?* Sudden certainty: *I'm not in the palace any more.*

Full memory returned between one breath and another: that last moment, two enormous shadows that became men—men in the nursery, waiting for them. One holding Iana, the other snatching at Amarni— Her blood ran cold. "Oh, *God*. The kids! I gotta get out of here, gotta find them, get us out of here." The ropes were too well tied; she didn't even bother with them. If she could shift, ropes and bonds shouldn't matter. *Shift*— But as hard as she tried, it wouldn't respond. The place that made the shift was there, but something thick and foggy shrouded it.

*   *   *

UNLIKE the boy who'd taken the message to him, Hesiom was a reasonable level-headed young man. The Sehfi healer had come up with him and was laying out her pastes and liquids on the bed, Aletto's man watching her closely and, Gyrdan thought, jealously—the woman was able to do something for the Duke he couldn't. Aletto was awake once more but he lay very still, eyes closed and lower lip between his teeth. Gyrdan gestured for the boy to wait in the hall for him and bent over the bed. "Sir, you're in good hands now, I'll come back in a while, if I may. News for you."

"Mmm—of course." Aletto's words were hard to understand; he kept a grip on his lower lip the whole time and his forehead was heavily furrowed. Gyrdan went out.

Hesiom looked nearly as anxious; his dark, heavy brows made one thick line above a long, freckled face. "Sir, the lady's carriage—"

"Yes, I know, it's gone. Unpleasant night for a drive, I'd have thought, but I understand there was an argument."

"Yes, sir, I heard that." Hesiom jumped as a faint cry came from behind the closed doors. "Thing is," he went on after a moment, "it didn't strike me odd *then*, but now—I'm not so certain that *was* the lady driving. And the little 'uns: You know how they are, sir. Ordinarily, they'd say something or call my name, being friendly, you know, sir."

"They didn't this time?"

"I didn't see them at all, sir. Just the—the person I thought then was Duchess Robyn, all bundled against the cool air. Now—I just don't know. It was dark, and she didn't say anything at all, just—just waved and went on. Out the gates."

"And turned away from town and the celebration," Gyrdan said.

"Yes, sir. I—that *did* strike me a little odd; there's not much that way, especially late, and on a night like this, man can't see any distance at all, where's the pleasure in a drive? But before I could worry about it much, word came out from one of the kitchen lads, the Duke was flat in the family dining, his ankle all turned under at an ugly angle, and that drove everything from my mind." A small silence. "I'm sorry, Sir," Hesiom added in a small voice.

"Mmmm? Oh. Not your fault, lad. No, I was thinking. Never mind, go on back down. You'd better find Joras for me, or Garret, if he's not busy with those prisoners. Send him here, I need him." Hesiom nodded, turned and sped away. Gyrdan sighed and went back into the Duke's chamber.

The healer—an extremely old village woman who'd moved to Sehfi only recently, when the town's last healer died—was gathering up her things and putting them back into an enormous roll of a satchel. Aletto's eyes were open and, while he was still quite pale, he no longer seemed to be in as much pain. The woman had securely wrapped the ankle in masses of dark cloth; Aletto's oddly shaped toes stuck out the end. She rummaged through her bag and came up with a flat leather flask. "Here, you," she said abruptly and shoved the bottle into Zepiko's hands. "A measure of that powder dissolved in a cup of water, three times a day. See he takes it all down, the foot will heal faster and cause him much less discomfort." She brushed past him and came up the side of the bed, shoved her fists into her waist and scowled down at the Duke. "And you, sir, if you've sense at all you'll stay flat in that bed for the next five days at least. Walk on that foot and the powder'll do you no good in this world."

"I'm not walking on it," Aletto whispered. He managed a half-smile. "Thank you, healer."

"Bah. Thank me by tending it properly. You've got this man, your lady—enough people to run your errands for you. You," she said, rounding on Zepiko again, so suddenly he stumbled and nearly fell onto the bed. "Someone must be with him at all times—if he needs the privy, one of you is there to hold him up. *No weight on that foot.*"

"No weight," Zepiko said flatly. He looked extremely irritated as he picked himself up. The healer turned on her heel, scooped up her large bag and settled the wide strap over her head and across her chest, sketched Aletto a very abbreviated curtsey and left. Zepiko scowled at her back.

"Go after her, Zep," Aletto said weakly. "Give her three silver, will you?"

"Three," Zepiko grumbled, but he nodded and went out. Aletto sighed and let his eyes close.

"Gyr?"

"I'm here, sir. The staff's gone back downstairs, everything's quiet once more. You look better, so I'll leave you."

"I feel better." As if to prove it, Aletto opened his eyes. "Not good, mind you, just—Gyr, would you do me a—a favor? Go to the nursery, and ask Robyn if she'd—if she'll—" His voice trailed away; his color was very high.

Gyrdan spread his hands wide. "I heard about the argument, sir."

"Mmm. Yes. No privacy in the fort. I—was trying to catch her when I slipped. I just wanted to—"

There wasn't any help for it. Gyrdan shook his head. "I'm sorry, sir. I've already been to the nursery looking for her; she's not there."

"Oh." Aletto considered this; his forehead puckered. "Oh?"

"Not there. Nor the children. The carriage is out—"

"She—surely she didn't take them out on a night like this?"

"I thought you'd know better—wait, sir, if you're going to sit, let me help you." Gyrdan came around the bed and got his hands under the Duke's arms and eased him up, then moved down to edge the pillow back under his foot. "I spoke to the boy at the gate who saw the carriage go." He made a succinct story of it. Aletto's frown deepened.

"She turned right? But—oh, no. She—she wouldn't." Gyrdan waited. Aletto shook his head. "Surely she wouldn't have set out tonight for Sikkre—but if she was truly angry with me—"

"Would she have done that, sir?"

"She's *threatened* it before this. Gyr, would you get me paper and a pen—the desk, over beyond the hearth. If someone would ride out to the telegraph tonight, send a message to Sikkre for me—"

"Of course, sir." Gyrdan fetched what Aletto needed, waited for him to write the message and fold it into quarters. "I'll find someone right away, we'll get it sent within the hour."

"Good." Aletto let his father's old armsmaster help him get flat once more. He edged his shoulders uncomfortably, finally sighed and closed his eyes. "That stuff she poured down me tastes awful, but I think it's working. Bring me the confirmation message as soon as it comes, will you?"

"Of course. Sleep in the meantime, sir, why don't you?"

"Mmmm. Think—I will." Gyrdan thought so, too. The Duke seemed to be already asleep when he turned back for a last look at the door.

*   *   *

IT had been hot all day in Sikkre, and the heat remained well after sundown, rising from packed earth or stone streets, coming in waves from the inner walls. The Thukara had spent most of her day in a sweltering office, typing up the points she would negotiate the next afternoon for a deal between an Italian trading family and the mining consortium northwest of the city—raw silver in exchange for even finer blade steel than the Rhadazi had, faceted topazes in several colors and brocades in wonderful patterns and extremely subtle shades that had the Weaver's Guild itching for the opportunity to duplicate them.

Just after sunset, Dahven had come looking for her. "My dear woman, why don't you dismiss these poor people and let them at least have a toast to the Emperor's birthday? And come watch me eat, if you're intent on starving yourself." Jennifer opened her mouth to protest, then grinned and shoved away from her desk.

"You're right." She stood, clapped her hands together. "All of you, this is a test! See how fast you can clear the room for the night, go join the party out there!" A ragged cheer greeted this, sporadic applause. Jennifer laughed, flapped her hands at them. "G'wan, shoo! I'll see you all tomorrow—and it's a long one again, sorry, folks, so don't celebrate *too* hard!"

"Enjoy yourselves," Dahven added. He wrapped an arm around Jennifer's shoulders and said, "I hope you were done, because I'm taking you out of this sweat-box right now. Food and a little conversation, please, a trip up to the tower to look over the market lights and the festivities, and an early night?"

"Mmmm." She stretched and yawned hugely, like a cat, then

slumped against him. "Yeah. Great idea. Wait—hold it." She slipped free of him and went back to her desk.

"No papers," Dahven began warningly. Jennifer shook her head, bent over and came up with her bo in her left hand. Dahven's eyebrows went up.

"Got in the habit of carrying it," she said mildly. "Don't know of any good reason to leave it behind yet, do you?"

"Don't exactly see any problems—"

"Nothing locally. At the moment." She smiled at him. "In another month or two, I'll need it to maneuver around the halls." She ruffled his hair. "Don't look at me like that; I feel fat and awkward, that's all. You knew it was coming."

"Fat," Dahven scoffed easily. "Fat, my—"

"Shhh." Jennifer shushed him, cast a sidelong glance at two of her young women clerks who were busy stacking string-tied folders in the middle of their desk. "Shell-like maiden ears, all right?" She waved at the girls, let Dahven lead her out into the hall. "What's for dinner—or do you know, either?"

"Staff said a surprise, in honor of," Dahven said. "Shesseran, of course," he added in response to her raised eyebrows, and, darkly, "I hope that doesn't mean Lowen's going to start playing with the food once more."

"Doubt it. She quit experimenting with the meals when I turned up pregnant, remember?"

It was, as always, exquisitely cool in the dining hall—almost cold after the heat of the office, Jennifer thought. *Wonderful. For the first time all day, I finally feel awake.* She settled into her chair, laid the bo on the floor next to it, eased the soft backless shoes off with her toes. Dahven took his place next to her, slid low in his chair and balanced his chin on steepled fingers; watching her, expectantly.

Something—what did he expect her to notice? "Very nice—roses in a bowl, the cloth Birdy's girls embroidered for us under them, new candles, our matched silver goblets, goodness! The whole nine—what's this?" She leaned forward, wrapped her hand around the bottle standing next to the roses and examined it closely. "Yours?" He shook his head, waited. "Nice bottle, anyway. Where's it from?"

"There were actually two bottles in the basket, there's a note—here." He fished through his pockets and finally came up with a square of thick, rough-edged cream paper.

"In honor of Emperor Shesseran's natal day, with his thanks

for valued service to Rhadaz—and with additional thanks from Prince Afronsan." Jennifer's eyebrows went up. "From 'Prince' Afronsan?" He'd never once addressed himself by the title, not to her or around her. The hair at the base of her neck prickled. *"Really?"*

"What it says," Dahven replied. He sprawled even lower in his chair, chin now in one hand, still watching her.

"And this being the Emperor's day, we're to toast him, I gather."

"Not bad so far." Dahven freed his hand so he could offer her silent applause, then hooked it back under his chin once more.

"With this—whatever it is—stuff."

"Brilliant. I knew I'd wed brains."

"Yes, and didn't you need them," Jennifer responded dryly. His lips shaped her a kiss, and he grinned. "Even though 'Prince' Afronsan is well aware I can't drink because I'm pregnant—and that we both have excellent reason to never accept gift wine?"

"Brandy," Dahven corrected her. "Otherwise—"

"And," Jennifer shook a finger at him, "if you'll allow me to finish, sir, although brandy starts out as wine, you know, *and*— oddest of all, I received a wire from Afronsan this afternoon, which made no mention at all of any gift." She paused; Dahven merely smiled blandly and waved her on. "Thank you, kind sir. I meant to tell you, the temporary telegraph station is finally set up—two of them, actually. One at the last pole heading north-west, coming out of his offices, the other at the southwest end of our line. He said there can't be ten days' work separating the two, and that's factoring in possible bad weather and breaks."

"I knew he was threatening to put in temporary stations—"

"Not just a threat, you know Afronsan; he couldn't wait to use that machine."

"Anything important, or just chatter?"

"Mostly chatter—a few points about a woolen mill that may be slated for the coast near Bez." She turned the bottle around once more, tipped her head to one side so light could fall on it and she could study the seal more closely. "*Pages* of chatter— well, two pages and a half, anyway. Plenty about the Emperor's natal day celebration in Podhru, and chatty enough that if he'd really sent this, he'd have said something about it—if only that he was aware I wouldn't be drinking any and to apologize for the temptation."

"Mmmm. Well, you'll notice I didn't crack the seal." Dahven

took the bottle from her. "It appears to be English—but I wasn't aware the English made brandies. And I'm reminded of something Chris said—what was it about brandies?" He frowned. "Can't remember."

"Not surprising, considering how many things he said while he was here." Jennifer touched the bottle with one finger, drew it back and stared down at it. "Maybe I'd better wire the Heir, tonight. I mean, this and a note like that with it—who else do you think might have one?" She looked up. Dahven slowly shook his head. "You, me—and every other Duke in Rhadaz? Maybe?"

"It sounds mad." Dahven sat up and drove both hands through his hair.

Jennifer frowned; a half-submerged memory . . . "Look, I'm probably wrong about this stuff." She unhooked his near hand from his hair and smoothed it. "He could have just got one of his clerks to send a note and bottles out; I know he's trying to delegate more small stuff these days. But let's ask—just in case, all right?" He groaned, nodded. "Good. God, it's been a hot day!"

Dahven grinned. "You had to pick sun-washed rooms for your offices, didn't you? You eat something, and we'll figure out a message for the Heir."

"One for Robyn and Aletto, too," Jennifer said. "Aletto *said* he was going to station a man at the end of their wire—"

"It might even be up to the fort wall by now." Dahven captured her hand. "But you eat first."

"That's an easy promise to keep; I'm starved." She glanced toward the kitchen. "Speak of which, what's taking them so long down there? You don't suppose Lowen got creative after all?"

"Deliver us." Dahven got up and walked over to the door that led to the long hall which eventually came out in the kitchens; as he opened it, Jennifer heard a high-pitched babble, shrill and frightened-sounding women, a man shouting them down. She turned in her chair, came halfway to her feet. Dahven shut the door. "Something's wrong down there—I can't decide what." He slid past the waterfall and ran toward the entry. Jennifer was on her feet. Dahven held up a hand, listened intently, then turned back.

"Don't know. I can hear plenty of yelling down that way. Could be someone at the guard station— Wait here, I'll go check."

"You only *think* I'm staying in this room without you!"

Jennifer replied vigorously. She knelt, scooped up her bo and rounded the table at a barefooted run. "Remember last time I got caught in here alone?" He cast her a startled look, compressed his lips. "Come on, let's get out of here, the damned room's wide open."

But before she could reach him, Dahven began backing into the room, one arm outstretched to catch her. "Grelt's whistle—did you hear it? Attack from outside, armed men! And," he added softly, "it's coming this way. I can hear shouting out in the courtyard—ours or not, I can't tell—" She heard it too; then the unmistakable flat crack of rifles and the higher, sharp snap of pistol fire. Coming from outside and down the long hall both.

"Cisterns," Jennifer said crisply as he hesitated.

"Cisterns," Dahven agreed. "Go, wait for me." He bounded across the table as Jennifer skirted the pool at the far end of the room. She listened intently at the door there before opening it, and the bo was up and ready as she unlatched it, then eased it stealthily with her foot. No one there—this time. She drew a deep breath and expelled it hard. Dahven was back at the serving doorway to the kitchen; a plain sword belt hung from his shoulder. He glanced her way; she nodded and he closed the door, then ran over to join her. Jennifer led the way into the boxlike, windowless storage room. Her jaw was set, lips tightly compressed; her heart thudded heavily against her ribs. *I know they've cleaned this place, more than once. I swear I can still smell Anselm's blood.* And the stuff they'd drugged her with. She tightened her grip on the bo; Dahven handed her his sword belt and knelt to lay his ear against the floor hatch that led to the palace cisterns. Jennifer glanced over her shoulder. Louder out there . . . she took a step back, juggled his swords and her bo in one hand, pulled the door to. He already had the hatch up.

"Carry the belt for me, can you, Jen? And—here, wait a moment." He pressed her toward the steps, made certain she had the hatch under control and ran back into the main room, returning before she had a chance to open her mouth, the small box of blue-lights kept at the far end of the table clutched in his hands. "Go, I'll follow." He shifted the box and held it against his ribs, took the weight of the hatch on his shoulder. It came down with him, plunging them into utter blackness.

Jennifer stood very still, halfway down the steps, breath held, bo braced against the step below to help her balance. She could make out very faint sounds the way they'd come, she thought; a step above her, Dahven was fiddling with the box catch. *Thread*, she ordered herself. She wanted to shiver—dislike of enclosed places, mostly, though it didn't help she'd come this way before in—*call it unfavorable circumstances*, she thought. Thread. Something to concentrate on—and a useful weapon. She shifted into awareness: no one below them, at least. No one in the little storage room yet, either. The water-Thread and its New-Agelike sound overwhelmed nearly everything else, with the great stone pools so near.

She regained normal perception as blue-light flooded the narrow, steep passage. Dahven held out one of the thick glass balls for her and eased his sword belt out of her other hand. She glanced back up at him; he had the open box balanced on one hip, the sword belt slung over his shoulder and a long, slender sword in his hand. "You first," she whispered, and edged aside to let him pass. "Don't want you falling on me with that nasty thing out."

"Me, either," he whispered back. "I can light the steps for you and be there if *you* fall." He grinned as he slid by her; Jennifer stuck her tongue out and made a hideous face. "Anything down there? Or could you tell?"

"Just water—no one waiting."

"Mmmm. I'll keep this ready anyway." He went down the long flight of stone steps sideways, cat-footed, elbow high. The sword glittered. Jennifer juggled the blue light, finally shifted it into her left hand so she could get a better grip on the bo. It seemed forever down to level floor once again. Dahven glanced her way and gestured with his chin toward the arched doorway into the cisterns, five paces away. Jennifer set her blue-light on the last step, took a good two-hand hold on the long staff, and waited. Dahven stopped just short of the arch to set down the box of blue-lights, to ease the sword belt from his shoulder and draw his second blade; the belt hit the floor with a muted thump. Jennifer caught her breath harshly as he rounded the doorway and vanished into the enormous holding chamber, but he was back almost at once. She left the single blue-light where it was, picked up the box and followed him through the arch.

"You all right?" he asked in a low voice. Jennifer nodded, not trusting her own. Dahven laid his swords on the floor and drew her close. "Certain?" She nodded again. He looked around, led her a short distance to the broad stone lip of the nearest pool. "Sit, I'll be right back." He went back for his swords and back through the arch to retrieve the belt; he had both blades snugged under one arm and was fastening the belt around his hips with steady hands as he came back.

"What—what now?" Her voice was a little high, maybe. Not shaking. Good. He'd have enough to worry about, without fretting about *her*.

"Now? We wait a little. Once everything is clear up there, and Grelt finds the dining room empty, he'll send men down here. Only logical place for us to go, after all. And if no one comes looking for us after a while—well, then we'll wait until dark and go out the far end, just like we did the first time you left the Thukar's palace." He cupped her cheek with his hand. "I'm sorry, I know how you dislike places such as this."

"It's better than being used for a pincushion, or target practice," Jennifer replied dryly. It struck her as outrageous, all at once. "Someone's actually invaded the palace!"

"Sounds unlikely, doesn't it?" Dahven replied. "Even the Lasanachi didn't get that far against Dro Pent. Of course, they didn't have guns, either." Silence. "I've been thinking—that brandy. The celebrations for the Emperor's birthday tonight, all across Rhadaz. If one of the foreign lands really does want Rhadaz, as Chris thinks, the timing couldn't be better."

Jennifer frowned. "But we're still back to which one? I mean—the note could have been anyone."

"The bottle has an English seal."

"Yes, but the English don't export liquors. Not here, at least. I think the Mer Khani offered us beer or ale, early on. Of course, the French distill liquors—"

"Little brown sand gods," Dahven said suddenly. "I remember now—Dupret. Remember what Ariadne and Chris were talking about, that first evening?"

Jennifer nodded. "I—wait—about things being done to the Zero at his distillery and then it's sent to France, and Chris—Chris said, something about boxes of flavored brandies. . . ." She sighed. "Dupret's brandy. But *he* doesn't trade with Rhadaz, and the French have barely begun to work with us. So how did that stuff get an English seal and make it here?"

"Dupret." Dahven rubbed his chin against her hair. "In league with the English, the Mer Khani, the Gaelic States—?"

"Or Vuhlem?" Jennifer put in. "Lialla says he's bringing in Zero, remember?"

Dahven swore under his breath. "It gets more tangled and ridiculous by the hour!"

Jennifer shook her head. "I know. The wire I send to Afronsan later tonight is going to include some pretty pointed questions for Chris."

                          *   *   *

CHRIS at the moment had several pretty pointed questions of his own—his head ached with them. He glanced in Ariadne's direction, let his eyes close as she shifted her weight. All these hours in darkness, he could actually make out her face if she stayed within arm's reach—which meant she could see his, too. He wasn't entirely certain he wanted her to read his face at the moment. After all, she had the— *Chill, Cray*, he ordered himself hastily. *Remind yourself you'd rather have an assassin on your side tonight than a weepy girl-type you'd probably have to coldcock in order to get her off the boat quietly.* His stomach hurt. *Those afternoon talk show TV people back home would be all over me—Men Who Marry Terrorists and the women who cut them.*

Somehow he managed not to jump as Ariadne's breath tickled the hair on his neck; her hand edged up his shoulder and caught his earlobe and she spoke very softly. "How many hours do you think it has been?"

Chris edged around and replied in kind: "Heard the midnight bell up there. We're moving pretty fast, too."

"So. We could be near this Bez—when?"

"Before daybreak, with a good set of sails, good wind and guys who know their job." She kept her hand on his ear, withdrew into herself for a long moment. Leaned back once again.

"Then it is time for us to act." She looked at him, searchingly, he thought. Seeing if he was scared, probably. "You are ready?"

"Nearly. Gimme a minute to get my arms and legs loosened up again, okay?"

"Well thought." She let go of him, moved back and seemed to flow to her feet and across the room. Chris started after her, then checked the movement as his left foot tried to cramp. She wasn't going anywhere, though: Faint light coming through cracks between the boards making up the bulkhead between storage and hall showed her clearly. She had her head turned, ear to the wall most likely. After a long moment, she nodded, then bent forward, hands working at her lower back. Chris stretched out his left foot until it quit protesting, then drew his knees up to his chest one after the other, swung his arms back and forth and tried to work the kinks out of his neck. He clasped his hands, stretched them carefully. *No gross popping noises, please, guys. They'd hear it up on deck and she'd kill me.* He glanced at Ariadne, who was coming up from a deep squat. *Literally.* Nice thought. He sat down and worked his feet out of the soaked boots, pulled up his thick socks and went over to join her. Ariadne nodded and moved to the door, slid the blade into the narrow crack between door and door jamb, all the way down and then high as she could. She shook her head, leaned against the crack to listen intently. Chris held his breath. Nothing moving out there. After a moment, Ariadne turned and tugged at his shirt; he bent down so he could whisper against his ear. "No one there. A man at the head of the steps, however, on the deck." *Oh, yeah?* But Jennifer could have told him that, and so could Li. Just one more thing Ariadne hadn't bothered to tell him about. *Well, hey, maybe Dija got her a market charm, who knows? Ease up,* he ordered himself. Ariadne tugged at his earlobe to get his attention. "I open the door; you wait at the end of the steps. I manage that one."

He opened his mouth, closed it again. No point in arguing this again; besides, she had the knife. Ariadne gripped his forearm with her free hand; he laid his hand over hers and squeezed. A brief flash of teeth answered him; the hand fell away. She eased the door open, paused, then moved into the open. Chris took her place in the doorway and stared; she'd been wearing dark stuff anyway, for travel, but now everything except her eyes was swathed in those long, black scarves. Black gloves, the dark skirt—no boots, dark stockings. She went up the stairs without so much as a whisper of cotton against wood and nary a creak and vanished, a dark, small shadow moving into darker shadow.

The ship was creaking enough, out there, to cover his own noises—if they got that far. Chris watched as she disappeared up into darkness and bit his lip. He didn't have anything in the way of a weapon; if she screwed this up, he'd have to fall back onto his judo. *Of which there isn't nearly enough.* Something he could use as a bo—in that room they'd just left, or maybe in this hallway . . . but before he could even properly formulate the notion, Ariadne was back, crouched down on an upper step and beckoning urgently. Chris drew a deep breath and went as fast and quietly as he could. Not as quiet as she'd been—not bad, considering his big feet and greater size.

She withdrew in a crouch onto the deck, well in the shadow

of the shed roof covering the steps, used her hands to indicate he should stay low, too. *Like I'm that dumb, lady.* His irritation vanished when his knee came down on something soft. His hand went out, touched a bearded face; he snatched it back at once. He'd never felt a dead man before, but there was no mistaking this one.

She tugged at his shirt, leaning across the body and murmured against his ear, "Three men that I can tell on the deck; one above, in the sails. Do not look up—your face will show, and it is much paler than his." She found his hand, pressed a dagger hilt against his palm and closed the fingers over it. "That was his. How do we leave this ship?"

Chris set his free hand under her chin and turned her head in the right direction. He eased himself a little higher, settled back on his heels and cautiously pointed.

She nodded and was on her feet, bent low and moving swiftly and silently across the deck. Chris glanced in the direction of the bow and the helm—two men there at the wheel, he couldn't see anyone else. Maybe one man in the bow; that was usual when sailing at night without a moon. No one the other way—that he could see, at least. The guy in the rigging might hear or see him— *Go. Just—just go.* He felt enormous and awkward, all pale hands, heavy feet, buffalo-gaited; there was too much cloud for moon or stars but it was never totally dark at sea, and it seemed impossible he'd make it all the way to the rail. His forehead was slick with sweat by the time he gained the minimal shelter of the railing. He crouched there, fighting to breathe quietly; his left hand was already exploring the side. "Good," he whispered. "Cargo net right there—feel it?" He took her hand, guided it to the rope, then leaned close to her and breathed against her scarves: "Easy now, go as far down as you can and *wait for me.* We don't *even* want to get separated out there."

"No." She was gone, over the side, working her way silently down. He edged his way around so his back was to the rail, the knife in his hand, watching. Nothing. No one. Count of five— still quiet. He jammed the dagger through his belt at the small of his back, prayed it wouldn't poke him, and slid sideways over the rail, feet searching for holds. A very small hand gripped his toes, guided them into place; she had stopped just out of sight. Chris looked down at her and nodded. Ariadne began a slow, cautious climb down the wide mesh of rope.

Moments later they were both clinging to the lower edge of

the net, fingers and toes curled around thick, wet rope. Chris looked down. Still a bit of a drop—he'd never cared much for even low diving boards. *At least it isn't the ten-meter.* Ariadne watched him; her lip was caught in her teeth and she looked rather anxious, he thought. "Sure you can swim?" he whispered.

"I—can swim." She twisted around to eye the distant black highlands. "But that far and in a sea—"

"I can get us both to shore," Chris assured her. "Can you jump in and not panic?"

"I—?" For a moment she looked truly outraged; she shook her head. "I waste time. I can do what I must. Go, I'll follow."

"Nope. We go together, count of three. Keep your feet together, arms close to your body, legs straight. You'll go deeper that way but you won't make a splash." She nodded, watched his face as he counted and, at three, drew in a deep breath and let go of the net.

The water was cold, and it seemed to Chris he went down forever. *Thank God for all that skin-diving.* At lest his brain wasn't freaking that his lungs couldn't hack it. He broke the surface, shook hair and water out of his eyes and blinked rapidly to clear them. Ariadne trod water rather awkwardly a few feet away, her back to him; she was watching the ship continue toward the Bez straits without them. Chris swam toward her.

Ariadne grinned at him and her eyes were alight. "Her name was on the stern in so large letters even the blind could read them! *Windsong.* Have you heard of it?" Chris let his head fall back as he trod water; he had to fight not to laugh out loud, the ship was too close for that. A giggle escaped, all the same. Ariadne swam closer to him. "What?"

"Heard of it? Oh, lady, haven't I *just*!" *Picked us up, only just four years too late and outside the wrong city, going the wrong way—no big deal. Chuffles, old buddy, know what? I just found another reason to get out of this in one piece and it's called Nail Your Ugly Hide to the Nearest Wall.*

12

⌘

JENNIFER looked up as one of the household women handed her a cup and only just managed to stifle a grimace as her eyes made contact with the gruesome turquoise-and-gilt walls of the blue room. The woman would probably think her Thukara was scowling at *her*. And, Jennifer thought as she looked at the drawn face and overbright eyes, burst into tears. Half the kitchen staff was still hysterical. "Thank you, Hinerra." The woman inclined her head, turned and left; two guards went with her. Hinerra's daughter, Jennifer recalled, was one of the new kitchen girls. *Wonderful.* Her eyes rested on the door just closing behind the servant: Royal blue and turquoise, gruesome fat, smirking gold cherubs in some kind of relief work, reaching down for the latches. *Ugh. Those two. That blue. It's a conspiracy, these guys are trying to keep me so busy I* can't *redecorate the damned room.*

Ridiculous thought—not even remotely funny; all the same, it brought up a grin from somewhere, and momentarily loosened the tightness in her chest. *I feel like a few hysterics myself, at the moment.* She sniffed the liquid, then sipped cautiously—berry, slightly sweetened, no booze or other calming agents. One or two of the older women with country backgrounds couldn't be made to see her reasoning or the midwife's on the subject of alcohol and babies. This poor kid of hers had one involuntary black mark on its record already, thanks to Dahven's brothers and the dose of Zero she'd been fed; she wasn't going to add any deliberate blots on her own if she could help it. *Yeah. You and your peach dessert wine—just one swallow, now and again . . . You don't even like it that much. Stick to water, like a good girl.* She sighed, closed her eyes and slumped lower in the chair, then

204

finished the fruit drink and settled the base of the cup onto the three-sided table by feel.

Men were everywhere; three guards inside the blue room. She didn't like it much, but Grelt wasn't in a negotiating mood; when she'd tried to argue with him he'd said flatly it was this or one of the tower rooms, where she could be safely locked in. *Hah. He only thinks I'd go hang out up there again,* she thought sourly. Once, four years ago had been enough for a lifetime.

Dahven was helping with the search, out there somewhere with the guard combing halls and checking all the rooms. She didn't like that, either, but he and Grelt had both gone male and protective on her, and she'd finally backed down. They were right, anyway: She had more than herself to look out for. She shifted, crossed her legs—only barely above to do that with the extra weight, she realized moodily—and swung her free foot back and forth. *Great example you're setting for those kids in guard suits, lady.* Half the guard in here looked younger than Chris by several years, and she'd bet most of them were scared half silly behind those poker faces. She ought to summon the energy, sit up . . . *Yeah. Foreigners in the Thukar's palace. As Chris would say, like I could make them forget that. Rully.*

I should be hungry; we never did get dinner, and I was starving when we got to the dining room. She shifted awkwardly, drew one bare foot up under her, and rubbed her back against the rough cloth of the chair; the growing itch between her shoulder blades flared, subsided. Watch—she fumbled at her shirt pocket, swore under her breath as she remembered setting the heavy thing on her desk when it and the shirt underneath stuck to her skin.

The door opened; she sat up. One of the younger wall guards in very new sand-colored breeks and tunic came across blue carpets and knelt self-consciously at the foot of the dais. Eyes averted, he held out a long ribbon of paper. Jennifer resisted the urge to snatch it from him—an even stronger urge to order him to knock it off that she knew was created by lack of food, worry and the clashing shades of blue that never failed to set her teeth on edge. "It's all right, relax," she mumbled. Some of the newer guards really made her feel silly—all this bowing and scraping. Dahven was going to have to talk to the new under-armsmaster about this protocol stuff. "Give," she added, and extended a hand. That narrow paper came from the telegraph office; the Mer Khani had provided it, and the man who headed the Sikkreni

telegraph office was too frugal to waste it. "At ease," she added
dryly; the boy seemed locked in place. "In fact, you can go if
there's no answer—"

"They said wait," he replied earnestly, then blushed. "Um, I
mean, Thukara, pardon—"

"Never mind," Jennifer broke in hastily. "It's perfectly all
right, I don't eat guards, you know. Go sit—over there. I'll call
when I need you." Her eyes were running down the sheet.

The message was actually quite short—frustrating because of
it: THUKAR AND THUKARA BEWARE LIQUOR GIFTED
YOU ALSO WAS ATTACK ON WIRE TO BEZ AND SIKKRE
SO SUGGEST YOU SEND ARMED MEN TO CHECK WIRE
YOUR END AND WARN THEM RIDE WARY END. She
sighed heavily, turned the paper over—nothing. No who, no
why—well, the Heir likely didn't know either. She thought a moment, beckoned the boy over as she pulled the little table closer;
the cup went clattering across the dais. She was printing rapidly,
large block letters on the back of the message as the boy knelt
once more.

"Here—what's your name?"

"Japyr, my—"

"Good," she broke in hastily. "Japyr. Take this back to the
wire office, have them send it immediately." It was even more
terse than Afronsan's: RECEIVED BOTTLES. DID NOT
DRINK. PALACE ATTACKED TONIGHT. OK HERE. WILL
CHECK WIRE SIKKRE. The boy practically ran from the room;
the doors banged behind him. Jennifer got to her feet. "One of
you—go find Grelt or the Thukar. I have news for them."

But the door opened and Dahven came in; one of the household men followed bearing a laden tray covered by a heavy,
cream-colored cloth. "Lowen's compliments." Dahven held the
small table steady so the guard could set the tray down. "Thanks,
Feriman." The guard inclined his head, left. "She's afraid you've
already wasted away," Dahven added; he dropped heavily into
his chair and drew the cloth aside.

"A lot *she* knows."

"Yes, well, that isn't all fat, remember? She also insisted I
make certain you eat, and that I help you." Jennifer sniffed a
deep, two-handled cup of clear, steaming broth, snagged a thick
slice of brown bread and tore it into ragged chunks, dropped
them into the soup and drank. Hot, almost too hot to drink:
chicken, with parsley for flavor and nothing else. *Wonderful. I*

love this stuff before she starts messing with it. "She apologized because it wasn't much, not what she'd planned—"

"This is fine, honestly." She couldn't tell the head cook she preferred plain stock; the woman would be hurt. She blew on the soup, drank more. It warmed her throat, released the tightness in her chest she hadn't even realized was there. "We had a wire from Afronsan." Dahven looked across his soup mug; she repeated it, as close to word for word as she could remember.

"Oh, wonderful! Think anything else can go wrong tonight?"

"Drink your soup; you're supposed to be helping me with all this food," Jennifer replied mildly. "I sent a reply, just to let him know we were still alive."

"Yes. Well." Dahven tore his bread in half and dribbled honey on it. "The cut wires will have to wait until daylight; we haven't anyone to spare right now."

"The wire can wait; if it's been cut, the guys with the scissors are probably waiting for the repair crew."

"Grelt says the palace is clear; there's going to be an armed guard on our apartments tonight, though, and he's got men up there installing a heavy inside bar right now. The city—well, who knows? I haven't heard in a while but the city guard was combing the streets looking for the men who escaped the palace; I heard there was gunfire out there."

Jennifer spread butter on a bit of bread and tucked it in her cheek, poured chilled water into her cup. "Any other exciting news?"

He shrugged. "Nothing at the moment. Seven men dead, three injured—but not nearly as bad as I'd feared when I heard those guns. Seven prisoners," he added shortly.

"Prisoners—really! Who? I mean, what—?"

"*You* sort them out," Dahven snorted. "Seven men, and not one of them talking—but as far as any of us can tell, there's at least six different nationalities among them."

* * *

It was very much a party on the streets of Holmaddan City: Vuhlem had sent out casks of ale, beer and wine at sundown, to be stationed at the four main city squares and shared among the populace. For once, the weather was cooperating and as the night sky grew dark, it was almost temperate—the wind was gone, the air dry.

Three young women in subdued dark blue caravaner breeks and thick brown cloaks threaded their way down one of the main thoroughfares, skirting several men playing drums, tambors and a'luds. Black-clad women stood all around them, clapping in time and watching a long line of dancing men. A little farther on, two men danced openly with their young wives. Ryselle shook her head. "If my father could see this, he would die of it."

Lialla laughed. "As my friend Chris says, you *wish*."

Ryselle grinned. "It would certainly upset his stomach. And our young *friend*—I wonder what he would say if he saw them."

"I wonder," Lialla replied dryly. The three skirted yet another street band, and made a wide detour behind a mob waiting for the Duke's free wine.

Sil was clapping her hands in time to the music. "Yes. If we'd had any sense, we would have never let him out of the building this afternoon." She thought about this. "If we had real sense, we'd let him reap his own profits from this notion of his."

Ryselle snorted; they turned down on of the narrow alleys. "Have *you* tried stopping a Holmaddi male? But I'd have sat on him while you draped him in chains. Young fool."

"Better yet, I'd have locked him in the privy and left him there the night," Sil replied cheerfully. "I still say sensible women would let him go and get himself killed."

Lialla shook her head. "And if he's caught? The Duke would start pulling his teeth or set that Triad on him, and only *then* kill him."

"Mmmm. After he's named names. You *do* know how to choose a pleasant thought," Sil replied.

"I blame myself," Lialla said after a moment. "I had to mention the brandy in the first place; I could've kept my mouth shut until after he was gone, at least. Or kept him—"

"Don't blame yourself, Li," Sil said mildly. "If you hadn't said anything, we might not have found out where they took that Gray Haven cache. I can't quite blame him—he wants to *do* something, you know how boys are. And he had to go back or be counted a deserter, and Vuhlem wouldn't be pleased about that, either."

"Name me one thing that *would* please Vuhlem," Lialla said gloomily. They reached the end of the alley, emerged into bright lights, music and more people—a different mix of all three, since they were nearer the city barracks, away from the commercial areas. "He's too young for the guard, you know; they made him a messenger boy, but it's nothing official. He's not held to the same rules."

"Let's hope not," Sil said quietly as they skirted yet another group of male dancers—younger and mostly guard-clad here—and a group of admiring girls. A small military horn and drum band played for them. "If he's caught with his hands in those Gray Haven bottles, he'd better have a good lie ready." She was quiet as they slid between dancers and musicians and out into the open again. "So had we better, come to that. In case they catch *us*."

"I did tell you I could do this alone—"

"I know you did, Li. I remember my answer, too."

"And that's the last thing the boy said, isn't it?"

Lialla snorted, stepped into shadow and fished in her tunic. She pulled out a tangle of long chains, several small, odd-shaped pendants. "Here, take this."

"Blurring-charm?"

"Shhh—yes." Lialla separated the mass of chain into three separate chains, draped one over Sil's wrist and handed the second to Ryselle. "You know how this works? Put the chain around your neck but keep the charm away from your skin until we get near the barracks. I'll tell you when to slide it under your tunic, so it's touching flesh. It'll keep you unnoticed for as long as we need to be here—so long as you don't run into anyone. But you don't just want to suddenly disappear in the middle of the street."

"No. Oh." Ryselle laid the charm on her open hand and gazed at it curiously. "A thing this small—?"

"Just so." Lialla closed her fingers over it. "Better if you don't let people know you have it; they aren't exactly illegal, but guards don't like to see people with them."

"They don't?" Ryselle obediently drew the chain over her head.

"Thieves use them."

Ryselle nodded. Two days of city—she still felt very much like a goat in deep water. *Sretha was right; a city isn't just a village grown large.* At least these women didn't laugh at her for her foolishnesses. But there weren't any thieves in Gray Haven—what would anyone steal? She bit back a sigh. *Besides my fool brothers and their friends, who stole the Duke's goods.*

The street was wider here, all at once, not quite as well lit, the men almost all young and the women—Ryselle's eyebrows went up in astonishment as she nearly ran into one of them. *She must be half frozen, so much of her bosom out of her dress—and what is all that black stuff around her eyes?* Lialla and Sil took her arms and drew her on down the street, then into shadow between two dim blue-lights. "Almost there," Sil whispered. "Keep quiet here, all right?" Ryselle nodded; Lialla turned and ran light-footed between two low barracks, stopped at the far end of the skinny alley, then crouched low and moved along the back side of the right-hand building. Open windows here, hard-packed dirt and the smell of horses—no lights at all except for reflection against an inner wall from a blue-light even farther inside. She waved her hand, waited until the other two women caught up with her.

Sil edged to the fore and looked around, then touched Ryselle's shoulder and indicated direction: the thick hedge the boy had mentioned that separated the line of barracks from the stables. Lialla's fingers closed on her shoulder; she held up her own charm, dropped it inside her tunic. Ryselle shifted hers, hesitated. She didn't feel that different—that less visible. She swallowed, eased away from the wall and went crouching into the darkness. The hedge was very prickly; a cautiously drawn breath assured her it wasn't used for the purpose the men in her village would have put it to. She edged along it, hand feeling for some hole—two, three, four paces. A hard-packed path and a gap. Through that . . .

It was extremely dark back here, the smell of horses very strong; she could hear laughter from the street, back the way they'd come, see the outlines of the barracks roofs from the light out there. Lialla was with her then, and a moment later, Sil.

Sil's face was invisible in the deep shade of the hedge, Ryselle's just visible if Lialla leaned closer to her. The village woman raised her shoulders in an elaborate shrug and mouthed, *What now?*

Lialla nodded her head toward the building they'd just left and mouthed, *Wait and see.* She was playing it by the moment herself—the way her luck had gone ever since she'd first come to Holmaddan, the boy was out there in the street partying, or he'd already gone to sleep, and he'd had no intention of stealing a bottle of that brandy for her. The stables: She shifted into Thread-awareness. A man in the stables, among the horses—asleep or nearly so. No telling if that was the boy, if he'd come and gone—if the bottles were in there—if anything. *I had to talk about getting hard proof against Vuhlem while that fool boy was in earshot*, she thought gloomily. Asking for trouble.

Trouble for more than Kepron, if someone stumbled across

them. *I should have made them let me come alone.* Well, she'd tried; at the moment, she was rather glad of the company. A faint southerly breeze stirred the hedge and brought the warm, familiar odor of stables with it. *I can just imagine poor Jen out here, the way she hates the smell of horse.*

Time passed. Lialla stretched cautiously, extended her Thread-sense again. It was getting late; the boy was probably on the street somewhere or already passed out in his bed. Furtive movement in the stable, then, but not from the man she'd found earlier: He still slept. This— she still couldn't tell one person from another with Thread, but there was no doubt in her mind, the slow, careful way he was moving in there—what man with acceptable business in the stables would be skulking around that way? *Kepron—you young fool!*

Light stabbed from the nearest window of the barracks, then spilled over hard-packed, dry ground between building and hedge. Lialla raised a hand to shield her eyes and blinked rapidly; Sil tugged at her sleeve, indicating the hand urgently with her chin. Lialla tucked it inside her dark sleeve as a two-handed oil lamp, turned high, was set down with a thump just inside the open window. Two enormous men suddenly blocked the light; a mumble of voices reached them, growing clearer by the moment as the men neared the window.

"—only did what was necessary, sir."

"All the same, the Duke is grateful for your help, Ripliden. He'll send a cart for the boxes at first light, and there'll be a bit extra in the pay packet for you and your men this month. Duke Vuhlem likes to reward initiative like yours."

"Well—thank you, sir."

"The crates are in a safe place?"

"Out there—no guard but there's a man on duty at all hours."

"Good enough. Well—" The Duke's man stretched expansively; the shadow of his arms crossed the hedge and the women went quietly flat onto the dirt. "I'd best be gone."

"I'll light your way, sir." The lantern moved; Lialla felt cautiously for her knife.

Ryselle started violently, gripped Lialla's arm—hooves clattered into the stable and across loose planks. And then a high-pitched, startled yell from inside the stable; the women went face down and utterly still as the two burly guardsmen ran from the building, through the gap in the hedge and into the stables. Another yell, indignant and unmistakable: Lialla cast up her eyes and swore under her breath, then touched Ryselle's arm to get her attention and indicated the hedge with the least movement of her head. She eased herself slowly back toward the main branches, as far into shadow as possible. Ryselle edged herself in the same direction; Lialla could just hear furtive movement behind her that she hoped was Sil. Three men emerged from the stables: the two guards with the boy caught up by his arms and dangling between them. He clutched something to his chest. The far guard, a bear of a man in Vuhlem's colors, stopped short, dragging boy and guard captain perforce to a halt. He snatched a bottle from Kepron's hands and bellowed, "Explain yourself, boy!"

Kepron's voice was girl-shrill and tremulous. "I wasn't—I mean, I didn't—! I mean, sir, I—!"

"Silence! I can see for myself; Captain, you've a thief in your company! And a thief who steals from Duke Vuhlem—you surely knew those things were Duke's property, boy! Well? *Well?*"

"I—well, no, I—I mean, sir, yes, I—"

"You know what stealing that same Duke's property cost other men of late, boy?"

"I—but, but sir, I—" Kepron sounded very near tears. The Duke's man loomed hugely over him; his captain snagged both his arms and gave him a ferocious shake. Ryselle had to grab her lower lip between her teeth; her stomach hurt like she'd swallowed a stone from the fear that they'd be found the moment that man took his eyes off Kepron. At the same time, she was fighting a dreadful urge to laugh. *Serve the little fool right.* He looked just like her brothers—she bit down hard on the corners of her mouth and closed her eyes. All at once it wasn't the least bit funny.

The captain spoke up, his voice stern but mild compared to the Duke's man. "Just tell him, Kepron, don't dither so! Zerygos, he's a boy and it's the Emperor's fest-night, can't you tell he's already half drunk? I can vouch the boy's normally honest and honorable, like his father before him. Give him a chance to tell his side of things, why don't you?"

"Bah!" Zerygos spat, turned on his heel and stomped off toward the barracks. Kepron staggered; without the captain's grip, he'd have fallen. The captain gave him another shake, nothing as fierce as the last one.

"All right, boy. Partly my fault, I suppose; I thought everyone knew not to touch those crates, but you were gone when we brought them in, weren't you?" Kepron nodded cautiously. "All right. Buck up, then; I won't let the Duke's men eat you. But let this be a lesson to you, boy! A guardsman doesn't sneak things, or steal—not in this company, he doesn't!"

"Sir. I'm—sorry, sir." Kepron had gone weak-kneed; his whole body sagged; Ryselle watched, fascinated, as his near hand took on a life of its own, edged up under his tunic and withdrew another bottle; it slid from his grasp and fell less than an arm's length to land in soft dirt next to the worn path. The captain was laughing, covering whatever sound the thing might have made.

"Aye—well, all right. Not the worst thing you might've done, considering who your father was. Remind me, I'll tell you some of the scrapes *he* got into. Wonder to me our captain or the Duke himself didn't have the skin off the man once a week. Well—come on." He pushed through the hedge, pulling a very visibly reluctant Kepron after him. The outer door to the barracks slammed behind them but didn't catch; moments later the light faded as he picked up the lamp and carried it with them. Another door slammed—it was once again quiet and dark in the yard. The outer door creaked slowly open, with a faint growl of rusty hinges.

Ryselle worked her way from under the hedge and came up into a cautious crouch. Lialla's hand tugged at her sleeve; the Wielder breathed against her ear, "Careful!"

Ryselle nodded. "He dropped one." She went forward on her hands, feeling the ground. Just short of the gap in the hedge, she found something cool, smooth and heavy. Her fingers wrapped around it; she twisted around so Lialla could take it. "Now what?"

"We can't—is that one of the bottles?" Sil whispered. Lialla held it up; Sil touched it. "Good. Then let's get out of here."

"Can't," Lialla whispered back. "His captain won't be able to protect him, if Vuhlem's man decides to *really* question him."

Ryselle gripped her forearm hard. "You can't go in there! You said you wouldn't—!"

"I never said that." *And I don't want to,* Lialla thought grimly. *But that doesn't mean I can't.* "Go if you want." They shook their heads in unison; Lialla swore under her breath. "Then wait out here; stay close together, those charms should keep you hidden. You even think they're looking for you, don't wait to find out. I'll be fine." Both women gave her a clearly disbelieving

look. "This isn't the place to argue, all right?" Before either
could say anything else, she edged around Ryselle and into the
gap in the hedge. Both hands were deep in Thread by the time
she reached the barracks wall next to the door, and she was already drawing down the thick yellow blurring stuff to weave into
a compact net.

Thread: A net like this should protect against discovery by
anyone short of a Silver Sash Wielder—or a Triad. But she had
one small addition: Lialla stood still for one long moment, con-
centrating. *Not a shape or a sound—more of an almost-scent. I
think.* Whatever it was, it still lived under her ribs—she could
still Shape it: Light ran down the blurring-Thread and filled in
the mesh.

No one could see her now—perhaps a full Triad, but she'd
have been aware of one of those long before now. *Vuhlem's isn't
anywhere in the city; I can tell.* She dismissed that; she'd have
enough trouble seeing where she was going because everything
was laid over with Light and blurred or distorted. *Don't trip over
the furniture.*

There was just room enough for her to turn sideways and slide
into the room without touching that ill-oiled door.

Wall—over there, and bare floor between. Good. The inner
doors—three of them along the one wall—were closed tight. But
she could just make out voices now: Kepron's a little too high
and fast, and so very carrying; now the rumble of his captain's
as she came up to the wall. Vuhlem's man was growling like the
bear he resembled; probably scaring the boy half silly. But it
sounded like he might be backing down. She wrapped Thread
around her fingers in an elaborate cat's cradle and brought her
hands toward her face. Mumbling suddenly became clear words.

"You can see the boy meant no real harm. He simply saw the
bottles and was tempted. And we did recover the brandy, after
all."

"I'm—very sorry, sir," Kepron said. "I didn't know—I
thought it was the company's, and they—the men gave me wine
tonight, and I thought—it felt so good, I thought maybe a little
more, and I remembered those—"

The captain laughed, and he fell silent. "There, Zerygos.
Weren't you ever a boy and drunk a first time?"

"Well—by all rights I should report this. *You* know that stuff
isn't—"

"Yes, I know what kind of *brandy* it is," the captain said meaningfully. "D'you think it's important to the boy?"

Silence. Lialla smiled grimly: *Keep the dirty secrets from the babies, right?* "Well, then," Zerygos said grudgingly. "I suppose you can deal with this young fool. Make certain he remembers this night, mind now, Ripliden! No good saying he's young and drunken and forgiving him—they don't learn from that!"

"I know. I'll see he's properly punished, Zerygos."

"Good. And I'll see those crates are moved in the morning. Where's the inventory you made in that village?"

"You want it now? All right. Kepron, you're dismissed for now, but you're confined to barracks the rest of the night. You and I will discuss this in the morning."

"Sir. Thank you, sir." Lialla tensed as footsteps crossed the room on the far side of the wall and a door opened. It wasn't any of the three into this room, though. A moment later she heard Kepron tearfully curse under his breath.

Quick search—no one besides the boy close to this main chamber; he was coming her way. Lialla dropped the Thread/Light shielding, pulled the charm from inside her shirt, and dropped it in her pocket, just as the boy opened the door. He glanced back into the room he'd just left, listened intently a moment, then started light-footed across the main room, toward the outer door. His face was grim—*going for the rest of the evidence*, Lialla realized. And probably for the first time in his life aware there might be serious consequences if he were caught.

"Ssst! Boy!" Lialla hissed softly. His whole body jerked and he spun on one heel; his face was utterly white. "We have to get out of here, come on!" She grabbed his arm; he jerked it away.

"What are you doing in here?" His whisper was shrill; he clapped a hand over his mouth and goggled at her. When he spoke next the whisper was barely audible, near as she stood to him. "Why are you here at all? I have everything in control—!"

"Yes, so I heard," Lialla murmured. "Some control! We've got the bottle you dropped out there, that was good thinking, but the Duke's man is probably halfway back to Vuhlem with the inventory of those crates by now. Guess who he'll want to talk to when that top box comes up a bottle short?"

"I—" The boy's mouth sagged; he pulled it closed with a visible effort.

"You forgot they'd have a full count, didn't you?"

"Someone else might have—"

"Sure, anyone could've taken one. But they *know* you did, they caught you, remember?" He remembered all right, Lialla thought grimly. "Never mind, just let's get out of here." Scared as he was, he was still going to argue, she realized. Her fingers sank into muscle; he winced. "Look, kid: Come willingly, right now, or I'll put you to sleep on the spot and drag you." He glared at her, but there was no real strength in his anger; his shoulders sagged, the fire went out of his eyes and he nodded. She fished in her trous pocket and drew out a charm like the one she and the others already wore. "Put this on, it'll keep you unnoticed until we can put some distance between us and that Duke's man. Unless you'd prefer to see how Vuhlem decides to pry information out of you?"

Kepron closed his eyes and swallowed hard. He drew the chain over his head without further comment, stood quietly while Lialla slipped it under his shirt and into place against his chest, then let her lead him out the back way and into the dark.

* * *

IT was very dark on the north shore of the Sea of Rhadaz. Chris and Ariadne huddled under the edge of a low, crumbling stone bank, backs to a wave-pitted boulder: It was hard on the skin and still unpleasantly damp from high tide, but at least it partly blocked the erratic breeze coming from the east.

Ariadne leaned bonelessly against him, her cheek on his chest, her wool cloak wrapped around both of them—Chris had shed his halfway to shore when the sodden weight became a serious problem. There wasn't quite enough cloth to go around, full as her cloak was and close as they sat, but at least it was good wool, Chris thought, warm even when wet. *Give or take that damned wind.* Ariadne's icy little fingers moved against his shirt, sending a chill right through him. "Here," he said softly. "Let me, okay?" To his surprise, she simply nodded and let him take both her hands between his so he could rub them gently. "Hey. Worst is over, okay? You did real good out there."

Momentary silence. She fetched a deep breath. "I nearly—drowned you."

"Nah. You did all the right things. Honest." She had, too, he thought admiringly: admitted early enough on that she was half frozen and completely exhausted—while she was still capable of listening to him. At his suggestion, she'd quietly rolled onto her back so he could tow her ashore. She'd been a burden, small as she was, but she'd listened to him, kept quiet, held her breath as long as possible so she'd float better. "Good thing I swim best on my back," he added lightly. She didn't need to know that was a lie, or how near he'd been to total exhaustion by the time they hit the surf line. Ariadne merely nodded.

Her hands really were frigid and she was way too tense—fighting not to tremble, he thought. *Bad timing, all around.*

He couldn't remember this stretch of coast, not coming into it from out at sea and in the dark. No lights anywhere—but there'd never been much life along this southern stretch of Rhadaz. *I just hope we're past Disaster Central, and that damned Horde. All she'd need is a good dose of Weirdies on Donkeys right now.* It figured they *had* to be well beyond the spot where their company had been attacked four years earlier, though; the highlands came down to the water differently about there, making a steeper rise from the beach. Here, if either of them could work up the energy to move, they'd be able to climb right up onto dry ground. Besides, that ship had been moving at a pretty good clip; they'd be well past any point that far east. *Yeah. So now what?* he wondered bleakly.

Anywhere along the shore was out, once day came—those guys could miss them any time now and decide they were worth finding again. *Wonder who has the hit out on us—this time? And why?* Revenge; on him for knowing too much—on her from Dupret. He dismissed it; probably they'd find out, all too soon. The road—he didn't really like the thought of walking barefoot to Bez, however far it was. Besides, those guys could land in Bez, send mounted men back along the road. *Who do you dare trust? Someone in guard uniform might be in Chuffles' pay, or her dad's.*

If he could find the telegraph line, pull the stunt like they used to in the old westerns, where some guy climbed a pole and sent a message— *Sure. If I knew Morse code back home, never mind what they're using here. Don't even know local for S.O.S.*

"Better," Ariadne mumbled against his chest. He let go of her hands; she tucked them between her and him.

"Sorry we can't have a fire," he said after a little.

"I understand. It is all right."

"I've got Mer Khani matches in a waterproof tin, it's just we could be seen—"

"I know."

"Once it's light enough to see where we are, we'll find someplace safer, out of sight and I'll start one then, swear."

"All right." She didn't sound very interested—scary, he thought. She didn't feel cold enough for hypothermia—he didn't think.

"If—" He hesitated. "If you can sleep, go ahead. I'll keep you warm as I can, and I'll watch."

"Thank you," she whispered. She slept almost at once; Chris settled himself a little better against their stone windbreak and looked down at wildly tangled hair—all he could see of her. He drew her closer; she murmured something and snuggled into his warmth and, greatly daring, he leaned down to kiss her forehead; it was cold and tasted salty. *Poor kid. If this was her old man's doing, I swear he's toast*, he promised himself grimly. *I'll pull his card myself.* He shifted cautiously, easing down the rock a little so they'd both be more comfortable; something clattered on the stones. He freed a hand, felt cautiously. The dagger he'd carried all the way to shore had eased its way free of his belt. He grimaced, carefully felt for the hilt and moved it where he wouldn't accidentally cut himself if he fell asleep.

Knives. He really disliked blades, any of them—every pocket knife he'd had as a kid had left its scar on his fingers somewhere. *Great. I wind up with a girl who's kinky for 'em.* Or at least, not afraid to use them. At all. What she'd said, back in that dark little cabin, about using her knife—it sounded as goofy as Ernie's story about the sewing circle and terrorist society. *Yeah. Then she went out and used it to cut that dude's throat, every bit as quietly and efficiently as she'd said she could—oh, jeez.* He felt sick. *Will I* ever *dare close my eyes around her?*

*   *   *

"ARE you done yet?" Edrith inquired dryly. Enardi's tousled, damp head emerged from a thick drying cloth and he sighed happily.

"Clean, yes. And finally warm. And—"

"And clad in short order, I hope," Edrith broke in. He was sitting on a low, cushioned bench that ran the length of one wall, watching as his friend drew a clean shirt over his head. One leg jittered up and down as if it had a life of its own.

"You worry too much, Eddie." Enardi reached for the trous Vey had brought from Kamahl's. "The clothing only just got here, remember? And everything that can be done to find Chris is being done."

"I—yeah. I know," Edrith said gloomily. He ran his hands down clean, creased trous that had come from his luggage, pressed down hard on his knees. The motion in his right leg stopped. "What—so what's next?"

"You know as much as I, my friend." Enardi snugged his belt and drew on the heavily embroidered vest, then sat down to wrap his feet. "Once the Heir's clerks have statements from Vey and Dija about what they saw, then they ask us the same things. And then we are taken to rooms for what is left of this night."

"Great." If anything, Edrith sounded even more unhappy. "I hope they're better than the last room I had here."

"I don't doubt they will be. You aren't unknown this time, after all—"

"Yah. I'm still in the midst of trouble, just like when Dahven's brothers' men caught up with us."

"Yes, and look how well that turned out—eventually." He bent over to draw on his boots, came up rather red-faced and short of breath. "There, you see? Ready at last." Enardi bundled the still-damp and salt-stiffened clothes around his other boots and stuffed them in the bag atop Edrith's. "I think we may leave that here, for the moment. Come on. Back to that fire."

"You just go?"

"We both 'just' go, as the Heir said we should." Enardi gave his companion a shove.

The hallway was dark and notably cooler than the bathing room had been. Edrith, who was in the lead, came to an abrupt stop and, when Enardi would have passed him, held out a warning arm. Voices—someone was shouting furiously out there, and not Afronsan. Just ahead of them, a woman leaned out of a doorway and came cautiously into the hall.

Enardi edged around Edrith and quietly went toward her—it was Princess Alessya, as he'd rather thought. As he came up, she turned and looked at him blankly, then with recognition; she held a hand to her lips for silence and motioned him nearer. All at once, the shouted words became very clear.

"Alcohol! Liquor sent to my palace and to my city estate! To think of liquor as a gift I would appreciate is terrible, but now I learn from you that it is additionally tainted by the yellow foreign drug! And why are such products here at all? Because my Heir has opened his arms so widely to these foreigners, they now believe they can do whatever they choose!"

Enardi's eyes went wide, and he hastily clapped both hands over his mouth. The Emperor!

Afronsan's even, quiet voice came in the ensuing silence. "My brother, please. Let me explain to you the measures—"

"Measures." Shesseran spat the word; his voice rose to piercing. "Measures? They *dare* seek my death, they plot against the House of Shesseran, and you—what brilliant strategy have you, Afronsan? Tell me, please, how you will appease these barbarians next!"

"They are not all barbaric, my brother; even you have said so. I am doing all I can to discover which nation, if any, is responsible—"

"Which? What does it matter if it is these arrogant English or the brash Mer Khani—or the French, the Lasanachi, or all of them together? The thing is done! I warned you, Afronsan! This is what comes of throwing our borders open, and letting such peoples come into Rhadaz with whatever things they wish!"

"My brother, you know they don't—"

"Ah? No? And what of this yellow drug? And these weapons—guns? You tell them no, but so softly they do not even pretend to hear you! But you do not care what is brought here to ruin our peoples and our way of life, do you? So long as you obtain more of these foreign mechanical playthings—"

"My brother—"

"Silence! I am not finished!" Shesseran's voice echoed down the hall; Afronsan's lady sagged into the wall, and Enardi caught hold of her shoulders. "You will only tell me again how useful these things are, as you always do, but this time I will not hear your excuses! For five hundred years, we have managed our affairs as did our fathers before us, and we have remained a strong people because of it! Why is there now need for change? The foreigners are blinding you to common sense, Afronsan!" Silence. When the Emperor next spoke, his voice was under control, but not by much; it was still high and peevish. "Well, there will be a return to common sense here; I can see where my hand is needed, to guide Rhadaz back into the proper ways. You will return to your papers and your clerks in the morning, brother, and you will refrain from meddling in any other affairs whatsoever, if you know what is good for you. *I* will deal with this crisis at once—as you should have done long before now!" Silence again, broken by the sound of men crossing the room and the loud slam of the outer door.

Enardi cast a worried look over his shoulder; Eddie was all round eyes and sagging jaw. Alessya stirred, squared her shoulders determinedly and Enardi let her go. She gave him a brief smile and a low-murmured "Thank you," then walked into the main room. Enardi heard the Heir—or would he remain Heir, still?—sigh heavily. A very low-voiced conversation which he caught none of. Edrith tugged at his sleeve urgently, and he felt his face warm—eavesdropping, and on the Emperor, by all the gods at once. He began backing away, letting Edrith pull him along. But Afronsan's voice stopped them. "My young friends—?" And then Alessya was in the doorway, urgently beckoning them. Afronsan was pacing the room with long-legged, nervous strides; he stopped as the two younger men hovered uncertainly in the entry. "I am sorry you were party to that." He managed a smile, but his eyes were worried indeed.

Enardi shook his head. "Sir—"

"Never mind." Afronsan resumed pacing. "Well. This is— unfortunate. And this time, it may be a while before I can persuade him to sense; he's threatened lately that he'd close the borders and I fear he may try that this time; close the borders, shut down the harbors— We don't dare let him find you in Podhru—since you actively deal with the foreigners."

Enardi shook his head; he'd gone quite pale. "Sir, please, we'll leave at once."

"No—wait. Let me provide a way out of the city for you. And let me think for a few moments how best to arrange matters so I don't lose contact with either of you. Particularly if he *does* seal the ports." He crossed to one of the chairs near the fire and threw himself into it, stared at the toes of his low, soft house boots for some time. Alessya went back down the hall and Enardi heard a distant door close behind her. He and Edrith remained where they were, anxiously watching the older man as his lips moved and he held up a hand and began turning fingers down one at a time. He sighed, got back to his feet. "Well, his timing isn't good, but I did partly expect it, so it could be worse. Even if he decides to block all the ports, order foreign ships out and confine any Rhadazi who's involved in foreign trade, he won't achieve that tonight: I doubt he'll begin before tomorrow, if then. Which gives us time—" The Heir's voice trailed off; he shook himself and addressed his companions. "I'm sorry; discussing the matter with myself. We know there were men after you tonight; they may still be looking. So I suggest both of you and your two friends remain here as my guests for what is left of the night, get as much rest as possible." Edrith opened his mouth, close it again. "Tomorrow we may have news about Chris and his lady, and I'll have something arranged to get you safely out of Podhru. Fahlia, I think, would be best. Alessya's father would shelter you."

He looked up; Enardi managed a smile and inclined his head. "Sir. Of course we'll do as you suggest. And I truly appreciate your aid just now, with everything else on your mind—"

"Everything? Ah, yes." Afronsan sighed faintly; he looked extremely tired all at once. "Well, my brother can be reasonable if I approach him at the right moment." He got to his feet, pulled the bell-rope and, when one of the servants opened the outer door, added, "Your friends should be waiting for you. Go, sleep if you can; I'll send word in the morning."

The door closed behind them. Afronsan ran ink-stained fingers through his hair and collapsed into the chair once more. *Tired—I could sleep for the next full day, and still wake tired.* Well, there wasn't time for sleep just yet. There were messages which needed to reach certain ears in Bez and Sikkre, and down in Fahlia. *In case my brother decides the telegraph must go even before he closes the borders.*

One couldn't blame the old man, really; he must have been affronted to his very soul by that brandy. *But whoever sent it to him will owe me for what he's done.*

13

CHRIS came awake with a start and bit back a groan as outraged muscles protested. He'd managed some sleep after all: Last thing he'd remembered was a very dark night sky and now—well, the boulder at his back fortunately shaded them from what seemed to his aching head an excessively bright early sun. Ariadne had slipped down during the past hours and now slept with her head on his leg; her fingers still clutched his sleeve.

He shifted very slowly, flexed his arms, rotated his shoulders. *Leave the legs out of it for now, let the poor kid sleep while she can; bet she won't feel much better than I do.* At least she wouldn't have the headache *he* did; a night propped against a damp rock hadn't helped anything. *Hope the guy she took out last night is the one who clobbered me,* he thought sourly. Everything else ached, just not as bad as his head at the moment. He cautiously flexed his fingers—they felt like fat sausages. *Start a fire with those—sure.* Ariadne stirred, mumbled something, and shifted slightly under the cloak. He thought she still slept—decided not to lift the cloak to check on her. That would let light and cold air in, and she was surely warmer down there than he was at the moment; there was a thin haze of fog on the water and the air definitely felt foggish. At least there wasn't any breeze off the water yet. Small favors.

He eased his free arm out of the thick wool and tried to work the muscles at the base of his neck. After a few minutes, his left fingers almost felt like they were his again and he could turn his head enough to look north, toward where the road must be. It was higher and farther away than he'd thought last night: He couldn't see the telegraph poles, like he'd hoped. The shore was a fairly narrow strip of sand here; there wasn't much of a dry space between the ledge and the high-tide mark. *Hope there isn't a super high tide today.* He couldn't begin to remember when high tide would come, but a neap tide would take a dark moon, and that was several days away. *More small favors. Gosh.* Still massaging his neck, he tilted his head back and began studying the higher ground.

Ariadne stirred; her grip tightened on his sleeve. She groaned very softly and began flailing at the cloak. Chris found the long seam and murmured, "Watch your eyes, lady, it's bright out here. Cool, too."

"Watch my—? Ah. I understand." Her hand came down hard on his thigh as she pushed herself to sitting; Chris closed his eyes and fastened his teeth in his lower lip. The whole leg felt bruised, her hand like an iron bar. *Thought you were in shape, guy.* Ariadne's wildly tousled head broke free of the dark, damp wool; she shoved the tangled mass out of her face, two-handed, then snatched the cloak close around her chin. "*Dieu*, what cold!" In the early light, she looked haggard; the corners of her mouth dragged. "A—you said there could be a fire?" She sounded wistful.

"Yeah. Said that, didn't I?" He managed a smile. "We oughta get off this beach, anyway, we won't look like part of this rock once the sun gets a little higher. Besides, I can't begin to figure out where we are from down here." He eased onto his knees, closed his eyes as his left foot tried to cramp. When he opened them again, Ariadne was studying him, and he thought she looked worried. "Little stiff," he admitted ruefully. "Nothing much."

"As you say," she replied. She didn't look convinced, though; and when he tried to ease his way from under her cloak, she gripped his arm and shook her head.

"You are still wet and it is terrible cold outside; we will manage this together."

"Yeah—well, know what? I sure won't argue with you on that one." In fact, it took both of them helping each other to get onto their feet, and it was several long minutes before Chris located a place on the bank behind them low enough that he could scramble up it; he had to lift her. Ariadne huddled against him for warmth as he turned to survey the land around them.

"There is nothing here," she whispered. "Nothing at all."

"Oh, it's not quite so bad as that," Chris replied easily. "There aren't any villages, but I knew that already. There are plenty of streams along here, so we'll find water. And I'm not great at it, but my mom did teach me a little about how to forage, so maybe I can find us a *little* something to eat." Maybe. Ariadne was trembling; he wrapped his arm around her shoulders and pulled her closer. "We'll be all right. Let's get you a fire, that'll help. Okay?"

Somehow at the moment, he couldn't feel too down: Unless he was very mistaken, they were much closer to Bez than he had hoped—not that many miles from the place Aletto's company had camped four years earlier, waiting for Casimaffi's ship to take them to Podhru. He'd know better once they got up to the road.

That would have to wait, of course, until they had a chance to get dried out—and warm. But there were a couple of dead-looking trees, not too far away or too much of a climb even for a couple of gruesomely stiff people. Small stuff that would make a quick, hot fire.

It wasn't at all easy walking uphill together over rough, un-even ground and loose rock; Chris's wet trousers were chafing his legs and while the cloak was no longer actually dripping, it was heavy and uncomfortable. But the sun felt warm against his back, the sky was clear, and just beyond the trees he'd picked out, the ground leveled off and in a couple of places dropped into shallow hollows.

He left Ariadne in the most sheltered of these, clearing a place for a small fire; he'd have left the cloak with her but she turned stubborn for the first time since they'd left the *Windsong* so abruptly. "I am below any wind here; you need it to hide your shirt and hands from sight. If that ship comes back—"

"Yeah. I'd draw them right to us. Good idea." He drew the thick fabric close. "I won't be long, it really can't be much of a fire, you know."

"I know. Go."

The wood he found was tinder-dry, and what little smoke it made drifted north and flattened out almost at once. "Okay," Chris said as he knelt next to her and held out one wing of cloak. She edged back under it and sat cross-legged, hands outstretched to briskly crackling warmth. "Let's see how dry we can get first. After that, I can climb a ways, see how close the road is, see if I can't figure out how far we are from anywhere safe."

Ariadne laughed grimly. "Yes. Safe. There *is* such a place?"

"Well—hey. Yesterday, I'd have said the Emperor's city.

Today—all the same, I know people in Bez I really, truly would trust with my life. If we can get to them, we'll be fine. Now," he sighed faintly, eased himself down onto his backside and pushed his feet toward heat. "Walking might be a problem, both of us without shoes and all—I mean, my feet are tough—"

"I have gone enough places without shoes that my feet will manage."

Manage. What she said about swimming. And high places. Well, she wasn't as heavy as Robyn; if need be, he could always carry her. "Well, then," he said aloud. "Once I figure out where we are, water's the next thing."

"Yes," Ariadne replied simply.

Chris looked down at her; he felt a sudden surge of pride. "You know—you really are amazing."

She shook her head, glanced up at him and quickly away. "No. I—one does what one has to do."

"Well, sure. You know that, and so do I. But most people do a lot of whining about it in the meantime—ah, complaining."

"Oh. Well, but—what good does the complaining do, if it does not make things different?" She shook out the hem of her skirt, balanced it across her knees. The long Mer Khani machine-knitted stockings were torn in several places, and she made a vexed noise over them, then sighed. "Well, I could not wear them to walk in without the shoes. Turn away your head." Chris turned his head as ordered; his face felt rather warm. Fabric rustled; her elbow caught him in the hip. "There—*bien.*" The ruined stockings lay in a wad between her feet, and her legs were bared to the knees—coppery brown, as though her shins got more sun than her face.

Don't stare. Don't even look like you want to touch, Chris reminded himself. Ariadne gave him a quick, sidelong glance, let the skirt down a few inches, and edged her feet nearer the fire. The silence stretched for some time, broken only by the crackle of fire, or the snap of a branch as Chris broke larger sticks across his knee. The sun moved toward midday, warming the little hollow to the point that Chris was able to spread the cloak across two medium-sized stones at the back side of the hollow. He turned for another look out to sea: no sails in sight anywhere. He turned around so the sun and fire could dry the back of his shirt. "You also," Ariadne said suddenly. "You do not—whine?— complain about things." He turned his head cautiously, met her eyes. "There is blood on your neck, a little from your hair. You were hit that hard, last night?"

He reached back carefully; his fingers came away red. "Didn't know. But it felt like he broke my head in two, quite honestly."

She edged over to kneel in front of him, gazed into his eyes anxiously, then held up a hand. "How many fingers are there?"

He bit back a smile. "Four fingers and a thumb, my name's Christopher Robin Cray, you're Ariadne Dupret, and it's the day after the Emperor's birthday, which makes it—"

She laid the fingers over his mouth, silencing him, and shook her head. "Ariadne *Cray*. My wretched father, he is Dupret. Let me see where that *canaille* broke open your head."

"Look careful," he warned. "And don't touch."

"I—"

"Do *not* touch. Hurts like hell, okay?"

"I do not touch," Ariadne replied, a little stiffly. He could feel her breath stirring the hair at the base of his neck and he bit his lip; but she was as good as her word. "It is a swelling and a cut, but not so bad as I thought—I think it is not. Your eyes are normal, anyway."

"Yeah. Remember how far I swam last night with that; it can't be as bad as it feels."

"Perhaps. With water, I could clean it at least."

"Yeah. Well, leave it alone for now, please; I have a nasty headache but *I* can manage. He didn't crack my skull in half, and it won't turn green and gross before we reach Bez."

"Only so long as you swear I can tend it then," Ariadne said flatly.

"Well—you or someone with the stuff to clean it up. I'm not gonna go around with a headache like this any longer than I have to. Trust me, okay?"

"Trust—" Ariadne stopped, considered this, then suddenly laughed. But Chris couldn't find out what she thought was so amusing.

The sun was high when he kicked dirt over the last coals and checked for stray embers. Ariadne stuffed the tattered stockings in one of the skirt's deep pockets and began picking her way up the bank. Chris joined her a moment later, then led the way uphill. The ground flattened out not far ahead. "Hey. Look there—telegraph poles, and road." He turned to help her; she waved him on.

"Go. See if you can tell where we are. I am following." But

as he turned back to start climbing again, Ariadne tugged urgently at his trouser leg and pointed east. "There—that way! I hear horses—"

Chris dropped down, bringing her with him. "Oh, hell, my damned luck! Well, but they could be—" She shushed him vigorously.

The road bent away from the sea and ran down a hill to the east, making it impossible to see anything; Chris could now also hear horses—several of them, coming at a walk. *Resting, or looking for someone?* He eased up cautiously, ducked back down as the first rider came around the bend; a moment later, he ignored Ariadne's fingers on his sleeve and edged up to look once again. At least a dozen of them, he thought—and two wore the distinctive red and gold of the Podhru guard. "Okay," he whispered. "I think they're all right. You wait here and I'll—"

"You are not certain? What am I in this place without you?" Ariadne demanded in a low, furious voice. "I go also."

He couldn't really argue with that; she wouldn't stand a chance out here on her own. He hesitated. The lead rider, a dark-haired man in plain brown riding leathers, reined in not far from them and stood in his stirrups, then turned and held up a hand. "We'd better walk them all the way to water; it's been a long night." His voice was resonant, carrying—unforgettable. Chris was on his feet and halfway up the slope before Ariadne could react.

Someone on the road shouted; the lead rider turned, then dismounted as Chris came onto the road. Ariadne climbed up the bank and stumbled; one of the men leaped from his horse and ran to steady her. Chris turned to give her a nod and a reassuring smile, then held out a hand to the lead rider. "I don't know your name, but you're Afronsan's man, I saw you in his office two days ago, remember? You cannot believe how glad we are to see you."

The Heir's man gripped his hand. "It *is* the merchant Cray, isn't it? I am Hiwan. We were told to watch for any—any sign of you." He glanced in Ariadne's direction and prudently lowered his voice. "We didn't expect to find you anywhere along here, let alone alive. Can you ride? The Heir sent urgent messages for Bezjeriad and also there is word for you."

"We can ride," Ariadne said. The guard had brought her up; Chris wrapped an arm around her shoulders.

"Right," Chris said. "If you were trying to catch that ship—

Windsong, by the way—good luck; it's long gone. We swam ashore last night—hours ago. Of course, they might come back to look for us, you never know."

"*Windsong*—you are certain?" He glanced at Ariadne, who nodded firmly, then turned and looked over his company. "You and you—you've good eyes. Stay here, watch for activity out there or on the road, keep hidden. I'll send fresh mounts back for you once we reach the city." Chris managed somehow to pull himself into the saddle without aid; he wasn't certain he could stay there for very long if Hiwan set a fast pace. Ariadne let herself be helped up, tucked her skirts deftly between bare legs and saddle, and kneed the animal forward so she was next to Chris. Hiwan remounted and led the company up the road, still at a walk.

"We'll get you to Bezjeriad, sir, but it won't be quick, I'm afraid."

"It's quicker and easier than barefoot on this road," Chris said.

"Mmmm. There's nowhere to change horses along this road, and these have come all the way from Podhru." He freed a water bottle and passed it over to Chris; one of the other riders handed his bottle to Ariadne. "And there's no food, just water. Plenty of that, though."

"Water is enough for now," Ariadne said; she drank, then pulled a wad of handkerchief from her pocket and wet a corner to blot her lips with.

"Water's wonderful." Chris took a long swallow. "All right. Why don't you give me your messages, then we can tell you what went on last night."

It took most of the morning; the Bezjeriad end of the telegraph was in sight by the time he finished. Hiwan sent three of his men into Bez with the Heir's messages for Duke Lehzin and to get fresh horses for the men left behind. "Watch your backs, and don't be distracted or put off short of Lehzin himself!" A fourth man went with them to carry a message from Chris to Fedthyr. "We'll wait here," Hiwan added, "to guard the telegraph until Lehzin sends extra guards; also in case there is any reason whatever why the merchant and his lady will not be safe in Bez." He looked at Chris, who was already easing himself stiffly from the saddle.

"Yah," he mumbled. "What I'd give for a hot tub right now." Ariadne slid to the ground, clung to the stirrup to hold herself upright, then tottered into Chris, who wrapped both arms around her. "C'mon, lady. We got a warm place here to sit down for a while, and I got a nice long wire to send."

*   *   *

THE second-floor hall of Duke's Fort was unusually quiet for midmorning; Gyrdan came up the broad steps two at a time and tapped at the door to the Duke's apartments, pressed impatiently past Aletto's man when he would have held the door to a crack. "Move; I've messages for your master."

"Gyr?" Aletto sounded groggy; Zepiko pushed his way around Gyrdan and the bed to help the Duke sit up and shoved pillows behind his back. "Any—anything at all?"

"News," Gyrdan said; he held up a sheaf of messages. "Nothing particularly good, though." He eyed Aletto critically: The younger man's eyes were red-rimmed, as though he hadn't slept properly and he was clearly in pain. "The telegraph is operational at our end, but it must be down elsewhere; your man says he can't raise Sikkre or the Podhru station. The—" He hesitated, drew a deep breath and said rapidly, "The lady's carriage hasn't been found, but my man rode well down the road toward Sikkre and he says there's no sign of tracks that way."

Aletto shook his head. "I don't understand. She can't have gone—where could she go? There's no other road going west from Sehfi that a carriage could travel."

"I know, my Duke. I gave him some extra men and sent him back out a short while ago. They'll find her. Don't worry, sir," he added. "There's bound to be a sensible explanation."

"Of course," Aletto replied; Gyrdan wasn't convinced, and he didn't think he'd convinced Aletto. He set the pile of messages on the bed. "There's nothing urgent in these, I'm told."

"Good."

"One last thing, though: You remember I told you last night, we took two men and a quantity of Zero, up near the Cornekkan border?"

Aletto shook his head. "Can't remember, Gyr. I'm sorry."

"Not surprising, sir. We still haven't learned anything from them, but I've got men working on the problem. Thing is—I'm certain they're Vuhlem's men."

"Vuhlem's—" Aletto sighed, briefly closed his eyes. "It doesn't surprise me; you saw the message my sister sent, didn't you? She says he's behind the Zero coming into Rhadaz; she was hoping to learn where he got it."

Girl's mad, Gyrdan thought, but he kept the thought to himself. She hadn't listened to him, either. "I'm sure she's right," he said grimly. "But we'll get proof."

"Good. Let me know." Aletto's man handed him water; he drank thirstily and let the man ease him back down flat. "I'm sorry, Gyr; I'm not much company at the moment."

"Anyone can see you're hurting, sir. I haven't anything else at the moment anyway—but you'll know as soon as I do." Aletto merely nodded and waved a dismissive hand; his eyes were closed, and Gyrdan thought he was already half asleep. He let himself quietly out of the apartment and went back down to the barracks. Better make certain, he thought, that those boys were doing a proper job of questioning Vuhlem's messengers.

Down the hallway, a door latch clicked, very quietly; the par-Duchess leaned out and glanced warily up and down the hall. She ducked back into her apartments, emerged moments later with a small bundle wrapped in black scarves. She hesitated in the doorway: Aletto's man was on his way across the hall, down the main stairs; he was pulling a thick cloak around his shoulders. She watched his head until it was out of sight, then walked quickly down the hall and tapped on the door of the Ducal apartments, let herself in and closed the door behind her.

Aletto stirred, opened his eyes. "Mm—Mother?"

"They said you were hurt, last night." She set her bundle in one of the chairs by the fire and came across to him. Her face was very pale, and at the moment the resemblance between mother and son was quite strong. Lizelle's lip trembled. "You should have sent for me."

"I—didn't want to worry you, Mother."

Lizelle managed a watery smile. "You mean, you thought I wouldn't come, after yesterday. I—" She turned away, clutched her hands hard against her breast. "I'm not certain how well I can Wield, any more—I was never much good at healing. But once it's dark, if you like, I can—I'll try to help you."

"Thank you, Mother."

"Does it hurt—much?"

"It hurts. The healer left a powder, it makes me sleepy but doesn't seem to help otherwise."

"I—" Lizelle caught her breath, swallowed loudly.

"Mother?"

"Never mind. I heard about the quarrel—last night. The boy—Amarni—?"

Aletto groaned. "I didn't know—but I'd never have left it at that—"

"I heard what you said. The whole household knows, of course."

"Gods," Aletto murmured feelingly.

"You know there aren't any secrets from the household, Aletto. But when I heard what you said to her—that it was her fault—"

"I never meant it; I would've taken it back—ah, what use?"

"No, listen. Please." Lizelle turned back to face him. "I should have told you—a long time ago. It didn't seem important. It's—you can't just inherit that kind of—of talent from one parent. However Robyn had it, at least—*we* can't." She hesitated; her hands seemed to have a life of their own, knotting and unknotting. Aletto stared at them, seemingly fascinated. "Your father was able to shift, he had the talent but he chose never to use it. It was there, all the same. It's—that was why Light took him the way it did; it responded to the talent, not just to a man falling into it. You have that because of him, and so does Lialla, of course. It's why she Wields—the way she does. And because of you and Robyn, your children—" Her voice faded to nothing. Aletto's eyes were closed, his face so expressionless he might have been sleeping or dead, but a single tear beaded his lashes. Lizelle turned away and bit her lip. "I'm—Aletto, I'm sorry. There just—there was never a reason to tell you before; it didn't seem likely you'd—that you would marry or get children. And then, of course, I didn't know—about Robyn— Oh, son, please don't—" She drew a shuddering breath, crossed to the bed and sat on the edge, took his head between her hands and held him. Aletto leaned against her for some moments, then pushed away; his eyes were red. "You're in pain, I shouldn't have—"

"It's all right. I can bear the pain, I'm good at it. This thing—" He sighed, very faintly. "I don't think I can bear this. I don't know where she went, what she's thinking—she may never know I was trying to come after her, to apologize—!"

"Shhh. She knows *you*, Aletto; she'll realize when she begins to think properly. Your Robyn isn't the sort to hold a grudge, and you know she loves you. She's probably on her way back, she and the babes."

"I—yes. Well—" He shifted, gasped and lost color alarmingly.

Lizelle caught hold of his arm. "Let me—I can get you something, ease the pain—"

She stopped; his lip was caught between his teeth and his face haggard but his eyes narrowed. "The stuff you use? Your Zero? Robyn warned me you might—"

"Might what? Try to help you?"

"Mother, you've ruined yourself with it—"

"Aletto, no! I *need* it—!" She closed her eyes; her shoulders sagged. "I'm sorry. I didn't mean to—never mind. But I would never offer you—that. It's—I brought you a bottle—"

Aletto sighed. "I don't drink, either; you know that, Mother."

She shook her head, held up a hand. "Please—let me finish? This isn't—it's not what you think. It came yesterday, early, a gift from the Emperor and his Heir, for the Duke's house, to celebrate Shesseran's birthday." She crossed the room, came back with the bundle of scarves and unwrapped a small, finely blown glass bottle. "This is yours, the box came to me, a bottle and one for you, there's a card, somewhere. I—I had a little last night to toast Shesseran's health, like the card asked—just a swallow or two. Aletto, you *know* I don't believe in drink! This isn't wine, it's like fruit and then it fires the throat, warming and soothing all at once—" Her voice faded away.

He took the bottle she pressed into his hands, turned it over and frowned at it and then at her. "I *can't* drink, Mother—I don't dare, you know that."

Lizelle sighed. "You've told me so many times how you and Robyn won't any more. As if you couldn't control yourself, son! But—I told you yesterday how my back hurts so I can't even stand some mornings? Well, that one swallow of this last night— the pain was gone completely, and it wasn't anywhere as bad this morning."

"Oh, Mother—!"

"It's true!" she snapped; her face softened; she laid one trembling, cool hand against his cheek. "My poor son, don't you realize what it does to me to see you in such pain? This isn't like the wine you used to drink, you could never drink this like wine. You're Amarni's son, Aletto; I know you're stronger than Robyn thinks. But I wouldn't have brought this to you just to drink. Only because it helped me, and I thought—"

"I know. It's all right, Mother."

"It's not all right. At least try this, please. For my sake." She stepped back. Aletto shook his head and tried to hand the bottle to her but she backed away, scooped up her scarves and walked toward the door. "I'll come back after dark—to see if I can

Wield for you. Keep that, please, son. Just—you might change your mind. Keep it, in case you do."

He wanted nothing more, suddenly, than to be rid of her—her raddled, dragged-down face, her anxieties. *Her drugs, which set Robyn and me at each other last night in the first place.* "All right, Mother. Leave it here; I'll think about it." He set it on the chair Zepiko had left next to the bed and managed a smile for her. "There—better?" She blew him a kiss and left.

The smile slipped. Amarni, his father, a *shapeshifter*? It sounded utterly unreal. But Robyn: He drove his hands through his hair, fell back on the pillows and stared at the ceiling. Where was she? What was she thinking? She must hate him, to take the children and just—go. "Wherever she is, I can't do anything about it—I can't even move from this blasted bed!"

She could've gone to Sikkre—Gyrdan's man could be wrong about the cart tracks. *She had to have gone that way; where else is there? Back to her own world?* She couldn't—he didn't think so, at least, but just now he was miserable enough for anything awful to seem likely.

He shifted; his ankle throbbed ferociously from just that tiny movement. "Ah, hells." He hadn't felt a mood this low or this black since the afternoon Jadek beat him in front of half the household and old Merrida. *Mother's magic potion—but it might work. Better than that mess of the healer's. I could try it, I suppose. It's some kind of strong drink, if it's a toast for the fete, but just one couldn't hurt.* He turned his head, eyed the bottle. Swallowed and made himself look away from it. A moment later, he was staring at it again. Such a small bottle. The Heir knew he didn't drink and why; Shesseran didn't hold with wine or anything like it. *They'd never have sent me this if it—if I could—* The thought trailed off; too much effort to think it through.

He could remove the wax and the cork, see how it smelled. If it was wine, well, he'd recork it and have Zepiko dispose of it right away. Somehow, he was cautiously halfway on his side, the bottle in his hands, the English seal a shattered pile of red wax on the edge of his covers. The cork— He drew a deep, steadying breath, glanced toward the door as footsteps neared. They went on by; not his man, then. Or Gyrdan.

It wasn't wine; it smelled like wonderfully ripe peaches, something else that stung his eyes and warmed his nostrils, and then his throat. Just a taste—a swallow. Well, perhaps a second. He sat very still, assessing the stuff as it slid down his throat and warmed his belly, then smiled faintly and closed his eyes as he brought the bottle up again. His mother was only partly right; he could still feel that ankle, but he didn't really care any longer.

Warmth wrapped him, a surge of euphoria: He didn't need them, any of them. He could do anything, he, himself. As for Robyn— "Ahhh—to hell with all of them," he laughed, and took a third, very deep, swallow.

*   *   *

A little light trickled through thick, dust-laden drapes—just enough that Robyn could make out the size and shape of the room where she'd wakened hours before, and the boy who held a spoon to her lips. The room was an ugly, utilitarian block without furnishings except the rug she sat on. The boy was younger than her Chris, and visibly scared half silly. Trying to tough his way through. Robyn shifted her weight carefully, tried the bonds that held her wrists behind her, and the boy drew back at once. "Sit still," he ordered flatly, "or—or I'll go and leave you to starve!"

"All right." She spoke calmly, soothingly—*keep them relaxed, make them think of you as a friend*. She'd read that somewhere, or seen it on TV. Get them to identify with you. "I can't harm you, not like this." She drank broth from the spoon. "I'm— awfully thirsty," she said finally, tentatively. The boy set the spoon down and held up a cup. She tested the contents cautiously—it was water, nothing more so far as she could tell, at least. "Thank you. That helps a lot. My—can you tell me if my children are all right?"

For a long, frightening moment she thought he wouldn't answer. Maybe he had a reason he couldn't say—? But he set the cup aside, glanced at her, away again, finally nodded once, curtly.

"Can I see them?"

"I—" He bit his lip, bent down to pick up the soup spoon again. "I don't know," he said finally and Robyn thought he sounded very unhappy about it. "They didn't say."

They. She thought about this as he fed her the rest of the broth. "They" could be a lot of people, just like "here" could be almost anywhere. He gathered up the empty soup plate and the spoon, got to his feet. Robyn swallowed the last of her pride. "Before you go—um. All that liquid, you know? I need a toilet." He really *was* young, she thought, and the thought amused her: Even in the dark little room, she could see him flush bright red. He set the plate down once more, eyed her warily.

"You swear you won't—try to escape?"

"I don't see how I could," Robyn replied frankly. "Do you?"

He stood motionless, considering this, apparently; finally, he walked behind her and knelt to untie her wrists. As she drew her arms in front of her and began massaging her hands, he skipped back, gathered up the empty vessels and was at the door in one swift movement.

"There is a privy, there—" He indicated with a nod, shifted the cup and plate to one hand and backed toward the door. "If you take off the chain, they'll b-beat me—but they'll kill you." A moment later, he was gone, the door shut hard behind him. Robyn caught the unmistakable click of a latch.

The privy was where he said. It was musty, as if the sanitation hadn't been kept up any more than the dusting had. She didn't think this place had been in use for some time. "We have to be close to the fort, but where?" No answer. We: Were the children here also? She had no way of telling. She tugged at the chain around her throat, at the bit of silver which hung from it. Take if off—she wasn't sure she believed the boy. But she wasn't going anywhere without Iana and Amarni.

*   *   *

In Podhru, the streets were quiet at this hour before sunset; signs of the previous night's celebration were everywhere. Fog shrouded the harbor, where one of Afronsan's men was questioning the harbormaster again.

Beyond the gates of the city, there was little movement; along the Podhru–Sikkre road which paralleled the nearly completed telegraph line, a lone man rode toward the Thukar's city at a gallop: Vey had left everything behind, including his change of clothes and the spare horses, accepting instead the loan of Afronsan's fastest mare and a light saddle. He carried nothing but his own weight and a thin message pouch personally handed to him by the Heir at midday. As the light faded, he crouched low on the mare's neck and calculated distance: There were two places along the road he'd be able to change horses, thanks to the Heir's badge; he would need both changes and the luck of every god available, if he was to reach Sikkre by midday the next day.

In the civil service building, the man who was still the Emperor's Heir sat in the growing dark, a cup of cold coffee forgotten between his hands as he considered the situation: Shesseran was still furious; he hadn't yet disinherited his brother, but he'd already sent orders to immediately close all ports to outside vessels and expel foreigners; Afronsan suspected other orders had gone also, to keep Rhadazi ships in port when they came home, and possibly to make certain arrests—the merchant Cray certainly among any such men taken.

But Shesseran had agreed to leave the telegraph alone. Thanks to the wire, Afronsan already knew Chris Cray and his lady were still alive—that Lehzin had blocked the isthmus but too late; *Windsong* was long gone. Casimaffi would again say he'd been used, of course—if anyone dared confront him.

Vuhlem: Afronsan considered the message received several days back from the Thukara, passing on word from the sin-duchess Lialla. He personally didn't doubt Vuhlem was using the foreigners for his own end, and that he wouldn't scruple at drugs. But Shesseran—he and Vuhlem had schooled together; the Emperor wouldn't hear a word against his old friend.

The Heir also knew Vuhlem: Vuhlem was one of those cold-blooded men who saw only his own wants and the quickest path to achieve them. But to join in a plot to take over all Rhadaz? Afronsan couldn't decide, and he still had no real proof against the man. Nothing short of utterly solid proof would convince Shesseran.

Afronsan set aside his cold coffee and lit the lamp, found a pad of paper. There were messages to go out at once—lest Shesseran change his mind about the telegraph before morning. To the Thukara—yes; that young guardsman of the Thukar's had most of them, but he had a little more to tell her. To Lehzin; another the telegraph office could pass on to young Mr. Cray and his lady. He could only hope the Bez Duke appreciated all he'd done to improve outside trade, that he'd help the Heir in this hour—to a certain point, at least. And getting Mr. Cray and his lady out of Rhadaz, across the isthmus and safely on their way to Fahlia, wasn't much. Alessya's brother the Duke could send them on south; the Gallic railway abutted his Duchy.

He'd have to send the rest of CEE-Tech away within the hour; Fahlia could help them also. If Shesseran had been aware of their presence earlier, there'd have been a true disaster—but he hadn't been. And no one on the Heir's staff would tell him.

"My poor brother," Afronsan murmured as he finished yet an-other message and blotted it. Shesseran had been one of the finest Emperors Rhadaz ever had. But he was growing old, and ill, and so set in his exceedingly strange ways he was easy play for the foreigners: Look how he played into the hands of those who dealt the drug Zero by closing the ports! Rhadaz surely would have allies among the foreigners—either against any who would take over a land the size of Rhadaz, or simply those who fought the drugs. If Shesseran sealed Rhadaz against outsiders once more, no foreign ships would bother to make the long journey to Bez. And whichever of them intended malice would have a free hand.

It would take a strong man to guide Rhadaz through the days to come, and Shesseran was not a well man: His hands trembled uncontrollably at the best of times, and when he raged, his lips turned faintly blue. Afronsan knew me must tread with care, lest another such rage be the death of his brother; this was no time for the chaos brought on by a change of heads under the ancient crown.

Messages—he wrote down the last of those to be wired to the Thukara: CHRIS AND ARI SAY TELL YOU THEY ARE FINE, ON WAY SOUTH VIA FAHLIA. WATCH FOR CASIMAFFI SHIPS OFF SIKKRE COASTLINE, ALSO HOLMADDI SHIPS OF ANY KIND. REPLY ASAP VIA WIRE, BROTHER MAY REMOVE SAME AT ANY TIME, AFRONSAN.

                              *   *   *

THERE had been celebration in the city of Holmaddan the night before, but no one would have known it: All signs of the Emperor's fete, and any other street trash, had been efficiently cleared away.

A lone caravaner woman moved quickly down the near-deserted street, along the outer wall of the caravaner's storage; she slipped through a low postern and into the stables, found her way across the floor by feel and took the blue-lit steps by twos.

There weren't many people in the shared second-floor space this night: Green Arrow had pulled out the day before and the small coastal branch of Gray Fishers wasn't due for two more days. The near hearth was dark and reeked of soaked ash; a low fire burned in the far hearth.

Lialla got to her feet as Sil tossed back her scarf and came across the floor. "News? Any at all?"

"More news than a rational woman can sort through," Sil replied flatly. She laughed suddenly. "But since none of us are *ra-*

tional! Vuhlem's guard is seeking the boy, but not openly; there's word been quietly put about the market, here and there." She met Kepron's wide-eyed gaze; he was pale and looked ill. "They're confident someone will turn you in, boy. As a thief."

Lialla waved that aside impatiently. "And?"

"Word from the south, I had it via that sole Silver Hawk wagon that tends the inland hill tribes: attacks on all eight southern Duchies the past night, during the Emperor's fete."

"And?"

"And?" Sil shook her head. "I'm sorry, Li. No solid word, and the rest isn't good; they say an armed attack on Sikkre, but driven off; another on Bez via the ports, also pushed back. Fahlia and Derra Vos—well, who pays heed to either Duchy, south of the sea as they are? But in Podhru, liquor sent to the Emperor and his Heir both, in hopes either man will drink, and die."

"Zelharri? Duke's Fort?"

"I don't know. Cornekka—they say the Duke is very ill, but after all his lady runs the Duchy. Nothing from the fort, save rumor the Duchess has taken the children and gone back to her own kind."

"The—Robyn? No! She'd never leave Aletto—where would she go?"

Sil shrugged, came over to warm her hands at the fire. "You asked for rumor; there's no trustworthy word from Zelharri."

The boy got to his feet, began pacing the hearth. "You should not have taken me away from my company; I was mad to listen to you—!"

Lialla spun around, gripped his shoulders and shook him fiercely. "Act the fool, go ahead! Who's being sought right now, by his own company, for stealing the Duke's drugged brandy?"

"You don't know it was drugged," he said stiffly.

"Try the bottle yourself, boy," Ryselle put in. "I'll laugh while it kills you." She glared up at him from the hearth where she crouched and turned baked tubers; he pursed his lips, turned away as if she counted for nothing. In his eyes, likely she did.

"No one tests that bottle," Lialla said flatly. "It goes out tonight, still sealed; with any luck the Thukara will have it by midmorning. Sil?"

"Yes?"

"The small caravan leaves at dawn?"

"Last I heard," Sil replied. "I spoke to Ghillian; she'll carry it

down, then take to horse at the Holmaddi border and make
Sikkre with the bottle by sunrise. Good enough?"

Lialla bit her lip, turned away from them all: Too much riding
on her not nearly strong enough shoulders; too many trusting her
to separate the issues and see the right thing done. "More than
that, it's fine. Thanks." She considered this, managed a faint
laugh. "At least Vuhlem's only one Duke and not the
Emperor—I'd go mad, trying to juggle matters for nine Duchies."

"Vuhlem could be Emperor, given the chance," Kepron said.
Ryselle snorted; Sil laughed. Kepron sneered at both. "Go on,
laugh at me while you can! Why do you think he's brought in
the Zero to begin with? Don't know, do you?"

"But you can tell us," Lialla said evenly, before either of the
other women could respond. "Why?"

Kepron preened. "I heard my captain talking about it: Drugs—
men pay for them, or course; the man who imports them makes
more money than those he sends out with the drugs. You see,"
he added as he gave Ryselle a pitying glance, "there is more to
this than you mere women suppose."

Lialla quickly nodded, forestalling other comment. "I see. He
makes money—but what could he possibly want with it?"

"Power, of course: A man with position and money can hire
more men to serve him."

"Yes." Lialla nodded again, sent a warning look and a swift
hand-sign toward Sil as the caravaner gaped at her: *Keep still,
listen!* Sil caught the intent, if not the meaning—she clamped her
lips together, folded her arms, and strode away. Kepron's young
lips twitched.

"My captain says Vuhlem has companies outside the city—at
least ten such companies, and large ones: men who will serve
him for coin and do whatever he asks, no matter what the Emperor or his weak Heir asks of the Duke."

"How lovely for him," Lialla exclaimed dryly. "And when the
Heir becomes aware of all this trafficking and sends his headman
with a sharp axe?"

"He will not." Kepron folded his arms across his chest.

Lialla folded hers. "No? Then we 'mere' women are in great
trouble, I suspect—and all the caravaners here, since Vuhlem's
never hidden that he dislikes women with any brains at all, and
the caravans are not useful to him beyond a certain point. Now,
the boy who stole a bottle of brandy, and endangered the Duke's

entire plot: Well! He's surely safe, isn't he? His captain was
ready to stick up for him; the Duke's man was sympathetic to his
drunken desire for more wine—and of course, he is male, like
Vuhlem—!" She stopped; Kepron made a faint, unintelligible
noise and closed his eyes.

"Boy," Sil spoke against his ear suddenly; Kepron gasped,
eyed them all wildly and again tightly closed his eyes. "A sensible boy with the brains he credits to all men—such a boy
would begin to think, 'How does all this matter to me? Who is
my friend?' Or, at least, 'Who will for whatever reason aid
me?' " Kepron was watching her warily. Sil gave him a dark-
eyed, lips-only smile. "Consider who risked all to free you from
Vuhlem's guardsman, who took up the bottle you dropped."
Kepron glared at her; she smiled sweetly in reply. "Why—
women. What *man* has done as much for you—ever?"

Kepron spun away from them all. Lialla eyed the other
women, shook her head. "Kepron," she said, quietly. Silence.

"Well?" Just as she decided he wasn't going to speak, he did.
"Women." He spat. "My mother, my father's sisters—my mother's aged sister Sretha, she could have taught me to Wield, if
she'd had the courage—!"

"If she'd sought a quick way to die," Ryselle cut in. Kepron
glanced at her, looked away again. "We village women don't
choose our lot, it's chosen for us. By *men*. You can't expect me
to weep for you, boy, because you wanted something you
couldn't have. We live with that all our days."

He shook his head. "And which of you truly wants more than
a hearth and a man to take care of her for life? I didn't ask for
that kind of free passage, I wanted—"

"Choice," Ryselle said flatly. "What else matters?" Before he
could answer—if indeed he wanted to—she turned away from
him. "Ursiu—Lialla. Why is it Sretha Wielded all about me since
my babyhood and I was never aware? But you went into that
barracks and suddenly—I *saw* the thing you did."

Lialla had been pacing the hearth; she froze. "You—you saw.
What?"

Ryselle shook her head. "I—don't know. For certain. Something like—a stretch of fishing net, curled in on itself, pale yellow or maybe even greenish, a pattern of that color, a line . . ."
She shook her head again, visibly frustrated. "A ball of tightly
woven string—"

"Dear gods," Lialla whispered. Ryselle looked at her. "You—you saw Light."

"That—was Light?"

Lialla crossed her legs at the ankles, sank onto the hearth and *reached*. A faint sound—perhaps two. When she regained reality, Ryselle was cross-legged on the hearth before her, wide-eyed. Kepron glaring at both impartially from a few paces away. "I was right," Ryselle whispered. "I did see something! But—Light's evil!"

At least here, she was on solid ground: Lialla shook her head. "No; magic is. I know: Good or evil is in the way you use it, not in the magic itself. But—Light? You truly saw that? Sensed it?"

She half expected Ryselle to bolt. But the girl remained where she was, eyes closed and lips firmly pressed together. She shook herself. "Light. Magic. Real magic. Sretha said—you could use both. You—can you teach *me*?"

Lialla smiled, and caught hold of the other's wrists. "I'll be honored."

A snort above them; Kepron. "Light?" he demanded; his voice soared and cracked. "No one clean uses Light—!"

"Wrong, boy," Lialla replied flatly. "I do. And so will Ryselle."

"You dare not—!"

"I dare whatever I choose. *Boy*." Lialla looked at Ryselle, who was visibly dazed; then at the boy, who seemed both stunned and furious at once. "Even to teach a pubescent male to Wield Thread—"

Ryselle tore her arms free of Lialla's grasp and leaped to her feet; red blotched her cheeks and her eyes were black. "Wield? You'd teach that—that—?"

"I intend to teach you both," Lialla said flatly. "If any of us should live so long."

14

JENNIFER pushed away from her desk and stretched, hard; her eyes felt like someone had filled them with sand, and her back was board-stiff. "Comes of not sleeping the past two nights," she muttered. "I'm too old for this."

"That's two of us." Dahven slouched in the chair across from her. The enormous office was deserted except for them; late afternoon sun cast long shadows across the courtyard below.

"Mmmm." Jennifer eyed the desk with distaste, finally pulled over the just-delivered pile of narrow paper. *More telegraph messages from Afronsan. I suppose I should be grateful Shesseran's left the wire in place, instead of griping about Afronsan overusing it: I'd go mad not knowing what's going on out there.* It was hard to not panic, just now. She dredged up a smile for Dahven, shoved the lightweight dispatch case toward him. "And you used to be a pro at long nights. Here, make yourself useful for something besides holding the chair down; go through this again, see if I've missed anything vital."

"It was a different kind of long nights," Dahven said. Jennifer laughed, shook her head. "I know, Jen, spare you the details, yes?" He sat up and took the case, drew out three long, thin sheets of paper. "His printer couldn't have found a smaller type, could he? This is terrible."

"Could be worse; ordinarily, Afronsan uses both sides of the paper. That's on one and it has margins all around." Jennifer was juggling a long strip and scanning down it rapidly. She let out a sigh of relief. "Well, there's one piece of good news, anyway: Chris and Ariadne are safely out of Bez. This is from Lehzin, via Podhru, he had them escorted across the isthmus just before day-

243

break yesterday, and he sent a couple of his guards with them, to
see they make it into Fahlia all right."

"Fahlia? Why go there?"

"Thought I told you." Dahven shook his head. "It was Chris's
idea, actually—if I deciphered that wire of his right. When they
first got into Bez, day after the Emperor's birthday?"

"I remember—didn't remember Fahlia."

"Maybe I didn't say. Chris was more cryptic than usual, which
hardly ever makes sense. I think he was trying to keep it secret
from anyone else who might read the message."

"What—Afronsan?"

"Silly." Jennifer made a face at him. "Whoever planned the
birthday attack, more likely; I have a sneaking hunch Chris left
out plenty he thought I'd be better off not knowing." She considered this. "What I got from the Heir was bad enough; those two
are lucky they're alive. I wouldn't feel safe on a ship either, just
now."

"No. So—overland from Fahlia. That will take forever."

"There's railway in the Gaelic States, of course; Chris says
they'll pick it up just across the Fahlia border and go south.
Damn. I wish they'd just come back here."

'Yes. It's so safe *here*," Dahven said dryly. "Or in Podhru."

"Or anywhere in Rhadaz; tell me about it." She read in silence
for some moments, set one sheet aside and picked up another.
"Ah. More news on the same general subject; the Heir sent
Enardi and Edrith down to Fahlia so they could meet up with
Chris, and Dija's with them. Couldn't persuade her to come back
home, I guess. What a mess." She picked up another message.
"From Lehzin—I sure do wish we had a direct line to Bez, it
seems such a waste of time sending to Podhru and *then* here."

"Faster than the post."

"Yeah. Four years away from L.A. and I still want a fax.
Lehzin was sent bottles—and the same kind of note we got. He
and his lady were ill the whole night, but didn't attribute it to the
booze at the time. He sounds harassed." She handed the message
over; Dahven read it and handed it back.

"I'd be: Emperor's guard everywhere, the port closed, their
main source of outside money completely shut down."

"You *should* be; anything new from the guard out there?"

"Same—" Dahven sighed. "Twenty men, women, and children
killed, just—so they'd know the guns were deadly. The last tally

I got on outsiders caught was thirty-seven, but I haven't talked to any of the city guard tonight."

"We're fortunate they didn't murder more people than twenty," Jennifer said.

"And that some of the guard know the lower market as well as they do—Vey's back out there again, on night search."

"Well—he knows the risk he's taking, and he's cautious."

"Yah," Dahven scoffed. "Remember what happened to him last time?"

Jennifer set her pages aside and reached for his hand. "You bet, he was right where I needed him. Don't worry; he isn't so cocky these days, he'll be as safe as anyone out there." She went back to her sheets. "Wonder what Shesseran thinks we're going to do with that stranded pack of Mer Khani traders down in the Feathers, since he sent their ship away without them?"

Dahven shook his head. "Hope he goes easy on them; there's no point in marking all the foreigners with the same daub."

"No. I talked to those men yesterday, remember; I think they were as surprised as we were."

"Convince Shesseran," Dahven said gloomily. "I didn't know the old man had that much action left in him." He held up the top sheet from the dispatch case, laid it back on his knee and read in silence for some moments. "Afronsan says he had the bottles analyzed and Edrith was right—it was a fancy fruited brandy, very strong and sweet, enough flavor to hide more Zero than was in it—though his man thinks it would be enough to at least incapacitate an ordinary person, and probably kill someone like a Wielder." He read in silence for some moments. "Ah, hells, word down from Cornekka and Zelharri: Jubelo's very ill; they got brandy, three bottles. No one drank it but him, and he only had a toast's worth."

"What's the word from Zelharri? I haven't seen anything since that short thing from Aletto, asking me to send Birdy home. Robyn's got great timing, hasn't she?" Dahven frowned, shook his head. "She'd never take off like that, not tell anyone where she was going, unless they'd had a really nasty fight. I'm ready to strangle both of them, just now. At least someone could have bothered to tell us they're all right."

"I know." Dahven's finger moved down the page. "No, I don't see anything—wait." He read in silence once more. "Well. Now I see why we didn't hear anything out of the fort, they've been busier than we have. Fete night, Gyrdan brought in some of

Vuhlem's men, and one of the guard caught Lizelle with a fresh supply. Let's—here, Gyr says one of the men has admitted they'd carried Zero down from Holmaddan, it came in via Lasanachi ship—but the Lasanachi are only transporting the stuff."

"Holmaddan." Jennifer slammed the desk with both open hands. "I *knew* it! What about Vuhlem?"

"No—don't see anything here." Dahven ran a hand over his eyes. "Much more of this and I won't be able to see at all. The wire was cut—well, we knew that—but it's repaired, west and south both. Something about the gift bottles—"

"I wish someone would *use* the damned telegraph up there," Jennifer grumbled. "Let us know what's going on—oh, God." She clutched the telegraph sheet. "This *is* from the fort, from Joras, Aletto's guard captain—"

"Not from Aletto?" Dahven set his sheets and the case back on the desk and came around the desk to read over her shoulder.

"No. Aletto fell the night of the fete, did something awful to his leg. Gyrdan went to question Lizelle's girls and found one of the brandy bottles there, so he took it to Aletto to show him—" The color drained from her face. "They found the other, empty, Aletto drank it and they can't wake him, and Robyn's still gone—!" She dropped the sheet and looked up at him. "Dahven, that's four days ago now!" She shoved her chair back; Dahven caught hold of her shoulders and pulled her close.

"Sit still; you can't help him or Robyn by panicking. There has to be a sensible explanation."

"Sensible!" Jennifer's voice was muffled by his shirt. "After everything else that's gone wrong? I can't—"

"Jen, listen to me." He shook her gently. "Take a deep breath, please." He waited until she did. "You know better than this. I know you're afraid. You can't help them by panicking."

Silence. Jennifer drew a deep, shuddering breath and finally nodded. "I—all right. I know that."

"Gyrdan and Joras are good men; probably they'll do a better job of sorting things out than either of us could—or than Aletto could."

"I know." She nodded again, leaned her cheek against his chest and gripped his sleeve with both hands. "I—I want to go there, right now—don't look at me like that, I know you're doing it and you don't have to say it, I know it isn't practical."

"Or possible," Dahven said. "Because even if I was fool

enough to let you out of the palace, Grelt would never allow it."
He gave her another gentle shake. "All right?"

"No." She let go his sleeve, rubbed her eyes vigorously. "But
I'll manage." He went back to his chair; Jennifer picked up the
telegram from Duke's Fort and read the rest of it to herself.
Dahven waited. She offered him a shaky smile. "I'm glad there
isn't a copper-per-word charge on these, like there was in my
world. There isn't much else here, though: They haven't found
the carriage, or any sign of where it might have gone since it left
the fort. Gyrdan doesn't think Birdy was driving it. He's sectored
Zelharri into squares and got plenty of people to search. Lizelle
admits giving Aletto that bottle, she thought it would work better
than whatever the healer gave him for pain—" Jennifer crumbled
the message in her fist. "I'd like to kill that stupid woman.
Aletto's stayed dry for all this time—!"

"She probably feels bad enough, Jen."

"Gyr said they had to get the healer in for *her*; to quiet her. A
lot of use that is! And—that's all." She looked at the wad of
message, dropped it and smoothed it with careful fingers.

"Sent when?" Aletto asked.

"Mmmm? Oh." She glanced at the sheet, set it to one side.
"Midday."

"Ah. This reached Afronsan yesterday. I wonder if—" He
turned as one of the gate guard came into the room. "Yes?"

"Sir? There was a caravaner outside, just now, with a
message—from Dro Pent." He set a flat, sealed and waxed
packet on Jennifer's desk and left.

"Dro Pent?" Jennifer echoed. "Now what? Wasn't there a
message from Wudron in there, saying they were all right?"

"Didn't get that far," Dahven admitted. He broke the seal,
pealed off the outer wrapping and unfolded a single sheet of paper; one side had been used before and was heavily crossed over
with a thick nib. He turned it over. "It's from Krilan—the boy,
remember?"

"The boy who got duped by a couple of would-be Thukara assassins? You think I'd forget Krilan? What's *he* up to?"

Dahven shook his head, held up a hand. He finished the page,
handed it to her. "Read it; you won't believe me if I tell you."

"Nice." Jennifer looked at the sheet and made a face. "Is this
his bad writing, or did he find the worst scribe in all Dro Pent?
I can't—oh." She was quiet for some moments. "He's—no, with
everything else that's happened the past few days, I can't say

he's kidding. Foreign ships in the harbor—and Vuhlem's men in the palace since the night of the Emperor's fete? That's mad!"

"No—it's Vuhlem, in league with someone from outside."

"In league with, maybe," Jennifer remarked sourly. "But he's not under anyone else's thumb."

"No, he wouldn't be."

"He has Dro Pent, and Wudron's playing window dressing because Vuhlem has Wudron's wife."

"Well," Dahven said thoughtfully. "If he'd done the same here, I'd have cooperated with him; you can't blame Wudron."

"I wasn't—I didn't know the man was that clever."

"Frightened, more likely. But there's a bit of curious luck for you—here I sent the boy to Dro Pent, gave him a letter for Wudron, and told him to watch for Zero—and he actually saw something useful. Two things: Vuhlem's men selling it in the taverns, and then this. I didn't expect it."

Jennifer picked up the letter again, ran her finger along one of the lines. "I'll wager Wudron will be glad—if we can do anything for him before it's—God. You don't suppose Vuhlem took Birdy, do you?" Jennifer swallowed. Dahven leaned across the desk and gripped her hands.

"That might be the best possible thing that could've happened—they'd want to take very good care of her, if they planned on holding her for Aletto's good conduct, don't you think?"

Jennifer nodded. *But they could have killed her and the kids at any time and how would Aletto know the difference?* "Do you think—" She swallowed. "Would you mind getting someone to go down to the kitchen and have them send me up some cool juice, and maybe a roll? And see if they can hold dinner until after we've readied the return wires? I'd—I'd like to get all this out of the way before—"

"Of course." He went. Jennifer swallowed again, and scrubbed at her eyes. *I am not going to cry; he'll know the minute he comes back.* A tear slid down her cheek; she swallowed salt. "Oh—damn you, Birdy. You'd better be all right. You and those kids—" She swallowed again. "You'd—just better, that's all." Vuhlem in Dro Pent—Vuhlem behind all those bottles of spiked brandy. She shook her head. Funny—at the moment, Lialla was probably safer than any of the rest of them; Vuhlem was so busy outside his Duchy, he couldn't be paying close attention to anything going on inside it.

Then again—the caravaner woman who'd delivered Lialla's messages and the bottle said the Duke's guard had nailed a notice to the gate of the caravaner house, ordering the house vacated and expelling the caravans from his Duchy by next full moon.

What next? she wondered tiredly. He must think he could figure a way around Shesseran; one of the few things that could get action from the Emperor these past years was any kind of complaint from one of the grandmothers. *Maybe he's figured out a way to polish the old man off—I've heard often enough how ill he is, and everyone knows what Vuhlem thinks of Afronsan. Paper-pusher is probably the nicest thing the old chauvinist ever called him.*

She could hear Dahven out in the hall, talking to one of the boys on guard. She rubbed her eyes once more and drew the pile of telegrams over. Somewhere in all this, there had to be a little more good news. *Can't let the whatchits grind us down before we've had a chance to fight back. They haven't even technically won the first skirmish, after all.*

Whichever of the foreigners was pushing Zero—well, they couldn't have much support from the other nations: She had Chris's input on that, and her own observation. If it was all right, why sneak around like this? And Vuhlem didn't have all the odds stacked on his side. *We'll make it. God, we'd better.*

*   *   *

ROBYN came awake suddenly; the room was lighter than it had been—moonlight finding its way through the shutters that blocked the only windows. She sat up slowly, chafed her arms. *Cold.* Chill air moved across the floor; the door stood ajar and someone—she swallowed, began to edge away, but it was the boy. He knelt beside her. "Lady? You're awake?"

No, I always sleep sitting up in the middle of a bare room, Robyn thought sarcastically. She resisted the urge to say it aloud. "Yes. Why?"

"The—" His voice trembled and she thought he was very near tears; the hand that brushed against her hand was icy. "Lady, I don't know what to do! The—the men who—they were supposed to come, to bring food and give me orders, and they haven't, and there's nothing else to eat, and I don't know—!"

His whisper was spiraling toward hysteria. Robyn gripped his arm and gave it a shake. "It's all right. If you don't know what to do, will you at least listen if I suggest something?" His teeth were chattering; he nodded. "Let me have my children—they're still here? Still all right?" Silence again. He nodded again. "That's good. Thank you for telling me. You've been as kind to me as you dared, and I appreciate that. Let me have the children, and—and get us out of here and back to Duke's Fort."

"I—I can't! If they came—!"

"No, listen." Somehow she kept her voice low and soothing, when she wanted nothing more than to grab him and scream in frustration. "It's all right. When were they to come?" Silence. She shook his arm again. "When?"

"Three—three days ago."

"That's a long time. Something must have happened to them, so they can't come. Don't you think so? Let me have the children, then come with us, back to the fort. Duke Aletto won't hold this against you, I promise I'll speak for you. I won't let him or anyone in the fort hurt you."

"I—I don't dare. They—they said the Duke would—that he'd kill me—" He wrapped his arms around his narrow chest and shivered. "He has a Triad, they said he'd tell the—tell them to—" He shook his head violently.

"Duke?" *Where's Jen when I need her? I'm no good at pulling words out of people!* "Which—no, let me guess. Duke Vuhlem?"

"I—how did you know that?" the boy whispered.

She bit back laughter. "Lucky guess. Please. This is your chance to save yourself and do a good deed; wouldn't you feel safer if you were inside the fort, not out here waiting—?" He was shaking again. She crossed her fingers and waited.

"A—but a Triad—!"

"A Triad couldn't get at you in the fort, it's sealed against that kind of thing." It wasn't; so far as Robyn knew that wasn't possible. Then, she knew that but he might not.

Apparently, he didn't. "You swear that?"

"The usurper had one there once, remember? When Aletto took the fort, he wanted to make certain they couldn't come back. Boy, listen to me, please. Get us back to the fort, so we're all safe. Duke Aletto won't let anyone harm you, he'll be too glad to have his children back again." *His children, anyway; God knows how he feels about me.* She'd nearly forgotten, these past dreadful days—that quarrel.

The boy got to his feet; her heart fell. But he held out a hand and pulled her up; his palm was cold and wet. "Come—with me."

She followed him to the door, fought for patience while he peered fearfully around the sill, then followed him down the length of a cold, dimly moonlit hallway, past a glassless window and a hinge-sprung door that must lead outdoors, from the feel of the frigid air that came past it. "What is this place?" she whispered. "Where are we?"

He glanced back at her. "It's a—a hunting lodge, on Lord Carolan's old estates. M-my father used to serve him."

Another hallway, at right angles to the first. There was a lamp at the far end, and here, a blue-light in a holder. The boy dug it free and opened the door beside it. Robyn made herself remain still until he'd gone into the room; she wanted nothing more than to shove him aside and run, but the boy's control was so fragile, she might ruin everything.

The room was smaller than the one where she'd been held, and most of it was filled with an enormous, heavy bed. The boy brushed aside the hangings. Amarni lay on his side, curled in a ball; Iana's arms were wrapped around his neck, her head on his shoulder. The boy eyed her warily. He licked his lips.

"I—they said to let them wake once a day, to feed them and give them a powder with the food so they'd sleep, and be less trouble. I—"

"What powder?" Robyn whispered. She laid a trembling hand on Amarni's forehead, Iana's throat. The boy's face was warm, but not overly so; Iana's pulse was fast—too fast. *Don't blow it now. Don't*— The boy took a step away from her.

"I don't know—a powder, the box is here."

"I'll take it; the fort healer will need to test it."

"I—I didn't give them as much as they said to, lady. I swear it! I—you can tell, if they'd slept all that time they'd be—" He swallowed. "They're clean. You can tell."

She hadn't thought of that; after all those days, the air in this room would be utterly foul. "I believe you."

He turned away, held out a small box. "I have a little sister; I couldn't—"

Robyn's fingers closed on the box; she shoved it into her pocket and eased Iana's hands away from her brother. "Let's go, now. Get out of here. You can tell me once we're moving, if you want to talk." He shoved the blue-light in his shirt and took the girl from Robyn; she settled Amarni's damp, tousled head against her shoulder, let him lead the way back into the hall. Amarni's breath was warm against her ear.

Another door, a short, brisk walk across dry grass or weeds to a smaller outbuilding; frost crackled underfoot, gleamed white where moonlight found a way between thick trees. The boy shifted Iana, drew out the blue-light and led her inside.

On the far side of the stable, she could hear horses shifting; her carriage blocked the way. But when she would have set Amarni inside, the boy shook his head. "No. If—if they come, they'll know which way we went, there's only the cart track we could have taken, and they'll come after—"

"Yes, all right," Robyn said hastily. No point dwelling on horrors.

"Can you ride like that, lady? If—there's a trail that starts a little ways from here, I think I can find it, and then—they don't know Zelharri, lady."

"I can ride like this," Robyn assured him. "Here—I'll wait in the carriage with them, you deal with the horses." She looked around the dark stable and bit her lip. "And—hurry, can you?"

It couldn't have taken more than two hours, judging by the moon, but the trail the boy chose was all steep climbs and descents. By the time they came into the open and a place she recognized, Robyn was ready to drop. Relief weakened her further: *I didn't realize how scared I was that he wasn't gonna bring us back to the fort—until now. Get us back to the fort and once I'm sure the kids are all right, I'm just going to collapse.* Minutes later, the boy reined in at the edge of the Zelharri–Sikkre road. "I—I could just—you could find your own way in," he said doubtfully.

"I can't carry them both," Robyn replied. "And that's no answer, not if you want to live. They'll get you out here. Your only chance is the fort." He looked at her. "I trusted you; it's your turn now." He shook his head, but before she could say anything else, he nudged the horse and started east—up the road toward Sehfi.

A curve in the road, a low, long incline—she'd see the first houses when they crested that. *Not far, not far at all.* She shifted Amarni cautiously; the arm that held him against her was growing numb.

The boy on watch at the gates gaped as she rode in. Men on the walls—men in the courtyard. One of them ran across and took the boy's horse by the bridle; another turned to shout, "Tell the captain, the Duchess is back!" He caught Robyn's mount.

"One of you, go warn the household and someone come help us over here!"

Someone took Amarni from her; someone else helped her down from the horse and, when it was clear she couldn't walk on her own, wrapped an arm around her. She shook her head; tried to make the words come. "The boy—he got us free. I swore to protect him if he did."

"It's all right." Gyrdan was at her other side. "He found you?"

"He—guarded us. My word—"

"It's all right, tell us later. We'll put him somewhere safe for now, and we'll keep your promise, no one will lay a hand on him. Someone, take this young fellow down to the guardhouse. You're all right, lady?"

Robyn laughed breathily. "I've—been better. But, the children—they were given a powder, something for sleep; someone send for the healer."

Gyrdan's face was suddenly grim. "She's already here." Someone held the door for them. She stared up at him; he scooped her up as her knees gave. "The Duke drank something, three nights ago, and we haven't been able to waken him since."

Robyn let her eyes close. *I think I'll cry—I can't deal with this. I can't.* Gyrdan's hands tightened around her as he took the stairs. She could hear a low, worried buzz of voices, then Gyrdan's sharp, "Zepiko, open up! It's Duchess Robyn!" More whispering. Zepiko opened the door and stepped aside to let Gyrdan carry her inside.

"Oh, God, it's warm in here." She wrapped arms around herself. "I didn't think I'd ever be warm again." Zepiko brought her a chair and she sank into it. "The children—?"

"Coming now," Gyrdan said as the door opened again. "One of you send for someone to tend the lady! Something hot to drink, at least!" He went to the door and shouted orders to someone out there. Robyn bit her lip. The healer was just stepping back from the bed. Aletto lay very still; he was so pale, at first Robyn couldn't tell if he was alive. The covers rose a little, fell again.

"What—" Her voice cracked; Robyn swallowed and tried again. "What's wrong with him?"

The old woman snorted inelegantly. "The stuff he drank. By itself, an entire bottle of strong liquor, it would have given him a three-day headache." Robyn shook her head.

"But—he doesn't drink! Not any more."

"Never mind," Gyrdan had come back into the room. "I'll tell you what we know later. This—his mother thought it came from Podhru because of the fete."

"Lizelle gave it to him? *Lizelle?*" Robyn struggled to her feet. Gyrdan shook his head.

"Never mind about Lizelle just now; she's remorseful enough that the healer had to give her a calming powder and set a full-time watch on her. The drink contained drug."

"Zero," Robyn whispered. She blinked rapidly, looked at him for a long moment, then transferred her gaze to the healer. She didn't like the old woman much; didn't feel comfortable talking to her as she had with the previous healer. One more thing. . . . *I can't take it, I just can't.* She bit back a sigh. *As if I had a choice.* "Is—will he live?"

"He hasn't died yet," the healer replied flatly. "Which I'm told is a good sign. He is nearer true sleep tonight than he was this morning."

"He'll live," Robyn said, as flatly. She leaned across the bed and felt under the covers for his hand. "The children—there's a box of stuff, here." She fumbled it from her pocket and held it out. "They were given this; they're sleeping and I couldn't waken them." The old woman pried the lid up, stirred the contents with her finger. "The—boy who gave it to them said he'd made it so they would wake after sunrise, but—"

"A sleeping powder for babes—was he mad?" She set the box on Aletto's small writing table and crossed the room; Amarni and Iana had been settled on the cushions next to the fire. Robyn eased herself out of the chair and onto the edge of the bed, drew Aletto's hand out from under the covers; tears blurred her vision.

"Sweetie? Babe? Aletto, it's me, Robyn. Birdy." His hand lay limp across hers. "Aletto, you're going to be all right, everything is." Her fingers tightened; she slid his hand back under the blankets and got to her feet. Gyrdan held the door for one of the kitchen girls with a tray; the girl set it on the small writing table and waited while Robyn drank strong, sweetened tea, then a mug of steaming broth. The healer picked up her bag.

"I'll take the powder with me, learn what I can of it, but the babes seem to be merely asleep. I'll come in the morning."

Robyn nodded, blotted soup from her lips. "Thank you." She watched the woman go, then turned to the kitchen girl. "Avran, I'll need blankets brought here from the nursery; find someone to manage that, will you? And another mug of the soup, maybe some bread." The girl took up the tray, curtseyed and went. Robyn sat very still for a moment, bit back a sigh. There wasn't any excuse now; no more putting it off. "Gyrdan."

"Lady?"

"Who's been managing things here—since—" She shook her head. "Since everything?"

"I have, mostly," Gyrdan said.

He was more than competent enough to manage, Robyn thought. She wanted nothing more than to leave it all in his hands. *But all that, on top of everything else he has to do.* She wasn't very happy either, at the moment. *I hate this; I'm no good at taking charge, and I just hate it.* That wasn't going to change anything, either. She brought up a smile for him. "I'm glad you were here to take care of things for us, Gyr. Can you still, at least for the night?"

"Of course."

"Good." Robyn squared her shoulders. "Tomorrow morning, please, come here at second bell. You and I will have to decide what needs to be done to get the fort back to normal."

*   *   *

CHRIS stared out a long narrow window framed by an ornate sill, and watched the French Gallic state streak by. *Wow. Maybe a whole fifty miles an hour, you think?* But it was hard not to enjoy the ride, despite everything. Last time he'd driven a car, he hadn't been doing fifty. At the rate the narrow-gauge steam train ate up what he still thought of as Mexico, they'd reach the bottom curve of the Peninsula in another day.

Barring odd problems, like the cattle on the tracks two days earlier. Still, they'd reach Pinareo on the swampy Caribbean coast days earlier than the fastest ship could.

Of course, you still gotta factor in the trip down to Fahlia and then through southern Fahlia— Dry, hot—serious desert. Duke Adreban hadn't come right out and said he'd be for it, but Chris thought there was a good chance he could persuade the man to bring the tracks right up to the city walls. He rolled his eyes. Once the Heir got things under control again, or course. Adreban tended to do things his own way, and kind of shine the Emperor, when the two didn't see eye to eye; Shesseran wasn't any better than any other Rhadazi: He tended to forget the southernmost two Duchies.

The tracks bent left; brilliant sunlight hit the window. Chris blocked his eyes, felt for the curtain and pulled it partway across.

Red velvet; that and the gold-plated windowframe makes the place look like a bad movie cathouse.

The first-class accommodations hurt his eyes—and his normal frugal spending habits; it wasn't cheap. But first class carriages were one or two rooms to a car, with a corridor running along the side to let them move around, or have food or bedding brought. They were roomier than any ship's berth he'd taken to date, and a lot cleaner—and fully contained. And gruesomely ornate. But after the Podhru docks, Chris wasn't ready to mingle with the rest of the passengers at meals—or anywhere else.

He glanced at the bag he was presently using as a footstool; it was probably half paper—messages from Afronsan and just about everywhere else.

The seat he had by the smaller window was at least comfortably padded and high-backed; Dija was behind the screen on a low couch, sleeping; Edrith prowling the halls, keeping an eye on things or just trying to work off excess energy. *Wish he'd quit; if someone spots any of us—* But they were supposed to be in Bez, or possibly back in Podhru, inside sealed borders. Maybe things had gone right for once.

Maybe Ernie's right and we're nuts to be heading south again. But if we weren't safe in Podhru, then why bother staying home? Besides, if he lost this deal on iceboxes, a whole house of cards could come down. *I tried poor when I was a kid; I'd like to opt for something else for a change.*

If he'd stayed in Rhadaz and gotten locked in, he'd stand absolutely no chance of learning anything useful about the Zero traffic.

Ariadne wore brown; not the best color on her, but practical for traveling by steam train. She was presently curled up in a low chair under the large window, turned so the light would fall on her book—some dry-looking thing Adreban's lady had pressed on her. He wondered how well she was doing with a collection of essays in Rhadazi. But she'd been at it most of the day.

Quiet, really, since Afronsan's men found them on the coast road. Downright subdued. *Either the whole thing freaked her out, or she's sorry she said anything back on that damned ship.* Five men. . . . He looked up; Ariadne had let the book fall to her lap and she was watching him, almost as if she'd been aware of his thought. "You comfortable?" He couldn't think of anything else to say.

She nodded. "Thank you, yes."

"Not sorry you came along?"

"No." She smiled suddenly. "Not now. Perhaps when we take ship, if there is again a difficulty."

"Nothing like an interesting trip."

"Interesting—yes." She picked up the book, sighed, closed it and set it aside. "Talk to me, please. Tell me things."

Tell me things. Jen had made Lialla's life miserable for weeks with that phrase. *Hey, we were in a tough spot for sure back then, and we came through all right.* He laughed. "Sure. What kind of things you have in mind?"

She considered this. "Where we go, once we leave this train. Why."

"The Portuguese big island—I still think of it as Cuba, after all this time. Business is why. If—if everything's okay when we get to the coast, though, I'm hoping we can take a couple of days to play. I love the water along there."

"Water." Ariadne shuddered.

"Yeah, me too, after that last swim. But this is like your island, water's clear and warm, lots of colorful fish to look at once you get under the surface. Anyway, maybe. Depends on what's going on down there. After that—I'll have to do some checking, get Eddie to talk to people, see if it's still safe for us to head up to the mainland. And after *that*, we may try to get passage to England."

"And if the English or the Mer Khani are those who threaten Rhadaz?"

"It could be; but you know, more I think about the whole thing, it's weird. I'm dealing with a few fairly high-ups in both governments—I've been in and out of major cities, read newspapers, talked to people—I can't believe it could be a whole country doing this to us and *nobody* knows about it. In my world, when the English shoved opium at the Chinese, it was a just a big trading company trying to be sure there'd be enough tea for the folks back home, and that it wouldn't cost 'em too much, and there was plenty of talk: argument in the papers, people upset and others all for it because who cared about the heathen Chinese? All that. It's hard to keep anything like that quiet, word leaks out, and the more people involved, the harder it gets. I keep trying to figure it, you know? But there's no tea-equivalent in Rhadaz: All we've seen are, oh, a small group of Mer Khani with the telegraph, and another bunch buying cloth, a few Eng-

lish doing something else—it isn't organized, there's no overall
pattern.

"If they want the land—well, that could be the Mer Khani de-
ciding they should have everything from sea to shining sea, just
like the world I came from; could be the English, keeping a good
post for the Pacific trade and making sure the Mer Khani don't
get too spread out."

"Or the Gaelic states, who fear if the Mer Khani begin to take
more land, they will not stop until they have all," Ariadne said.
"The Mer Khani already put pressure on the islands; I heard my
father and some of his friends, a year or so ago, talking about it.
But—you are right. When the Mer Khani made pressure, everyone knew of it."

"Yeah. Like I figure."

"But companies—there are some my father deals with and
others not—because, let me think how he said it—" She
frowned, pushed stray hair back from her forehead. "Because
they were tied to other companies, many of them all together but
secretly, so it was difficult to make money from any deal with
them—he said—" She chewed on her knuckle, stared into space.
"Yes! He and his friend Sorionne, they were talking over dinner
one night about how Sorionne had finally put his accounts man
to reading everything he had from these companies, and there
was one name, a man who had a part in each—"

"Conglomerate," Chris breathed. "Oh, hey. I don't suppose
anyone mentioned the name?"

"No—or if so, I was distracted by someone else at the table.
I never heard it." She shook her head, eyed her knuckle with distaste, and rubbed it dry on the back of her other hand. "I'm
sorry."

"No—really. That's all right. It may not be what I think, but
it's someplace to start looking—and my aunt Jen is just the person to do it. Her and the Heir both. Hah!" He clapped his hands
together, let his head fall back and laughed. "Hey, what a stitch
if whoever it is gets nailed by a couple paper-pushers!"

"It helps?"

"It could. We'll send a message back up to Afronsan right
away, let them take care of that end of things. Get something out
as soon as we hit the coast, maybe find someone Eddie trusts in
New Lisbon to carry one around by—hell, I forgot, ship's out.
We'll get something to Fahlia, they'll sneak it up to the Heir."

"New Lisbon: You think this is safe?" She put a dry accent on the last word. Chris grinned.

"Like anywhere we've been is, right? But if there are any rumors around, that's one of the best places to pick them up, and Eddie's real good at it."

"My father does business in New Lisbon," Ariadne said.

"Yeah, I know. But only in the main port on the south side of the island, and he's not liked there, some kind of slick trick he pulled on the locals, I don't know what, but Eddie does. Anyway, we aren't going to the main port city; we'll be on the northwest tip, clear across the island."

A familiar tap at the door; Eddie stuck his head in. "We're coming in to a station, some big river town. You better stay inside; I'll go look around." Before Chris could say anything, he was gone again, the door shut behind him.

"Oh, swell," Chris said sourly.

Ariadne set her book aside and got to her feet so she could look out the window. "Don't be angry with him. Even I would not have looked at him twice under that hat; it changes him."

"Yeah—I guess. I just don't like having him stick his neck out for me like this, but you can't convince *him*."

"No. I understand that." He glanced at her sharply; her attention was fixed on the landscape outside the window. "Did you mean it," she asked quietly after a moment, "when you said you had never killed a man?"

He blinked. "I meant it. Not that I wouldn't have, a few times, when we first came here; either because I was really mad or it was self defense; I had plenty of chances to think about that 'him or me' thing, you know? Back home, I used to say it all the time, but everyone did—*you* know: 'I'm gonna kill that guy,' but it just meant you were mad. My mom—she wouldn't step on a spider, she never has believed in fighting and wars and all that. I'm not as good that way as she is, but it's something I learned young—you know." He smiled faintly. "Hard to break that kind of habit."

"I know about habits learned young." Ariadne's eyes were fixed on the rolling brown hills, the distant line of green that must mark the river. "My mother, the other women of her class, the women of my father's class—men treat them as property. Not as—property which has value and must be kept nicely—" She shook her head.

"I know what you're saying; they don't just get someone to

sleep with and make sons for them, or someone to dress pretty and show off how rich their men are—they get a punching bag at the same time. Someone to beat up on who can't hit back." She turned, visibly surprised. "Hey. I told you about my mom. She's had more black eyes and bruises—and half the time the guy was someone *she* chose, someone she brought home. You figure."

"It does not stop among my father's friends at bruises," Ariadne said. "Not—by some of them. Still, there are some few kinds of places a woman can go, without men: My mother and some of the women who became her kind because of my father's rank—they met to drink tea and to sew and to gossip. And after a while, to learn from each other ways to manage such men. My mother's mother in Afrique, she was good at liquids and powders to put into a drink, to send a man to sleep or to kill him, and so my mother had that to pass on; another woman who had always worked magic for healing spells learned how to use that power in other ways; yet another had learned blades from her brothers—" She was watching him steadily, waiting for his reaction.

"You do what you have to, to protect yourself," Chris said. "I can't argue with that."

"In France, things are not so difficult for women as in Jamaica, though not what I would name good. In Jamaica, there is no law save what men like my father decide, there is no guard other than the men they hire. They blame the heat, or the wind, or the drink—"

"They all do that; it's not just a local thing," Chris said. "Wasn't my fault, I was drunk, I was depressed, she asked for it—I've heard all that crap."

"Yes—well. By the time my mother began to bring me to these meetings, she was already unwell, and my father—" She stopped, swallowed, turned away to stare out the window again. "She thought I would be able to continue what she did, with the powders and so on; but I have no gift for them, and only a certain little ability with the magic. The blades: I could use them, and I liked them—the feel of them, and that I could deal with any man of Philippe-sur-Mer."

"So—five men." He kept his voice level, unchallenging. "How come your father wasn't one of them?"

"Many reasons." She shrugged. "He is more suspicious of everyone than most, and a superb duelist. The men I killed—one had fallen just outside his club and lay snoring against the wall; two others were so drunken, they were unaware of my presence at all. The other two—but my father seldom drinks to such a degree, and he is wary."

"Yeah. Tell *me*."

"Yes. You know. Also." Her shoulders sagged. "I was the fool; I thought I had more claim upon him as Marie's child and all he has left of her. But this Zero—"

"Yeah. Letting him know you knew about it probably wasn't a great idea."

"Yes, tell me this *now*," she replied dryly. Her mouth quirked. "And another thing, which has only occurred to me since I left his house. He spoke often of somehow returning to France, to take the estates of my grandfather when he dies. For that, he would need to take the place of my uncle Philippe, and I did not think he could."

"Not so hard," Chris said. "Bottle of brandy laced with Zero, and bye-bye, Uncle Philippe."

"It would be enough if my grandpere thought Philippe took the drug—any drug. He has strict notions of what makes a nobleman, which is why my father has the Jamaican properties, and his not-too-clever youngest brother Armande the mines to the south, on the north side of the lake. My grandpere might dismiss any of his sons entirely for behaving like common men, and if he thought my father dispensed this drug for money— To produce it for France or for Orlean is not bad, but to sell it—poor and low men do this." She spread her arms. "And so, I think, if my father hopes to return to France and inherit Orlean, he would never take a daughter such as myself. Dead, I only am the child of a boy's foolish young love."

"You think you're worth more to him dead?"

"Do you doubt it, Chris? Or you, also?" He shook his head. She picked up the book and added, "I will take this where Dija is, and perhaps sleep also. It is a good book for sleep."

"Sure. I'll call you in time for dinner." *Called me Chris. Never did that before.* He liked how she said it: way in the back of her throat. He resettled his shoulders against the padding, and eased the curtain aside a little. They were coming into a large town— plenty of buildings and people everywhere. He wasn't about to get out, but it was something to look at.

People—any of them could be Dupret's or part of the crowd trying to take over Rhadaz. If that was what they were after.

Maybe just looking for a new dope market. He sighed, and bent down to open the bag he'd been using to rest his heels. Maybe read through that long wire from Jen again, see if there was anything useful he'd missed. "Christopher Robin, out to save the day," he muttered as he searched for the tied bundle from Sikkre. "Right." At the moment, he felt extremely foolish. "The only guy who can figure out who the bad guys are; remember what you told Jen?" He glanced out the window as the train slowed, then ground to a halt. A long, shaded platform out there, and people all over the place. As he watched, a tall, lean man in very nondescript brown pants and shirt and a wide-brimmed hat walked past the window and eased into the crowd. Eddie looked, Chris decided, like one of the natives cleaned up for a trip to town—no one paid any attention to him.

He could hear Dija's voice, blurry with sleep; Ariadne's low-voiced reply. He smiled. "Owe you one, lady," he said softly, to himself. "We get out of all this in one piece—and I'll really owe you one."

Consortium—an East India Company. Maybe. Worth a look, anyway, and if there was something to be traced, Jen would find it—if Afronsan and his palaceful of clerks didn't beat her to it. He stretched hard, settled back on the bench and opened Jen's thick telegram: It wasn't just him, going after the windmills—he had help. "The best." And somehow, it was going to be enough.